Mark shot Ramsey a look. "I think half of what the kids told us is fueled by that blasted legend folks 'round here insist on feedin' regularly."

"Legend?" The case file contained only the facts of the case. But when facts were in short supply, other details took on more importance.

"Guess you'll be hearin' it from 'bout every person you talk to in town. I know I can count on you, out of anyone, not to be distracted by nonsense." Still, it seemed to take him a few moments to choose his words. "We've got somethin' of a local phenomenon here called the red mist. Someone else could explain it better, but it's caused by some sort of reaction from some plants 'round here and contaminants in the air . . . Once every blue moon, the fog in low-lyin' areas takes on a red tinge for a day or two. Nothin' magical 'bout it of course, 'cept the way it makes folks 'round here take leave of their senses."

"So the kids that found the body saw this red mist?"

"That's what they're sayin'. And I do have others in these parts that claim they saw the same thing, so might've been true. But local legend has it that whenever the red mist appears, death follows . . ."

WAKING EVIL

THE MINDHUNTERS

KYLIE BRANT

BERKLEY SENSATION, NEW YORK

THE BERKLEY PUBLISHING GROUP
Published by the Penguin Group
Penguin Group (USA) Inc.
375 Hudson Street, New York, New York 10014, USA
Penguin Group (Canada), 90 Eglinton Avenue East, Suite 700, Toronto, Ontario M4P 2Y3, Canada
(a division of Pearson Penguin Canada Inc.)
Penguin Books Ltd., 80 Strand, London WC2R 0RL, England
Penguin Group Ireland, 25 St. Stephen's Green, Dublin 2, Ireland (a division of Penguin Books Ltd.)
Penguin Group (Australia), 250 Camberwell Road, Camberwell, Victoria 3124, Australia
(a division of Pearson Australia Group Pty. Ltd.)
Penguin Books India Pvt. Ltd., 11 Community Centre, Panchsheel Park, New Delhi—110 017, India
Penguin Group (NZ), 67 Apollo Drive, Rosedale, North Shore 0632, New Zealand
(a division of Pearson New Zealand Ltd.)
Penguin Books (South Africa) (Pty.) Ltd., 24 Sturdee Avenue, Rosebank, Johannesburg 2196,
South Africa

Penguin Books Ltd., Registered Offices: 80 Strand, London WC2R 0RL, England

This is a work of fiction. Names, characters, places, and incidents either are the product of the author's imagination or are used fictitiously, and any resemblance to actual persons, living or dead, business establishments, events, or locales is entirely coincidental. The publisher does not have any control over and does not assume any responsibility for author or third-party websites or their content.

WAKING EVIL

A Berkley Sensation Book / published by arrangement with the author

PRINTING HISTORY
Berkley Sensation mass-market edition / October 2009

Copyright © 2009 by Kim Bahnsen.
Excerpt from *Waking the Dead* by Kylie Brant copyright © by Kim Bahnsen.
Cover art by S. Miroque.
Cover design by Rita Frangie.
Interior text design by Laura K. Corless.

All rights reserved.
No part of this book may be reproduced, scanned, or distributed in any printed or electronic form without permission. Please do not participate in or encourage piracy of copyrighted materials in violation of the author's rights. Purchase only authorized editions.
For information, address: The Berkley Publishing Group,
a division of Penguin Group (USA) Inc.,
375 Hudson Street, New York, New York 10014.

ISBN: 978-0-425-23071-8

BERKLEY® SENSATION
Berkley Sensation Books are published by The Berkley Publishing Group,
a division of Penguin Group (USA) Inc.,
375 Hudson Street, New York, New York 10014.
BERKLEY® SENSATION and the "B" design are trademarks of Penguin Group (USA) Inc.

PRINTED IN THE UNITED STATES OF AMERICA

10 9 8 7 6 5 4 3 2 1

If you purchased this book without a cover, you should be aware that this book is stolen property. It was reported as "unsold and destroyed" to the publisher, and neither the author nor the publisher has received any payment for this "stripped book."

For Michelle—
who was brave enough to join the family first
and has been enriching our lives ever since.
We love you!

Prologue

The canopy of trees blocked the full moon, allowing only an occasional sliver of light through the dense foliage. The branches were intertwined, like the fingers of lovers, but there was nothing romantic about the still, waiting air of the woods. Even the nightly serenade of nocturnal creatures was silenced for the moment in an eerie lull.

"C'mon." Robbie Joe gave a slight tug to Becky Ritter's hand as he sent a quick glance behind them. No lights. The others hadn't gotten this far yet. "Told you this was a short-cut. We're goin' to beat everyone for sure. The trail is right over here."

"That little bitty thing?" Becky came to a complete halt, playing the beam of the flashlight over the direction he'd indicated. "Robbie Joe Whipple, that is not a trail. It's barely an animal path and leads right through those brambles. My legs are goin' to get all scratched up if we follow it." To remind him of the seriousness of the possible damage, she shone the flashlight on the legs in question. And they were, to Robbie's adolescent mind, the stuff of fantasies, left bare by minuscule denim shorts. He could imagine how they'd feel under his hands, sleek and smooth, or better yet, wrapped around his hips, tight and demanding.

But even more vividly, he could imagine beating everyone else back to Sody's parking lot, lording it over the rest of the losers when they came straggling in. Or better yet, rubbing his feat in the face of that hotshot Timothy Jenkins, who was really such a candyass he probably would never get out of the car if he did make it to the woods.

When Becky didn't respond to a discreet tug on her hand, he switched tactics. "Girl, I purely can see why you wouldn't want a scratch on those fine legs of yours." He didn't have to feign the admiration in his tone. "And I swear on my granddaddy's grave, if you get one little ol' mark on 'em, I will personally apply my grandma's special ointment to every square inch. Scout's honor."

She giggled and gave him a slight push. "Don't you try your fast talk with me, Robbie Joe. I've heard 'bout your reputation."

"Now don't you go believin' everythin' you hear." Wise advice, since anything that would have reached her ears had been manufactured, exaggerated, and repeated by him in a diligent and as yet unsuccessful quest to end his blasted state of virginity. "If it gets too thick in there, we'll turn back. You have my word on that."

But still she hesitated, looking over her shoulder and inching closer to him. "What about those sounds I heard earlier? The ones that sounded like screams."

"Told you, it was probably just a bobcat. And they're scared of humans, so it'll make itself scarce when it picks up our scent." He hadn't actually heard the sounds she referred to, doubted that she had either, but he wasn't going to quibble with an opportunity to get his hands on the girl the football team called "Backseat Becky." Slipping his arm around her waist, he gave her a light hug and hoped her reputation was more deserved than his own. "I'm not lettin' anythin' happen to you. And I'm not gonna let Cami or Merilee get that batch of switchgrass back to Sody's before you and blather about it for the rest of the summer."

"That's true." To his relief, she began moving toward the path. "Cami does like to go on. And if Merilee and Jon win, we'll never hear the end of it, either." Merilee was her latest frenemy, although the girls spent so much time together Robbie had to wonder when Becky had had occasion to earn her famed reputation.

"Here, give me the flashlight." He noted that the beam had gone dimmer and prayed the batteries lasted until they got out of the woods. He hadn't made this trip for years, not since he was a kid, and never at night. With false bravado, he said, "I know this area like the back of my hand. We'll be back at Sody's before the rest of those guys even get here." Already he was wondering how many of the other couples *would* make it this far. Easy to talk big back at Sody's. But laughing at local superstition safely in town was a lot different than being smack-dab in the center of the woods at near midnight.

He swallowed, wished for some water. The night air felt thick and close, as if the dense canopy above shut out oxygen the way it did light.

It was slow going, seeing as how he had to hold the briars out of the way each time for Becky to walk through. And the trail had gotten more overgrown since the last time he'd been here—what? Three years ago? He hoped they'd still be able to get to Ashton's Pond this way. Becky would never forgive him if they had to turn back without getting that batch of switchgrass that would prove their bravery to the others.

"Oh my gosh, this is so spooky." Becky's giggle sounded a little strained. "How much farther to the pond, do you think?"

"It's not far now," he lied, although, truthfully, Robbie couldn't recall exactly how much longer they'd have to walk. He tripped, nearly fell, and threw a hand up to halt Becky while he played the light over the ground beneath him. "Watch out for this log. Almost fell on my ass."

But when he tried to help her over it, Becky stood stock-still. "What . . . what's that?"

Those looming shadows had to be trees, didn't they? Trees and thickets and overgrown brush. He played the flashlight around, saw nothing but a pair of yellow eyes peering at him from a low hanging branch.

Relief flooded him. "That? It's just an owl, Becky. Can't hurt you."

"Not that, 'tard. That!" She flung her hand out, her voice growing shriller. "Where's that fog comin' from?"

He saw it then, little curls of vapor rising from the ground. Wrapping around tree trunks, winding through bushes. A sheet of ice kissed his skin. Because this was no ordinary fog, that was for damn sure. This was red mist. The stuff of local legends.

For an instant, for one terrifying moment, Robbie Joe was afraid he was gonna pee himself then and there. He didn't even have time to be grateful for the way Becky launched herself into his arms, barely registering that the position had her boobs flattened against his chest. He could only focus on the fog—the red mist—and how it wound around his legs, seeming to grow thicker by the moment.

"Shit," he whispered, his mind blank with panic. His muscles went tense as he poised to run, to race the hell out of there, the dare be damned. But then he saw the lights. Little dancing balls of it, flickering all around them, bouncing high and then skipping from shadow to shadow. He went limp with relief. "Sheeeee-it," he repeated, louder this time, and added a laugh for emphasis. "If that's the best you can do boys, you need to spend more time in chemistry. Mr. Stokowski would be purely disappointed that you couldn't come up with anythin' better than this."

"What?" Becky hissed her fingers clenched on his sides. "What is it?"

With his free arm he guided the girl in the direction of the pond again, kept his voice loud enough to be overheard by the guys who must be hiding nearby. "Just some of the assholes thinkin' they can scare us with some lame-colored smoke and covered flashlights." Leastways, he figured that's how they did it. Chemistry, or school in general, wasn't his strong suit. "C'mon, we gotta hurry."

He held tight to Becky, and she stumbled along beside him, questions spilling from her lips. "How do you know it's them? How do you know it's not . . . ?"

"Because there's no such thing as the red mist," he said grimly. "It's all a bunch of superstitious shit dreamed up by drunks in our parents' generation." But there wasn't a doubt in his mind that it was *his* generation responsible for him nearly disgracing himself back there.

Already he was plotting revenge. Which ones were in on the joke? Arends, for sure, that rat bastard. Maybe even Gallop. Yeah, this was Lenny Gallop's speed, all right. He heard nothing around him. Certainly not Gallop's obnoxious donkey bray of a laugh. Which meant the guys were already heading back to Sody's to tell how they scared the shit out of Robbie Joe Whipple.

And everyone would have a good laugh at his expense. The knowledge burned in his chest. He'd never hear the end of it, no matter how many times he denied falling for the prank. Unless he put a spin on it, walked back into Sody's with a handful of the switchgrass everyone was supposed to get, and act like he hadn't been phased a bit. *Shoot, was that s'posed to scare me? Must not have spooked me much if I went ahead to the pond and got this.*

Becky was breathing hard, but he barely noticed. He was too concerned with the upcoming scene back at Sody's. Yeah, that's how he'd play it, calm and unconcerned. *Looks like I was the only one with the balls to go clear to the pond. So who you callin' the candyass?*

"You're sure it was some of the guys?" Her voice was shaky. "Because the fog's up here, too."

"Yeah. But we're goin' to show them all up when we get back with that switchgrass." They broke through the trees ringing the water then, stepped into the clearing with a suddenness that was disorienting.

"They must be still 'round here," Becky whispered. "The lights . . . see them? If they're doin' that somehow with their flashlights . . ."

"Maybe that part wasn't them." And he was in no mood to linger here, even if his friends were still somewhere in the woods behind him. Ashton's Pond wasn't inviting in the daylight, and night didn't improve the atmosphere. Its deep, dark depths were still, and he knew from experience that the waters held a smell that didn't wash off the skin, no matter how you tried. He'd seen copperheads here before, and Robbie played his flashlight carefully over the area to be sure they wouldn't encounter one.

"Those lights are probably just caused by fireflies. They have those special ones in the Smoky Mountains. Ever hear 'bout that? They all turn on and off at the same time."

"Oh." Becky's voice was steadier now. "It's sort of pretty. And . . . wait!" She grabbed his arm, guided the flashlight to the weeds growing near the water's edge. "There's the switch-grass. All we have to do is cut some and head back. Where's your knife?"

He dug in his jeans for his pocketknife and opened it before handing it to her. She walked gingerly on the mucky ground surrounding the pond before squatting next to the weeds, while he trained the flashlight on the clump she was interested in.

"If you're right, and some of the guys were back there, then some of the girls are in on it, too," she said, her voice muffled by her position.

Robbie was only half listening. Her shorts were low riders, and her position gave him an excellent view of the crack of her ass. He was more a tit man himself—at least he'd like to be—but Becky did have a very fine ass. Timothy Jenkins claimed to have tapped it on prom night, but Jenkins was a liar about most things, so his story about pounding it to Becky doggy style in the back of his mama's van was most likely a fantasy. But the vision did hold an allure that Robbie Joe couldn't help but contemplate.

"If I find out that Merilee planned this with Jon, I'll slap her senseless." She sawed at the clump with determined motions. "You and I will have to synchronize our stories. We don't want them tellin' everyone that we . . ."

Her scream then echoed across the pond and back, reverberating through his skull, bouncing off the trunks of trees surrounding the area. She scuttled backward, whimpers coming from her lips in staccato bursts. When she hurtled into his arms, the flashlight went sailing from his limp fingers. He stared in horror at the sight she'd uncovered.

The flashlight rolled, its beam bouncing crazily until the Mag-Lite came to a rest shining on the spot where Becky had been cutting switchgrass at the pond's edge.

Spotlighting the human foot that had been hidden by the tall grass.

Attached to a body immersed in the cool dark water.

Chapter 1

The helicopter landed in the clearing with a slight bounce before settling on the ground again for good. Ramsey Clark shouted her thanks to the pilot, shoved open the door, and jumped lightly to the ground, her lone bag slung over one shoulder. She ran in a crouch to avoid the rotors, heard the *whop-whop-whop* behind her indicating the pilot taking off.

She jogged toward the cluster of four people waiting nearby. The three men wearing suits each held a hand over his tie to prevent it from dancing in the breeze generated by the chopper's rotors.

"Director Jeffries." The hand she offered was engulfed in the older man's pawlike grip and squeezed until she had to hide a wince. The chief of Tennessee Bureau of Investigation hadn't changed much in the years since she'd left its ranks. His craggy face might be a little ruddier. His mop of white hair a bit shorter. But his six-foot frame was still military straight and as lean as ever.

"Good to see you again, Clark. I hear you've been makin' quite a name for yourself with Raiker Forensics."

Since the director wasn't prone to flattery, and since he could have heard it only from Adam Raiker himself, Ramsey allowed herself to feel a small glow of satisfaction. "Thank you, sir. I think I've learned a lot."

Jeffries turned to the two men flanking him. "TBI agents Glenn Matthews and Warden Powell. You'll be assigned to their team. If you need more manpower, give me a holler and I'll talk to the boss."

Ramsey nodded her appreciation. Jeffries had no superior at TBI, so they were being given carte blanche. Raiker had told her to expect as much.

The director turned to the man in the sheriff's uniform on her right. "I believe you know Sheriff Rollins."

Frowning, she was about to deny it. Ramsey knew no one in Buffalo Springs, Tennessee. But the sheriff was taking off his hat, and recognition struck her. "Mark Rollins?" She shook her former colleague's hand with a sense of déjà vu. "I didn't know you'd left TBI."

"Couple years ago now. Didn't even realize I was interested in movin' back home until the position of sheriff was open." Rollins's pleasantly homely face was somber. "Have to say, tonight's the first time I've regretted it."

"I assume you've looked at the case file."

Ramsey's attention shifted back to Jeffries at his comment. She nodded and he went on.

"Rollins has his hands full here calmin' the local hysteria, and after a week, we aren't progressin' fast enough to suit the governor's office. The area is attractin' every national media team in the country, and the coverage is playin' hell with his tourism industry expansion plans." The director's voice was heavy with irony.

"I understand." And she did. Being brought in as a special consultant to the TBI pacified a politically motivated governor and diminished some of the scrutiny that would follow the department throughout the investigation. If the case drew to a quick close, the TBI reaped the positive press. If it didn't . . . The alternative didn't bother her. Ramsey had served as shit deflector many times in the past in her capacity as forensic consultant. If the investigation grew lengthy or remained unsolved, she would be served as sacrificial lamb to the clamoring public. Or to the state attorney's office, if someone there decided to lay the blame on Jeffries.

"Raiker promised a mobile lab."

"It'll be here tomorrow. But for certain types of evidence, we may need access to the TBI facility on an expedited basis."

"We'll try to speed any tests through the Knoxville Regional Lab." Jeffries beetled his brows. "Just help solve this thing, Clark. It's causin' a crapstorm, and I don't want a full-fledged shit tornado on my hands."

Ramsey smiled. She'd always appreciated Jeffries' plain-spokenness. "I'll do my best, sir."

"Can't recall a time that wasn't good enough for me." Clearly finished, he turned to his agents. "I'll expect daily updates. And keep me abreast of any major developments." Without waiting for the men's nods, he turned and strode briskly toward a road about a quarter mile in the distance. Ramsey could make out two vehicles parked alongside it.

"I'm guessin' you'd like to get on into town, drop your stuff off in the room we lined up for you," Mark was saying.

Ramsey shook her head. "I want to see the crime scene first." Since diplomacy was often an afterthought for her, she added belatedly, "If that's okay."

The sheriff raised a shoulder. "It's all right with me. What about you fellas? Want to come along?"

The two agents looked at each other, and Powell shook his head. "We'll head back." He shifted his gaze to Ramsey. "We're set up in the local motel on the outskirts of town. One room serves as our office. We got you a room there, too, when Jeffries told us you were comin'."

And by not so much as a flicker of expression did he reveal his opinion on her being brought in on the case, Ramsey noted shrewdly. She'd have to tread carefully there, with both agents, until she was certain how her presence here affected them.

"I'll check in with you when I get to town, and you can bring me up to date on your notes so far."

When the agents headed in the same direction Jeffries had gone, she turned to Rollins.

"Let me get that for you." He reached for her bag, but she deflected the gesture.

"I've got it, thanks." She fell into step beside him as they walked toward the tan jeep emblazoned with SPRING COUNTY SHERIFF in black lettering on a green background. "Tell me about the case."

"Same ol' Ramsey." A corner of Rollins's mouth pulled up. "Always with the small talk. Chatter, chatter, chatter." His voice hitched up a notch as he launched into a mock conversation. "Well, I'm just fine, Ms. Clark. And how have you been? How's that new job of yours? The wife? Oh, she's fine, too. Still adjustin' to small-town life, but the two little ones keep her pretty busy. What? You'd like to see pictures? Well, it just so happens I have a couple in my wallet. Got them taken at the local Wal-Mart just last month . . ."

"I can play the game if I need to," she replied, only half truthfully. "Didn't figure I needed to with you."

He stopped at the vehicle, his hand on the handle of the driver's door, his face serious again. "No, you don't gotta with me. Figure we go far 'nough back that we can just pick up. But you'll find you'll get further with some folks in these parts if you put forth the effort. I know you never had much patience for mindless chitchat, but the pace is slower 'round here."

She was more familiar than he knew with the unwritten customs and tradition demanded by polite society in the rural south. Had, in fact, spent her adult life scrubbing away most of those memories with the same ruthless determination with which she'd eliminated her telltale drawl.

Rather than tell him that, she gave him a nod across the roof of the car. "I'll keep it in mind." She opened the back door and tossed her bag on the seat behind the wire mesh used to separate prisoners from the law enforcement personnel. Then she slid into the front passenger seat.

He folded his tall lanky form inside and started up the Jeep while she was buckling in. Several minutes later, he abruptly pulled off the road and began driving across a field. After the first couple of jolts, Ramsey braced herself with one hand on the dash and the other on the roof of the car.

"Sorry." Rollins seemed to move seamlessly with each jar and bump. "It'd take half an hour for us to get there by road. The kids that found the body hiked across through the woods on the other side, but going in from this direction will be an easier walk, though I'm told it takes longer. Brought the body out this way."

"Has the victim been ID'd yet?"

"Nope. White female, between the age of eighteen and twenty-five. Found nude, so no help with the clothin'." A muscle jumped in Mark's jaw. "Not from these parts, is all I know. No hits from any of the national missin' persons databases. The medical examiner took a DNA sample, and we submitted the results to the FBI's system, but no luck."

So a Jane Doe, at least for now. Ramsey felt a stab of sympathy for the unknown woman. Maybe she hadn't even been reported missing. She'd died alone and away from home. Was that worse than being murdered in familiar surroundings? Somehow it seemed so.

"How valuable have the wits been?"

"What, the kids?" Mark shot her a look. "Told us what they knew, which didn't turn out to be much. Both scared silly, of course. Spoutin' nonsense about red mist and screamin' and dancin' lights . . . Tell you what I think." The Jeep hit a rut with a bone-jarring bounce that rattled Ramsey's teeth. "I think half is fueled by that blasted legend folks 'round here insist on feedin' regularly."

"Legend?" The case file contained only facts of the case. But when facts were in short supply, other details took on more importance.

Rollins looked pained. "Guess you'll be hearin' it from 'bout every person you talk to in town. I know I can count on you, out of anyone, not to be distracted by nonsense." Still, it seemed to take him a few moments to choose his words. Or maybe he was saving his strength for wrestling the Jeep. Beneath the spread of grass, the terrain was wicked.

"We've got somethin' of a local phenomena called the red mist. Someone else could explain it better, but it's caused by some sort of reaction from certain plants in the area comin' in contact with iron oxide in stagnant water, coupled with contaminants in the air. Once every blue moon, the fog in low-lyin' areas takes on a red tinge for a day or two. Nothin' magical 'bout it of course, 'cept the way it makes folks 'round here take leave of their senses."

"So the kids that found the body saw this red mist?"

"That's what they're sayin'. And I do have others in these parts that claim they saw the same thing, so might've been true. But local legend has it that whenever the red mist appears, death follows."

The Jeep hit a rut then that had Ramsey rapping her head smartly on the ceiling of the vehicle. With a grim smile, she repositioned herself more securely in her seat and waited for her internal organs to settle back into place. Then she shot the man beside her a look. "Well, all nonsense aside, Sheriff, so far it appears, your local legend is more grounded in facts than you want to admit."

Rollins brought the Jeep to a halt a few hundred yards shy of the first copse of trees. "Don't even joke about that. My office is spendin' too much of our time dealin' with hysterical locals who set too much store by superstitious hogwash. The truth is, this is a quiet place. The crime we do have tends to be drunk and disorderlies after payday at the lumber mill, or the occasional domestic dispute. Once in a while we have a fire or a bad accident to respond to. But violent crime is a stranger here. And when it appears, people don't understand it. They get scared, and when folks get scared, they search for meanin'. This legend is just their way of gettin' a handle on how bad things can happen near their town."

Ramsey got out of the car and stretched, avoiding, as long as possible, having to look at that expanse of woods ahead of them. "That's downright philosophical, Mark. Didn't learn that in the psych courses at TBI."

He reached back into the car for the shotgun mounted above the dash, and then straightened to shut the door, a ghost of a smile playing across his mouth. "You're right there. I understand these people. Lived here most of my life. I know how they think. How they react. Don't always agree with 'em. But I can usually figure where they're comin' from."

They headed for the woods, and Ramsey could feel her palms start to dampen. Her heart began to thud. The physical reaction annoyed her. It was just trees, for Godsakes. Each nothing but a mass of carbon dioxide. And she'd mastered this ridiculous fear—*she had*—years ago.

Deliberately, she quickened her step. "You hoping to go hunting while we're here?" She cocked her head at the shot-gun he carried.

"Not much of a hunter. But we do have some wildlife in these parts. Those kids were downright stupid to come in here at night. There's feral pigs in these woods. An occasional bobcat. Seen enough copperheads 'round in my time to keep me wary."

When her legs wanted to falter at his words, she kept them moving steadily forward. Felt the first cool shadows from the trees overhead slick over her skin like a demon's kiss.

"Wish I could tell you there was much of a crime scene," Mark was saying as he walked alongside her. "But apparently a bunch of kids dared each other to come into the woods and fetch proof they'd been here. First ones back to town got braggin' rights, I 'spect. So they paired off and trooped out in this direction. Shortly after the two found the victim, a few others arrived. And then the whole thing became one big mess with tracks and prints all over the damn place."

Ramsey felt a familiar surge of impatience. No one liked to have the scene contaminated, but one of the few down-sides to her job with Raiker Forensics was that she was rarely called to a fresh crime scene. By the time their services were requested, the crime could be days or weeks old. She had to satisfy herself with case files, pictures of the scene, and notes taken by the local law enforcement.

"The way Jeffries talked, you've gotten more than your share of unwanted media attention." They stepped deeper into the woods now and the trees seemed to close in, sucking them into the shadowy interior. She resisted the urge to wipe her moist palms on her pant legs. "Seems odd for national news to be interested in a homicide in rural Tennessee."

"I suspect some local nut job tipped them off. It's the leg-end again." Mark's face was shiny with perspiration, but Ramsey was chilled. She would be until they stepped back out into the daylight again. "Every two or three decades there's this red mist phenomena, and a couple times in the past there's been a death 'round the same time. The two circumstances get linked, and all of a sudden we have people jabbering about secret spells and century-old curses and what have you."

She made a noncommittal sound. Part of her attention was keeping a wary eye out for those copperheads he'd mentioned so matter-of-factly. But despite her impatience with idle chit-chat, she was interested in all the details that would be missing from the case file. Evidence was in short supply. It was people who would solve this case. People who'd seen something. Knew something. The tiniest bit of information could end up being key to solving the homicide. And with no murder weapon and no suspects and little trace evidence, she'd take all the information she could get.

"Have you eliminated each of the kids as the possible killer?"

"Shoot, Ramsey they're no more than sixteen, seventeen years old!"

When she merely looked at him, brows raised, he had the grace to look abashed. "Yeah, I know what you've seen in your career. I've seen the same. But 'round here we don't have kids with the conscience of wild dogs. They all alibi each other for up to thirty minutes before the body's discovery. Witnesses place the lot of them at Sody's parking lot for the same time. Pretty unlikely a couple hightailed it into the woods, committed murder, and dumped the body knowin' more kids would be traipsin' in any minute."

Unlikely, yes. Impossible, no. But Ramsey kept her thoughts to herself. She was anxious to hear what Agents Powell and Matthews had to say on the subject.

There was a rustle in the underbrush to her right, but it didn't get her blood racing. No, that feat was accomplished by the trees themselves, looming like sinister sentinels above her. Hemming her in with their close proximity. She rubbed at her arms, where gooseflesh prickled, and shoved at the mental door of her mind to lock those memories away.

Some would have found the scene charming, with the sun dappling the forest floor and brilliant slants of light spearing through the shadow. They wouldn't look at the scene and see danger behind every tree trunk. Wouldn't feel terror lurking behind. Horror ahead.

The trail narrowed, forcing her to follow Rollins single file. "Whose property are we on?"

"Most of it belongs to the county. We've got little parcels that butt up against the land of property owners, but we're standin' on county ground right now." They walked in silence another fifteen minutes, and Ramsey wondered anew at any kids foolish enough to make this trek at night.

Sixteen or seventeen, Mark had said they were. She knew firsthand just how naïve kids that age could be. How easily fooled. And how quickly things could go very wrong.

One moment they were deep in the woods. The next they walked out into a clearing with a large pond. It was ringed with towering pines and massive oaks, their branches dripping with Spanish moss and curling vines. The land looked rocky on three sides, but it was boggy at the water's edge closest to them, with clumps of rushes and wild grasses interspersed between the trees.

Ramsey's gaze was drawn immediately to the crime scene tape still fluttering from the wooden stakes hammered into the ground. A plastic evidence marker poked partway out of the trampled weeds near the pond, overlooked by the investigators when they'd packed up.

And in the center of that taped perimeter, crouched in front of the pond, a man repeatedly dunked something into the water and then held it up to examine it before repeating the action yet again. A few yards away, a jumble of equipment was piled on the ground.

She eyed Rollins. "One of yours?"

Looking uncomfortable, the sheriff shook his head. "Now, Ramsey," he started, as she turned toward the stranger. "Better let me handle this."

But she was already striding away. "Hey. Hey!"

The man raised a hand in a lazy salute, but it was clear he

was much more interested in the reading on the instrument he held than he was in her. Ramsey waited while he lowered the tool to jot a notation down in the notebook open on his lap then looked up and shot her a lazy grin. "Afternoon, ma'am."

"Interesting thing about that yellow tape all around you," she said with mock politeness. "It's actually meant to keep people out of a crime scene, not invite them inside it."

The sun at her back had the stranger squinting a bit at her, but the smile never left his face. And it was, for a man, an extraordinarily attractive face. His jaw was long and lean, his eyes a bright laser blue. The golden shade of his hair was usually found only on the very young or the very determined. Someone had broken his nose for him, and the slight bump in it was the only imperfection in a demeanor that was otherwise almost too flawless. Ramsey disliked him on sight just on principal.

"Well, fact is, ma'am, this isn't an active crime scene anymore. Hey, Mark." He called a friendly greeting to the man behind her. "Kendra May know you're out walking pretty girls 'round the woods?"

"Dev. Thought you'd be finished up here by now."

Ramsey caught the sheepish note in Rollins's voice and arched a brow at him. The sheriff intercepted it and followed up with an introduction. "Ramsey Clark, this is my cousin, Devlin Stryker. He's uh . . . just running some tests."

"Your cousin," she repeated carefully. "And does your cousin work for the department? If so, in what capacity?"

Rollins's face reddened a little. "No. He's a . . . well, he's sort of a scientist, you could say."

Stryker rose in one lithe motion and made his way carefully back to the rest of his belongings, which included, Ramsey noted, a large duffel bag with unfamiliar-looking instruments strewn around it, along with a couple cameras, a night vision light source, and—she blinked once—a neatly rolled up sleeping bag.

"Odd place to go camping."

"Can't say I used the sleepin' bag much last night." He

unzipped the duffel and began placing his things inside it. "Too worried about snakes. I thought I'd stick around awhile to compare last night's readin's with some from today."

With quick neat movements, he placed everything but the sleeping bag in the duffel and zipped it, standing up to sling its strap over his shoulder. "I'm done here for now, though."

"Done with what, exactly?"

Devlin sent her an easy smile that carried just enough charm to have her defenses slamming firmly into place. "Well, let's see. I used a thermal scanner to measure temperature changes. An EMF meter to gauge electromagnetic fields. An ion detector to calculate the presence of negative ions. Then there's the gaussometer, which . . ."

Comprehension warring with disbelief, Ramsey swung back to face Rollins, her voice incredulous. "A *ghost hunter*? Are you kidding me? You let some paranormal quack compromise the crime scene?"

Chapter 2

There was a glint in Stryker's brilliant blue eyes that might have been temper, but his voice was affable enough when he corrected Ramsey. "This quack tends to prefer the term parapsychologist. And I'm not huntin' ghosts. I'm searchin' for scientific data that will prove or disprove the presence of paranormal activity."

"My mistake," Ramsey replied, her voice heavy with irony.

"Need a lift back to town, Dev?" Rollins asked.

Stryker bent to snag the sleeping bag with his free hand. "Nope. I'll hike out. Got my car parked on the road by Rose Thornton's place."

"Careful she don't run you off with the business end of a shotgun," the sheriff warned. "Rose has gotten sorta cantankerous in her old age."

A masculine dimple winked in Stryker's smile. "Shoot, Rose was born cantankerous. Wasn't room to get much worse. I'll see you back at town." He shot Ramsey a smile. "Ms. Clark."

She watched him move away in a gait more an amble than a stride. Waited until he was out of earshot before turning to aim one long meaningful look at Rollins, who had the grace to look a bit discomfited.

"It's not what you think."

"Forget that he was mucking around in the crime scene," she said. It had been eight days since the murder. The sheriff's office would have worked the scene well before TBI was called in. Their investigators would have gone over it again. There was only an infinitesimal chance that any evidence would remain undiscovered. But as a law enforcement officer, Rollins should have been careful enough to protect that fraction of a chance. "But after all you said about the negative publicity and superstitious nonsense flying around about this crime, I would have thought allowing someone like Stryker in here would be the last thing you needed."

"This scene has been worked four times already," Rollins said stiffly. His posture was ramrod straight. She recognized the signs of bruised ego. "And I don't have the manpower to post a guard over it indefinitely to keep the curious away. If you thought you were going to waltz in here and find somethin' at the scene we missed, you're gonna be disappointed. I know my job, Ramsey. As well as you do."

Time to back off, Ramsey realized. And as frequently happened, that realization arrived just a bit too late. "I know you do. That's why I'm surprised you'd take the chance that this ghost . . . *parapsychologist* would get the townspeople in even more of an uproar than this murder has them already."

"Dev pretty much grew up in Buffalo Springs." And by his tone, Ramsey could tell she hadn't yet pacified the man. "Him and his family are known 'round here. I'm countin' on him to convince the town that this local legend is a bunch of bull, once and for all. His books do more debunkin' of this sort of stuff than not. Some people in these parts look up to him because of his degree and the books he's published. If allowin' him access to the crime scene after we finished processin' it will help toward that end, I thought it worth a shot. It's my decision to make, in any case."

Suppressing a wince, Ramsey nodded. Just because she knew Rollins, had once been his colleague, didn't mean she wouldn't have to step carefully to avoid antagonizing the man. Local law enforcement was notoriously territorial. She'd first learned that as a TBI agent. And though diplomacy didn't come naturally, it was a trait she was skilled enough at, when she took the time to employ it.

"Understood." Silent for a moment, she crouched down and scanned the area, absorbing the atmosphere as some people soaked up the sun's rays. With so few opportunities to be primary on a crime scene, she always insisted on visiting the scene herself, regardless of the timeline. Her boss, the legendary Adam Raiker, would say to understand a case, you had to see what the victim saw. Hear, smell, and touch what he or she did. Know the victim, know the crime.

The first step of knowing this victim was visiting the site where her body had been discovered.

"The case file said the kids found the vic at eleven P.M. Time of death estimated one to two hours earlier." She looked up at Rollins soberly. "You sure those witnesses didn't hear anything? See anything?"

"The girl, Becky Ritter, thought she'd heard screams earlier, but Robbie Joe claimed he didn't." Rollins pushed his hat back to swipe at his forehead. "Chances are he's right and she was just imaginin' things. When we first got the call, we figured it for a simple drownin', but once we saw the bruises on her throat, we started thinkin' differently. Medical examiner didn't find any water in her lungs, so we can be sure this was a dump site. Spent four days going over every inch of the surroundin' woods. Damned if we've found a thing to suggest she was killed 'round here. Most likely someone stopped on one of the borderin' roads and carried the body in. If those kids hadn't happened along when they did, the body was likely to never have been found. This pond is actually an old limestone pit. First settlers in town hauled stone from here to build their houses. Water is eighteen, twenty feet in places."

He pointed across the pond. "The second pair of kids came through that way. And between the four of them, I tell you, we would have needed God's own luck to get a decent footprint, even if the perp left one."

The radio on Mark's belt let out a burst of static. The disembodied voice of a dispatcher sounded. "Car one, what's your location?"

He unsnapped the radio and answered. "Car one. I'm down at Ashton's Pond. Go ahead."

Rising, Ramsey circled the edge of the water, eyeing the ground carefully before stepping. The police tape framed the area where the victim would have been found. She saw the half-cut weeds that the teenagers had been sawing at. Was the body dumped where it had been found, or had it drifted and gotten tangled in the rushes sprouting out of the water's edge like tiny hollow spears?

She eyed the water's surface. Calm, even stagnant. There was a faint odor to the water, something metallic with a slight sheen of decay. Barely a ripple marred its surface.

Her flesh prickled, and for a moment, just a moment, past and present collided with an impact that made them indistinguishable.

Running. One hand clapped over her mouth to muffle her panting as she stumbled through the boggy woods toward the swamp. Terrified of what lay behind her. What awaited her if she were caught. But danger lurked in every shadow ahead. Sounded in each small noise. The certainty of her own death growing clearer by the minute.

"Ramsey?"

She started, almost lost her footing, and her shoe slipped into the soft mud. Water pooled over it before she pulled it free, and she caught a flash of silver near her foot, as if something lurked beneath the surface waiting for an unsuspecting meal. "Yeah."

"I've got to get back to town. Got some news crew parked in my office, insistin' on gettin' a statement."

He was already striding in the direction they'd come, but Ramsey stopped long enough to wipe her shoe on the soggy grass a few feet from the water. Something made her look over her shoulder, a quick furtive glance. But the scene looked no different. A dank, still pool, calm and somehow unwelcoming, fringed by rock, swamp plants, and scraggly brush. A place that was no stranger to death.

She shook off the fanciful thought and forced herself to hurry after Mark into the thickening stand of trees.

The only thing worse than having to walk through those woods again would be to walk through them alone.

Motel was a polite term for the line of small cabins punctuating a rutted gravel drive on the outskirts of Buffalo

Springs. Ramsey stood in the doorway of number nine and took stock of her temporary home. Green carpeting—God was that shag?—had been ruthlessly vacuumed. The cheap paneling on the walls gleamed with polish, and she'd be willing to bet not a mite of dust would be found on the old TV or the chest of four drawers.

Although the place obviously hadn't been updated since the seventies, someone regularly took the time to keep it clean and comfortable. A quilt lay over the white iron bed, with plump pillows fluffed and resting against the headboard. There was an old hurricane lamp sitting on a crocheted doily on the bed stand, and through the open door of the bathroom, she could see a set of thick yellow towels hanging from a pitted metal bar.

"It's nothin' fancy," the owner, Mary Sue Talbot, was saying behind her. "Not what you're used to, I 'spect. But those other TBI fellas said you'd be okay stayin' here."

Mary Sue would have been pushing middle age when this carpet was laid, but she took as much care with her appearance as she did with the rooms she let. Her white hair was worn in a soft pageboy, and the crisp navy shirt she wore was spotless and tucked into a pair of trim starched jeans.

"It's fine," Ramsey assured her. "Homey. Beats lots of places I've stayed in, I can tell you."

The woman studied her, as if searching for sarcasm, but evidently what she saw in Ramsey's expression reassured her. "You need anythin' at all, you just lift that phone over there and give a holler. We don't serve any meals here, but there's a soda machine in the office, and every mornin' we have a tray of fresh doughnuts from The Henhouse. That's a restaurant on Main Street. Best breakfast in the area. I can sell you a doughnut and a cup of coffee for two dollars every mornin', but it's first come, first serve."

Since she wasn't much of a breakfast eater, Ramsey smiled politely. "Thanks. I may take you up on that." She waited for the older woman to take her leave, then dropped her bag and followed her out the door. She was anxious to talk to the TBI agents. She knocked on door eight, the cabin they were using as the investigation headquarters, and Agent Powell answered it in his shirtsleeves.

Without a word, he stood aside and allowed Ramsey entrance. Matthews, the younger agent, was there, too, sitting at a long folding table that served as a desk. Someone had prevailed on Mary Sue to have the bed removed from the room. A laptop, fax, and copier were wedged on another table against the window. Matthews had shed his suit coat, too, and his sleeves were rolled up on his forearms. The cabins weren't equipped with air-conditioning.

Ramsey looked at the older man. There was a nagging sense of familiarity about his name, but she couldn't recall having met him during her stint at TBI. "Had we met previously?" she asked, coming farther into the room. "While I was with TBI?"

"Don't think so." He was tall, with a runner's build, craggy features, and a fading gray crew cut. "Heard your name a time or two. I've been in the Knoxville field office for fifteen years."

Of course. A mental memory clicked. Warden Powell was lead agent in Knoxville's Criminal Investigative Unit. She recalled seeing him at the ceremony where her team had received a commendation for successfully cracking a baby-snatching ring. He'd been up for an award then as well. She should have known Jeffries would put one of his most trusted men to head the case.

She crossed to the far wall where they'd turned the paneling into a bulletin board, with pictures of the victim, maps, and crime scene photos taped to it. Ramsey had the fleeting thought that it would take Mary Sue hours to scrub the sticky residue off the paneling.

"Any thoughts from the scene?"

"Someone went to a lot of trouble to carry a body that far into the woods."

Powell nodded and joined her at the wall, stabbing one long index finger at an aerial map of the area. "The unknown subject knew his way around. No one would just happen into that forest near midnight and stumble onto that pond. He was headed there. It's plenty deep in the center. He didn't want the body to be found, that's certain."

Or he'd have dumped it in the forest, she thought, and let the animals finish the job he'd started. "He should have weighted it down if he didn't want it discovered."

She studied the wall for a few more moments. "So we have an UNSUB familiar with the area. Points to a local, or someone who once lived around here." She had a sudden thought. "Are these woods hunted?" Hunters would come from quite a ways for a hunting spot rife with the game in season. And hunting permits would leave a nice paper trail if they started looking in that direction.

"Sheriff says no. County doesn't allow it. But 'round these parts, you'd most likely be dealing with poachers."

"And any poachers are likely hillies."

She turned around to cock a brow at Matthews. His speech bore a faint but unmistakable Bronx accent. She took a moment to wonder how a New Yorker had wound up in the TBI before asking, "Hillies?"

He looked up from his paperwork long enough to throw her a glance. "What the townies call the rural people living in the hills outside of city limits. We've only been here a few days and already it's plain there's no love lost between some of the people in town and the hill folk."

That wasn't unusual in the rural south, she knew. Every culture had its caste system, and down here, the only "proper" home outside of city limits was an estate or ranch. And the people occupying the outlying areas could be just as distrustful of the city residents.

"Any word on the trace evidence you collected at the dump site?" Ramsey asked.

"The regional crime lab in Knoxville is matching every footprint, every fiber, to the clothing worn by the kids at the site. Once we have that eliminated," Powell shrugged, "then we'll see if we have somethin' to go on. Everythin' else we held back for the portable lab you've got arrivin'."

"Getting late." Glenn Matthews wheeled his chair back from the table and rubbed his eyes with the heels of his palms.

Ramsey pegged him as early thirties, dark complected, with a thick head of wavy black hair. "You up for dinner? There's a decent steak house in town."

At Powell's snort, the younger agent grinned. "Ward doesn't like the noise or the clientele, but the food's good."

"More of a honky-tonk than a restaurant," Powell muttered, turning back from the photos he was studying. "Music's too loud, and the customers are more interested in beer and pool than eatin'. But the food's not bad."

Even his half-hearted endorsement was enough to tempt Ramsey. The bag of chips she'd had on the way to the airport this morning was a distant memory. "That's good enough for me. I need to do a quick change first. I'll have to ride with you. My rental isn't due to be delivered until tomorrow." She made it as far as the door before pausing to look back. "I'd like to study the full autopsy report. I assume you have a copy."

Powell nodded. "I prefer nothin' leave this area. I'll get you an extra key."

Satisfied, Ramsey headed back to her room. She knew it would help to have a full stomach before she spent hours poring over the details of how their Jane Doe died.

———

Powell's description of the Half Moon was on the mark. Ramsey followed the two agents through the tavern-slash-grill, eyes immediately stinging from the smoky haze no ordinance would ever successfully ban. There was a he-done-me-wrong song blaring from a large jukebox wedged in the corner next to a small dance floor that was currently empty.

But there were an equal amount of diners and drinkers, and it was easy to see that the locals shared Matthews's opinion of the food.

The waitress, a sharp-featured thirtysomething with big bangs and tight jeans, seated them at a cramped table and slapped an extra table setting and menu down in front of Ramsey. "What'll ya have, handsome? The usual?" It didn't take brilliant deductive skills for Ramsey to guess the woman wasn't addressing her or Powell.

"Steak and a beer." Matthews gave her an easy smile. "You've already got my number."

She gave him a slow wink from a blue encrusted eyelid. The woman obviously applied her makeup with a trowel. "I know you like your beer cold and your steak hot, but how do you like your women?"

"Spicy."

While the two laughed, Ramsey followed Powell's lead and opened the menu, ignoring their exchange. The entrees ran to meat and potatoes, which at the moment suited Ramsey fine. When the waitress finally tore her attention away from Matthews, she said, "Rib eye, medium well, potato baked, and just water to drink."

Powell snapped his menu closed. "Grilled chicken breast, rice, and a glass of low-fat milk."

As the waitress walked away, an exaggerated sway to her hips, Matthews told Ramsey confidingly, "Ward's got ulcers. Can't eat anything that isn't bland."

"Got them from keepin' young turks like you out of trouble," the other man said sourly. He rubbed at his gut as if in pain. "The diet they have me on is enough to ruin anyone's appetite."

"I'll bet." Ramsey was distracted from the conversation by a familiar blond head seated a few tables away. Her own appetite ebbed at seeing Stryker for the second time in one day.

Her reaction to him wasn't totally objective. Realizing that didn't make it any less real. Nor did it make her tone welcoming when he got up and headed their way.

"Evenin'." Although his greeting was directed at the table at large, his gaze was on Ramsey. "Nice surprise to see you again, Ms. Clark."

She could feel the two agents' eyes on her, but she didn't bother with an introduction. "Stryker. Funny place to look for ghosts."

"Never know." His mouth quirked up in a smile. He was, she decided, entirely too easygoing. "They've got ol' Gil cookin' back there. That could be a direct line to the afterlife." He circled their table to stand behind her and pulled out her chair. "Mind if I borrow her for a few minutes, fellas? Promise to bring her back in one piece."

Rather than engage in the explanation necessary to erase the men's quizzical expressions, Ramsey gritted her teeth and rose. "Excuse me, would you please?" But when Stryker took her elbow to guide her back toward his table, she shook off his touch.

"I don't appreciate being commandeered." She saw then, for the first time, the woman seated at the table he'd vacated. The one he was steering her toward. "Who's that?"

"Leanne Layton. She's a real nice gal, so don't go bein' mean to her. She wants to meet you."

She shot him a look filled with dislike. "I'm not mean."

His smile widened. "You purely are. Surly even. 'Course some guys might find that edge attractive."

She snorted. "Like I care whether . . . Hello." She was forced to swallow the rest of her retort as the woman smiled at her.

"Dev, you rude ol' thing. I didn't mean for you to go steal her away from her friends." Leanne Layton smiled sunnily up at Ramsey. "My fault. I was wonderin' about you, and Dev here said he'd met you. I told him I'd like to talk to you some time, and off he goes and whisks you over here."

"I thought Ramsey would be interested to hear you tell her about the local legend." He pulled out an empty chair and sat Ramsey down in it with one hand to her shoulder.

She sent him a killer look, which seemed to slide off him. "Actually . . ."

He bent down to murmur in her ear. "Open your mind a little, Ms. Clark. I promise your brains won't fall out." Straightening, he said in a louder tone, "How 'bout I go up and get you both one of Gil's special lemonades?"

"Doesn't do any good to get mad at him."

Ramsey shifted her gaze, which had been drilling into the man's back, to the woman next to her, who was smiling ruefully.

"I mean you can try, but seems like a good mad just doesn't stick when you're dealin' with Devlin Stryker."

"You know him well?"

"Known him since we were both in strollers. Even after his family moved away, he came back regular to visit his granddaddy."

Interest sparked among her ire. He was as good as a local then, but with an outsider's objectivity. As such he might be of use filling in details about the people in town if they started profiling suspects.

Temper easing, Ramsey took another look at the woman next to her. With her cap of sleek brown hair, red sundress, and manicured nails, she'd look at home on a magazine cover featuring Southern belles.

"Stryker . . . Devlin tells me you're an authority on the legend of the red mist."

Her fire-engine-red nail polish flashed as Leanne gave a dismissive gesture with her hand. "Not me. But I can repeat what my mama has told me since I was little. Donnelle Layton," she said in an aside. "She's sort of a volunteer historian for the local historical museum. I'm not sayin' she puts a lot of stock in the story, but she's very exactin' about writin' down the history of people and places around here. It's all part of the color, you understand, of who and what formed our town."

Ramsey always forgot the roundabout path conversations took in the south. She took a deep breath, squelched her impatience, and tried to summon a polite smile.

"You've probably noticed it has been a little nuts 'round here since the murder. Well, maybe you haven't noticed, since Dev said you just arrived, but it is. And I don't mean just the news crews either. A murder always gets people in these parts spooked, because of the legend. On account of the murders happenin' in threes." Leanne paused to dig around in a purse too small to be of much use, and extracted a package of cigarettes.

"There have been other homicides here?" Rollins had mentioned deaths occurring around the same time as the appearance of the red mist. But he'd neglected to mention they'd been homicides. Ramsey's interest in the legend kicked up several notches.

After lighting a cigarette and inhaling deeply, Leanne continued. "There are different versions of the legend, you understand. But the facts that remain the same are that every generation, give or take a few years, we'll have a sightin' of the red mist followed by a death. And shortly after the first one, two others will occur. Of course they aren't always violent deaths. Maybe someone will have a heart attack or die in their sleep." Leanne seemed fuzzy on the exact details. "But the red mist is always sighted before the first body is found."

"You mean by whoever discovers the victim?" Ramsey asked. She was intrigued in spite of herself.

"Oh no." Leanne shook her head emphatically. "There'll be several reports of people claimin' to have seen it. Gets some of the folks worked up, you understand, when they hear 'bout it. Children aren't allowed out after dark. The streets just roll up at dusk. Some people even leave town for a while."

"Sheriff Rollins said there's a scientific explanation for the color, and that it's just low-lying fog."

Leanne lifted one smooth shoulder left bare by the sundress. "He'd know, I 'spect. Come to think of it, our chemistry teacher tried to explain it to us back in high school. Can't say I ever paid it much mind back then." She gave Ramsey a mischievous smile. "When we were kids, it was more fun scarin' ourselves with the legend, you know?"

"I can imagine." Ramsey thought for a moment. "What about those details you talked about? The different retellings?"

"You should really talk to my mama. I'll just mess it up. Never could keep them all straight. But they are interestin'."

Making a mental note to do just that, Ramsey asked, "How far back does this pattern go? The red mist and murders, I mean?"

Leanne sat back as Dev arrived at the table and carefully set two glasses of frothy lemonade in front of them. "Thank you, honey." To Ramsey she said, "How long? I'm not sure. About a hundred years or so." Her inflection made it more a question than a statement. "The one thing that can't be denied is that there *is* a pattern. It's just one of those things."

A helluva pattern, Ramsey agreed silent. And one of those things that Rollins had glossed over in their earlier discussion on the topic.

"Where can I find your mother if I want to hear more about the legend?"

Leanne set her cigarette in the ashtray and reached for her glass, sipping daintily from the straw. "She works part-time at the mill in Clayton. That's about fifteen miles from here. But most Wednesdays she's at the Historical Museum on Main Street."

"You can't miss it." Stryker spoke for the first time since returning to the table. "The storefront has been restored to reflect the architecture of the 1800s. Narrow gray buildin' on the north side of the street."

"I'll remember that." She shot him a meaningful look. "That is, if my brains don't fall out before then."

"Stop in and see me sometime, too." Leanne reached over to rake a hand through Ramsey's hair, causing her to jump. "Sorry." She smiled ruefully. "Habit of mine. I own Sharp Cuts on the corner of Fifth and Maple. And you have a decent enough cut; you just need a trim." Her gaze turned assessing. "Do you highlight it?"

"Uh, no." How did they go from discussing century-old legends and deaths to hair?

Leanne lifted one smoothly arched brow. "Lucky you. Like I say, stop in. I talked too much and didn't get to hear a thing about you. We do manis and pedis, too."

Ramsey must have looked as blank as she felt because the other woman went on. "Manicures and pedicures. We're full service."

Curling her fingers with their ragged nails into her palms, Ramsey decided it was time to take her leave. "I should get back to my . . . friends. It was nice meeting you, Leanne. I'm sure I'll be seeing you again." Although not, if she could help it, by making an appointment with the woman.

Rising, she glanced at Stryker, who was watching her with an amused glint in his eye. "Later," she said shortly, her voice full of promise.

"Countin' on it." He picked up her glass, offered it to her. "Don't forget your lemonade."

Ramsey hesitated for a minute, then took it from him and walked back to her table, where the food had arrived.

"Sorry," she said, slipping into her chair and unfolding a napkin across her lap. "That took longer than I expected."

The two men were already eating. "How'd you meet Stryker already?" Powell cut off a piece of chicken and put it in his mouth, chewing with a resigned air of a man eating purely for fuel rather than enjoyment.

"He was at Ashton's Pond when I got there with Rollins." As she cut her steak, she gave them an abbreviated account of their first meeting.

"Don't know what Rollins was thinking," Matthews said when she was finished. "He knows better than to let a civilian tromp around in a crime scene."

"We're not going to find anythin' else there," Powell said flatly. "We've eliminated the area around the pond as the primary scene. Our best chance of solvin' this thing is to discover where the victim was killed."

"And to ID her," Ramsey put in. Matthews had been right. The steak was better than average. She slathered her potato with butter until she caught Powell watching her and decided not to rub it in. "That woman Stryker introduced me to told me a little about the legend of the red mist. Have you heard about it?"

"Hard not to." Powell speared rice into his mouth and then took a long drink of milk. "Every wit we interview goes on 'bout it. Just a bunch of superstitious nonsense."

She didn't disagree. "But what if someone is playing on that superstition with this homicide?" She was thinking out loud. "Get people this agitated, and it can cloud an investigation. Make it difficult for investigators to separate fact from fiction."

"Right now we've got damn few facts," Powell said grimly. He'd finished his meal and was eyeing her steak avariciously. "First thing in the mornin' we'll bring you up to date with what we do have and consider our next steps. Assign duties."

And he was in charge of doing so. His message was clear. Ramsey didn't mind. Eventually, though, she'd have a few ideas of her own for tracking down the identity of their Jane Doe.

She'd barely finished eating when Powell was shoving his chair back, reaching for his wallet. Ramsey got her purse and placed some bills on the table.

"I'm going to stay for a while," Matthews surprised her by saying. "I'll catch a ride later."

Powell lifted a shoulder. "As long as you realize no matter what time you come draggin' in, I'm getting you up at seven."

The younger agent was already turned away, scanning the crowd. "I think I can handle it."

Ramsey caught Stryker's gaze on her before she turned away to follow the agent out of the tavern. The man was a bona fide pain in the ass. But tonight, at least, he'd at least been a somewhat useful one.

Chapter 3

They might not know the victim's name, but it was evident that she'd died unhappily.

Ramsey held the autopsy report, with the crime scene photos arrayed on the table before her. Their Jane Doe hadn't spent enough time in the water to bloat up the way a floater would have. Less than two hours, according to the medical examiner.

Flipping a page of the report, Ramsey continued reading. She still couldn't believe their bad luck. They'd had teenage kids running all over those woods, and none so far admitted to having seen a car or stranger there that night. Given the timeline of when the kids were seen in town and how long the body had been in the water, they may have missed the killer by as little as forty-five minutes.

Assuming, of course, that the same person who killed the woman was the one who got rid of her body.

Ramsey lingered over the description of the Jane Doe. Five-six, one hundred thirty pounds. Between eighteen and twenty-five. Brown hair and eyes.

Settling back in her chair, she put her feet up on the supporting bar beneath the table and used the descriptors to work up a mental picture of the victim. Not as she was when her body was found, broken and violated. But of whom she may have been before she'd met her killer.

Ramsey would need that in her brain, a visual of the woman as she had been alive. Young. Vibrant. With a future that had been snatched from her. Already that familiar burn had lodged in her chest. The one that wouldn't go away until justice had been delivered for the unknown victim.

The next page revealed the woman had had her appendix removed no more than three years ago. Two small tattoos adorned the body. The TBI agents had run the vic through the state and national crime databases. Neither her fingerprints nor the tattoo identifiers had hit, so the woman didn't have a record.

Ramsey reached forward for a handful of pictures. The body had been found facedown in the pond. The small amount of water in the lungs indicated the organs had just begun to passively fill. She'd been dead before she'd been dumped there.

She lingered over the photos showing the bruises to the woman's throat. Death by manual strangulation. A very personal way to kill someone. The report indicated violent vaginal and anal sexual intercourse prior to death. Bruising to the vulva and upper thighs. Anal fissures and perineal lacerations. The extent of the trauma suggested possible multiple partners. If any trace evidence had transferred from one of her attackers to the body, the time in the water had destroyed it.

And that, Ramsey thought grimly, might have been another reason to travel so far into the woods to dump the body. Water was a great decomposer of evidence. What the fish left would have been unrecognizable after a day or so.

But the killer hadn't been given days.

She looked at her watch. It was nearing midnight. But it would be a while before she'd sleep, especially with the woods still looming large in her mind. Slumber could take an experience like that and magnify it to nightmare proportions. Linking past and present together so realistically that she'd wake with her heart hammering in her chest, her pulse sprinting, and the taste of raw panic choking her. Leaving her feeling despicably weak and vulnerable.

Ramsey didn't do weak or vulnerable. Not anymore. Not in a very long time.

Determinedly, she turned another page of the report. She was used to coming in later on a case and needing to play catch-up until she was as well-versed in the details of the investigation as the primaries were. And she preferred to look at the notes with a fresh eye, before anyone had told her too much, skewing her perception and perhaps blinding her to a novel direction.

The photos drew her attention once more. Strangulation was sometimes a crime of passion. But there were no finger-prints left on the body, meaning either its short stay in the water had erased them or the killer had worn gloves. Which would point to premeditation.

Ramsey turned her focus to the next page in the medical examiner's findings. She skipped over the data revealing the weight and mass of the victim's internal organs and found the part that reported the contents of her stomach.

A small amount of water and an unknown substance that was identified only as a "plant derivative" had been digested shortly before death. Cocking her head, she considered just what that term might mean.

A food item would have been easy to test and identify, but a plant derivative? Ramsey was at a loss. What else would fall into that category? Leaves? Tree bark? Roots?

Puzzled, she leaned back in her seat, threading her pen through her fingers. There were always those who experi-mented with new ways to get a buzz. And herbalists abounded who concocted nonpharmaceutical answers to disease. Even drug companies were experimenting with different types of tree bark for various medicines.

Reaching for her notepad, Ramsey jotted down *stomach contents—plant derivative??*, underlining it twice. She men-tally crossed her fingers that the ME had saved the unknown substance for further testing.

Exhaustion was starting to gray the hem of her concentra-tion. She'd already put in a long day. But she wanted to finish this report and mine it for leads she thought most relevant.

It would be interesting tomorrow morning to compare her conclusions with those of Powell and Matthews.

A vehicle sounded on the gravel on the drive out front. Ramsey didn't look up until headlights flashed across the window. Then she rose, report still in her hand, and crossed to lift a corner of the shade. Even in the darkness, she recognized Matthews as one of the two figures getting out of a car and heading into a cabin two doors down.

Feeling like a voyeur, she dropped the shade and went back to her chair. It hadn't taken the agent long to make friends tonight. She'd figure Powell to be on the other side of this room, which meant the younger man would be next to him. She wondered what the senior agent would think of his colleague's extracurricular activity. She didn't know him well enough to hazard a guess.

She continued reading the report until something in it made her sit straight up in her chair. Leaning forward, she grabbed the photos taken by the ME, flipping through them until she found the ones she was looking for.

The body had been found facedown in the water. One lower leg—foot to knee—had been exposed enough to catch the attention of the teenagers. And on the back of the ankle, the ME had found a substance he had been able to identify.

Bleach.

———

"I think identification of the victim should take precedence," Ramsey stated firmly. "Once we know who she was, where she was from, we can narrow our search for her attacker."

"Agreed, but we've got lots of different threads started on this investigation, and we need to follow up on all of them." Powell was sipping from a glass of milk he must have picked up in the motel's main office. "Startin' with fully checkin' out the witness accounts."

"The sheriff told me the teenagers had been alibied for the night of the crime."

"We haven't talked to everyone who claims to have seen them that night. And a few we've tried to talk to haven't been especially forthcomin'. We need to continue interviewin' everyone who lives along that road closest to the woods. They might be able to identify a vehicle seen on it that night."

"We could get a forensic artist to make a sketch of the victim," Ramsey suggested. Matthews still had said nothing. He was seated at the table wolfing down his second doughnut with a cup of coffee. If he was feeling any effects from his late night, it didn't show. "Send it to neighboring towns."

"No one's reported this woman missing." The younger agent finally spoke in between bites. "It's been all over the news, and none of the calls the sheriff's office has fielded so far have matched the vic's description."

"All the more reason to get her face out there," Ramsey pressed. "Maybe no one knows she's missing. She could be a runaway. Homeless. Or someone who has been so isolated her loved ones don't even know she's gone." Batterers regularly cut off their wives or girlfriends from their family and friends. Their Jane Doe could have died at the hands of a husband or boyfriend and not even be missed yet by those who cared about her.

"I'm not releasin' her likeness to the press," Powell said firmly. He was dressed in the same suit he'd worn yesterday, a nondescript dark color with another white shirt. Only the tie was different. "Jeffries would have my ass if I fed the media anythin' else to keep their interest alive. My job is to handle them as quietly as possible."

Before anything could be resolved, a knock sounded at the door. Powell opened it to a middle-aged man in a deputy's uniform. "'Mornin'." He uttered the obligatory greeting as he stepped inside, a sober expression on his face. "I'm Chief Deputy Phil Stratton. Sheriff Rollins had me stop on my way home from my shift. He's handlin' some distraught parents at the office." His gaze traveled from one face to another. "Local folk, Jim and Linda Grayson. They just returned from a stay in Knoxville. They're afraid the victim might be their daughter, Joanie Lyn."

———

Ramsey doubted she was who Rollins had had in mind when he'd sent the deputy to have someone meet the parents at the Spring County morgue, located in the center of Buffalo

Springs. But she'd volunteered for the duty, and neither of the agents had seemed inclined to argue with her. Dealing with heartbroken parents was a grim reality of the job, and not one that anyone relished.

But she'd wanted to see the victim. Wanted to talk to the ME who'd performed the autopsy. This would give her an opportunity to do both, and to take pictures to fax to the forensic artist, Alec Bledsoe, back at Raiker Forensics headquarters. Once she had a likeness of the victim in hand, Powell could hardly resist at least distributing it to nearby law enforcement agencies.

She'd discovered a new model silver Ford Escape left at the motel office in her name, and she found it fully equipped, complete with an in-dash GPS. Ramsey wasn't surprised. Adam Raiker was a demanding employer, but she never had a complaint about the timeliness of the agency's resources.

Armed with the deputy's directions, she turned left out of the motel parking lot and headed into town. With just over two thousand residents, Buffalo Springs was the largest town in Spring County, a mostly rural area that included hills and parts of the Great Smoky Mountains. The mountain range had unexpectedly lovely valleys in between that marked eastern Tennessee. Buffalo Springs was located in one of those valleys. According to the map she'd consulted prior to her arrival here, the rest of the towns dotting the county were less than half its size.

She wasn't familiar with the area. Ramsey had worked for TBI seven years before joining Raiker Forensics three years ago, but she'd worked out of the Memphis office.

Ten minutes later she was pulling up to the one-story stone utilitarian-looking building that the deputy had directed her toward. She spotted Rollins's car moving slowly up the street toward her, so she waited outside the building.

A man in the passenger's seat got out and joined Mark before they approached Ramsey. He was on the wrong side of sixty, gray and balding, with clothes that hung slightly on his frame, as if he'd recently been sick. He shuffled rather than walked, and Ramsey knew she wasn't the only one dreading the upcoming scene.

Mark made the introductions. "Ramsey, this here is Jim Grayson. Jim, Ms. Clark is a special consultant workin' with TBI on this case."

Ramsey surprised herself by laying a hand on the man's arm. She was not normally a toucher. "I sincerely hope that's not your daughter in there, Mr. Grayson. But you have my word we'll do everything in our power to make sure justice is served in this case."

He looked at her then. Really looked at her. And she revised her original estimation. This man wasn't just sick. He was dying. She could see it in the yellow rims just inside his eyes. In the creases pain had carved into his face. He reached up to cover her hand with his. His palm was dry and papery. "I don't know what to hope for anymore, Miss. I surely don't."

She trailed behind them as the sheriff led the man through the building's lobby and down a long hallway to a doorway with a man in scrubs standing outside it.

"Here." The stranger handed Mr. Grayson a mask. "You might want to put this on." He offered nothing to Rollins or Ramsey, so she mentally steeled herself. A moment later, she walked into the morgue after them, and the familiar odors assaulted her senses. She had a moment to be grateful she hadn't eaten that morning before following the trio to one of the small compartment doors that lined one wall.

The man grabbed a handle and pulled the steel gurney out. He took his time folding the sheet back to reveal the body, and Ramsey knew he was giving the man time to ready himself.

But a moment later, Grayson's shoulders slumped forward, and he slowly swung his head from side to side. "Not her," he croaked. "That's not my Joanie Lyn."

He turned away, his expression so shattered that Ramsey leaped to his side, certain he'd crumple. She and Mark assisted him out of the morgue, back down the hallway, and out to the street without the man saying another word.

Rollins left his side to open the car door for him, but before he got into the car, Grayson turned to Ramsey again. "Four times now." Her gaze sought Rollins, uncomprehending, before the man continued. "Four times I've come to a place like this in the last six years. Sometimes hoping, God help me, that I'd see my daughter on that slab. At least then, we'd *know*."

"It has to be the most agonizing task a parent can do," she murmured, her throat tight.

"Find out who she is, Miss Clark." His brown gaze traveled back to the building, lingered. "That's all I ask. Find out that girl's name so her daddy don't have to go to his grave without ever knowin' what happened to his li'l girl."

"We'll do our best." She knew better than to issue promises. But once Grayson was in the sheriff's car, as it pulled away from the curb, she made the promise silently anyway. Because she knew herself well enough to know she wouldn't rest until she'd done just that.

———

"You've got the report." The medical examiner, Don Wilson, the man in scrubs she'd seen earlier, pulled out the gurney of the victim one more time, this time with less grace. "I don't know what else I can tell you."

Ramsey took out her camera and began snapping photos of the bloodless face of the victim. "I'm interested in the stomach contents. I was wondering if you saved them for testing."

"Turned it over to those TBI guys. Figured they sent it up to the Knoxville lab where the test will, given their schedule, sit there until sometime next year."

She suppressed a sigh of relief. So the substance had been saved. Powell had mentioned the physical evidence from the scene and the fingerprints had been sent to Knoxville. Everything else was probably being kept at the sheriff's office until the mobile lab arrived. Including the stomach contents. There was no way of knowing if further testing could be done on it but the scientist Raiker was sending was a whiz, if a bit on the bizarre side. If there was more to be learned, Jonesy would find it.

She stepped closer to the corpse and angled the camera for a closer photo of the marks on the corpse's neck. "The report said the hyoid bone was broken."

"I also found fractures to the cartilage of the windpipe and larynx. See this?" He reached past her to point at the victim's eyes.

"Pinpoint hemorrhages."

"That's right. Death was by manual strangulation prior to her bein' dumped in the water."

"I agree. But your findings were in the report. I'm interested in things that weren't included in it."

"Everythin' was in the report," insisted Wilson. "I know the regs. Whatever we're required to include was there."

Ramsey lowered the camera. "I'm not talking about what you're required to include. I'm interested in what you couldn't add to the report because you lacked the evidence. Impressions that occurred to you while you were conducting the autopsy."

He was silent for a moment, regarding her from midnight dark eyes. "My job isn't to . . ."

She gave a mental sigh. "You're human, aren't you?" Human enough to begin to be irritating. "You start to form opinions as you work. Some are validated, some aren't. And some you just don't have enough information to be sure whether you were right or wrong."

"That's what you want to hear?"

"That's what I want to hear." The camera clicked again as she took another shot.

"Because you like opinions unsubstantiated by fact."

Lowering the camera, she eyed him. "I still believe the Cubs can win the World Series."

His raised brows showed the words had done the trick. "That's not just unsubstantiated, that's pure fantasy." Convinced, he stepped closer, the smell obviously not bothering him. Ramsey had long suspected that MEs early on lost the use of their olfactory senses altogether.

"Okay, there were a few things. For instance, take a look at the hands." He pulled the sheet back to the body's waist. "See the length of the nails?"

She blinked, surprised. Most of the time the ME or investigating detective clipped the nails of a homicide victim close and bagged them for evidence. No one had bothered doing so with the Jane Doe. But that wasn't what Wilson was talking about. "You didn't find anything beneath them." She recalled that fact from his report.

"Not a speck. Violent assault like this, she didn't strike her assailant?"

Ramsey eyed the hands he was holding up. The nails were medium length, badly broken in spots. "Even though it appears she may have broken them defending herself." Or perhaps she'd been held somewhere and had been trying to claw her way out. In either scenario, there should have been evidence beneath the nails.

He nodded. "Exactly. Which then makes you wonder if the nails had been scrubbed before the body was dumped. No way to be sure, so I didn't put it in the report. Just put down that nothin' was found."

But something else was bothering Ramsey about the nails. "I can see the clear polish on them." It was a little embarrassing to admit her ignorance of manicures. "But what do they call it when they put that white stuff along the tips like that?"

Wilson looked at her like she was crazy. "Out of my area of expertise." But he held the hands up so she could take several pictures of them.

When she'd finished, she rubbed at the lacerations on the back of the victim's wrists. "If she'd been restrained by rope or cuffs, I'd expect to see abrasions around the entire wrist, not just here." The wounds made her wonder if the assailant had held the victim's wrists down as he assaulted her, rubbing them raw as they were pressed against something hard and rough.

The ME just lifted a shoulder. "With the bleach I found on the back of one foot and the lack of any evidence beneath her nails, it's plausible to guess that the entire body had been scrubbed down. Of course," he hastened to add, "I can't prove . . ."

"I know, I got that." Satisfaction flashed through her. Because the same thing had occurred to her. She thought for a minute. "I'd expect some sort of evidence beneath her nails around each break. Is it possible that her time in the water would have destroyed all of it?"

"It's possible. The only trace evidence I found was the bleach on one heel."

"She was facedown in the water," Ramsey said slowly. "The kids sighted the foot of the body first."

"Of course, she could have stepped in somethin'. She could have brushed up against it, and that would account for that residue on her skin. So again, all I put in the report was the substance and where it was located." As if growing uncomfortable with his conjectures, he covered the body up with the sheet again. "Like I said, all the facts are included in the report. The rest . . . it doesn't mean anythin'."

"Maybe not." Ramsey was in unfamiliar territory herself. Facts solved crimes. Built cases. But sometimes speculation led to a valuable lead.

And there was at least one lead she wanted to follow as soon as she downloaded these pictures.

———

The last person Dev expected to see walk into Leanne's Sharp Cuts at ten o'clock in the morning was Ramsey Clark.

He caught sight of her in the mirror first, in between exchanging flirtatious rejoinders with Maddie Simmons in the next chair. Maddie was twice his age, and perhaps double his weight—he wasn't going to go there—but she was a woman, and he'd never met one yet who didn't enjoy passing the time with a little innocent repartee.

Enter then Ramsey Clark, serving as the exception to the rule.

She stopped dead when she caught sight of him, and he

enjoyed betting that her clenched jaw meant she was gritting her teeth at his presence there. No one else had noticed her yet, or the way she was inching back toward the door.

Because his mama had taught him to be neighborly, he called out, "Why, if it isn't Ramsey Clark. You're a sight for sore eyes this summer mornin'." Leanne twirled around and squealed in delight.

"Ramsey! Dev and I were just puttin' our heads together tryin' to figure how I was goin' to see you again. I have so much I want to ask you, you just have no idea."

The smile on Ramsey's face looked forced. "I had a question I thought you could help me with. But I can come back. It looks like you're busy."

"Shoot, Dev's done and Hailey here is working on Maddie."

Leanne approached Ramsey in that friendly way of hers, and Dev got out of the chair, intrigued. He didn't know much about Ramsey Clark, but he knew enough to recognize she was about at ease in a place like this as a long-tailed cat in room full of rocking chairs.

She slanted a look at him. "Does Superman know you've stolen his cape?"

He grinned, unabashed and reached up to take off the red protective plastic cape that was emblazoned with the salon's name. "Actually he gave it to me on account of me achievin' superhero status."

"Get along, Dev." Leanne shooed him away. "She didn't come to see you." Turning her attention back to Ramsey, she said, "What can I do for you, hon? A trim? We do a facial here that will have your face skin feelin' as fresh as dew on a rose petal."

"Nothing like that. I wanted you to look at a picture and give me your professional opinion on something."

To her credit, Leanne managed to contain her shock and excitement with an aplomb Dev could only imagine was costing her.

"Sure thing. Why don't you come back to my office?"

His own curiosity piqued, Dev trailed at a distance to the

back of the shop. When he arrived there, he saw Ramsey taking some papers out of her bag. "I downloaded some pictures from my camera and ran them off. I'd like you to take a look at the hands in these photos. I'm wondering if the nails were professionally done."

Leanne peered at each digital photo in turn. "Doesn't take care of her hands, that's for darn sure. I'll never understand why people take the time, some even pay good money for a manicure, to be this careless with their nails. We're runnin' a special on manis and pedis next week. Probably shouldn't tell you that, bad for sales, but if you're interested it would be a great opportunity to . . ."

Her voice trailed off as she lingered over one of the pictures. Dev came closer to see for himself, his presence still not commented on by either woman.

"I know that's a special kind of manicure, right?" Ramsey tapped the photo Leanne was looking at. "What do you call it when the nail tips are polished that way?"

"It's a French manicure," she responded absently. "Probably done in a salon. Lands, look at all the breaks she has. Was she diggin' ditches?" Without a breath, she shifted back to her assessment. "Of course I can't tell for sure, because there are certainly plenty of women who do their own. But see this?" She traced a line on the nail. "It takes skill to get the smile line that perfect on every finger. Real hard to do on yourself. If I had to guess, I'd reckon this is a salon job."

If the pronouncement affected Ramsey, there was no sign of it. Her voice was even when she asked, "Any way to tell approximately how long ago it was done?"

Leanne sucked in her bottom lip, a habit of hers Dev recognized from the time they'd been kindergarteners. "Probably within the last week, week and a half. See that clear polish she has over the nails? There's not a lot of outgrowth showin', which means it had to have been done fairly recently."

She handed the pictures back to Ramsey, who refolded them and slipped them back into her bag. "I really appreciate this, Leanne."

"Hope so." She smiled brightly. "'Cuz when this is over, I'm goin' to pump you somethin' unmerciful about all this. I figure you can't say anythin' now."

Dev recognized the relief that flickered over Ramsey's face. He was a bit shocked himself at Leanne's restraint. The woman had many admirable qualities, but patience wasn't one of them.

"No, I can't. But you have been a great help. Thanks a lot."

Ramsey turned then and nearly bumped into Dev, who had, he'd admit it, sidled closer to get a better view of the pictures.

"You're constantly underfoot," she noted, in a tone far different than the one she'd used with Leanne. "Don't you have ghosts to bust?"

Something devilish in him had him taking his time moving out of the way. "Bagged my quota last night," he replied, tongue planted firmly in cheek. "Wouldn't be sportin' of me not to leave some for the next quack who comes along."

She brushed by him, and because he wasn't a man to waste an opportunity, he turned to observe her retreat. It was, he noted with appreciation, a sight well worth watching. The slim-fitting black pants she wore did an admirable job showcasing those trim hips and long legs.

"Dev." Leanne grabbed his arm and shook it, and reluctantly he shifted his attention back to her. "Do you know what I just did?" Without waiting for a reply, she continued on a suppressed squeal, "I just helped in a murder investigation!"

"Now, Leanne," he started, warningly.

"I know, I know," she raised her clasped hands to her lips, her brown eyes sparkling. "But that just had to be pictures of that poor gal they found in Ashton's Pond last week, didn't it? I mean, that's what brought Ramsey down here, so it goes to figure."

"Maybe," he allowed, although it was probably true enough. "But this isn't one of your television shows, so don't go gettin' carried away."

She gave him a slight push with the ease of a woman who'd known him all his life. "If it were an episode of *CSI*, the thing would be solved in fifty-three minutes. But just because I like watchin' those shows doesn't mean I'm naïve about how things really work." Leanne nodded toward the direction Ramsey had taken. "For instance, I know a bit about that outfit she works for. Raiker Forensics. Bet I know more than you do."

He didn't want to admit to the interest her words sparked in him. "How would you know about that?"

"There was somethin' on *Primetime: Crime* about it just last year." A bell rang and she ducked around him to see who had come in the front door. Turning back to him, she said, "That Raiker fella, he used to be one of the FBI's top profilers. They mentioned all the famous cases he was involved in. But then he was on the trail of that serial killer—'member the one that killed all those kids in Louisiana?—and he saved a victim but ended up gettin' captured himself." She waited expectantly, but Dev merely shrugged. He didn't share Leanne's fascination with grisly crimes. For all her elegant appearance, she was frighteningly bloodthirsty.

His lack of reaction seemed to annoy her. Her bottom lip, slicked with bright red lipstick, jutted out briefly. "Anyway he was held captive and tortured for days before escapin' and killin' the guy. He retired from the Bureau and started his own agency. You know what they call it, right?"

Because he felt guilty for being such a poor audience, he searched his memory and came up with the name she'd mentioned. "Raiker Forensics?"

"Not the real name, dummy." Leaning past him, she called out, "You just go ahead and sit down in my chair, Eileen, I'll be with you in minute." Turning back to Dev, she lowered her voice even more. "They call his outfit The Mindhunters. On account of them being called in on the most puzzlin' crimes. Think of that. One of the Mindhunters in li'l ol' Buffalo Springs." She sent him an arch look. "If you don't see how special that is, Devlin Stryker, you've been livin' under a rock."

"Sounds like you've been talkin' to my housekeeper."

He trailed after her as she bustled out to greet her newest customer, his hands shoved deep in the pockets of his jeans. Despite his expressed disinterest, he was mulling over what Leanne had revealed.

He wouldn't be a bit surprised to discover the woman knew what she was talking about. As if in response to the quiet small-town life of Buffalo Springs, she was voracious in her hunger for sensational crime. It came, he supposed, from being born and raised in a town where an enthusiastic case of TPing made the weekly paper.

But he was less intrigued in the history of Ramsey's employer than he was in the woman herself.

He ambled to the door, pausing to lay a couple bills on Leanne's desk, and responded to Eileen's greeting distractedly. What kind of woman, he wondered as he pushed open the door to the sidewalk, would voluntarily immerse herself in this kind of gruesome job, day in and day out?

It was different for Leanne. She had an almost voyeuristic interest in true crime, a distant view from her secure perch in a sleepy little town. The murder that had rocked Buffalo Springs was, for Ramsey Clark, a commonplace occurrence.

Because there was nowhere in town far enough that he couldn't walk to it, Dev set off for the house left empty when his granddaddy had gone to the assisted living facility.

Easy enough to see where Ramsey's edge had come from, he reflected, making his way up the street at an easy pace. A woman in an occupation like that would have to be tough.

And he was contrary enough to wonder what all lay beneath the woman's tough exterior. And if he'd ever get a chance to discover that for himself.

Chapter 4

"You're Robbie Joe, right?" When the teenager in the store uniform turned around in the grocery line to look at him, Dev gave him a friendly grin. "Devlin Stryker. Knew your daddy when I was in school. He still workin' at the mill in Clayton?"

The kid looked seventeen or so, still in that gangly awkward stage that every living boy paused at on his way to manhood.

"Yeah, that's right." The kid shuffled up to the cashier and laid a small fortune worth of junk food and a half liter of pop on the counter. "He's a supervisor there now."

The bored-looking cashier, who looked to be a few years old than Robbie Joe, rang him up and announced the total. As the boy fumbled for his wallet, Dev dropped some bills on the counter.

"Let me get that for you. Least I can do for a local celebrity."

Looking considerably more cheerful, the kid said, "Thanks, Mr. Stryker."

Dev fell into step beside the boy as he headed out the automated double doors of Easley's Supermarket. "You done for the day?"

"Uh-uh." Robbie Joe was already digging into the plastic bag holding his purchases. "I'm on lunch break."

Remembering the contents he'd bought, Dev suppressed a wince. Hopefully the boy's belly was up to the punishment it was about to get. "Mind if I hang 'round while you eat?"

Shaking his head, Robbie pulled out a package of Nutter

Butters and opened it. "I guess you recognized me from TV, huh? I've been on lots lately. One was even national news."

"Actually I recognized you because you're the spittin' image of your mama in high school," Dev said. They stopped at a bench located several feet away from the store and sat down. He'd always liked the boy's mama, though his daddy had been something of an ass. After he'd gotten his girlfriend pregnant and dropped out of school, Dev had rarely seen either of them. When it occurred to him that Robbie Joe must be the product of that encounter, he could practically feel his bones creak.

"I'm interested in what you saw that night, Robbie." Dev watched in unwilling fascination as the boy washed half a package of cookies down with the soda. "Before you found the body."

"You mean the red mist and stuff?" Unconcerned with social niceties, the kid wiped his mouth on the back of his hand. "Tell you the truth, Mr. Stryker . . . it all seems like sort of a dream."

"I'll bet." Dev dug in his pocket, pulled out his card, and handed it to him. "I make my livin' checkin' that sort of thing out. Write books about people's experiences with paranormal events and phenomenas. I'd like your perspective."

The boy took the card but didn't look at it. "I recollect your name now. Heard my daddy mention you a time or two."

Since Dev's opinion of Robbie Joe's daddy was handily reciprocated, he didn't dare ask for more details. Instead he pulled a slim miniature recorder out of his pants pocket and held it up so the boy could see it. "Mind if I ask you a few questions then? With the recorder on?"

A measure of enthusiasm showed in Robbie's expression for the first time. "Are you gonna put me in your book?"

"Depends on whether I get enough material while I'm in Buffalo Springs to interest my editor in the project," Dev hedged. Everything inside him shied away from using the events in this town for a new release. It was too intensely personal. And way too painful.

But even that nonanswer was enough to loosen the teenager's lips. He embarked on a highlight of the events of that night, and Dev listened without comment until the boy ran down. Then he said, "Let's back up to those lights you saw. The ones you thought were the guys' flashlights."

Robbie had worked his way through the package of cookies and was making serious inroads on a second Twinkie. Dev didn't know whether to congratulate him on his intestinal fortitude or hand him a Tums.

"Yeah, I thought the guys were behind me. Just funnin', y'know? But then I figured, shoot, it could be fireflies. Probably was, just like I told Becky."

"So these lights were the size of an insect?"

Robbie scratched his head with the edge of Dev's card. "Well . . . no, they were bigger than that. Like I say, they looked like they coulda been from flashlights, except dimmer, y'know? Like maybe when the battery's runnin' low. But in some parts of the Smoky Mountains, they got those special fireflies that all glow at once, don't they?"

"Synchronous fireflies," Dev said absently, thinking about what the boy had revealed. "So you're sayin' you only saw one light at a time?"

"Sometimes there was just one and sometimes there'd be a bunch of them hoppin' around. Just like bugs do. That's what I'm sayin'. The biggest one was like four inches or so. But then when I saw the smaller ones, they were half that."

"And the lights were solid white?"

Robbie started to speak and then paused. "Tell you the truth, Mr. Stryker, I'd be makin' it up if I told you I noticed. They made me think some of the guys were there, and then I started thinkin' about *that*, not what the lights looked like."

Dev didn't press. Becky had insisted the lights had a violet ring around them—she'd been very specific about the color—but he wasn't going to relay that to Robbie and influence his opinion. Instead he drew him out at length about the fog the boy insisted had come out of the ground, starting at his feet and winding around his body before spreading across the entire area.

"I heard Butch Tippon saw the red mist, too," Robbie added. He was clearly anxious to prove he wasn't imagining things. "And Becky said Silas Parker and Wally Greenberg did, too."

Dev had heard the three men's names as well and, in fact, had already talked to those men, and at least five others who had made similar claims. If their accounts were to be believed, given their separate locations at the time, the red mist had covered an outlying area of town of at least five miles. Dev made a habit of eating breakfast every morning at The Henhouse because there was no better place to overhear interesting tidbits like that to follow up on.

He saw the boy glance at his watch and, taking the hint, switched off the tape recorder. "I'm guessin' you need to be getting' back to work soon."

Tilting the soda to his lips, the kid guzzled from it like a fraternity pledge on hell night. Once he'd lowered it, he said, "Yeah. And my daddy will check up on me to be sure I'm here all night." His voice held a dejected note. "I got grounded on account of going to Ashton's Pond after dark, which is bogus. Hardly none of my other friends did."

Here was a topic which Dev could fully appreciate. He'd experienced that particular parental punishment frequently himself as a teenager. "It'll pass. You've still got most of the summer ahead of you."

"Yeah." Clearly unconvinced, Robbie Joe stuffed the remaining candy bar and bag of sunflower seeds in his pants pockets and rose. Dev hoped it would be enough to sustain the boy until he got off work. From what he'd witnessed, he had his doubts.

"Good talkin' to you." Giving the boy a clap on the shoulder, Dev left him as Robbie crumpled his trash and two-pointed it into the nearby waste can.

"Nice meetin' you, Mr. Stryker."

Barely restraining a wince, Dev headed home. Having a kid address him like that was a none-too-gentle reminder of the passage of time.

There were other reminders, of course. He considered

them as he strolled back to Benjamin Gorder's house. There had actually been a few unfamiliar faces in town since he'd arrived five days ago, despite the fact that he made it back here three or four times a year to see his granddaddy.

And there had been others missing. Mike and Mona Reed had retired and moved to Chattanooga. Crystal Meinders had married—for the third time—and gone to live in Clayton with her truck driver husband. Since Crystal had given him his first French kiss in seventh grade and an eye-popping lesson on the female anatomy, he regarded her kindly enough to wish her luck this time around.

He passed a familiar picket fence and felt his heart grow a little heavier. Time was when he used to take a stick and run it the length of that fence, just to hear the racket. Got chewed out regular for it, too, and one summer had to give it a coat of paint because his granddaddy had agreed with Ida Trivett that he'd probably worn the paint clear off just with his antics.

Ida had died the past winter at the age of eighty-four, and her death made him all too aware that his time with his granddaddy was running out. Of course, Benjamin was five years younger than his neighbor. But his last stroke had left him weak enough that moving him into the assisted living facility had been the only solution.

The time would come when his closest family in this town would be gone. He gave a stone on the sidewalk a kick, just to see it bounce and roll, and considered that future. He'd been born in Buffalo Springs. Had spent most of his summers here. Had even attended the local high school. Would the connection weaken with Benjamin's death?

Not likely. He turned up the narrow walk to the neatly kept story-and-a-half home with its wide front porch. This town had a grip on him. It always would.

At least until he could put the past to rest once and for all.

He went inside and booted the computer, bringing up the voice-recognition software that would surely go down in history as one of the most useful inventions known to mankind.

Removing the recorder from his pocket, he rewound it, then pressed play. The computer would type up the notes of

Robbie's interview, and all Dev would have to do was clean up and edit the passage when it was finished.

He hooked a nearby stool with his foot and dragged it over. Settling back in the computer chair and putting his feet up, Dev listened to the interview with a critical ear. No new information had been garnered, but he'd talk to every teenager who'd been in those woods before he was done, and interview any other person in the area who claimed to have seen the red mist.

He'd already decided Silas Parker was fabricating. His accounts didn't match any of the others and was spare on details altogether. Dev was used to separating fact from fiction as he traveled around investigating reports of paranormal phenomena. It wasn't unusual for people to claim they'd experienced something they hadn't. Dev almost preferred it to the ones who were purely convinced they *had*, despite all evidence to the contrary.

Toeing off his shoes, he crossed one foot over the other and idly watched Robbie's words dance across the computer screen.

According to Mark, the sheriff's department had determined that none of the other teenagers had been behind Robbie Joe and Becky in those woods. None had shown up on the scene for at least several minutes after the two had found the body, and they'd come from a different direction altogether.

As for the firefly theory . . . Dev listened again as the boy verbally tried to persuade them both that insects could have made the lights the kids had seen. Although he hadn't tried to convince the boy differently, Dev discounted that idea as well.

A more reasonable explanation, he thought, folding his arms behind his head and contemplating the familiar hairline crack in the dining room ceiling, was that the lights had been reflections of some sort. Or that they'd come from someone else with flashlights behind them, as Robbie had suspected, not wielded by his friends, but by someone who hadn't yet come forward. Maybe even the killer himself.

Dev had suggested as much to his cousin, and to his credit, Mark had seemed to take it under consideration. But it had been easy to see that the sheriff hadn't put much stock in the theory.

Of course, he could wonder about a whole different direction altogether and contemplate whether the lights were in fact spiritual orbs.

He'd encountered countless "evidence" over his career that reputed to be exactly that—balls of light that were physical manifestations of a spirit's energy. Of course he'd mostly debunked such happenings. Those showing up on photographs could too often be attributed to poor lighting, reflections, or camera malfunction.

But he wasn't a total disbeliever. Not by a long shot. During the course of his career he'd seen things, heard things, that couldn't be explained away by facts or the physical world. Been scared out of his long pants a time or two, he admitted without embarrassment. And had learned along the way that most so-called paranormal events could be explained by science.

Others had to be accepted as something else.

The pounding on his front door put an abrupt end to his ruminating. Dev's feet hit the floor, and he rose as the first shout was heard.

"Stryker! Get on out here so I can speak at ya!"

The voice was vaguely familiar, but he couldn't put a face to it before swinging the front door open.

He recognized the man standing on the porch with little enough effort, though. Banty Whipple—nicknamed for the banty rooster he resembled—was red-faced and looked ready to chew a strip off someone.

Dev propped one hand on the doorjamb and rested the other on the doorknob. "Afternoon, Banty."

The other man looked like he'd sucked a bag of lemons. "My name's Robert."

"'Course it is," Dev said agreeably, although if he'd ever known the man's given name, he'd long since forgotten it.

"Heard you was talkin' to my son over to Easley's Supermarket. Clem over to the Gas 'n' Go saw ya. Said it looked like you two had yourselves a nice long conversation."

"We did," Dev said, growing more mystified. He crossed one stockinged foot over the other. "Nice kid. Favors his mama." Which was plain good luck any way you looked at it.

"Stay 'way from him, you hear me?" Banty slammed his palm against the screen door for emphasis. "We needed to give permission to the sheriff and those state guys to talk to him. Even had to sign somethin' before the media folks could get near him. So who the hell do you think you are to waltz up and sit him down pretty as you please and fill his head with nonsense?"

"Well, the fact is, Ba—Robert," he corrected himself, "I'm not the law and I'm not the press. So technically I don't need your permission to pass a few minutes shootin' the breeze with your son."

"The hell you don't!" The second assault on the screen door came from Banty's fist. "My kid's not gonna be one of them weirdos you write about spoutin' crazy talk about haints and zombies and whatnot."

He was about to point out that he'd never written about zombies—although he would if he found an interesting case—but the man's next words had the statement drying in his mouth.

"Don't know as I'd want him talkin' to you under any circumstances." Banty spit his chew on the porch in disgust. "Hell, ever'body in these parts know what you come from, what your daddy was. Maybe some folks can ferget that sorta thing, but I ain't one of 'em."

Dev slapped his palm on the screen door and pushed it open so abruptly that Banty had to back up a few steps to avoid being struck by it. "Care to expand on that?" he said in a deadly controlled tone.

The shorter man thrust out his jaw. "Yer daddy's a killer. Can't deny that even if you want to. And now we got us another murder 'round here and who shows up? In Buffalo Springs, havin' your family 'round is plain unlucky for some folks. I ain't the only one thinks that way, neither."

"Thinkin's not your strong suit, Banty." Dev took another step toward the man. Felt his fingers curl into fists. "Never was. Now you've had your say. Better leave before I kick your ass." Although he saw the car roll in front of his house, he didn't take his eyes off the man in front of him.

"Shee-it." Banty spat again and rolled his shoulders. "You couldn't kick the ass end of a fly. You always was a . . ." His fist swung out, nearly connected, its speed surprising. But Dev was ready for him.

His foot hooked around Banty's ankle at the same moment he sent a vicious right jab to the man's jaw. Banty's head snapped back and the momentum had him tumbling backward off the porch, landing on his backside in Benjamin Gorder's azalea bushes.

"What seems to be the problem, fellas?" Mark Rollins strolled up the walk, looking sternly from one man to the other.

Whipple scrambled to his feet, wiggling his jaw gingerly. "I come here to tell Stryker to stay the hell away from my kid, and he went crazy and started swingin'."

"Now, Banty, I stood right here and watched you throw the first punch," the sheriff said reasonably. "You really want to stick to that story?"

The man's face flushed an ugly shade of red. "I want him to keep away from my kid. A man's got a right to protect his own son from Stryker's type. He's got bad blood. That's probably what made him some weirded out haint chaser." He scrambled to his feet and took a step in Dev's direction.

"You said your piece. Now it's time to move on." Rollins inserted himself between Banty and Dev. "Go on with you now," he said, when Banty showed no signs of obeying. "I've already run you in once this year on assault charges. The judge won't be so lenient second time 'round."

Whipple finally brushed himself off and turned to go. "I'm leavin'. But don't you ferget what I told you, neither, Stryker. Keep away from my kid."

Both men watched as Banty climbed into his souped-up dually truck and roared away. When Mark looked back at

Dev, a small smile was playing around his mouth. "You always did have a way of stirrin' things up."

Dev lifted a shoulder. "He was just blowin' off. Beat up the screen door some, but no harm done." Easy enough to see now why Robbie Joe had tried so hard to convince them both there was a rational explanation for the red mist and the lights he saw. Banty had seemed much more comfortable about his son finding a dead body than witnessing a possible psychic phenomena, but Dev was in no mood to appreciate the irony. "Hell, I talked to all the other kids with no problem."

Mark pushed his hat back and wiped at his forehead. "Well there was never any love lost 'tween you and Banty, so you shoulda known he'd call you out if you gave him the least reason."

No, there had never been any love lost between the two of them. And the man's words about Dev's daddy were the main reason. He'd heard them before, or others much like them, from the guy for two decades.

They weren't any easier to hear now than they'd been when he was twelve.

"Kendra May's been houndin' me somethin' fierce 'bout you comin' over to dinner soon. Says she hasn't seen near 'nough of you since you got to town."

"Sure." Dev strove for a lighter tone he was far from feeling. "Tell her to give me a call. We can sit 'round and talk over old times again. Bet she's never heard the one 'bout you gettin' caught top down and pecker up with Carolyn Grimes in your mama's convertible near Tackett's woods."

The man looked pained. "Just remember, if I land in the doghouse with her, I might end up bunkin' here with you."

"I'll keep that in mind."

They parted on a friendly wave, and Dev went back into the house. But it failed to seem as welcoming as it usually did. The echoes of Banty's words rang in its empty rooms. Rattled around in Dev's mind even when he tried to shake them free.

Yer daddy's a killer . . . I ain't the only one thinks that way, neither.

No, Banty hadn't been the only one to utter those words to him over the years, although he imagined they were whispered behind his back far more often. This town had passed judgment on his father nearly thirty years ago.

Dev swung the front door shut behind him with a decisive bang.

It was high time to figure out once and for all if the town had been right.

Chapter 5

"I faxed the vic's picture to headquarters earlier today." Not finding either of the agents back at the motel room, Ramsey was checking in with Powell by cell phone. "It shouldn't take more than twenty-four hours to get an artist's sketch back. We can make copies and have them distributed to law enforcement and nail salons in a fifty-mile area."

"Good catch on the nails. If we can get the ID done quietly without havin' to involve the media, I know Jeffries will be much happier."

And the governor would be happier still, Ramsey thought cynically, but the comment remained unvoiced. "I talked to the sheriff and suggested he have the ME clip the victim's fingernails and bag them as evidence. You never know, maybe we'll get lucky enough to come up with a match on the polish. Has the TBI lab come up with anything yet on the footprints or fibers?"

"Nothin' yet. I planned to call and give them another nudge today."

"What about ViCAP? Has a report been submitted?" The Violent Criminal Apprehension Program's national database would spit out any crimes with similar elements.

There was a moment of silence. "Check with Rollins on that. I thought he was goin' to take care of it. If he hasn't, you could submit the form from his office."

"I'll do that." Hearing the crunch of gravel under tires, she lifted the shade and looked out. Felt a jolt of satisfaction. "The mobile forensics lab is here that Raiker promised. You've got evidence at the sheriff's office, right?" Running the tests from the mobile lab would mean the results would be available in hours rather than days or weeks, moving the investigation into a much faster pace.

"Everythin's there except the latents, casts of footprints, and fibers. Rollins will probably want to have a deputy deliver it all, but you can put the request in when you stop by his office." Switching topics, Powell went on, "Matthews is out makin' a second pass on the interviews of the kids. I'm door knockin' on the properties fringin' the woods to see if anyone claims to have seen anythin' that night."

From the disgust in his voice, his lack of progress was clear. But Ramsey asked anyway. "Getting anywhere?"

"Lot of nothin' so far. People who don't like talkin' to law-enforcement types." The phone crackled, as if he were traveling farther out of range. "Give me a call when you finish at the sheriff's office. I could use a hand out here."

After promising to do so, Ramsey disconnected and went outside, jogging across the parking lot to where two people were standing near the mobile lab and the midsized SUV that had followed it in.

"You two must have really pissed Raiker off to have drawn this duty," she joked, joining Abbie Phillips and Ryne Robel next to the lab. "Where's Jonesy?"

"Inside unpacking his baby." Robel stretched then slipped one arm around his petite wife. "And Raiker sent us because we're on our way to Lexington."

A dart of jealousy stabbed her. "Get out." She gave Abbie a light shove. "You two are working the Lexington child-snatching case?"

Her friend nodded, satisfied. "That's right."

"How about you?" Ryne's faint Boston accent sounded foreign to Ramsey's ears after only a day of the rural dialect of Buffalo Springs. "How's the case shaping up?"

She gave them a rundown in a few succinct sentences, welcoming the chance to bounce even a few of the details off her colleagues. Both looked pensive for a moment. "Jeffries is making your job IDing the victim a bit difficult with the media blackout."

"I've got an idea I'll be following up tomorrow, or as soon as Bledsoe faxes back a likeness to distribute. We'll keep it out of the press unless we have no choice."

The other two nodded. They worked with her at Raiker Forensics, Ryne most recently when he quit his job as a Savannah police detective to move closer to Abbie. Both were familiar with the dynamics politics could play on a case.

"Maybe the killer's a ghost and the red mist is its disappearing act," Ryne suggested, sober-faced.

"You're a funny guy. I'm surprised Abbie hasn't beaten that sense of humor out of you yet." The other woman was lethal with Muy Thai.

"She's tried," Ryne's grin was wicked. "But I'm a fast runner."

Abbie checked her watch. "Uh-oh. We need to get moving to make it to Lexington for our case briefing." She and Ryne moved in tandem to the car.

"Good luck," Ramsey called as she headed toward the sleek black RV. The pair waved and got in the vehicle.

It still gave her sort of a jolt to see Abbie with Ryne, relaxed and . . . happy was probably the word she was looking for. A few months ago Ramsey would have guessed the woman was destined to remain as solitary as she was herself.

But Abbie's new relationship, as unexpected as it was, wouldn't be affecting Ramsey's lifestyle. She'd long ago learned that a no-strings private life worked out the best for her in the long run.

She climbed the two steps to the lab and pulled the door over. "Jonesy. Ready to go to work?"

"You're joking, right? Tell me you're joking." The most brilliant scientist on the Raiker team—and that was saying something—pulled his head out of a lower cupboard for a minute to glare at her. With his smooth baby face, he looked like a twelve-year-old on the verge of a tantrum. "It's going to take hours to get organized. And I still have to get hooked up to a water and electrical source. The supply I have on board isn't going to last long."

Ramsey returned his stare and wondered what the TBI

agents would make of the man. Jonesy—she'd never heard his complete name—was dressed all in black, as was his norm. His hair this week was shaved on the sides, the center worn in a Mohawk, also dyed black. With all the piercings on his face, she'd always half expected him to spring a dozen leaks when he took a drink. He had two sleeves of tattoos, which ran from shoulder to wrist. She'd once heard that Raiker plucked him away from the FBI's crime lab to come work for him. Since the feds were notoriously uptight, she had a hard time believing Jonesy could have lasted a day with them.

"Talk to Mary Sue Talbot in the office," she instructed. "Apparently this place is equipped with a couple campsites, and she'll direct you to one of them."

Jonesy had returned to his task in the cupboard, so Ramsey was talking to his back. And a wedge of blindingly white skin as his shirt rode up.

It was too early in the day for her to deal with seeing any amount of the man bare. She closed her eyes for a moment to erase the image. "Give me your cell phone."

After digging around in his pocket, he handed it to her, and Ramsey programmed her number into it. Then she repeated the action, inputting his number on hers.

"So far we only have results on the latents. There were no hits on the Automated Fingerprint Identification System. I'm on my way to the sheriff's office to get the evidence transferred back here that wasn't taken to the TBI lab." And she knew which test she was most anxious to get his take on. "I'd like you to identify something found in the stomach contents. Something the ME defined only as a plant derivative."

"I'll run that test. I'll run any test. As a matter of fact, I will run around the RV naked if you just get out and let me set up here."

"God knows no one wants that," she muttered. The scientist could be a bit dictatorial about the order in his lab, but his work would be worth it.

Shutting the door of the RV, a thought brought a smile to her face. It was going to be worth the price of a ticket to see how the people of Buffalo Springs reacted when they got a load of Jonesy.

It was another couple hours before Ramsey finished at the sheriff's office. Rollins wasn't there, but she spoke to him by cell about sending a deputy to the mobile lab with the rest of the evidence. She convinced him to do it right away without, she thought, being overly pushy. Then she inputted the necessary information for the ViCAP form and submitted it on the office's designated machine and called Powell. He gave her directions to the property owners he wanted her to speak to. But it took her another quarter hour to speak with the dispatcher, Letty Carter, who provided her with maps of the area before Ramsey set out.

The roads twisted and climbed without any visible rhyme or reason. She consulted the maps she'd gotten from the dispatcher—with the warning of dire bodily harm if she didn't return them—and made note of the properties that butted up against the forest engulfing Ashton's Pond. With Powell working from the northernmost end, she decided to start with the southernmost property owner, a—Ramsey squinted at the small print—Duane Tibbitts.

Obligingly, a mailbox with that faded last name on it signaled the place, so Ramsey turned off on the narrow rutted drive. It was nearly overgrown with underbrush in places, and if it had once seen gravel, that time was in the far distant past. A few inches of rain would turn the drive into a quarter-mile-long mud slick.

The trees grew denser, as if crowding close to swallow up anyone stupid enough to approach. Grimly, Ramsey kept her eye on the road and her mind firmly rooted in the present.

Swinging the vehicle around a sharp curve, she came to a jolting stop before a ramshackle dwelling. Chickens scratched listlessly at the dirt on either side of her.

The house slouched like a sullen teenager, its once white paint chipped and peeling. The porch sagged beneath a drooping roof propped up by a trio of tired two-by-fours. The screen door was only a frame, and the window in the front door had what looked like a bullet hole in it.

But there were curtains at the windows and geraniums in pots on the steps. A gray tiger cat sunned itself where a slant of sunlight pierced the trees and painted the porch with its glow.

It opened its eyes in a slit as Ramsey got out of the vehicle. But when she approached the porch, it jumped to its feet, arched its back, and hissed a warning.

A warning Ramsey should have heeded. Because a moment later the doors swung open and a woman stepped out on the porch. At any other time, Ramsey would have been wondering at the black eye she sported. But right now, she was too busy regarding the shotgun the woman carried, aimed right at her.

"Good afternoon." With effort she kept her voice pleasant. "Is this Tibbitts' place?"

"Won't matter none to you with a hole through ya." The woman jerked her head toward the drive. "Get on outta here. A person's got a right to privacy on their own property."

A trickle of perspiration snaked down Ramsey's spine beneath her black suit jacket. It was too warm to wear it, but it hid her shoulder harness. She dearly hoped she wasn't going to have to pull her weapon.

"I'm not here to invade your privacy. I suppose you've had plenty of visitors already, with the media types that swarmed the area after that murder."

There was no response. Nor did the woman lower the shotgun.

With a nonchalance she was far from feeling, Ramsey leaned against the open door of the vehicle. She could dive inside if it looked like the woman was about to follow through on her threat.

A bleached blond about five-six, the stranger could have passed for fifty with her facial wrinkles and lack of teeth. But the hands gripping the shotgun were smooth, and the figure beneath the tight tank and jeans was youthful. Ramsey was betting she was at least twenty years younger. A meth head, from the looks of her. Ramsey's gaze went beyond the woman to the front door she'd left ajar.

"My name is Ramsey Clark, and I'm working with the Tennessee Bureau of Investigation on the homicide that occurred in the woods behind you a few days ago."

"Don't care who y're," the woman said in her heavy drawl. "I got nuthin' to say, and you need to git on outta here afore I start shootin'." She hefted the shotgun meaningfully. "I got a shell loaded and ready."

A man's voice sounded from the confines of the house. "Hurry up and get rid of 'em and get yer ass back in here, Mary."

Making a sudden decision, Ramsey gave her an easy smile and made to get back into the SUV. "No problem. I'll just go on back into town and get a warrant." She took her time sliding into the car.

The woman—Mary—looked torn. With a glance behind her, she lowered the shotgun to rest it across one arm and came off the steps to approach the vehicle.

Ramsey tensed. She left the car door open, but one hand crept inside her jacket and unsnapped the guard on her holster. Her fingers settled on the grip of the weapon, ready to draw it if necessary. In times like these she blessed Raiker's insistence that his operatives be issued concealed and carry permits in whichever state they worked for the duration of the case.

"Hold on, now." Mary tried a smile that showed gaping holes where her missing teeth should have been. "No need to make two trips out here, is there? No need to make one, truth be told. We can't tell ya nuthin' 'bout that night. Din't hear or see a thing."

Convenient. "I'm talking about June fifth, around ten P.M.?" The woman shook her head. An accompanying bolt of frustration twisted through Ramsey. "Wait, I guess it was the sixth."

Mary froze mid head shake, recognizing the trap, but then recommended it even more violently. "We mind our bizness 'n' 'spect everyone else to. We got nuthin' but trees 'tween here and Ashton's Pond. What you think we're gonna be able to see clear over there?"

Ramsey's hand relaxed a bit over her weapon. Mary had the shotgun cradled in her arms now, not seeming worried that it was loaded—according to her earlier claim. As long as it was no longer pointed at her, Ramsey wasn't worried either.

"That's what I'm asking."

"We din't hear nuthin'." She spit the words out, her earlier show of pleasantness evaporating. "Din't see nuthin' neither. We're isolated out here, and that's the way we like it."

"What about Duane?" Ramsey let her gaze drift to the house. "Maybe he saw something."

"He didn't. He works third shift over ta the mill in Clayton. He wasn't even here."

But Ramsey's attention had been diverted. There was a flash of something in the trees beyond the house. "Is someone out in those woods?" She pointed a finger. "I saw something move."

The woman gave a quick glance over her shoulder. "I don't see nuthin'," she said, her words an ironic echo of her earlier declaration. "Pro'bly a deer."

"This deer was wearing overalls and a flannel shirt," Ramsey said drily. "Is Duane out there?"

"He's in the house. Y'heard 'em earlier, din't ya?"

Ramsey's attention returned to the woman. "Anyone else living here with you?"

"We don' got no kids, Duane 'n' me. Maybe someday."

Ramsey took the moment to fervently hope not. Digging into her pocket for a card, she held it out to the woman. "If you think of anything that you've forgotten, please call me at the number listed there."

"Ramsey." The woman studied her name as if she hadn't heard it earlier. "Odd sorta name for a woman."

With a tight smile, Ramsey started the vehicle. "I'm an odd sort of woman." And that was probably one of the few truths spoken here in the last few minutes.

Mary retreated toward the house, and Ramsey attempted

to turn the car toward the drive without backing over one of the chickens.

In her rearview mirror, she saw the man again, this time taking cover in the trees lining the rutted drive. Maybe there was a meth lab somewhere in the woods surrounding the house. Certainly there was some reason Mary had grown more accommodating when Ramsey had bluffed about a warrant.

She'd mention it to Rollins and let him worry about it. It would be easy enough to check out whether Duane Tibbitts worked third shift at the mill, too. But as she bumped along the road watching for the lane to the next property, she had a feeling that the rest of the afternoon was going to be just as fruitless.

Dusk had settled, painting the normally sunny kitchen with shadows. "Please," Beau Simpson croaked. He tried to rise from the round-backed kitchen chair. A tap of the rifle barrel to his shoulder had him sinking again, fear congealing in a tangled knot in his stomach.

He swallowed, throat dry as dust despite the beer he'd just finished. "It don't gotta be this way."

"It has to be just this way, Beau." The other man's voice was calm. "You were trusted to do one job. And you fucked it up. They're goin' to identify the woman eventually. Do you get what that means? They'll identify her, and it's all your fault, because she never shoulda been found to begin with!"

Beau tried to think of something, anything to say. Could come up with nothing. If only Marvella would come home early for once from her Wednesday night pinochle game. Just once if she'd cut short the gossip and dessert, pick up Pammy Jo from her mother's, and come home and interrupt this scene. Give him time to think of another way.

"I thought someone was comin'," he defended himself. He'd seen lights in the woods. He *had*. "I figured dump her quick before I get discovered. Better that she be found than I be caught haulin' a dead body on my back."

"Better that you did your job and we wouldn't be in this mess. What was your job, Beau?"

He wasn't a man given to tears, but he started to cry then. Sobs racked his big frame. "I did what I could."

"What. Was. Your. Job?" The rifle barrel punctuated each word with a jab to the shoulder.

He didn't want to say it. Saying it would make it sound like he'd failed, and he'd done the best he could! And there'd been no harm done. Not really. Even discovering the woman's name wasn't going to lead anyone to them.

But in the end, the look on the other man's face had him swiping at his eyes with the back of his hand and obeying. Because that was what Beau always did when this man told him something.

"Wrap the chain around the body and dump it off the north side." The north side of the pond had the sharpest incline, reaching eighteen feet deep barely a foot from the edge.

"That's right. Instead you dumped her in a coupla feet of water and didn't weight her down at all." The voice had gone calm. Deadly calm.

Beau knew how dangerous this man was. Knew it didn't pay to cross him. But still he gaped in stunned disbelief when the shotgun, taken from his own gun rack, was shoved into his hands.

"You're gonna do the right thing now." The tone was low, persuasive. Beau stared at the gun barrel disbelievingly. Raised his gaze to see the man pull a handgun from his waistband at the small of his back. His gloved hands aiming it toward Beau.

"You're gonna wrap your lips 'round that barrel." The words were so cool and easy. As if describing how to take apart a carburetor. "Far enough inside that the bullet goes into your skull and not through the roof of your mouth. That's how you'll make this right."

"I ain't killin' myself . . . You're crazy!" Beau shoved to his feet, only to be stopped by the pistol pressed close to his temple. Slowly. Slowly he inched back down into his seat again.

"Yes, you are, and I'll tell you why. Because if you don't, I'm comin' for Marvella next time. You remember everythin' we did to the last one? What *you* did?" He waited for Beau to nod. "Well, it'll go worse with your wife. I'll make sure of that. Or maybe I'll just wait a few years and snatch Pammy Jo. Do her the same way."

The tears scalded his eyes now. Fear shredded his heart. "She's just a little girl!"

"You're the one needs remindin' of that, not me. You fucked up bad, but you can do the right thing here. You can save your family." The man reached over and guided the barrel to Beau's lips. "Otherwise . . . they're damned, Beau. All because of you."

Panic flooded his mind, a rising tide of fear. He couldn't think. Couldn't, not when the mental images the man's words had planted bloomed. Of Marvella stripped and stretched out like a whore. Of sweet li'l Pammy Jo, wrecked and ruined.

He began to shake, sweat dripping down his neck, his mind scrambling for a way out. But he realized there wasn't one. He'd seen what was done. He'd participated. And he knew what this man was capable of. He'd feared this all along, hadn't he? He'd *known* that failure wouldn't be tolerated.

His lips parted. He tasted cool metal and gun oil.

Listening to this man now wasn't his biggest mistake. It was listening to him in the first place.

He thought of his wife and little girl, and mourned wildly for the sight that would greet them when they walked in the back door.

And then he pulled the trigger.

Chapter 6

Ramsey unlocked the mobile lab with one of the two keys that had been provided, and stepped inside. She'd worked with Jonesy enough to first pause in the small outer area to slip on a lab coat, shoe and hair covers, and plastic gloves before continuing into the lab. A frown of annoyance crossed her face when she didn't see Jonesy at work.

It was nearly eight A.M. Not exactly the middle of the night. Maybe the scientist had worked late getting the lab set up, but she'd explained she was in a hurry for the tests to get started, hadn't she?

She walked farther into the lab, looking more closely at the tubes and vials and machines covering its counters. One of the machines—she couldn't name it on a bet—was humming and a red light winked from its front panel. Maybe Jonesy had gotten started last night. Maybe he'd worked all night and was just now getting some sleep while the tests were . . .

A slight sound had her whirling toward the back of the RV. Just in time to see a bare-assed Jonesy coming out of the bedroom lodged in the rear.

The sight of his nudity seared her retinas. "Jesus!" Ramsey clapped a hand over her eyes. "Strike me blind now."

"God almighty, Ramsey." Jonesy squealed like a girl. She heard a door slam and sincerely hoped he was on the far side of it. "What the hell are you doing here at the butt crack of dawn?"

"Poor choice of words," she muttered. In a louder voice

she called, "It's almost eight. Figured you'd be working by now."

"I'm not punching a clock, for Godsakes." She heard a door open a few moments later, followed by the sound of furious footsteps. "If I were, I wouldn't have been working my ass off until after two this morning. You want strictly eight to five, let me know right now. And take your damn hand away from your face!"

Ramsey cracked her fingers a fraction to make sure it was safe before lowering her hand. Jonesy was dressed—thank God—in a clean set of scrubs and booties on his feet.

"So you got started on the tests last night?"

The man glared at her. "You're a piece of work."

Belatedly, she reached for tact. "I appreciate the hours you're putting in. Really. Especially after the long drive yesterday. Ah . . ." She searched for more pleasantries. "Have you had breakfast?"

"I'd be having it now if you hadn't barged in."

"Because I'll be glad to get you something." If bringing him a doughnut and coffee from the motel office would placate him, she figured it was little enough to do. A happy scientist got quick test results. At least that's what she was counting on.

"Really?" He cast a wary glance toward her, obviously still smarting from their earlier encounter.

She could have told him she was the one who was going to carry *those* emotional scars for the rest of her days, but wisely kept the comment to herself.

"I wouldn't mind a cheese omelet. Maybe some hash browns. Do they do biscuits and gravy down here? I'll bet they do. A couple pancakes. Blueberry if they have them. Maybe you should write this down."

Ramsey opened her mouth to protest. Going a few yards to the motel office and heading downtown to a restaurant for take out were two very different things. "I was on my way to the sheriff's office." The look on his face had her acquiescing with ill grace. "But I can stop first and bring something back for you." She seemed to recall Mary Sue mentioning a place that served breakfast in town.

Ramsey waited while Jonesy rummaged around for a paper and pen to write down his order, the irony not lost on her. Her playing nice would keep the man happy. But it wasn't going to do a thing to erase the sight of his nudity from her memory. It was enough to make her wish for selective amnesia.

———

The din in The Henhouse almost had Ramsey, by no stretch of the imagination a morning person, backing out again. It was packed, and the voices of its many occupants melded into a drone reminiscent of its namesake. With a quick glance around, she saw that all the booths were filled, but there was an empty stool at the counter, so she slipped onto it.

A harried-looking waitress stopped to fill the coffee cup of the woman next to her, so Ramsey said, "Excuse me, do you . . ." And then stared at the woman's back when she flitted away as quickly as she'd stopped, refilling cups all the way down the counter.

"You'll have to be faster than that if you expect to get Vicki's attention," observed the woman at her side.

"I guess." Ramsey looked at the woman and was struck with a vague sense of familiarity. "Do they have take-out here?"

"Yes, and you really won't have to wait long for Vicki to come zippin' back so you can order. She's got a method to her, and if you let her go, she's pretty systematic."

"Thanks." Ramsey studied the woman for a moment longer. "You wouldn't be related to Leanne Layton, would you?"

"I would think so. I'm her mama." The woman flashed a smile reminiscent of her daughter's. "Proud one, too. That girl is makin' somethin' of that shop of hers. You ever been there?"

And it was, Ramsey thought ruefully, a charmingly worded hint that she could use an appointment. "Actually I have. I spoke to Leanne yesterday. And the night before. My name is Ramsey Clark. She was telling me that you're somethin' of an expert on the legend of the red mist."

"Well, bless her, I'm no such thing." Donnelle Layton patted her lips gently so as not to disturb the lipstick that looked to be the exact flaming shade her daughter wore.

The waitress stopped in front of Ramsey then, so she switched her focus long enough to place the order and then looked back at the older woman. "I'd like to come by and talk to you sometime about the history you've done of the town. Especially the different accountings of the legend."

Donnelle picked up her fork and toyed with it while maintaining a pleasant expression. "What brings you to Buffalo Springs, Ramsey? My, that's an unusual name. Pretty, too." Effortlessly she segued back to her original question. "Do you have kin nearby?"

"I'm from Virginia. I'm working with TBI on the murder that occurred near here recently."

"Must be an excitin' job." Donnelle lowered her voice. "My daughter can't get enough of those gory crime shows. I'm all the time tellin' her it's just not feminine to be that enthralled with all that killin'." She smiled sunnily. "Not that you aren't feminine. What I wouldn't give for your height." She stood, withdrew her wallet from her purse, and selected some bills to lay on the counter.

"About the legend . . ." Ramsey began again. "Leanne said I could find you at the Historical Museum on Wednesdays."

"I'm afraid I'm busier there than a one-eyed cat watchin' two mouse holes. But I do wish you well with your work, Ramsey." The woman slipped the strap of her purse over her arm. "And you make an appointment with my daughter, y'hear? She's a wonder with a pair of scissors. That's not pride talkin'; that's fact."

Ramsey was nothing if not persistent. She twirled on the stool as the woman prepared to walk away, unwilling to take no for an answer.

But before she could open her mouth, she heard the woman say, "Devlin Stryker, as I live and breathe."

As if her morning hadn't already started off ignobly enough, Ramsey thought sourly.

The second-to-last man she wanted to see—with the first being a nude Jonesy, but it was too late for *that*—was easing back from Donnelle's enthusiastic hug, one of her hands in both of his. "How's the beauty of Buffalo Springs?"

Ramsey managed, barely, to avoid rolling her eyes.

"I'm put out, is what I am." If Donnelle wanted to sound angry, she should eliminate the adoring lilt to her voice. "Leanne tells me you've been in town for days, and you haven't stopped by for dinner once."

"Just bidin' my time, Donnelle. How's Steve doin'?"

As the two commenced speaking of people that were unfamiliar to her, Ramsey lost interest and instead listened to the snippets of other conversations drifting around the restaurant.

". . . blew his head clear off, I heard . . ."

". . . Marvella is a case, I'll tell ya. Don't know what will happen . . ."

". . . know why he done it?"

". . . seen him yesterday and looked a might down to me. Thought to myself at the time that he . . ."

Shamelessly eavesdropping, Ramsey strained to hear more, but the fragments of conversation intermixed into an incomprehensible chatter. What she could make out was Donnelle's voice, clear as a bell.

"You come see me real soon. Stop down at the Historical Museum on Wednesday, why don't you? I'd love to spend some real time catchin' up."

Fuming, Ramsey threw a glance over her shoulder just in time to see Donnelle heading for the door. Dev turned and caught the full force of her glare and stopped midstep, his hands rising in surrender.

"I don't start full-on sinnin' 'til nine most days, so I'm pretty sure I'm innocent."

Ramsey faced forward at the counter again. "Of what?"

"Of whatever you're wantin' to slice me up over." Without waiting for an invitation—which she wouldn't have offered—he slipped onto the stool at her side and cocked his head at her. "Don't tell me. You're not a mornin' person."

"I sat right next to that woman and asked her if I could come by the Historical Museum and speak to her about the legend," Ramsey informed him, heat tingeing her tone. "She told *me* she was much too busy."

"I'm sure she didn't mean anythin' by it."

"I speak y'all, Stryker. No matter how politely it's worded, I can recognize the brush-off buried in the politeness."

"Well if you're that familiar with southern folk, you shouldn't be surprised to discover them closemouthed with strangers." To the waitress who hovered near him, he shot a smile and said, "Just bring the usual for me, Vicki."

"Sure thing, hon."

He returned his attention to Ramsey. "You actually carry a double whammy. Not from 'round here, and workin' for the law. I can't believe this is the first person you've run into who's not anxious to sit down and answer a bunch of questions."

Point taken. Ramsey reached for the water glass the waitress had set in front of her. "I suppose I should be grateful that I didn't get run off with a shotgun this time."

The humor vanished from his face. And she was left to wonder at the lethal look that could show in his eye when he wasn't wearing that incessant smile. "Someone pulled a gun on you?"

She debated how much to share with him before giving a mental shrug. So far she'd gotten nowhere asking questions of the locals. Stryker did nothing *but* talk. He may as well make himself useful. "Mary Tibbitts was not anxious to speak to me yesterday. Tried to run me off with the business end of a shotgun."

He grimaced and sipped at the coffee that Vicki had placed before him. "Not hard to believe it. Glad to hear she didn't use the gun. Way I hear it, the Tibbitts aren't known for their restraint in that area."

"Duane was supposedly inside but didn't come out. I was wondering if there was meth lab somewhere around there. She looks like a user. And I saw a man in the woods behind their house watching me."

"It was probably Ezra T., Duane's younger brother. And if the Tibbitts are usin' meth, it's a pretty good guess that they're buyin' it these days rather than manufacturin'. That family learned a pretty hard lesson years ago." He paused to add some cream to the coffee, stirring it with a spoon before taking another drink. "The story I heard was that Ezra T. was no more than two, sittin' in a high chair in the kitchen when his parents were cookin' meth in the house. There was an explosion, killed them both. Blew Ezra T., chair and all, through the wall."

"But he survived."

"With serious brain damage. He spent the next dozen years in residential care in Nashville. Duane and Mary brought him home a few years ago."

Shrewdly, Ramsey said, "I'm guessing it wasn't familial devotion that motivated them. His disability check now comes directly to them as his caregivers, right?"

"Wouldn't know 'bout that." With a clink of stoneware, Dev set his cup back on the saucer. "Ezra T. is harmless. Runs the woods most of the time, but he seems to be happy 'nough. He's a heckuva mimic. Hard tellin' his animal calls from the real thing. I think he was hangin' around watching' me a lot of the time I spent at the pond that night. He stayed back of the trees most times. He doesn't mean any harm."

"If he's in the woods so much, he might have seen something the night the body was dumped. Heard something." Had he been questioned by Rollins office? She didn't recall mention of it in the case file, and she'd been up until late last night going over it again.

Dev was shaking his head. "He'd be of no help to anyone. He's hardly a reliable source. He's got the judgment and the intellectual level of a four-year-old. No one would credit anythin' he had to say, especially about somethin' as important as murder."

"Maybe not." But Ramsey mentally filed it away to ask Rollins about later.

"So." He turned to face her more fully, a slight smile playing about his mouth. "'Bout your unpopularity in these parts . . . I can probably help you out with that."

She eyed him suspiciously. "Thanks, but I'm fine."

"Oh, really." His brows rose. "How are you plannin' on workin' a sit down with Donnelle to hear more about the legend?"

Lifting a shoulder, Ramsey craned her neck to see if any familiar dishes were lined up on the cook's counter. "It's not like the information is pertinent to solving the case." It was background, nothing more. Filler that explained the whys and hows of people's attitudes and beliefs, which, come to think of it, *could*, in a roundabout way, affect what they told law enforcement.

Vicki set a pile of disposable containers down in front of Ramsey. "That will be nine fifty. You can either pay at the register or I'll take your money right here."

Ramsey opened her purse and fished out a ten and two ones, handing it to the woman. "Thanks."

"You have yourself a good day, hon," the waitress said, heading to greet another customer.

"I'm surprised you think that way, after what happened yesterday evenin'."

She stood, reaching for the containers. "Why, what happened?"

He jerked his head toward the full restaurant behind them. "Haven't you been listenin'? Everybody in town's talkin' 'bout it, seems like. Beau Simpson killed himself last night."

Pausing in midmotion, she looked at him. "And who's Beau Simpson?"

"Has the hardware store here on Main Street. Took it over from his folks some years ago. Nice guy. Hard worker." His expression was somber for once. "Left a wife and little girl."

"Tragic, but what does that have to do with me or the case?"

"It's the second death after the red mist was sighted.

That's what people are sayin'." Vicki set his plate in front of him, and he looked up and smiled his thanks before returning his attention to Ramsey. "And if you were findin' folks close-mouthed before, they're really gonna button up now. At least those who hold with the legend. And others who don't but won't push their luck."

Intrigued, she sat on the edge of her stool facing him. "And why is that?"

He reached for the maple syrup and spread it liberally on his stack of pancakes. "Because the way the legend goes is that the deaths—some call them murders, but history doesn't necessarily bear that out—happen in threes. And there are some who believe the subsequent ones occur because of people askin' questions and stirrin' up things that should just be let be."

"Just ignore homicide, in other words."

"Didn't say I agreed. Just tellin' you the way some folks 'round here think." He lifted a bite of pancakes to his lips and chewed, his eyes sliding shut in an expression of appreciation. Swallowing, he added, "Donnelle is the one to see if you want the full story and all the versions of the legend. I can help you out with that. You heard her invite me to call on her at the museum tomorrow. I could take you along. She might not open up to a stranger, but she'll talk to me."

"She might speak to me if I stop in on my own tomorrow."

He took another bite, then reached for his juice. "She might."

She heard the doubt in his tone. Based on the woman's friendly dismissal earlier, Ramsey doubted it, too. "Or maybe I could get Leanne to intervene somehow."

"She'd probably be glad to. If you let her get her hands on your hair. Probably have to throw in a manicure and pedicure, too, but most women go for that sort of thing anyway, so it's not like it'd be too taxin'."

Shrewdly, she assessed his too-innocent expression. The man observed entirely too much. "But you'd let me go with you?"

"Sure." He paused long enough to cut more pancakes, rubbing them generously in the syrup pooled on his plate before bringing them to his mouth. "For a price."

"I should've known," she muttered, disgusted with herself for wasting time with the man. Rising again, she grabbed the containers and prepared to leave.

"Whoa." His eyes twinkled as he reached a hand out to stop her. "All I'm talkin' 'bout is a date."

She stopped, eyed him jaundicedly. "A date."

"Has to include a meal," he said judiciously, "to count as a real date. Dinner would be best."

"Breakfast," she counter offered.

"I've seen your mornin' mood, remember? Lunch."

"Done." With a sense of resignation, she gave in. "But not until after we've talked to Donnelle."

He studied her then, his eyes brimming with merriment. It occurred to her that some men could be too handsome for their own good. "Okay. I'm gonna trust you. That you won't think of some excuse to beg off after you've gotten what you want from me."

Because it'd only barely occurred to her, she said tartly, "And I'm going to trust you to get Donnelle to open up to me."

"Don't worry about that. I've got a gift for gettin' people to talk to me. I often thought I should have been a priest 'cept for one li'l thing."

"Let me guess."

"I'm not Catholic." Grinning, he shook his head and speared another bite of pancakes. "But I like the way you think."

Out of patience, she rose, this time intent on making her escape. "I'll meet you at the museum tomorrow at . . ."

"If that isn't just like you, Dev, to hoard all the pretty gals for yourself."

Ramsey and Dev looked up at the newcomer in unison.

"Hey, Doc." With a look of genuine pleasure on his face, Dev got up and shook the newcomer's hand. "You still chasin' Jenny 'round the office in between patients?"

"Gave that up long ago. She got too fast for me." The

stranger looked at Ramsey. "Gonna introduce us, Dev, or are you afraid I'll steal her clean away from you?"

"Ramsey Clark, this old coot is Doc Andrew Theisen. Been 'round this town long enough to know where the skeletons are hidden. Come to think of it, given his bedside manner, he may have contributed to a few of them."

Ramsey found her hand engulfed in Theisen's. "Listen to the ungrateful wretch. I brought him into this world, and he's been bitchin' 'bout it ever since."

She smiled, unwillingly charmed. He was seventy if he was a day, but fit, with a receding hairline that had long since gone white. His hazel eyes behind the dark framed glasses were kind, inviting her to share the joke.

"You should have filmed the moment you slapped him after birth. I think it would have achieved bestseller status."

The older man laughed, dug an elbow in Dev's ribs. "I like her. She's not meltin' in a gooey puddle at your feet. Show's she got character."

"She's got plenty of that."

"Here, take my seat." Ramsey took the food containers and stood. "I have to get these back to a friend."

"Let's say ten o'clock at the museum tomorrow," Dev said as Doc slipped into the seat she'd vacated.

"See you then." She smiled once again at Doc and said, "Nice meeting you."

"My pleasure."

Ramsey turned to go, fighting her way through a crowd that seemed to have doubled since she came in. Driving back to the motel, one of the containers tumbled off the pile, and she muttered a curse, reaching for it with one hand while driving with the other. Jonesy better appreciate her efforts. And he damn well better have some news for her on those tests sometime today.

Having learned her lesson earlier that day, she knocked on the lab door first. Or, since her arms were full, at least tapped it impatiently with her foot. She stepped back as he opened the door for her, delight written on every bit of his face that didn't have a piercing through it. "Room service. My favorite."

Rather than letting her into the lab, however, he came out, and she followed him to a nearby picnic table. "I've got tests running. I don't want to risk any contaminants." She sincerely hoped he was talking about the food and not her.

"Listen, Ramsey . . ." Jonesy was popping open all the containers and taking out the plastic silverware. He seemed to have trouble coming up with words. "About earlier this morning . . ."

Nearly grinding her teeth, she said, "We are definitely not going there."

Doggedly, he went on. "I don't know how much you saw . . ."

"Let's call it too much and leave it at that, shall we?"

But he wouldn't give it up. "I just want you know, there's a difference between guys. Now me, I'm a grower, not a shower. What I mean is . . ."

Ramsey abruptly turned to go. "We are not having this conversation." Swiftly, she started toward the motel, where she hoped to find Matthews and Powell.

"All I'm saying is, don't judge the gift by the package, if you get my drift."

"Call me when you have some results. That I'll want to hear. The rest of it . . ." The mental image flashed across her mind and she winced. "We will never talk about that again."

———

When she got to the office the TBI agents were using as headquarters, Powell was already gone. Matthews was sitting at the table, his laptop before him, sipping coffee and typing up yesterday's interviews in a desultory manner.

"Where's Ward?" she asked him.

Matthews winced, holding his head. "Inside voice, Ramsey. Have some pity on the walking dead."

"Did you tie one on last night?" she asked unsympathetically. "How do you stand staying out all night and getting up the next morning?" She'd heard him come in again last night. She'd just gone to bed herself. But she didn't spend much time sleeping anyway.

"Not well. This morning, not well at all. Powell got an early start to try to catch some of those property owners you guys missed yesterday."

"Hope he has better luck today than we did yesterday." She went to the fax machine, made a sound of satisfaction when she saw Bledsoe, the forensic artist, had sent the sketch of the victim resembling the way she would have looked alive. She plucked it off the paper tray. "Thank you, Alec," she muttered.

She opened the cover of the copier, pausing a moment to study the rendition. This was what was needed, she recognized, at least for her. A reminder of who the woman was before she'd become a victim. When she still had a life to lead, errands to run, problems to solve, friends to enjoy.

Before she'd come to the attention of her killer.

A few minutes later she grabbed a stack of the copies she'd made of the sketch and showed the top one to Matthews. "I'm going to deliver this to Rollins's office and have him distribute it to all the law enforcement offices within fifty miles. You're going to help me track down all the nail salons in the same vicinity and show this sketch, see if we can get a lead on the victim."

Matthews cocked a brow, gave her a cynical look. "Oh, am I?"

"I suppose you could go help Powell," she said, considering. "Yesterday I had a hillie point a shotgun at me, but that was probably an exception." She paused a beat. "You know what nail salons are full of, Matthews. Women."

The agent didn't look as enthusiastic at the prospect as she'd hoped. "I've about had my fill, thanks."

"Now why do I have a feeling I should tape record that remark for posterity?"

"Well, not forever," he amended, continuing to type slowly. "But the crazy gals in this town . . . you know two of them nearly came to blows last night at the Half Moon over me?"

"Don't tell me," Ramsey said drily, going back to check on the copies being spit out. "You've brought a different one of them back here at different times, and last night they were both in the same place at the same time, comparing notes. You're a prince, Matthews."

"And then," he continued aggrievedly, "after I separated them and tried to smooth things over, they both turn on me." He shook his head in disgust. "By the end of the night, they're acting like best pals and I'm being treated like the scourge of the town. I will never understand women."

"Yeah, we're a mystery, all right." It sounded as though he were lucky to get away without being castrated. No female liked being slapped in the face with the realization that she was only one of a string.

Unwillingly, her mind flashed to Stryker. Women of all ages seemed to respond to him, and she'd be willing to bet he'd cut a pretty wide swath through the females in town. Maybe he was that most rare of male creatures, a good breaker-upper. A man that stayed on good terms with former girlfriends had a gift.

And a bone-deep charm it would pay to remain wary of.

Chapter 7

Ramsey got a later start than she would have liked after stopping by the sheriff's office. When she discovered there were already results for the ViCAP report she'd submitted, she decided they could wait until tomorrow morning. She was anxious to get started with the nail salons.

She was unsurprised to learn Mark Rollins wasn't in.

"He got a call last night on the Simpson suicide," the dispatcher, Letty Carter, confided. "Beau blew his brains out while Marvella was at her card club, and the whole town's buzzin' 'bout it. Some are sayin' the store was in trouble and he was 'bout to lose the business his daddy built. But if you ask me, there's been emotional problems in the Simpson line for generations. Beau's grandma was a drinker, and his great-aunt Beulah was given to talkin' to people no one else could see."

Ramsey digested the gossip silently. She'd be willing to bet Letty was old enough to have been acquainted with both Simpson's relatives. The dispatcher was as wizened as a dried apple, and by the end of her shift each day, her makeup settled into the deep creases in her face. Her hair was a brassy blond color that even Ramsey could tell wasn't professional. She wore bright pink lipstick and matching fingernail polish.

Noticing the nails jerked her attention back to her task. "I'm sure the sheriff has his hands full right now, so I'll catch up with him later." She handed a copy of the sketch to the older woman. "I'd like this faxed to every law enforcement entity in a fifty-mile radius. Let them know we're looking for an ID on a homicide victim."

Letty studied the sketch. "Pretty girl." Regret tinged her tone. "It's a cryin' shame what was done to her. I'll take care of it right away."

———————

But hours later, Ramsey reflected that Letty's swift follow-through might well be the last bit of assistance she received that day.

She turned right as prompted by the in-dash GPS, and made her way into the town of Steadmont, population two hundred fifty. Armed with a stack of sketches, the maps she'd pried away from Letty again, and a Yellow Pages listing of salons in the vicinity, Ramsey had so far covered six towns east and south of Buffalo Springs. She'd decided to hit the smallest ones first, figuring a person would be missed more quickly in a town of seventy-two than one of three thousand. So far, her methods had met with a noticeable lack of luck.

She'd taken time to swing by Leanne's place and show the sketch around, but no one there recognized the victim. That fact hadn't been surprising.

Since she wasn't cursed with a Y chromosome, asking for directions didn't bother her. And it hadn't taken her long to figure out the fastest way to find the addresses on her sheets was to stop at the first gas station or woman on the street and ask. When she spotted a female out watering flowers, she did just that and was directed to a small pretty shop around the corner from the main thoroughfare.

But the owner at Pine Creek Nails shook her head when shown the picture of the woman. "No, she don't look familiar. Not one of my regulars, that's for sure, and I'd remember a walk-in that came in that recently. A French manicure, you say?" The operator squinted at the picture again. "I don't get much call for that here. Did you try Susie at Look Sharp? She's just a few blocks west of here."

"I'll check there next, thanks." After leaving the sketch and her card with the woman, Ramsey headed back to her vehicle.

When her cell rang, she recognized Matthews's number and answered. She'd dropped off a copy of the nail salons on her way out of town and requested that he head out the opposite way from Buffalo Springs to begin canvassing the places. "Tell me you're having better luck than I am." As she spoke, she pulled away from the curb and headed in the direction of the other salon.

"Possibly." Matthews sounded a great deal more chipper than he had that morning, so maybe his hangover had subsided. "I'm in Tallulah Falls, northwest of Buffalo Springs about thirty miles. And I have an operator here who thinks she recognizes the sketch as a woman who came in a couple weeks ago. Thing is, she swears this woman she worked on didn't have any tattoos. Said they'd talked about them and that both had agreed they didn't go in for that sort of thing."

"It's possible the victim was lying, I guess," Ramsey said slowly. "The tattoos aren't new, the ME said. His estimate was a couple years old for the one on her back and older than that for the one on her ankle."

"Anyway, I'm here while the operator is talking to the other workers trying to come up with the woman's name. If it pans out, I'll stick around and follow up, see if I can find out where she lived and worked."

"Great." A hum of interest sparked. "Keep me posted."

Ramsey knew better than to hang her hopes on the lead he was following, but it was more promising than anything she'd come up with today. Her fortunes continued as the next operator denied recognizing the sketch but told her of a woman who did nails out of her home. Ramsey had a similar lack of luck there, so she checked off the town and headed to the next, but not before hitting a fast food drive-through on the way back to the highway.

As she munched on fries and a sandwich, she thought about the tattoos Matthews had mentioned. They'd follow up on them if this lead didn't pan out, but tattoos were notoriously hard to trace. People didn't necessarily get them close to home, often bringing one home as a "souvenir" from vacation. Ramsey couldn't imagine wanting to risk carrying hepatitis back as a souvenir, but there was no accounting for taste.

It would be difficult to trace the artist and find records far enough back to identify the victim, especially since neither of the tats had been especially unique. And she knew from experience on other cases that tattoo places regularly went out of business, making them even harder to trace. If the ID process boiled down to tracing the tattoo, it was going to be an exercise in frustration.

Keeping an eye on her mirrors, she punched the accelerator. It was getting on toward late afternoon. She'd likely have time for only two or three more towns before they closed, unless she found a salon that kept evening hours.

The town of Kordoba bore more than a passing resemblance to many of the towns she'd visited that day, and according to the map, boasted slightly more residents than Buffalo Springs. There were four places listed on the White Pages printout for nail salons, but the owner of the first informed Ramsey that one of them was out of business, and a third had moved her salon to her home in the country.

Given the time, she didn't linger, leaving the picture and card with the woman to head to the other salon in town. This one was right on Main Street and outfitted with a candy pink and white striped awning and enough pink adornments inside to make Ramsey feel a bit nauseous.

The operator though, a redhead by the name of Tammy Wallace, reminded Ramsey of Leanne with her sense of style. She came bustling out of the back room when fetched by one of her employees, wiping her hands on a towel and wearing an expression of polite puzzlement.

Ramsey showed her ID, saying, "I'm working as a consultant with TBI, and we're seeking information about the woman in this picture." She handed her the photo of the sketch. Saw the woman's gaze drop to it and widen a bit.

Instinct had her pressing, "Do you know this woman?"

Her manner decidedly cooler, Tammy looked at Ramsey. "Why did you say you're lookin' for her?"

Adrenaline was firing along nerve endings. "It's very important that you tell me what you know about this woman, ma'am. You recognize her, don't you? Has she been in here before?"

With a little sigh, she said, "Follow me." Ramsey trailed after her to the back room, which turned out to be a small office. Tammy reached past her to shut the door, saying, "Bless their hearts, but those girls out there have the fastest tongues this side of the Mississippi. That woman in the picture? Her name is Cassie Frost. I've done her nails every month or so since Christmastime, I guess." A little smile played around her mouth. "French manicure, clear polish. She's not much for change. But she's a real nice gal. Have the feelin' she's had some hard luck lately, not that she's ever complained to me. Real pleasant." She gave a helpless shrug. "That's all I know. Tell me I didn't just land her in a heap of trouble."

Adept at evading questions in such matters, Ramsey said, "When was the last time you saw her?" And found herself holding her breath until the woman's answer came.

"I don't know. I'll have to check the appointment book. Sometime within the last couple weeks, I think."

"Would you happen to know where she lives? Where she works?" Ramsey pulled a notebook out of her pocket. She'd look at that appointment calendar. Check out everything this woman told her about the woman in the sketch.

But her gut told her Cassie Frost was the name of their Jane Doe.

———

"Yeah, she worked here." The owner of the Thirsty Moose, clad in a filthy white apron, desultorily wiped the bar. "She don't no more, and next time you see her, you can tell her that for me, too. Hasn't shown up for work in more'n a week. I figured she skipped town, but either way, she don't need to be stoppin' by for her last check. Left me high and dry lookin' for a bartender, and I'm keepin' her pay for my troubles. I gotta right to do that, too."

He had a unique grasp of the law, but Ramsey was more interested in details he could provide about Cassie Frost. "How long did she work for you?"

The man lifted a beefy shoulder. "I gave her a job before Christmas, I guess. My other guy quit on me suddenly, and I was desperate, same as I am now that she left. Claimed she had bartendin' experience and proved it by mixin' some decent drinks for me."

"She provide you with ID when you hired her?"

Ramsey slid a glance at the uniform at her side. After her conversation with Tammy Wallace, she'd contacted Powell, who'd sounded decidedly more cheerful when she filled him in. He'd promised to round up Matthews and anyone he could from Rollins's department and join her here. As per his instructions, Ramsey had placed a courtesy call to the local police to let them know the investigation was moving to their town. Kordoba PD in turn had sent Officer Michael Dade to accompany her to Cassie Frost's last employer.

"Sure. I need it to fill out the paperwork for her W-2, don't I?"

"Can we see it?"

The owner jerked his head to the half dozen patrons in the place. "Look, I got customers to tend to. I don't got time to . . ."

"We certainly understand if you're busy right now, sir," the young officer said politely. "And we can do this later." Ramsey opened her mouth to protest as he went on. "We can send someone back after closin' time. Should we say two A.M.?" He pulled out a notebook and pen, moving over to peer at the liquor license posted on the wall, jotting down the number. "That will give us time to check a few things out."

Ramsey hid a smile. The officer might be young, but he was no rookie. She watched the hidden threat register on the middle-aged man behind the counter, saw the moment he finished weighing his options before giving in ill-temperedly.

"All right, then." He jerked a head at Ramsey. "She can come with me and you stay here and watch my register. These thieves will rob me blind if someone don't watch 'em."

She trailed after him to the back of the dimly lit bar, into a rabbit warren of cramped back rooms piled with stock. Wedged into the corner of one of the rooms was a metal desk and file cabinet, apparently the sum total of the man's attempt at business organization.

He yanked open one of the drawers of the cabinet, muttering something under his breath she was probably better off not hearing. After leafing through files for a few moments, he withdrew one.

"Here." He jammed it into Ramsey's hands. "This is all I have on her. Like I say, she wasn't here long."

Ramsey flipped through it. Inside was a copy of the woman's social security card and a job application printed out in neat handwriting. She took a notebook out of her purse and started copying down details. "Was she still living at the address listed here?"

The man was craning his neck, trying to see out into the bar. She wondered if he was worried his handful of customers had mounted an attack on Dade en route to the cash register.

"Far as I know. She never said nuthin' 'bout movin'."

She set the folder down on the desk and followed him back out into the bar. "What about friends? Did you ever see her with anyone here? Did she talk about anyone?"

"She wasn't exactly the friendly type," the man said sourly. "She could mix drinks, but she didn't chat with the customers, know what I mean? I had to talk to her a time or two 'bout her attitude. I mean, nice lookin' gal like that, if she just worked it a little, she coulda brought in more business. Could be she was battin' for the other team, ya know? Maybe that's why she didn't like guy attention."

Ramsey shot him a look filled with dislike. She didn't envy Frost her time working for this jerk. She didn't bother telling the man that it was obvious the woman had attracted someone's attention.

And she'd ended up dead because of it.

———

Cassie Frost had rented a one-bedroom apartment over a department store on Main Street. And standing in the woman's home now, Ramsey felt an overwhelming sense of sympathy.

There were few personal belongings scattered around to stamp the room with her personality. The landlady, Phyllis

Trammel, had informed them as she'd let them in that the apartment had come furnished and the tenant had paid promptly the first of each month.

The elderly lady sat on the sagging couch right now, clutching the sketch she'd identified as Frost in one hand. "Kept to herself," she said now, her voice quavering. "Was never any trouble, but not one to chat either. I know I haven't seen her car move for near two weeks. Price of gas, it just don't pay to drive if you can walk."

Powell and one of the deputies were searching the car parked out front now. Deputy Leroy Ross was searching the kitchen. Ramsey was in the bedroom, and the apartment was small enough to hear the entire exchange between Phyllis and Officer Dade. With her gloved hands searching the dresser drawers, Ramsey pulled out a small bound book.

Flipping through it quickly, she called out, "I've got an address book." At least it had a few addresses in it, complete with telephone numbers and e-mail addresses. But she hadn't noticed a computer in the apartment.

For that matter, there wasn't a telephone.

She dropped the address book in a clear evidence bag, sealing and labeling it. Then she stepped out into the main room and addressed Trammel. "Did Ms. Frost have a cell phone?"

The older woman looked at her with eyes rheumy with tears. "I believe she did. Yes, because I offered to have a landline hooked up for her—that would be thirty dollars extra a month—and she said no, she had a cell phone and she'd just use that. Never got one for myself. Don't see the need for all this new technology takin' over. . . ."

Ramsey had quit listening. "You find a purse, Matthews?" Few women would leave home without one. If she'd taken it with her, it could mean she'd gone willingly with the attacker. Or that she'd been snatched outside of the apartment.

"Not yet." He walked out of the miniscule bathroom with several evidence bags in his gloved hands. "Got a little recreational pot and a prescription for birth control pills from a local pharmacy."

Having finished in the bedroom, Ramsey moved into the small kitchen. The deputy was going through all the drawers and cupboards. There was an outside door with a deadbolt and, pushing it open, Ramsey saw it led to a rickety fire escape. She crouched down outside the door and examined the lock, but it didn't look like it had been tampered with. Pulling the door shut firmly, she waited a moment and tried to open it from the outside. She couldn't.

She had to rap her fist on it a couple times before Matthews opened it a crack. "Forget your key again, dear?"

"Both her doors were locked, Glenn. No signs of forced entry."

The agent shrugged and opened the door wider for her. "Maybe she knew the guy and let him in. Maybe he was never here at all, and she met up with him elsewhere."

"The bar owner said the last time she worked was Friday, June fifth. Didn't show up for her shift the next day." And since she'd left at three A.M. and was due back on duty at five the next evening, they now had a window of time in which she must have met up with her killer.

"The body wasn't discovered until near midnight on the sixth."

"Yeah." She cocked a brow at the deputy, who was crouched down to look in the oven. He shook his head.

"Nothin' yet."

"Can you help me a minute?" Without waiting for Matthews's answer, she strode back to the bedroom where she'd left her evidence kit and the crime scene tools she'd retrieved from the trunk of her car. Reaching into one duffel bag, she withdrew a portable alternate light source and donned the goggles.

"You want to pull those sheets back for me?"

When the agent did so, Ramsey began to move the ALS meticulously over every inch of the surface of the fitted sheet. She indicated every hair found for Matthews to pick up with the forensic tweezers, wrap in tissue paper, and place in an evidence bag. Both sheets and the bedspread got the same treatment. But at the end of forty minutes, she turned off the

ALS and pushed up her goggles. "The bedding can be bagged." Whoever raped Cassie Frost hadn't done it on the bed.

She turned to leave the bedroom and found Officer Dade standing in the doorway. He gave her a sheepish grin. "Sort of interestin' to watch you work. Where you from, Ms. Clark?"

With a polite smile, she started to brush by him. "Mississippi." She froze a moment, shocked that the truth had slipped out. She never admitted that. Tried as hard as she could not to remember it at all. "I was with TBI a while back. I've lived in Virginia for the last few years." She forced herself to move again.

"You're from Mississippi? Well, shoot, I'm from Mississippi, too!" The officer's delighted voice sounded behind her. "I'm from Biloxi, born and raised. Whereabouts did you live?"

"Cripolo."

She went to the couch and switched on the ALS, pulled down the goggles, and hoped he'd leave it alone. But the man trailed out into the room to stand next to her.

"Cripolo? That seems like a right nice li'l town. Driven through it a few times on the way to the coast. You ever get back to Mississippi?"

"Not much, no." Not ever, if she could help it.

Matthews was beginning to dust the surfaces in the apartment for prints. She directed the landlady to the only chair in the room and began to meticulously run the ALS over the couch. It was old and decrepit enough to hoard stains from a couple earlier decades. When she finished, she gave the carpet the same treatment. Next they'd bag any fibers or hairs, then photograph the area.

But she already had the feeling they'd discover Cassie Frost hadn't been attacked in her apartment at all.

———

She dreamt of Mississippi that night. Exhaustion had lowered defenses she usually kept well honed, and the images crept in, melding details—some eerily accurate and others oddly misshapen—in a seamless fabric only a dream state can achieve.

Ramsey moved restlessly under the sheet. Somewhere in that stage between dozing and the sucking depths of slumber, she fought a silent battle to wake and avoid the unconscious mental movie about to unfold.

The officer she'd met that day was there, his smile wide and friendly. *You're from Mississippi? Well, shoot, I'm from Mississippi, too!* But then his face blurred at the edges, took on another form as he mouthed words uttered by people he'd never met.

I say we fuck her now. What if she gets away?

Whereabouts did you live? Cripolo? That seems like a right nice li'l town.

The dark forest, its gaping shadows yawning like a huge mouth teethed with trees, was fringed with swamps that were inhabited by gators and cottonmouths. Her body shook as the decision loomed again in a terrifyingly identical replay. A hideous death ahead. A horrific experience behind.

Shit, where would she go? Into the swamps? It's no fun when they can't run. We'll fuck her later. First we hunt.

You ever get back to Mississippi?

Hands trying desperately to cover her nakedness. To fight off the cruel fingers that groped and pinched and penetrated.

Better run, cunt, less'n you want to start suckin' right now.

The girl in the dream ran.

Yee-haw!

The familiar echo careened through her mind, shot chills up her spine. Brought her upright in bed, quivering like she'd been afflicted with palsy.

It took several attempts for her trembling hands to grasp the hem of the sheet. To wrap it around her frozen body. And supreme concentration to push back the remnants of the haunting scene that still lurked, just waiting to spin out again when sleep disarmed her.

She drew in a deep breath. Followed it with another. And let the simple act press back the images that threatened to swarm.

Calmer now, she rested against the headboard, her heart galloping like a Thoroughbred under the wire. The girl in the dream didn't exist anymore. She'd made certain of that. Ramsey would never be that vulnerable again. And the memories of when she had been that helpless no longer had the power to weaken her.

She told herself that over and over as she resisted sleep and stared at the shade covering the lone window. Waited for the sky to lighten and send slivers of light around its edges. The only thing left of her past was memories, and those couldn't hurt her.

But even as the mental reassurances calmed her pulse and steadied her breathing, her gaze remained fixed on the window. And she silently counted away the hours until morning.

Chapter 8

Lounging on the curb in front of the Historical Museum, Dev watched Ramsey pull up fifteen minutes after ten. He was about to open his mouth and say something clever about not expecting her to be the type of woman to keep a man waiting, but her face, when she slammed the car door of the SUV, had the words dying on his tongue.

"What's wrong?" He rose to meet her as she rounded the hood.

"Nothing. I hope you haven't been waiting long."

He laid a hand gently on her arm as she would have walked past him, halting her. "What's wrong?" he asked again.

She looked at him then, really looked at him, and it was like taking a fist to the solar plexus. Those green gold eyes of hers were ringed with shadows. But it was the haunted look in them that had alarm running through him.

"We've identified the victim. She'd been living a couple counties over. Her sister's arriving soon to identify the body. Then there'll be friends and neighbors to interview. I'll have to take a rain check on the lunch."

He shoved both hands in the pocket of his jeans and strolled along beside her to the museum door. "Seems like a good enough reason to break our date, so you've got your rain check." He paused a beat. "'Course I'm gonna have to upgrade that date to dinner, now, rather than lunch, as sort of an inflation."

She smiled a little, as he'd meant her to. "Why am I not surprised?"

He pulled open the door and waited for her to walk through it, noting as he did that he'd yet to see her without some sort of tailored jacket over pants. The temperatures were mild in this part of Tennessee, barely reaching eighty, but she still should be plenty warm in that getup.

In the next instant it hit him that she must wear it to hide a weapon, and the realization made his interest only burn hotter. Took a contrary man, he reflected, following Ramsey into the cool dim interior of the museum, to find the thought of an armed woman so arousing.

But then Ramsey Clark was no ordinary woman.

He slipped ahead of her at the last minute so he'd be the first to greet Donnelle. And her expression, when she looked up from a display she was assembling, was welcoming.

"Devlin, you ol' heartbreaker. I'm so pleased you stopped in!" Her delight dimmed an instant later when she caught sight of Ramsey behind him. "Ms. Clark. How nice to see you again."

Because he was listening for it, Dev caught the reserve couched in the polite tone. His smile bumped up a few amps to put the woman at ease. "Seein' as how Ramsey and I have similar interests in the history of the legend, we thought we'd save you some work. You can just tell it once to us both."

She demurred. "You've heard all this before, Devlin. Don't know why you'd want to go through it again."

Crossing his arms, he smiled easily at her. "I'm lookin' to refresh my memory. And it just so happens I find myself free for lunch, so I thought when we're done here, you might let me ruin your reputation by bein' seen downtown with a younger man."

"I think my reputation could stand a little jolt, actually." Her charm fully restored, she motioned them to follow her back to another room.

"If someone comes in, I'll have to see to them, but it's been quiet as a mouse wettin' on cotton so far this mornin'. Sit yourselves down at the table there. Can I get either of you coffee? Made it fresh about an hour ago."

"None for me, thanks," Ramsey answered.

"I'll take some, Donnelle. With cream, if you have it." A third cup of coffee wasn't going to do him any harm, and he recognized that the business of playing hostess would soothe the woman's nerves.

He could feel the impatience emanating from Ramsey as they spent several minutes swapping small talk and looking at pictures of Donnelle's newest granddaughter, making the appropriately appreciative noises. He was a man who understood the small tasks of putting people at ease in order to draw the information out of them in their own time, and in their own words.

Ramsey, he imagined, was just as adept at extracting information, but he thought her techniques might be found a bit abrupt around these parts.

Eventually Donnelle relaxed in a chair across from them and brought her mug to her lips. "Feels good to sit a minute," she confessed. "I swear there's enough to do here every week to keep me runnin' all day."

"I appreciate you takin' the time with us. Guess I don't have to tell you that Beau Simpson's death has whipped up some talk about the legend again."

"It always does. I recall the last time, especially after your daddy was killed in prison, folks 'round here were in a fever 'bout the whole thing."

He felt rather than saw Ramsey's jolt at the words. Had a hard time concealing his own. There were some memories that throbbed like a wound despite the passing of time.

"The legend is, of course, rooted in fact." He recognized the note that had entered the older woman's voice and knew she'd settled into her role of historian. "Many superstitions are, before embellishments are added. What we do know, what we have records of, is that the red mist was first sighted nearly ninety years ago."

Her spoon clinked against her mug as she paused to stir in more sugar. "There are, of course, different versions of the legend. One has it that a man named Harold Bean killed his wife in a fit of jealous rage in 1922. Killed her with an ax, the story goes, out behind the woodpile beyond their cabin. He hid the body, but the blood had turned to gas in the air, creating the red mist. Her lover, a man who had never been identified or caught, recognized his love's blood in the red vapor and came to avenge her, usin' the same ax on Bean and leavin' his body dead where he fell."

"That's only two deaths," Ramsey pointed out. She'd been uncharacteristically silent, Dev thought, and wondered again at the toll her recent findings had taken on her.

Donelle nodded. "Names and dates of each deceased are written in the history I've been keepin'. Actually, I had the whole thing written out in long hand, but now the museum board wants all notes transcribed into the computer." She smiled prettily. "I'll admit I'm not as handy with technology as I might be, so it's been slow progress.

"One other death occurred within a few days of the Bean family, and in this retellin' it's unrelated. A Lora Kuemper was found dead in her family's well. The story went that she must have tripped and fallen in on her way back from the outhouse late one night."

"But her death is connected in other accounts?"

By only a flicker of expression did Donnelle show her annoyance at Ramsey's question. "Another version puts a spin on the story that's a bit more salacious. This one has it that Lora and Wilma Bean had been carryin' on a lesbian affair. That Lora was the one exactin' revenge, only to return to the farm she shared with her husband. He drowned her in the well for her sins."

The stories were starting to ring a bell for Dev. He'd heard them a time or two over the years, or at least one form or another.

"The third account brings in an interestin' twist. Seems the Beans had a Negro girl as live-in help. There was talk that perhaps Mr. Bean and the girl were . . . friendlier than they ought to be. While Harold was at work one day, Mrs. Bean had the girl follow her to the woods and bring a basket to collect berries along the way. She killed her there and pushed her body into Ashton's Pond, though there's no record of it ever being found.

"Now Harold, comin' back from the field, was surrounded by the red mist and knew at once what his wife had done. When he confronted her with his suspicions, she attacked him with the ax and inflicted serious wounds before he got it away from her and killed her. He ended up dying from his injuries."

"Making Lora Kuemper's death unrelated."

Donnelle nodded. "Similar threads in all three versions, although they don't all connect to form the same picture. Technically, since the colored girl at Bean's was never found, she can't be counted as a fourth death." The woman gave a shrug. "She may have headed up north and gotten a job in the city."

"How long before the pattern was repeated again?" Ramsey asked.

"Nineteen fifty," Donnelle answered promptly before sipping from her coffee again. "The records are much more accurate from then on. The red mist was first sighted three days before a death. Cal Hopkins was found out in his garage, hanging from a beam. His neighbors, Lucien and Rachel Tarvester, swore they saw a car drivin' off from his house at the approximate time of death. But they weren't tellin' that story very long as Lucien was struck by a hit-and-run driver not a week later. Died up in the Knoxville hospital. His wife packed up and moved that same week. Less than two months later the house she was rentin' in Nashville burnt to the ground while she slept."

Dev slanted a look over to the notes Ramsey was writing. *Red mist as a premonition to deaths or subsequent to?*

"I think I'll have a look at that written history after lunch, Donnelle," he said. It occurred to him to do a little checking into the dates of deaths occurring around each of the dates. He hadn't run any tests at the local cemetery, though he'd have to be cautious doing so now. Nothing got people up in arms more than the thought of someone disturbing their loved ones at peace. But he was curious to know whether there was any activity around the graves of those affiliated with the red mist in another generation.

Ramsey checked her watch. "I have to go." He heard real regret in her voice. It was second nature to rise when she did. "I do appreciate you taking your time to talk to us today, Donnelle."

"Nice to see you again, Ramsey. You look like you're workin' too hard. Leanne's offerin' a facial half price with any trim next Friday, if you get a free minute." Lowering her voice, Donnelle went on, "Don't tell her I told you. But it'll be in the paper in a couple days. So you cut out that coupon and plan on usin' it, hear?"

Dev nearly smiled at the pained smile Ramsey gave in return. "That sounds . . . tempting."

"Don't forget dinner," he reminded her. And it pleased him to see her eyes heat and narrow with irritation. "Problem with inflation is if you don't pay it down, the cost just keeps increasin'."

"I'll keep that in mind." And her tone, as she uttered the words, was only slightly less sincere than her answer to Donnelle had been.

They both watched her walk away in that rapid, no-nonsense stride of hers. She wasn't a woman to use her retreat in a way guaranteed to catch a man's eye and ante up his interest. No, Dev mused, Ramsey put on none of the usual wiles and ways of her gender. And was all the sexier for it.

When his attention reverted back to Donnelle, she was eying him archly. "Not your usual type, is she Devlin?"

He slipped his hands in his pockets, rocked back on his heels. "What is my type, Donnelle?"

"Single, willin', and attractive, for starts. Oh, she may fit on two of those counts, I'll grant you." The woman stood gracefully and crossed the room to the desk to take her purse from a drawer. Turning to face him again, she continued. "But there's no softness in that one. It wouldn't pay to trifle with her."

He recognized the concern in the older woman's eyes and was touched by it. "You're right there. That's why I'm willin' to make the supreme sacrifice and allow her to trifle with me. And when I'm nursin' a broken heart, I'll 'spect you to be suitably warm and sympathetic."

She continued to regard him anxiously for a moment before visibly relaxing. As she approached him on stiletto-thin heels, she responded airily, "I'm not going to worry 'bout it, because with all due deference to your success with women, somethin' tells me she isn't going to fall for your usual line. That one's here for one reason only, and when her work is done, she'll be off again. You'd do well to remember that."

As Donnelle clicked up to him and took his arm, Dev reflected there was a measure of truth to the woman's words. Ramsey would be here only a short time and so would he.

But he couldn't think of a reason in the world not to spend that time as pleasurably as possible.

It was with a sense of déjà vu that Ramsey stood outside the medical examiner's office and watched a dark sedan roll up to the curb. But this time Mark Rollins was at her side, and the car's occupant was female rather than an ill older man.

But when the young woman got out, showing a tear-ravaged face that bore a striking resemblance to the victim, Ramsey braced herself for the upcoming emotional scene.

She let Rollins take the lead, approaching the woman, Sarah Frost, and making introductions while he led her up to the door.

Barely acknowledging Ramsey, the woman was saying, "I'm sure this is all a mistake. The last time I talked to her, Cassie was in Chattanooga workin' as a legal secretary. What would she be doin' in a Kordoba bar? She's not a bartender."

The lobby of the building seemed to echo with their footsteps as they made their way across it. Rollins nodded to the clerk manning the desk, who buzzed them through the door that would lead to the morgue.

"How long has it been since you've talked to your sister?" Ramsey inquired.

The flicker of guilt on the woman's face didn't go unnoticed. "About six months ago, I guess."

Ramsey exchanged a look with Rollins. "Would you say the two of you were estranged?"

Sarah's head came up sharply. "Of course not," she snapped. "We've always been close. We . . . there was some stuff recently, but we'll work through it. We will. Because I don't think this is Cassie. You've identified the wrong person."

"I hope that's true, ma'am." There was an unfamiliar tech awaiting them outside the morgue door. Ramsey took a moment to wonder where Don Wilson was before pressing Sarah, "What sort of problems were . . . are you having with your sister?"

There was another flicker on Sarah's face, strengthening Ramsey's earlier impression. "Oh . . . you know. Guy problems."

She subsided then, because the tech was leading them to the wall of metal drawers. Pulling out the gurney holding the victim. Ramsey and Mark surreptitiously moved to flank the woman as the sheet was pulled back on the corpse.

Sarah Frost's weak scream bounced off the walls and gleaming stainless steel tables in the room. Ramsey caught her in the next moment as the woman's knees gave out.

"Cassie! Oh my God, Cassie!"

Rollins motioned to the tech to re-cover the victim as Ramsey turned the woman toward the door. She was sobbing now. Great wrenching bouts of weeping that racked her body. With an arm around Sarah's shaking shoulders, Ramsey moved her down the hallway, to the lobby, where the clerk, with one swift look in their direction, disappeared into a back room to give them some privacy.

"I'm so sorry for your loss, Sarah," she murmured, her throat tight. She recognized the guilt in the woman's devastation. The tragedy of loss always made survivors feel their flaws more deeply. Magnified each slight they might have dealt the victim. Reminded them of everything done or not done.

"It's my fault." Ramsey could barely make out the words, but she noted Rollins's attention to them. "She wouldn't have been here if it weren't for me. It's all my fault."

Guiding her to a bench in the lobby, Ramsey helped the woman sink into it before sitting beside her. Rollins stood next to them, his discomfort showing in his expression. It was clear he was fine with Ramsey taking over with the distraught woman.

"Why do you say that?" Tissues sat on a nearby table— probably for just this sort of occasion—so Ramsey snagged some and handed them to Sarah.

"Quinn . . . he was engaged to Cassie." Her breath heaving, Sarah managed the words between sobs. "They were supposed to get married last year. But we . . . he and I . . . it was just so strong, y'know?" She raised swimming eyes to regard Ramsey imploringly. "We didn't mean for it to happen. But it was like we were meant to be together. Cassie was so hurt. So . . . devastated."

"So she broke the engagement?"

"Quinn did. We told her together. It was a pretty bad scene." The woman's face seemed to crumple again. "We all said some hurtful things. A couple weeks later she packed up and left town. I've only talked to her a few times since." Rollins had pulled open his notebook and flipped it open.

"What's Quinn's last name?" Ramsey handed the whole box of tissue to the other woman.

"Sanders. He has a fitness gym in Memphis. That's where we're from."

"How long ago did Cassie leave town?"

"April of last year. They were plannin' to get married in May."

"Has Quinn talked to Cassie since then that you know of?"

Sarah shook her head and blew her nose violently. Although her manner seemed calmer, the tears still flowed freely down her cheeks. "We thought it best for him to cut off all contact. And I tried to call her more frequently, but she didn't often answer my calls."

"What happened the last time the two of you spoke?" When the woman just looked at her, Ramsey expanded. "You said you hadn't talked to her for six months. But sometime after the last conversation you had, it sounds like she quit her job and moved away. Did she say anything to let you know why?"

The tears seemed to flow faster. "I thought enough time had passed, y'know? That maybe she'd gotten over . . . everythin'. At first we had a real good talk, and it was almost like things were back to normal between us. But when I told her that Quinn and I were gettin' married, she just hung up. And no matter how many times I called since, she wouldn't answer."

"Did she threaten to make trouble for the two of you?" There was a reason they always looked at family first in homicide cases. Strangling someone took a certain amount of passion. Emotions ran deepest with those who knew the victim.

"No, she would never do anythin' like that." Sarah blew her nose again, regarding Ramsey with bleary eyes. "Cassie wasn't like that. She just got real quiet and then she hung up."

"Sarah, we're going to do everything we can to find your sister's killer. I know you want to do what you can to help us." Ramsey caught the warning in Rollins's eyes, but it was unnecessary. She knew how to extricate the information she needed without shocking the interviewees into lawyering up. Waiting for the woman's jerky nod, she went on. "We're going to be talking to everyone who knew your sister and asking them the same questions I'm going to ask you. We want to build a picture of her last hours."

The other woman took a fresh tissue and wiped at her mascara, smearing it worse beneath her eyes. "But none of my friends have talked to Cassie since she left."

"She was last seen at three A.M. on June fifth. For our records, can you tell us where you were between the fifth and sixth of this month?"

The woman stopped wiping ineffectually at her ruined makeup and shot a sharp look at Ramsey. "What are you askin'? Are you suggestin' that I . . ."

"I'm suggesting that you want to help us solve your sister's murder," Ramsey put in smoothly, cutting through the woman's outrage. "We'll ask everyone who knew her well the same question. We'll check their stories. And when we find the person whose story doesn't hold up, we'll look closer. That's how it's done, Sarah."

Her throat worked for a moment, and she glanced down at the hands she had tightly knotted in her lap. "Quinn and I . . . we were at our engagement party that weekend. A bunch of us booked a place on Pine Lake for a few days." Her voice trailed off as if the thought just struck her. And Ramsey could read the abject misery in her expression. "Are you tellin' me . . . that my sister was killed while we were celebratin' our engagement?"

"Well, that's karma coming back to bite you in the ass." Glenn Matthews broke the silence that had stretched after Ramsey had relayed her earlier conversation with Frost to him and Warden Powell.

It was nearing ten o'clock. They'd returned to the motel only a couple hours earlier. After the scene at the ME's office, Ramsey had driven to Kordoba to join the agents in interviewing locals about Cassie Frost, to a noticeable lack of success.

"I got a list of the other people attending the engagement party and compiled their names and addresses, as well as that of the operators of the resort Frost says they were at." Ramsey batted Matthews's hand out of the way as he moved to snag the last piece of pizza. She hadn't eaten that day, and the agent had practically inhaled the whole thing himself.

"We'll need to look at the ex-fiancé," Powell put in. He was chomping morosely on a deli sandwich. "Husbands and boyfriends are always at the head of the list for a homicide like this."

Ramsey nodded. But she was betting they were going to

find that Quinn Sanders was tightly alibied for the time in question. Kordoba was across the state from Pine Lake. "That's what Rollins said. But it doesn't sound like Cassie had much to do with either Sanders or her sister after he called off their wedding. Of course, we don't have her cell phone, so we can't be sure. But it shouldn't be much longer before we get the Local Usage Details for it."

"Couple days," Powell agreed. They'd put in a request the day before and had had no difficulty obtaining a judge's signature for it. Wadding up the wrapper to his sandwich, he tossed it into the nearby trash. "What's the latest on the test results your guy is runnin'?"

She finished chewing before answering, and moved her slice of pizza farther from Matthews's reach. She didn't like the avaricious look in the man's eye. "Jonesy was able to tell that the substance in her stomach came from some sort of plant root. Plenty of people experiment with plant parts that give you a buzz. But whatever she digested didn't show up in her blood under any of the tox screens that were run, so apparently it doesn't act as a stimulant."

Taking another bite, she chewed reflectively. "Might be worth it to pursue a line of questioning with local healers. When I was with TBI, I heard plenty of stories about people who claimed to heal all sorts of disease and illnesses with herbs and plants and stuff."

"The autopsy report didn't show any signs of disease," Matthews pointed out.

"But people self diagnose all the time. Try holistic remedies for anything from headaches to menstrual cramps. If we can get a list of things used in the area by these people, we can get samples for Jonesy to compare to the stomach contents." She thought of something else the scientist had mentioned. "He's more specific than the ME was in his report about when the plant root was ingested. There are no signs of digestive acids mixed with the root. He believes it was eaten shortly before she was strangled. Maybe only minutes earlier."

"Meanin' she almost had to have been given it by her attacker."

She finished off the pizza and wiped her fingers on a napkin, studying the wall postings that acted as a murder book of sorts. Their findings in the last twenty-four hours hadn't been added yet. In the excitement of following up new leads, it was hard to take the time out to do the necessary information logging, but the task would have to be done to maintain a complete picture.

"People are buzzing about that suicide in town." Matthews stood and stretched. "Lots of hogwash about the legend and deaths in threes and all that."

"That's all it is," Powell said. He rose, as well. "Bunch of superstition. Just makes it harder for us to get answers from people in these parts."

"I got a quick lesson on the origins of the legend today." Ramsey got up and threw away the pizza box, then wiped off the table with a spare napkin. "Figured it always helps to know what sort of superstition you're dealing with."

"Who'd you get that from. Stryker?"

She glanced at Matthews. Didn't like the sly look in his eye. "He was there," she said coolly. "Lady at the Historical Museum gave us both a rundown on local lore. I had to leave early for the ME's office when Frost showed up, though."

"I'd have thought he could fill you in himself." Matthews cut off as Powell announced he was going to bed and left the room. Resuming, he said, "In a roundabout way, he's sort of linked to the last so-called red mist murder. Way I heard it, Stryker's father went to prison for committing it."

Chapter 9

"Your light was on."

It wasn't much of an excuse, Ramsey reflected uncomfortably, for knocking on someone's door at eleven P.M. But the urgency she felt to talk to Devlin Stryker wouldn't be assuaged.

And the irony of *that* was hard to ignore.

If he was surprised to see her, it didn't show in his expression. He regarded her somberly with one hand propped against the doorjamb. And she had the fleeting thought that he already knew what had brought her here.

"Light's on because I'm still up." He reached forward to push open the screen door, and with only a second's hesitation, Ramsey walked into the house.

It wasn't his. She would have known that even if she hadn't been told as much when the man walking his dog down the street had directed her here. There was no stamp of Stryker's personality in the worn leather furniture or the wildlife prints on the walls. But there were plenty of photos framing his famed grin. A computer on a desk in the corner of the dining room had notes and piles of books next to it. And a familiar looking heap of cases and tripods were stacked neatly on the floor a few feet away.

She eyed them, searched for something to say that wouldn't sound sarcastic.

"Ah . . . you're working tonight?"

"Planned on it. Jotted down names and dates from Donnelle. Wondered if recent events would result in any activity 'round the cemetery this time."

Ramsey was not often at a loss for words. But she was struggling now not to blurt out what was on her mind. Especially knowing that it would undoubtedly be a painful subject for him.

His mouth curved slightly, but the smile wasn't reflected in his eyes. "Don't know as I've ever seen you look so uncomfortable. So I reckon you heard some talk 'bout the last time the red mist occurred here."

Her gaze fixed on his. "You have to realize what a conflict of interest this is for you."

Brows raised in real surprise, he folded his arms across his chest. "Really? Don't see how. I'm not the media or the police. It doesn't really matter what my bias may be. That's the nice thing 'bout chasin' ghosts. They don't much care one way or 'nother."

She didn't rise to the verbal bait. "If I hadn't gotten called away today from the museum, you would have let Donnelle start in about the last murder in Buffalo Springs? Even as it implicates your father?"

He crouched down and began zipping up the cases of equipment he had piled on the floor. "She wouldn't have done that. A true Southern gentlewoman would never discuss somethin' so indelicate in front of the murderer's son."

It was difficult to say which of them was more surprised when she placed a hand lightly on his arm. "Dev."

He stilled, staring up at her, and it occurred to her that was the first time she'd called him by name. Embarrassed, she withdrew her hand and clasped both of them in back of her.

Heaving a breath, he rose. "I was going to tell you at lunch. Been half waitin' for you to question me 'bout it up to now. With the murder first then Simpson's suicide, there's no shortage of talk 'bout the deaths back then."

"I'm sure." Even if none of it had reached her ears until an hour ago, she was intimately acquainted with small-town memories. No single event could ever be lived down. Very little was forgiven. Nothing forgotten. And each time the gossip raged again, the retelling took another step further from facts and became the new truth. And living with that, *in that*, was the cruelest life imaginable.

"I'm gonna have a beer. Do you want anythin'?" Before she could answer, he was striding through the small dining room to the kitchen. Slowly, she trailed along in his wake, lingering over the collection of photos that covered walls and shelves. If they were put in order, one could see Stryker's development over the years from a towheaded toddler to a gap-toothed schoolboy, then to a young teen, already showing promise of those fallen angel looks, to a college grad. The sheer number of images astonished her. Ramsey couldn't recall seeing more than three pictures of her that had been taken during her entire childhood.

He came back from the kitchen, shoved a beer she didn't want into her hand.

"This is your grandfather's house?"

"Yep, it is. Put him in assisted livin' last winter, but he won't hear of sellin' the place. Gives him the feelin' he still has a choice about his last years. I guess that's important."

She sipped from her bottle. "I guess."

Reaching behind her, he pulled out a dining room chair. After she sank into it, he sat down as well. "I was two the last time the red mist was sighted in Buffalo Springs. Don't remember anythin' 'bout that night, of course. But the facts I've heard in the time since stay pretty true. Seems a gal by the name of Sally Ann Porter disappeared one day. Her mother—Jessalyn—was pretty upset. Sally Ann's daddy was out of the picture—messy divorce years earlier—and Jessalyn was convinced Sally Ann had fallen victim to foul play."

He'd shifted into the role of storyteller, she realized, as if that eliminated a bit of the sting from relaying a tale that held such a personal punch.

Tilting his bottle to his lips, Dev took a drink before continuing. "The sheriff at that time was my daddy's brother, Richard Rollins."

Jolted at the news, she interrupted. "But your name isn't Rollins."

"My mother remarried two years later and my stepfather

adopted me." There was a flicker of distaste on his face, as if the memory gave him no pleasure. "As I was sayin', Uncle Rich tried to soothe Jessalyn's fears, as it was his supposition that Sally Ann had taken off for New York or California or some such. Seems Sally was a free spirit. Liked experimentin' with drugs and men, usually in unison. She'd talked about leavin' town for a couple years. Everyone, even her friends, believed she'd finally done it."

"But not her mother."

"Not Jessalyn. She became more and more distraught. Can't blame her there. And maybe she felt a little bit of guilt, on account of she and Sally Ann hadn't been getting on up to then. They'd had harsh words over Sally Ann's lifestyle and her taste in men. And since Jessalyn was known for her ability to tear a strip off a person and wrap them up in it, people started sayin' as how they could see the girl wantin' to get away."

Maybe she was getting reacquainted with the roundabout way of speaking, but Ramsey felt no impatience creeping in as she listened. She had a feeling that this story would tell far more about Devlin Stryker than any of the words they'd exchanged so far.

He rubbed his thumb over the condensation forming on the bottle. "Jessalyn grew more and more disenchanted with the investigation and the entire Rollins family. Said she was going to look into things herself. But mostly what that amounted to was a lot of trash talk. Got to where she was even tellin' anyone who'd listen that my daddy and Sally Ann had been lovers. That of course upset my daddy, so he resolved to go talk some sense to her." He drank deeply, eyeing her over the rim of the bottle. When he lowered it, he continued, "Next mornin' Jessalyn was found dead on the floor of her bedroom. Strangled. My daddy was passed out drunk next to her body."

A bolt of pity twisted through her. She couldn't imagine willingly returning to this town every summer trailing that kind of background behind. She hadn't been back to Mississippi for more than a few days total in fifteen years.

"And that was enough to convict him?" It would have been more than enough, she imagined, nearly thirty years ago in a small southern town shaken by its first violent death in decades. Especially with the local legend thrown in to stir things up.

"That and the fact that he couldn't remember anythin' to defend himself. Said he couldn't recall a thing past the time he'd had a beer with his best friend Lon Chelsey at Suds right before headin' to Jessalyn's. Now this is where the facts stop and talk takes over. People sort of figured he'd faced Jessalyn, got a tearin' into for his efforts, and slunk off to pick up some liquid courage. Drank enough to work up a good mad and went back over to her house, tried again. This time with different results."

"But there was nothing in the police report validating that? Interviewing people who might have seen him during that time? Someplace who sold him the beer? Neighbors who saw him come back? Heard something?" She broke off at the smile curling one side of his mouth. "What?"

"Nothin'. Just . . . you think like a cop."

"What would you expect me to think like, a trapeze art-ist?" It would be interesting to see if that police report still existed. To track the course of the investigation and draw her own conclusions about its findings. "Your father was killed in prison?"

"Three weeks inside and he was stuck with a shiv during a prison riot. By that time, my mama had taken me to go live with her grandparents in Knoxville."

Because her throat felt tight, Ramsey took a long swallow of beer. "That had to be rough on you."

"Rougher on my mama, I 'spect. At any rate, she found husband number two quick enough. Later on it became a real good idea to separate the two of us for the summer each year, so she'd send me back to stay with my granddaddy."

Her mind backed up to what he'd said earlier. "That's only two deaths. With your father and Jessalyn, I mean."

"Figured you'd key in on that. 'Bout eight months later some boys were hookin' school and hangin' 'round Ashton's

Pond, lookin' for bull snakes. They saw somethin' in the bushes and investigated. Found human hair. Took four days, but Uncle Richard and his deputies finally fished the body that belonged to it out of the water. Near as they could figure, it was Sally Ann Porter."

Instinct flickered to life. "Ashton's Pond again."

He shook his head. "Nothin' like this last time. There was barely enough left of her to autopsy after the fish had feasted on her for so long. They figured she'd been hangin' out down there, doin' some speed, puttin' some space 'tween her and Jessalyn, and fell in. Too doped up to swim to the edge and pull herself out."

Maybe. Any pond or lake was bound to have a death or two reported within a thirty-year period. But Ramsey was more determined than ever to look up the old case files, if they still existed.

Every town had its share of tragedy, regardless of its size. But as Leanne had mentioned, there was definitely a pattern in Buffalo Springs. And she was becoming more and more interested to discover if there was any tangible link between the deaths she'd heard about. Not one that depended on ghosts and red mist and all that rot. But one that laid the blame for each death squarely where it was due—at some human's feet.

And three decades ago that human had been Dev's father.

Absently, she ran her thumbnail under the bottle's label to loosen it, surveying Dev soberly. "I can understand that you have questions. But I don't see how coming back here now, with all that"—she jerked her head toward his mound of equipment—"is going to provide you any further information about what happened with your father."

"See, that's where I figure you're wrong." He drained the bottle and sat it on the table in front of him. "I know you're one of those types who don't believe anythin' you can't see and feel and examine."

"I believe in facts," she put in.

"Facts are nice when they exist. But I'm here to tell you I've seen a few things in my time that science can't explain. Not often, mind you. I see far more that turns out to be nothin' but hype and hoax. And I spend plenty of time in my books exposin' those. But there have been a few times . . ." The look on his face almost had Ramsey asking for details. Almost.

"Anyway, now's the perfect time to explore the legend of Buffalo Springs." He stood, walked back to the kitchen to put away his empty bottle before rejoining her. "And the thing I've noticed about murder is that it tends to get people agitated. And when they're agitated, they talk. Not so much to outsiders, but they'll talk to me. Most of it isn't worth listenin' to, but every now and then details come out that are sorta interestin'. I'm hopin' enough of those details emerge to help me get a clearer picture of what happened the last time the red mist was sighted."

It seemed like a masochistic way to get information, but since she could now understand what drove him, she remained silent. It was, she admitted, a braver way to deal with his past than leaving the state and refusing to go back the way she had.

Not that she was about to rethink *that* decision.

"Well." She slid her half-empty bottle away from her and rose. "I guess I shouldn't keep you." She stood, glanced at the equipment in the next room and then back at him. "I mean . . . I suppose midnight is the time you want to be in the cemetery, right?"

From the grin on his face, it was apparent she'd said something idiotic, but to his credit he said only, "The time really isn't important. Other than being out of there before dawn. People don't take kindly to having others lurkin' 'round the graves of their loved ones, no matter what my intentions are. I've alerted Mark's office that I'll be there, in case anyone reports lights or some such."

Ramsey's impression of his intelligence had marginally increased since hearing his take on the supernatural events he explored. But it still seemed like a strange way for a person to make a living.

But then there were some, including her own family, who often pointed out that traveling around from one location to another investigating the most violent of crimes didn't exactly fit within the "normal" range, either.

She made her way through the room with him following her and stepped carefully around the stacked cases of equipment. But something stopped her as she had her hand on the door.

Turning, she surveyed him soberly. "I'm sorry about your father, Stryker." And she was. The failures of the parents inevitably impacted the child. She wondered now if that seemingly incessant affability of his had developed as a defense mechanism against some of those blows.

He closed the distance between them. "Have to admit, I'm not sorry you know the whole story. Half promised myself you needed to know that much before I did this."

She knew him well enough to mistrust that gleam in his eye. But obviously not well enough to guess what it meant. Because when his mouth lowered to cover hers, she could only stand there, stunned. Oh, she could feel. God, yes, she felt. As his lips molded hers, there was a kick to her system that jumpstarted her pulse. Fired tiny missiles of heat to parts of her body that hadn't been warmed in . . . The thought grew fuzzy. Jesus . . . God, he was good at this.

She reached out a hand, clutched at his shirt. And indulged in the hard hot pressure of his mouth for a few more seconds. Returned it.

He nipped and stroked with teeth and tongue, pressing her lips open to draw a response. Because she wasn't dead, he succeeded. She drew him closer, went on tiptoe to get nearer still. To warm herself at the flames flickering between them.

He eased his mouth away to nip at her throat. A rocket of heat shot straight up her spine. "I don't have to go out tonight."

Ramsey was having trouble comprehending the words, accompanied as they were with the stinging kiss he placed on the cord of her neck. "You . . . what?" She shoved her free hand in his hair as her throat arched beneath his teeth. And felt her heart straining like a long-distance runner on the last lap.

His palm cupped her butt. "I could stay." His lips did a slow, thorough search along her jaw and settled to worry her earlobe. "So could you."

The offer was pure temptation. Every nerve in her body quivered with the need to accept. There was more here than she would have imagined. More than she'd *let* herself imagine. And that in itself was the impetus she needed to reach for reason, which seemed strangely fragmented.

"No." Because the word sounded on a moan, she tried again. "No." And released the grip she'd had on his shirt. Withdrew the hand she'd had in his hair. Strove to quiet the inner chorus of disappointed hormones.

"No?" Since his hand showed no inclination to leaving her bottom, she stepped away from him. Would have tripped over one of his blasted cases if he hadn't steadied her with a hand to her arm.

"Listen . . ." She had no idea what she should say. But clearly something was in order. "I don't do this."

He cocked a brow, clearly intrigued. "Ever?"

Ramsey felt her teeth grind. Obviously the easiest way to diminish his appeal was to allow him to talk. "I mean when I'm working. It would be a mistake to mix business with pleasure." Hadn't Matthews found that out just the other night in a sort of divine kismet?

His mouth was quirking. "Even if I don't mind bein' the pleasure part?"

There was a zing to the pit of her belly just thinking about it. And it hardened her resolve. "Especially then." More cautious this time, she took another step away. And then another. And when he went to follow her, a little thrill of alarm zipped through her veins.

Obviously seeing it, he stopped. "What? I was just gonna walk you to your car. It's the gentlemanly thing to do."

"I walked from it to the house without incident." She doubted the same could be said if he insisted on accompanying her back to the vehicle.

He stopped and leaned a shoulder against the wall. "Okay."

"And you can drop that easygoing affable bit," she informed him, feeling surer of herself now that there was some distance between them. "I know it's just a facade to get what you want."

"Just because it gets me what I want doesn't make it a facade," he pointed out.

Ramsey waved a hand dismissively. "Whatever. It doesn't work with me. I'm not going to sleep with you, so you'd be wise to save your energy for . . ." She gestured to the equipment. "Your work."

"Good advice." He let her walk through the door. Get as far as the porch before adding, "Thing is, though . . . you kissed me back. I want you to remember that, Ramsey. 'Cuz I'm gonna have a heckuva time forgettin' it."

Up t' no good, the man was. Yessiree.

Ezra T. peered from behind the cool mossy tombstone at the person crouched in the center of the cemetery. That's what people said 'bout him sometimes, out in them woods. Up t' no good. He liked the sound of that. Made him feel like one of them spies in that show on TV.

He squinted his eyes. The man was too far away to tell who it was. But he seemed to be alone.

Disappointment surged. So it wasn't the couple he'd seen here once, he could tell that much. He'd watched them havin' butt sex in one of them little buildings with the dead people inside. Crept up real close, so he saw the whole thing. Got himself a good ol' stiffie, too.

Ezra T. knew 'bout butt sex. You got it when you was bad or done somethin' wrong. He and some of the other boys at the home in Memphis was bad sometimes. When he was, one of the workers, Tommy Lee, would creep in his room late at night. And would put a pillow over his head while he was hurtin' him, all the time whisperin' that was what happened to bad boys. Yessiree. And he'd get worse, lots worse, if'n he ever told anyone.

He'd never told. But when he got bigger, Tommy Lee started leavin' him alone, even when Ezra T. was very bad.

And one time he'd been walkin' by and seen the man moppin' the floor real close to the big ol' steps leadin' up to their floor. Ezra T. had reached out quick as a snake and pushed Tommy Lee, hard. And stopped to watch him bounce and roll down to the bottom of the steps. Everyone said later that somethin' musta attacked Tommy Lee's heart and that's why he died. But Ezra T. knew better. 'Cuz that's what you got when you was bad. Yessiree.

He crept closer, quiet as a fox sneakin' up on a rabbit. The man wouldn't hear him, neither. Ezra T. could imitate any animal in the woods. The calls they made. The way they moved, all silent and quick. He was fast, though not as fast as the deer or the rabbits. But faster than the boys who chased him sometimes, chunkin' rocks at him and callin' names. Those boys didn't know what could happen to 'em when they was bad.

The man had set up some sort of light. That was stupid. Dead people didn't need lights. And he was takin' a bunch of stuff outta bags and turnin' them on with clicks and whirs. Ezra T. remembered that stuff. He'd seen it down at Ashton's Pond.

He'd seen that man there, too. Stryker, Duane had said his name was when Ezra T. told him 'bout it. Said the man chased haints and goblins and stuff.

That was stupid, too. Ezra T. coulda told the man dead was dead. He'd seen dead before, hadn't he? He oughta know.

Growing bored, he looked back toward the fence he'd climbed to get inside. He could go home. Or back t' the woods.

He gave a little shiver. But at home, Mary and Duane would be smokin' the smelly stuff and yellin' at him to get on outside. And the woods . . . he hunkered down behind another tombstone and wrapped his arms around his middle, rocked a little. He didn't want to hear the screams again. It was gettin' harder and harder to tell if they was in his head or comin' from deep inside the woods.

All he could be sure of was that woman they'd found—the one in the pond—had been very, very bad.

Yessiree.

Chapter 10

If he hadn't stopped that afternoon and looked at a map of the cemetery, Dev would have been reduced to stumbling around for hours, shining a light on tombstones to find the one he wanted. As it was, he'd had little problem finding the first ones he was interested in located in one of the oldest parts of the area.

He wore a camper's light on his cap to keep his hands free. He shone the light on the stone in question. Despite their violent parting, Harold Bean and his wife Wilma rested for eternity side by side, sharing one stone. Squatting down to read the faded inscription, he realized with a jolt that the couple had been younger than he when they'd died. Wilma had been—he did a quick estimation—twenty-two and her husband eight years older. There were no children listed.

He scooped up the multifield meter and the temperature sensor. Neither had picked up anything out of the ordinary remaining stationary at the gravesite, so he'd walk around a bit to see if he got any activity.

With the Beans being the first identified victims associated with the pattern of the red mist, he'd figured they were the likeliest place to start. But before the night was over, he'd take a reading at the gravesite of each victim Donnelle had mentioned.

Including his daddy's.

There were many in town who wouldn't list Lucas Rollins in the victim column, but until Dev was finished with his own investigation here, he'd reserve judgment on that himself. Regardless what anyone else thought of him, or of his profession, he was first and foremost a scientist. He was interested in proof. What constituted that just differed a bit from what satisfied the law.

He stepped surely around the overgrown graves, headed by pitted and crumbling headstones. The cemetery was located on the outskirts of town, with the newest area on the other side of the site, its markers gleaming and shiny. But he'd always preferred this section, with the huge old trees seeming to spread their branches protectively over the dead.

He'd played here as a kid, he recalled, with friends from town. They'd fought their fair share of Indians and waged more than a few intergalactic battles before invariably being shooed away by the groundskeeper.

The memory brought a smile. Eddie Hammonds had been in charge of the place then, and he'd always pretended to turn a blind eye to their presence for a couple hours before chasing them off. The new guy he'd met this afternoon had gotten all pinch-faced and disapproving when Dev had shown him the note from Mark, typed on sheriff's department letterhead, requesting he'd be allowed access to the place tonight. But there had been little he could do, other than to snappishly demand that Dev lock the old iron gates behind him when he left.

It was a pretty certain guess that kids weren't allowed in here to play these days.

Lora Kuemper hadn't been listed on the plot chart he'd checked this afternoon. But ninety years ago, people were as likely to bury their dead on their property as in town in a cemetery, especially farm dwellers. Cal Hopkins's name, though, had been found, and it was to his grave that Dev made his way now.

He'd spent his fair share of nights in cemeteries over the years, but this was the first time he hadn't had to drag along machines specifically to detect hidden sound or technological equipment. He didn't have to worry about disproving alleged hauntings this time around.

As he walked, he idly played the laser pointer of his infrared digital thermometer around the area. The temperature

sensor gave an instant reading, and more than once it reflected a relative cold spot, what some would insist indicated
a spiritual presence. Dev would have liked to investigate the
spots further, but he forced himself to stay on task. It really
wasn't important whether former residents of Buffalo Springs
were resting peacefully. What mattered was whether those
associated with the red mist still felt the need to make their
presence known.

In the end, he found no signs that Cal Hopkins's spirit
was raising paranormal hell. Lucien Tarvester hadn't been
buried here, so he made his way across the graveyard to a
slightly newer section.

To the section that housed his daddy's grave.

He stopped at the sites of Jessalyn and Sally Ann Porter
first. Paused a long time, watching the illuminated dial of the
multifield meter intently. Interestingly, there was a bit of
activity, with the needle swinging slowly back and forth before settling into a normal setting. Which made him wonder
whether that was . . .

"What do you think you're doing?" A hard cold hand
landed on his shoulder.

"Jesus!" Dev jumped like a flea off a wet dog. Logically,
he knew it wasn't Jessalyn Porter demanding he state his
business. But he was startled enough that he stumbled backward a bit, landing against a body that was all too solid.

Swinging around, recognition flickered. The person was
only slightly more welcome than had it been one of the long-
time residents of the cemetery resurrected to accost him.
"Ah . . . evenin', Reverend."

Reverend Jay Biggers glared at him, shielding his eyes
from the glare of the illuminated lamp on Dev's cap. "Stryker."
Somehow he'd always managed to make the name sound like
a curse. "What are you up to sneakin' 'round here in the
middle of the night? Decent people are sleepin' at this hour,
not out desecratin' the graves of others' loved ones."

"You'll be happy to know I only desecrate on the third
Wednesday of the month. The graves are safe for the time
bein'." Dev shifted a bit to avoid stepping on the nearest plot

as he put a little distance between them. Biggers had the dour demeanor of a revivalist preacher at an atheist convention and had always smelled, Dev thought fancifully, a bit of brimstone.

The man stared distrustfully at the instruments he still held. "Tell me you aren't despoilin' this hallowed ground by your ghost-huntin' antics. This is an abomination, Stryker. I demand that you leave immediately."

"I'll be done in another hour or so."

"Right. This. Instant!" The man's voice quivered with the same fervency he usually reserved for the pulpit. But his zeal was lost on Dev.

"The thing is, Reverend," Dev started reasonably, "You don't really have the right to be orderin' me off the premises. This isn't church property, it's county. I have permission to be here, which, I have to point out, you don't. So technically . . ." He paused a moment to watch the vein in the man's prominent forehead begin to throb. "You're the one without a right to be here now, not me."

"Right? Right?" The man's face, usually sallow, went florid. "My position grants me the right. God himself grants me the right."

"A powerful friend, but in this case, he's trumped by the sheriff. I'll leave when I'm done here and not before."

The man's large worn hands clenched at his sides. "I have to say I'm not surprised at your flagrant disregard for simple decency. Given your bloodline."

The urge to punch the man didn't stem from his words. No, that temptation arose from Dev's sudden vivid memory of summer bible camp when he'd been about ten. The churches in town joined forces when it came to saving the local youngsters' souls from the devil that would likely lodge there given too much free time. That particular summer it had been Biggers's turn to supervise the events. One day he'd delivered a particularly impassioned sermon on sin, and with his gaze fixed on Dev, had assured the unruly group that murderers burned in hell for all eternity.

It had been the last day his granddaddy had forced him to spend in bible school.

"I'm sure you've saved many a soul with that Christian attitude of yours," Dev said tightly. Because it seemed wiser, he began moving away. "Maybe if your tolerance was as well-developed as your self-righteousness, your wife wouldn't have run off with the Schwan's man a few years back." A low blow, but Dev didn't mind fighting dirty with bullies, especially so-called moral ones.

"You'll be condemned to perdition, Devlin Stryker," the man's voice thundered behind him. "You'll burn in hell for this godless activity you embrace."

"See you there. In the meantime, you're violatin' a county ordinance by bein' here at night. I'd advise you to leave before I tip off the sheriff."

———

"We've got a couple prints that can't be matched to any of the kids' shoes. Here." Powell tapped one picture from the array on the table in front of them. "And here."

Ramsey narrowed her eyes as she studied the photos. Most of the kids had been wearing sneakers, which seemed to be part of the teen uniform these days. But Robbie Joe had had boots on that night. And from the look of these photos, someone else had, too.

She snatched up the magnifying glass a second before Matthews reached for it and took a closer look. *Trampled* was the best description of the area around the shore of the pond. Print over print. But with the magnification, she could see that the sneaker prints, and the boot print attributed to Robbie Joe, were on top of the faint boot marks that had been made sometime earlier.

"Still no way to know if those footprints were made by the perp," Matthews pointed out, leaning uncomfortably close to peer over her shoulder. Ramsey shrugged him away.

"Look at the heel marks on that boot print going toward the pond and the matching one leading away. The first one's deeper, isn't it?" If the UNSUB was carrying something heavy, like a body, the print going toward the water should be deeper than the one leading away from it.

Powell held up a sheaf of papers. "The techs made measurements from the casts we took and determined that it is. Glenn's right, there's no way to be certain. But it's sure possible they could belong to the perp."

Matthews straightened. "So all we have to do is check the boots of everyone in a tri-county area or so and we'll solve this thing."

Ramsey ignored his barely checked sarcasm. This gave them something to hold in reserve, for when they did get a suspect. Something that could tie the guy to the crime or eliminate him as suspect. As such, it was valuable, even if it didn't lead them to a specific individual right now.

"We should receive the LUDs for Frost's cell phone by the end of the day." Powell dropped the papers on the table and leaned both hands on it, looking from one of them to the other. "I'll update Jeffries while I'm waitin' for the phone records. I've already contacted the resort owner at Pine Lake. He affirms Quinn Sanders and Sarah Frost had reservations for the date in question. But someone needs to go down there and show him pictures of them and all the people they claim were with them. Get a positive ID, and then see if anyone there can alibi them for the time of death. Then we'll need statements from everyone who was in the Sanders group that weekend."

"I think Ramsey'd be best for—" Matthews started.

Powell interrupted him. "You're goin'. Do you good to give the women in Buffalo Springs a rest for a few days."

That surprised a half smile from Ramsey. She'd wondered just how much of Matthews's pastime that Powell was aware of. Apparently little got by the man.

"I'd like to run down that substance in the victim's stomach," she said. "Talk to the people around here who are known to dabble with healing or holistic health. See if I can get an idea of what the plant is, who uses it, and for what purpose."

Powell nodded. "I'd also like you to check in with that nail gal who gave you Frost's name again. Find out if the victim mentioned someone botherin' her. I have a meeting with Rollins this mornin', then I'll head back to Kordoba, too, and start talkin' to customers who frequented the bar, ask them the same thing." After a moment, he added, "How far have you gotten on the ViCAP printout?"

"Not far," she said blandly. In fact she'd looked at the huge stack of responses and immediately determined to narrow the search. "I want to resend a more specific request focusing on multiple attackers, foreign substance ingested, and the method of killing the victim."

He grunted. "That should keep you busy for a while. But in the meantime, start goin' through the responses we do have."

Ramsey caught Matthews's grin from the corner of her eye. Clearly he was feeling better about his assignment. Probably looking forward to a new locale for picking up unattached women.

But Ramsey was content enough with the tasks she'd been given, with the exception of the bottomless pile of ViCAP responses. She'd had a feeling from the beginning about the unidentified substance found in Cassie Frost's stomach.

Instinct told her if she found out what it was, it might just lead them to the killer.

———

After checking on Jonesy's progress sorting out the fibers they'd collected from Frost's apartment—and getting an unkind, growled response—Ramsey headed to her car. She figured she could put in a call to Tammy Wallace, the owner of the nail salon the victim had frequented, as she was driving into town.

The woman sounded harried when she answered. Ramsey had a moment to wonder just how busy a person could be who painted fingernails all day for a living before she began.

"I sure don't recall Cassie mentionin' anyone who was

botherin' her," Tammy said in response to Ramsey's first question. "I think I told you she didn't offer much personal information. I didn't even know exactly where she lived."

"So she never mentioned her ex-fiancé, either?"

There was a pause. "Is that what it was?" There was a measure of sympathy in her voice. "I got the feeling someone had hurt her badly. That she was sort of usin' some time to recover, you know? But she never seemed scared or anythin'. Just sort of . . . sad, I guess."

Ramsey paused her vehicle at the end of the drive, waited for a total of four cars to go by on the blacktop before pulling onto it. That constituted Buffalo Springs's morning traffic jam. "Did she ever talk about her sister?"

Again there was a short silence. She knew she'd taken the woman by surprise. "No-o." The word was drawn out. "If I'd had to guess, I'd have figured she didn't have one. Come to think of it, I think she might've told me she didn't have any family. That's odd, isn't it?"

Not really, Ramsey could have told her. God knew she didn't spend time talking about her own. Cassie had probably been doing her best to forget she had a sister. She'd been betrayed in the most intimate way possible by the two people she'd probably trusted most in the world.

Life, she reflected, could be a real bitch.

"Any of the other gals in your salon ever talk to her? Do her nails maybe?"

"Oh, no." It was clear from Tammy's voice that she'd ventured into a forbidden area. "She was my client, and no one else would have worked on her nails. But she got her hair cut here once. If you give me a few minutes, I can check on who cut it, if you'd like to talk to her."

Ramsey agreed to hold as she drove slowly into Buffalo Springs. It was, if one liked small towns, a sort of quaint place. The streets were wide and lined with storefronts, many of them still filled. Some had modern facades, but others, like the museum, had been restored to the original front, dating, she supposed, back well over a century.

Flags lined the streets, left over from Flag Day, and barrels of flowers dotted the curb and spilled bouquets of color in front of shop doors. And everywhere she looked, it seemed, there were small clusters of people passing the time of day.

Three older men sat on a bench in front of a barbershop that still had an old-fashioned striped pole. Kids rode bikes down the street with little heed for the intermittent oncoming traffic. A small group of people were gathered outside the car repair station; another set were talking on the steps of the post office. Most raised a hand in a friendly wave as she drove by, in the manner of people in a small town. Either they recognized you, figured they knew you, or soon would. Most would find the scene charming. Friendly.

Of course, most hadn't lived in a place similar enough for comparison. Most hadn't experienced walking by similar bunches of people. Hearing their conversations stop, only to start again a few moments later.

Most, she thought grimly, didn't realize the weight of the stigma that came from being born poor white trash in just this sort of town. How desperate the need to escape could be.

How that desperation could fuel decisions that were regretted for years afterward.

Tammy came back on the line then and introduced the hairdresser who had trimmed Cassie Frost's hair two months ago. Ramsey asked her much the same questions she'd asked Tammy, with the same lack of results. She disconnected the call just as she spotted a parking spot close to her destination.

Minutes later, she was pushing open the door to the Buffalo Springs Family Health Clinic to find herself in a surprisingly modern lobby area. She walked up to the front desk where a woman in her late fifties was multitasking by talking on the phone while typing at the computer. Her dark hair was liberally threaded with gray and worn in two soft wings on either side of her face. Her nameplate read Jenny Callison.

The woman smiled at Ramsey and lifted a finger long enough from the keyboard to indicate for her to wait a minute.

Ramsey used the interim to gaze around at the other occupants of the waiting area. There was a couple who were easily in their nineties, a bearded man holding a blood-soaked bandage to his hand, and a younger woman with a boy who looked as though his biggest health problem was boredom. He kicked at the legs of his seat with increasing volume as he stared in disgust at the ceiling while his mother flipped through a magazine.

When the receptionist disconnected the phone, she looked up at Ramsey with a warm smile. "Thanks for waitin'. How can I help you?"

"I'd like to see Doc . . . Doctor Theisen, if I could."

"And your name?"

"Ramsey Clark." When the woman immediately turned to the schedule on her computer screen, she hastily added, "I don't have an appointment."

Her smile decidedly cooler, the receptionist turned back to her. "Are you a pharmaceutical salesperson? Because the doctors here don't . . ."

"No, nothing like that." Ramsey dug in her pocket for a card and handed it to the woman. "I have a few questions about a case I'm working on that I thought he could help with. Maybe he could call me. My number is on the card."

Jenny craned her head to send a practiced eye around the waiting room. "If you don't mind waitin', he can probably work you in. Dr. Matlock is here today, too, so it shouldn't be too long."

Ramsey nodded and went to choose a chair. She didn't much like doctor's offices as a rule, but she was feeling more tolerant today, probably because she was here only on business. For something to do, she picked up a news magazine and started flipping through it, only to discover that it was six months out of date. Replacing it on the table, she settled in, ignoring the boy across the room when he stuck his tongue out at her.

A nurse in white slacks and a patterned smock came out to the room with a clipboard and called in a loud voice, "Esther Gentry."

The older couple took several minutes to get up and totter in the nurse's direction. After a few minutes, another similarly clad woman came out and called for the man with the injured hand.

Deciding that reading old news was preferable to watching the kid's rather substantial repertoire of rude faces, Ramsey picked up the magazine again and tried to read. Her time would have been better spent, she reflected after fifteen minutes crawled by, going over ViCAP hits. But Powell didn't want anything leaving the cabin serving as their office, so that hadn't been a possibility.

A half hour later, Ramsey had had ample time to consider that doctor's offices had a totally different concept of time than did laypeople. But she was surprised when the older couple shuffled out toward the front desk and Jenny looked up to smile in her direction. "Ramsey? Dr. Theisen will see you now."

A nurse showed her back to a room at the corner of the structure that, thank God, held no patient tables. A desk was wedged into one corner, with two chairs set next to it. The rest of the space was filled with bookcases that overflowed with medical journals and physician magazines.

She walked to the wall filled with framed diplomas and studied them. Theisen was a bit older than she'd presumed at their first meeting, closer to eighty than seventy by her calculation. She wondered why the man chose to continue working when most a decade younger would have retired to a life of fishing and driving the wife crazy with his constant presence at home.

The door opened behind her, and she turned to see the man Stryker had introduced to her at the diner.

"Ramsey Clark." There was real pleasure in his expression, in his voice, as he shut the door behind him and crossed to her, his hand outstretched. When she took it, he covered their hands with his free palm. "I knew you'd get tired of Devlin and turn to me. It was just a matter of time."

"Doesn't take that long to tire of Stryker," she agreed. And attempted to shake the memory of that surprisingly bone-melting kiss they'd shared the last time she'd seen him. "But I'm actually here looking for help."

He released her, gestured her to a chair. "Since you're the picture of health, I'm guessin' it's not for yourself."

She sat, waited for him to sink into the chair next to her. "It's not, no. It's regarding a case I'm working. I'm afraid I'm not at liberty to go into much detail . . ."

He waved a hand dismissively. "Don't worry about that. I have a bit of experience workin' with the police. No reason you'd know this, but I used to be the county coroner years ago, before the state went to all ME positions."

She looked at him, intrigued. "I didn't realize that."

"Served for nearly thirty years. I think they turned to MEs fifteen years ago." His brow above the dark glasses wrinkled for a moment before he shook his head. "Doesn't matter now. It was a good move. I learned a few things over the years, but I can't compete with the knowledge medical examiners acquire in their accredited classes."

"Nor did you want to," Ramsey guessed shrewdly.

His smile had his hazel eyes crinkling. "You're right. I served as a service to the community, but it certainly wasn't a position I relished. It was a relief to go back to treatin' patients full time and not get those phone calls in the middle of night. Tell you the truth, I don't think I was ever cut out for it."

A thought occurred. "You would have served as coroner when Sally Ann Porter's body was found."

A grimace flickered across his face. "I was, yes. Must have been . . . what? Twenty-eight, twenty-nine years ago. I recall it was the same year that Lucas . . ." He stopped, cut his eyes at her, and amended, "Twenty-nine years ago, it was."

She was curiously touched that he'd stopped himself before saying something about Stryker's father. The man was obviously well liked in town. And not just by women. "I just heard the story about her death and thought to ask. I was told the body was too decomposed to easily identify."

He nodded, crossing one long leg over the other and adjusting the crease of his dress pants. "Don't mind sayin' it was 'bout the worst I'd seen. Not enough flesh remainin' to determine any foul play. Certainly no broken bones indicatin' such. As I recall, the body was finally identified usin' dental records."

Which matched, more or less, what Dev had told her. She was still interested in looking at the police report regarding the matter. But she had to admit it was more for her own curiosity. It'd be a stretch to claim it related to the case that had brought her here.

"I heard that it was determined she'd probably fallen in and drowned."

He sighed, as if the memory was a sad one. "That was the most likely explanation. It was a sorrowful time in these parts, I don't mind tellin' you. Her mama had passed the same year. Had folks talkin', and that rarely serves a useful purpose."

She heartily agreed. "What I really came to see you about was to learn what you know about local healers in the area. Those that might use herbs and roots and things for various ailments." She caught him glancing at his watch, and she added, "But if you're busy, I can come back. Or you can call me later. I know you still have patients to see."

His eyes twinkled. "Don't you worry 'bout that. Just have Connie Streich out there with her son Bobby. She's a bit overprotective and runs him in every week or so with some imaginary ailment. Do them both good to sit a bit. Not much wrong with the boy that the business end of a willow switch wouldn't take care of."

She had to agree. "I was treated to some of his . . . ah . . . charms while I was waiting."

"I'll just bet you were." He clasped both hands around his knee and leaned his head back, as if thinking. "Let's see, now. Healers. The hills used to be full of 'em when I first went in to practice. Figure I only treated a hundred or so of the town's residents in the first two years I was open. Wasn't uncommon for even the townspeople to go to one for whatever was ailin' them. Times change slowly in these parts, and opinions even more so."

"But you won them over."

He threw her a satisfied look. "I did, yes. Took years of hard work. And a fair amount of education. But I built a decent practice, despite there still being some that clung to the old ways."

"Do you remember any names?"

"Shoot." He shook his head. "Most of those people would be long gone now. Rose Thornton used to dabble in it, but she's gettin' up there in years, just like the rest of us. At any rate, she's such a cantankerous old soul, I don't know that people could much stand to have her pokin' at 'em." His eyes twinkled behind the glasses. "Regardless of what Dev says, my bedside manner isn't all that bad."

She smiled, as he meant her to. "So you can't think of anyone else who still might have an interest in the area?"

Appearing deep in thought, he sucked in his bottom lip. "There was Selma Pritchard. Lived about five miles or so out of town in the hills. Can't recall whether she's still alive or not. Haven't seen her in years, but that's neither here nor there."

Stifling a stab of disappointment, Ramsey stood. She'd gotten at least a couple names, and by checking them out, she may get more. For that matter, it wouldn't hurt to ask Letty at the sheriff's office. Ramsey would be willing to bet she was close to Doc's age and may recall more names.

"I won't keep you any longer. But I do appreciate you taking the time to talk to me."

He rose and walked her to the office door, his manner courtly. "I may be old, but I still grab the chance to spend a few minutes with a pretty woman when the opportunity arises. You tell Devlin that I've been beatin' his time. Little competition would do that boy some good."

Since it seemed churlish to point out that Stryker wasn't in line for any such competition, she merely smiled and thanked him again before walking out the door he held.

The nurse must have been waiting for her exit, because before Ramsey was out of the hallway, she'd called the Streichs in. Stepping aside for the two to walk by earned Ramsey a hard kick in her ankle from the boy. She fervently hoped he'd need a shot during this office visit. One with an extra-long needle.

Jenny sent Ramsey a bright smile as she entered the lobby

area where two or three new patients had appeared. "Was Doc able to help you?"

Impulse had her veering course for the woman's window. "He was. Maybe you can, too. I'm looking for healers or people around here who deal with holistic herbal remedies."

A faint frown of disapproval marred the woman's brow. "I always tell people it can be dangerous to take things that haven't been . . ."

"No, I don't want to be treated," Ramsey assured her. "I just need to ask some questions."

There was a shrewd look in Jenny's brown eyes. "You're full of questions, no doubt 'bout it. Well there are a few in these parts. Probably more than I know. But you could start with Cora Beth Truman. I hear her name more than most. Lives up east of the bridge on old Highway Eight. Nellie Rodemaker is another one, but I've always heard she does more midwifin' than anythin' else. And Raelynn Urdall is another. She's got a fair reputation with some folks and is willing to trade services. I understand she treated Cleve Willits's whole family for bronchitis last winter and got herself repairs to her porch this spring in payment."

Ramsey pulled a notebook out of her back pocket and jotted the names down. Beneath them, she added the two that Doc had given her.

Jenny peered at her notes and shook her head. "Oh, no, dear, Selma Pritchard passed on nearly two years ago. As for Rose . . ." She sent her an arch look and lowered her voice. "That one's as likely to run you off with a load of buckshot as answer questions. You be careful there, you hear?"

"I will," Ramsey promised. "I appreciate the help." As she walked out of the office, she reflected that she wasn't particularly relishing being met at someone's door yet again with a shotgun.

One of these days the damn thing might go off.

Chapter 11

Lightning flashed as the skies opened up, threatening to drown Dev as he leaped across the growing puddles in the motel parking lot. He took a quick glance around. Ramsey's vehicle was parked in front of cabin seven, but cabin eight was lit up. He took a chance and knocked at that door. Sure enough, Ramsey opened it, looking decidedly unenthusiastic to see him.

"Your light was on."

She made a face when he repeated her words from a few nights earlier. "That's because I'm working."

"I have pizza."

Looking suspiciously at his empty hands, she asked, "Where?"

The overhang didn't offer much protection from the deluge. Water dripped from the roof and ran down the back of his neck. "In the car."

She looked torn for a moment before saying, "Bring it next door."

By the time he'd waded through the slick gravel and water-filled potholes to his car and back, she was standing in the open doorway to cabin seven. He ducked inside, shaking his hair out of his face. She took the pizza box from his hand, which, by this time, was looking a bit soggy, leaving him with the manila envelope he'd fetched along with it.

"Where'd you find pizza around here at ten o'clock at night?"

"The Kwik Stop on Main Street is open 'til midnight."

She appeared decidedly more cheerful as she served up

a slice for each of them on the napkins provided. He made a mental note that food tended to soften her up, and reached for the helping she handed him. He set the envelope down beside him and dug in.

"So." She finished chewing and swallowed. "You were just out driving around, got the craving for pizza, decided you couldn't eat the whole thing by yourself, and being in the neighborhood, dropped in?"

He grinned in spite of himself. He was contrary enough to find that sarcasm of hers sort of charming. "Somethin' like that."

She shook her head, took another bite. "I'm not the type to be swayed by a few kisses and pizza, Stryker."

"Swayed into what?"

"Into sleeping with you."

He choked a bit on a bite of crust. The woman had a habit of blunt speaking that was rare in these parts. And there was no reason on earth he should find that so alluring.

"I don't recall askin'." He waited a beat before adding, "But now that you bring it up . . ."

Ramsey eyed him knowingly. "Your reputation precedes you. Every female between nine and ninety may have a soft spot for you around here, but I'm not looking for a romance. Frankly, I don't need the distraction."

She may not have been looking for romance, he reflected as he reached for another slice, but he'd never seen a woman more in need of it. He wondered if she'd ever allow him close enough to provide it. "Heard you went to see Doc Theisen today."

Her pizza froze midway to her mouth.

Wondering at her response, he went on. "Ran into him at the Half Moon tonight. He was talkin' big about stealin' you away and runnin' off to Borneo with you."

Relaxing again, she continued eating. "He answered a few questions for me. He's a nice man."

"None better. Present company excepted."

"Of course," she said with mock politeness.

They ate in companionable silence for a few minutes,

during which time he wished he'd brought along something to drink. Now that he wasn't standing outside in it, the rain seemed cozy, with drops tapping the window and the thunder still rumbling ominously overhead.

"So does this count as our dinner?"

He shook his head sorrowfully. "Mighta known you'd try to welsh out on our date."

"I'm not welshing. I'm asking a question."

"No, this doesn't count as dinner. Obviously anythin' eaten after nine o'clock at night is a snack. For dinner, we're goin' to have to eat before eight."

"I stand corrected."

"Actually, after our conversation the other night, you got me to wonderin'." He picked up the damp envelope he'd carried in and handed it to her. "I stopped by the police station today and got a copy of the police report from the night my daddy was arrested."

She looked at him then, her expression somber. He found himself distracted for a moment by the gold flecks in her eyes. They matched the streaks in her short brown hair, which he recalled her mentioning earlier hadn't come from a salon. "Cost me two hours of waiting and ten dollars twenty-five cents for copies, under the Freedom of Information Act." It had also earned him a few odd stares from the officers on duty, and from Zelda Pike, the office assistant who'd run the copies. He had no doubt that his request would be fodder for speculation at Zelda's regular weekly coffee group come Saturday morning.

"Nothin' in it jumped out at me, but after those questions you asked the other night . . . thought you might pick up on somethin' I wouldn't." Her silence was starting to wear on him. He wished he knew her well enough to tell what she was thinking.

"I'll take a look at it. I have to admit, it didn't even occur to me that Buffalo Springs had a police department."

"It's small. There's talk every year of dissolvin' it as a way to save the town some money. With the sheriff's office stationed here, it seems like a waste to some folks." He welcomed the switch of topic. There had been something a bit voyeuristic in reading through those pages written in dry police-speak and knowing they were talking about his daddy. It had taken far more effort than he'd care to admit to shift part of himself away in order to reach some sort of objectivity.

"Spent the rest of the afternoon at the courthouse."

"For . . ." she prompted him.

He was gentlemanly enough to leave the largest remaining piece for her, but he helped himself to two others that were relatively puny to make up for it. "Lora Kuemper wasn't buried in the cemetery." He took a large bite, caught the dangling cheese with his tongue. "Not all of the red mist victims were. Thought I'd see if I could figure where they lived. Get permission to do some readings on the properties."

"What exactly would you be looking for?" she asked, real curiosity in her voice.

"Cold spots. Signs of radioactivity. Changes in the magnetic field." He shrugged. "There are all sorts of indicators of paranormal activity."

"And you're keying in on the so-called red mist victims because one of them is most likely to be haunting Buffalo Springs after this latest murder?"

He didn't mind the skepticism in her voice. Most of the people he knew were skeptical about things that couldn't be explained scientifically. "If there is any paranormal activity connected to the red mist, I'd expect to get readin's from one of the earlier victims. Since it all seemed to start with the Beans, and Lora Kuemper, they'd be the ones I'd focus on first."

"So you struck out at the cemetery?"

He thought of Reverend Biggers then, and of his fury with Dev's presence there. "You could say that."

"Well, I can't say I'm having any better luck than you are," she said in disgust, wiping her fingers on a spare napkin. "Some of the people I talked to today made Donnelle look positively chatty by comparison."

Intrigued, he looked at her. "Maybe I can help you in that

area again." His mouth kicked up at the narrowed look she sent him. "Came in handy the last time, you have to admit."

"I doubt it," she said shortly. "These were hill people."

"Their names?"

She looked at him impatiently. "Cora Beth Truman."

Her tone made the words sound like a dare. "Played summer ball with her youngest son." He smiled at her expression. "Who else?"

"Nellie Rodemaker."

He stretched his legs, his foot bumping hers in a friendly fashion. "I believe she's by way of bein' my mama's great-aunt's oldest daughter's girl." He waited for her to make the connection.

"Wouldn't that make her your cousin?"

"Second cousin, twice removed, I think."

"Why don't you just say that?" she wondered irritably.

His stomach pleasantly full, he sent her a lazy smile. "I just did. Were there any others?"

"Raelynn Urdall."

"Roomed next to her son my first year at the University of Tennessee." He shook his head as the memory took him. "That boy could actually slam a beer while standin' on his head."

Ramsey looked unimpressed. "Why would anyone practice doing that?"

"Posterity. Are those all the names?"

"The only other one was Rose Thornton. It was just after dark when I reached her place. But she didn't answer the door when I knocked. She may have been sleeping. I know she's older. She probably goes to bed earlier than most people."

"Either that or she was ignorin' you." But it would be odd for Rose to show such restraint. If she didn't want to talk to Ramsey, she'd have faced her down with a loaded shotgun. Dev had no doubt he'd get the same treatment, regardless of the fact that they weren't strangers. Rose had never been the welcoming sort.

"Maybe she wasn't home."

"She's home. Nowhere else for her to be. Only comes to

town every month or so for provisions. Doesn't have any family to speak of. Some distant cousins someplace north, I think."

Ramsey shook her head. "No, I mean maybe she was out in the woods beyond her house. I saw some lights in her yard, like someone was in the trees with a flashlight searching for something."

The thought of ol' Rose with a flashlight filled Dev with bemusement. He could still recall when the old cabin she lived in had been outfitted with plumbing and electricity back when he was a kid. Hers was an isolated property. It was flanked by a gravel road on the north, the cemetery on the west, and woods on the other two sides.

"I doubt it," he said dubiously. "Haven't seen her for ages, so don't know how she's gettin' 'round these days. But she has to be goin' on ninety. Can't see her out messin' in the woods at night, with or without a flashlight."

"Well, someone was there." Ramsey dropped her crust in the box and wiped her fingers with surprising daintiness. "Maybe it was that Ezra T. you told me about. He runs the woods, you said."

"He's as unlikely to have a flashlight as Rose . . ." Dev straightened in his chair as a thought struck him. "Exactly what did these lights look like?"

She looked at him with an expression of exaggerated patience on her face. "Like someone was at the edge of the woods, shining a light around."

"You saw just one light? Or several?"

His question seemed to take her by surprise. "It could have been several, I guess," she said slowly. "I thought it was one light flicking all over, but I suppose there could have been three or so. It seemed to move fairly rapidly around, so that's why I figured maybe someone was looking for something."

Dancing lights. That's how Becky had described what she'd seen in the woods. Dev continued staring at her, his mind working. Her words made him think of orbs, a manifestation of paranormal energy. Exactly one of the things he'd been looking for in the cemetery. Like what he'd be watching for at the old Bean or Kuemper places he'd traced through courthouse records.

"Quit staring, Stryker. You're creeping me out."

His mouth kicked up absently, but his mind was still racing. "Before we go back to talk to those healers tomorrow—"

"I never agreed to have you accompany me."

He ignored her interruption. "—I want to stop at the courthouse and trace the ownership on Rose's place."

Ramsey frowned. "What does that have to do with . . ." Comprehension obviously hitting her, she rolled her eyes. "Seriously, Stryker. I didn't see a ghost bouncing around, I saw lights. Don't go making this into something out of a Stephen King novel."

"Hard to say what it might be," he said mildly. He didn't expect her to share his interest in the paranormal, but it was starting to sting a bit that she discounted his expertise in the area. "But it's worth checkin' out. I definitely want to go to Rose's with you." When she didn't respond, he added, "Think of it this way. I make a bigger target than you. If she starts sprayin' us with buckshot, I promise to cover that very fine ass of yours."

She narrowed her eyes at him. "I'll take care of my own ass, thanks."

"I'd be willin' to bet you've been doin' so for a very long time." He didn't need her "damn straight" response to be certain he was right. There was a guard around Ramsey that would be difficult to penetrate. And he couldn't help wondering what had caused it.

She rose and began to tidy up, and he was content to sit back and watch her, even as he realized it was a prelude to suggesting he take his leave. Funny how he was becoming able to read her. And a little alarming, too. He made a point to get along with most people. But he didn't recall ever feeling this instant connection before.

A connection she'd deny if given the chance.

After folding the box in half and shoving it in the trashcan, she crossed to the table again and reached for the left-over napkins. Dev seized the opportunity to take her out-stretched hand and gave her a tug, landing her, with some strategic maneuvering, in his lap.

And then he took a moment to enjoy the way those green gold eyes of her heated.

"Do I look like a lap sitter to you, Stryker?"

Honesty forced him to admit, "No, you purely don't. But I've found it's the absolute best position for a little wooin'."

It was a pleasure to watch the expressions flit across her face before stunned surprise won out, settling there.

"Wooing?"

"Courtin'," he elaborated, bringing the hand he still held up to his lips. Pressing a kiss to her palm, he closed her fingers over it, one by one. "It occurs to me that's an area sorely missin' in your experience. I'm lookin' to fill the void."

"You're looking," she said dangerously, "for a broken nose."

"Too late. My stepdaddy took care of that when I was fourteen." And had taught him a valuable lesson in the process. If you're stepping into the ring with someone bigger, you better have some skills to make up for lack of size. He'd learned the skills, and they'd served him well enough over the years. But damned if he'd ever feel grateful to the man for that.

Ramsey stilled. "Your stepfather did that to you?"

He brought her hand to his lips, brushed a kiss to the soft skin beneath her wrist. He'd never noticed before how small-boned she was. Had been too busy looking at those long legs and fantasizing about the curves that just might lie beneath her jacket, if he ever could talk her out of it.

"Mm-hmm." He could feel her pulse beneath his fingers, the beat a little too frantic to feign disinterest. Because it pleased him, he dipped his head to nuzzle her neck.

"I hope someone threw his ass in jail for it."

It took a moment to register her remark. "No. It was an 'accident.' I was a smart-mouthed twelve-year-old when he started teachin' me to box. Had a lot of 'accidents' durin' the lessons." He traced the cord of her throat with the tip of his tongue before gently closing his teeth over it, satisfied when she shuddered. "I was sixteen the first time he suffered an 'accident' of his own. That's when I was sent to live with my granddaddy for good." As it had been what he'd wanted, there was no regret at the memory. Unless it was the way the incident had altered his relationship with his mama forever.

There was an intriguing hollow beneath her throat, and he explored it with his lips. Traced the surrounding bone with the tip of his tongue. She was a study of contrasts, cold logic and warm skin. Prickly edges and smooth curves. Made him want to discover every one of those contrasts for himself, puzzle over them one by one until he figured out which was real. Which was acquired.

"On our date, you have to wear a dress. Somethin' clingy and feminine." Strappy sandals with mile-high heels would be nice, too, but he didn't want to push too far.

As it was, her elbow came dangerously close to lodging in his gut. "Fat chance. You're a little late to start adding conditions at this point. I didn't bring a dress anyway."

"Okay." He was nothing if not a reasonable man. "You at least have to lose the gun. And the jacket."

"Listen, Stryker . . ." Her attempts to rise were placing her hip in painful proximity to his rising interest. "I've already told you this isn't going to happen."

He drew up one of her hands, then the other, to link around his neck. "What isn't goin' to happen?" He dropped a kiss beside her mouth before strewing a string of them along her jawline. "This?" He lingered over the baby-soft skin beneath her earlobe. "Or this?" He felt her hands tighten of their own volition around his shoulders and felt a bolt of satisfaction at her reaction.

"Yes, both. Nothing, I mean." The last words were muffled as he nibbled at her full bottom lip. And felt the hitch of her breath before she released it in one long stream. "Dammit, Dev."

Because he thought he read a measure of capitulation in the words, he covered her mouth with his and eased into the kiss.

The taste of her rollicked through his system, and alarms

rang dimly in the back of his mind. He had the experience to know that a mere kiss shouldn't be enough to fire his blood and send a dizzying arc through his brain.

And he was nowhere close to smashing through her famous guard. So reeling in his hunger with some difficulty, he resolved to chip away at it a little at a time.

He lingered over her mouth, taking care to draw out the moment. Enjoyed the glide of her tongue against his. The scent of her hair swarming his senses. The feel of her curves softening against his chest as she leaned into the moment.

She slid a hand into his hair and angled her lips beneath his. Her kiss was direct, much like her personality. And he found he liked that about her. Too much. He held her closer and increased the pressure of his mouth on hers, demand edging in, fierce and sharp as a blade.

He toyed with the buttons of her shirt, undoing the top two, then stroking the skin he bared. She was warm silk beneath his fingers, and the thought of freely touching that sleek flesh everywhere heated his blood like a fever.

Lights speared the room as a car pulled up, spotlighting them like a pair of necking teenagers caught on a gravel road in the beam of a deputy's flashlight.

And that description, Dev thought, as he painfully dragged his eyes open, tearing his lips from hers, was also from personal experience. Damned if he didn't feel the same urgency that had pounded through his blood back then when he'd had more hormones than restraint. Another few minutes and he'd have a helluva time taking it easy and slow. He knew instinctively that was the only kind of speed that wouldn't have her skittering away.

As it was, her eyes were a little dazed when she opened them half-mast to stare up at him. Her lips were swollen and red. And the sight of her all flushed and well-kissed made him want to throw his head back and howl in frustration.

"If you're plannin' to send me away tonight, it'd best be soon." Though he tried for humor, his tone sounded more ragged than anything. "Turns out my patience isn't as well developed as I thought."

There was a moment, one crazy instant, when he thought she might tell him to stay. He recognized the desire in her expression. Could almost feel the tug-of-war she waged between it and logic.

In the end though, the sound of a car door slamming outside seemed to help her recover some of that fabled guard he'd done his damnedest to dismantle. She shook her head, pulling away and swinging her legs to the floor. "I need to get back to work."

Ignoring the blade of disappointment twisting through him, he stood as well. "I'll leave you to it, then." He didn't bother to point out that most folks would be turning in at this time of night. Mostly because he didn't want to think about what that entailed. It would be enough—almost—for now, that she'd wanted him back.

And that the expression on her face when she watched him walk out the door was just a bit regretful.

He prowled along the blacktops, the hunger surging and clawing inside him for release. The last girl had only whetted his appetite. He needed another. One he could take his time with, one-on-one. No sharing. Just him and a soulless whore in need of saving.

One hand dropped to his lap, stroked his cock, which was already going hard. He could keep the next one for a while. No one would ever know. He'd keep her, and he'd do all the things he'd wanted to do to the last one but couldn't.

But this time, he'd have the time to do it right. Do *her* right. A silent laugh escaped him. But first he needed to find a bitch deserving of the act.

He found her two counties over, walking along a darkened rural road. Leashing his excitement, he slowed the vehicle and buzzed the passenger window down, trying to get a better look.

Definitely female. She threw him a quick look and walked faster. Maybe a little younger than he liked, but it was hard to tell in the darkness.

"Need a ride?"

"Nope."

He continued creeping along beside her. "Kinda late for you to be out."

"Just got off work. I live nearby."

She was a lying bitch, because there was nothing nearby for at least another mile or so. And if she lied that easily, there was no telling what other sins she needed to atone for. "Okay. If you're sure."

Relief in her face now. "Thanks anyway."

He raised the window and drove off, a Good Samaritan having done his duty. Then he found a place with decent cover to pull off the road, hiding his car from any traffic that might happen by.

His cock was rock hard now, anticipation hammering inside him. But he knew enough not to let excitement get the better of caution. He turned off the dome light before getting out of the vehicle. Left the back door open to ease getting her into the car. Then ran back the way he'd come, staying well hidden in the trees lining the road.

And waited.

She was walking faster now. Spooked maybe by his earlier invitation. Woman out alone at this time of night, she was asking for it, pure and simple. Just like the last one had, with her cold disinterest and sharp tongue.

Sinners, all of them.

He could hear her footsteps coming toward him. If another car came by, he'd have to stay put. But there was no beam of headlights in either direction.

It was a sign.

He nearly creamed his pants as she walked by his hiding place, unsuspecting. The urgency was a fever in his blood when he shot out of the trees, uncaring if she heard him. Wanting her to. Needing the thrill of the chase.

She made the mistake of turning around, wasting valuable seconds before stumbling into a run. Stupid, stupid cunt.

He had her around the throat in two long strides, one hand clapped over her mouth, dragging her back into the trees. She was stronger than she looked, though, slapping and kicking wildly.

He brought up the hand holding the stun gun and gave her a jolt. Her body went limp.

A grin crossed his face as he carried her to his car. It wasn't the last jolt she'd be getting tonight. He had plans for this one.

He just hoped he could keep her alive long enough to carry out all of them.

Chapter 12

"I finished the ViCAP responses last night," Ramsey told Agent Powell as he sipped from his glass of milk. Neither that nor the banana he had in front of him looked in the least bit tempting. She wondered if she could convince Stryker to stop on the way out of town for a bag of chips and a soft drink. The breakfast of champions.

"Find anythin' useful?"

"I put aside a few that were somewhat similar." She nodded to the neat piles she'd left on the table. All had come from the second request she'd filled out. "None match exactly. Amazing how many sexual homicide victims have a foreign substance discovered in their stomach."

"One more way to exert control over the victim," Powell pointed out, taking his time peeling the banana. He didn't appear eager for the meal.

"I think we're looking at an UNSUB who includes that as part of his ritual." Even as she said the words, she cautioned herself not to let instinct blind her to other possibilities. Powell could be right. The substance could be only about exerting control over the victim. If that were the case, any of the hits she'd set aside could tie to the UNSUB. "The ViCAP responses weren't detailed enough to describe exactly what it was the victims had been forced to ingest. I intend to follow up with the detectives listed on each hit. But first I'll continue to question the healers in the area to try to get an idea what that substance might be."

Powell grunted his approval. "And I'll follow up on the victim's cell phone LUDs today. Matthews is finishin' up the resort, but it sounds like the ex-fiancé and sister of the victim have solid alibis. He'll be drivin' to Memphis for the statements sometime today."

She nodded, unsurprised. "From speaking to the woman who'd done the victim's nails, it doesn't sound like Cassie Frost was the type to try and make trouble for the couple. More like she was running away, licking her wounds."

Powell bit into the banana and chewed morosely. "That's the take I got, too, from interviewin' patrons at the bar she worked at. Barely spoke to anyone. Did her job but not interested in getting friendly with customers. Hard to see how she landed herself in such trouble."

A quick shiver slicked over her skin. From an ease born of long practice, Ramsey pushed away the snippets from the past that threatened to surface. She picked up her purse, checked inside for her keys. "Sometimes you don't have to go looking for trouble. Sometimes it finds you anyway."

———

In the end, she had to compromise with Stryker. He agreed to make a stop at the Kwik Serv for breakfast—and hold the remarks regarding her eating habits—if she agreed to accompany him to the courthouse to pursue the line of ownership on Rose Thornton's property.

And the bag of Cheetos took enough of an edge off her hunger that she didn't grumble much when he nagged her into going inside with him.

The red brick structure had been built somewhere around the turn of the last century, but the halls were well lit and the floors polished to a shine. He led the way and skirted the elevator to climb a narrow stairway to the second floor.

"Devlin. You're back."

Ramsey managed, barely, to avoid rolling her eyes. Of course the Spring County auditor would have to be a woman.

"Didn't get 'nough of you yesterday, Hannah."

He turned, took Ramsey by the elbow, and guided her up to the counter. "Have you met Ramsey Clark?"

She froze, hand still in the Cheetos bag, fervently hoping she wasn't going to be called upon to shake hands. "Good morning."

The older woman's gaze met hers, the expression in them amused. "No, I don't believe I've had the pleasure." She was tall and still willowy, with brown hair going to gray and a pair of half bifocals perched on her nose. A decorative chain attached to their ends and looped around her neck. In her flowered short-sleeved dress and nylons with close-toed pumps, she reminded Ramsey of the stern librarian in her high school.

"Hannah pretty well runs things 'round here," Dev was saying, leaning his folded arms against the counter.

"Well, let's say I keep track of things," she corrected, her polite smile including Ramsey. "Which is lucky, since you've been full of questions this week."

But Ramsey was distracted from the conversation by the woman's nameplate setting on the counter. "Hannah . . . Ashton?"

The woman's brows rose. "That's right."

Feeling foolish with both the auditor and Dev staring at her, she said, "I recognize the last name. Ashton's Pond?" Then winced when Dev stepped deliberately on her toes.

"My great-great-granddaddy settled here before the town even existed," the woman said. "Many things in these parts still bear his name. A street in town, a park, the pond. There used to be a feed store on Main Street fifty years ago run by my granddaddy. Most Ashtons have moved away, but there are still a few of us around."

Shifting her attention to Dev, the woman's manner became more businesslike. "What can I help you with today, Devlin?"

"I was wonderin' if you could get me a property trace on Rose Thornton's place. I'm lookin' clear back to the original owner."

Hannah pursed her lips and looked up at him. "I'll be glad to do just that. But I can already tell you who the original owner was. It was my great-great-granddaddy, Rufus Ashton."

"No one on this list matches a name Donnelle gave us when she was talking about the legend," Ramsey observed. She was scanning the sheet Hannah had prepared for them as she drove.

"Pay attention to the road." He snatched the paper from her hand and skimmed it himself. "Well, it was a long shot."

"A long shot for what?" she wondered. "To find ghosts? Sometimes lights are just lights, Stryker. And that's all I saw on Rose's property last night."

He adjusted his seat belt to allow him to slouch more comfortably in his seat. "Everybody's seein' lights in the woods," he mused. "The kids at Ashton's Pond, and now you."

Because the obvious seemed to have escaped him, she pointed out, "We should be more focused on who's in the woods at night and what they're up to."

"Guess you'll be wantin' to camp out there and take a look for yourself some time."

Just the thought had her palms going damp, her stomach hollowing out. There was no way in hell she was going into those woods at night. She prayed it wouldn't become necessary. Maybe she could convince Rollins to check around. Some of it was county land, after all.

"I still think it was probably that Ezra T. you told me about. Or maybe a poacher." Both would have reason to be sneaking around the woods after dark.

Of course there were plenty of activities the woods would provide cover for. Because her throat had gone dry, she reached for her soda. Terrifying activities unsuspected in the light of day. Cassie Frost had discovered that.

So had Ramsey, once upon a time.

She glanced over at Stryker and found him with his head tipped back and his eyes closed. She felt a flash of envy. She'd been the one to spend hours after he left going over

ViCAP responses until her eyeballs bled. And if the activity had kept her mind from straying in his direction too often, she'd welcomed it for that alone.

It was still a bit disconcerting to recall how easily he'd diverted her attention. One moment she'd been cleaning up and preparing to kick him out, and the next she'd been wrapped around him playing tonsil hockey with a fervor that she still found more than a little embarrassing.

There weren't many men in her acquaintance who were satisfied with some light petting, especially sitting in a motel room with a perfectly good bed nearby. She'd been close enough to him to recognize his arousal. That had made it all the more surprising when he'd left without an argument.

Surprising . . . and maybe a bit disappointing, too. Enough so that she couldn't quite push away the thought that perhaps there'd be no harm if she didn't send him away the next time. She wasn't interested in anything more than the moment, and she hadn't met a man yet who'd quibble with a woman uninterested in strings.

Purposefully, she let the tires on his side leave the road, jolting him upright again. Smirking, she said innocently, "Here's the turnoff for Cora Beth's place."

"Like I said once before, pure mean," he murmured. His gaze was fixed on the scene outside the window. "Did you have a chance to look at the police report I left?"

His nonchalant tone didn't fool her. "I did." She slowed the vehicle to maneuver around the ruts the spring rains had carved in the secluded drive. Keeping her eyes on the bumpy path ahead meant she didn't have to risk looking at him. "Plenty of eyewitnesses placing Lucas in the vicinity of Jessalyn's place the first stop he made. Second time around, the next door neighbor, Alvin Crowell, swore he'd seen your father standing in the window of Jessalyn's bedroom." Never mind what the man had been doing looking into the woman's bedroom, Ramsey thought, as she wrestled the car over a teeth-jarring bump. If that particular question had been asked of him, the answer hadn't been included in the official report.

"So there's no question of his guilt."

His words were uttered just a little too easily for her to be unaware of the emotion bubbling just below the surface. "I didn't say that." Ramsey pulled to a stop before a simple framed house painted a cheerful yellow with white shutters. "There were lots of questions left unanswered. But the one that still bugs me the most is, where did your dad spend the hours between his first visit to Jessalyn's and the second? Seems like someone intent on getting that drunk, there'd be plenty of witnesses to that, as well."

She saw a curtain twitch at the front window of the house, knew someone inside was wondering at their presence there. "With his blood alcohol level, he had to have spent the interim doing little more than drinking. But your mother's statement indicated he hadn't done it at home. Hadn't even gone there in the interim. So where was he?"

He looked at her then, and the bleak expression in his eyes had her stomach twisting. "I don't know. But if that's the only question you've got after lookin' at the police report, maybe I should quit pokin' 'round."

"That's not the most outstanding question, Stryker." Shoving open the car door, she unfolded herself and sincerely hoped Cora Beth Truman was more forthcoming today than she had been during her previous visit.

Starting up to the house, she continued, "The most important thing I'm still wondering about is why there's no mention of it in the police report. Did they investigate it at all? If so, why wasn't it included? If not, why not?" And she wasn't happy with the random questions rattling around in her mind, either. Lucas Rollins had nothing to do with the investigation at hand. She couldn't afford yet another diversion while she was searching for Cassie Frost's killer.

She slid a glance toward the man at her side as they made their way up to the house. *Distraction* was a pretty accurate summary of his effect on her and her focus on this case.

She was fervently hoping that this time around he'd prove to be a helpful one.

———

There was the prerequisite small talk required first, of course. Ramsey had expected the woman's open delight at seeing Stryker. Had even accepted the green tea pressed on her and pretended to drink it, all the while longing for the Diet Coke she'd left in the car. But the familiar impatience had begun to burn when talk turned to Cora Beth's son while she caught Dev up on the happenings in his life for the last twenty-odd years.

The feeling faded momentarily when Cora Beth pulled out some faded photographs of two young boys sporting cocked bats and baseball caps pulled low over their eyes. She knew without asking that the blond one was Dev.

The famed grin was in appearance, of course. Along with an expression of enjoyment that would have been difficult to miss. The hot and cold running charm had been apparent even then. Giving him decades to hone that lethal charisma.

Finally, Cora Beth's attention turned to her. And Ramsey was certain she wasn't imagining the note of reproof in her mild words.

"You shoulda told me yesterday you were a friend of Devlin's, Ms. Clark. I'm afraid I'm a little wary of strangers, livin' up here the way I do. 'Specially since my husband passed five years back."

"I certainly understand your caution, Mrs. Truman." Whatever her feelings about having to use Stryker to get people to talk to her, Ramsey was eager to get some needed information now. "A woman livin' alone needs to be extra careful. But I've heard so much about your abilities as a healer, I've been mighty anxious to talk to you 'bout that." She ignored the startled glance Dev shot her. As she'd told him once before, she was fluent in y'all. And willing to use any tool at her disposal to loosen the woman's tongue.

Cora Beth settled her slight frame back against the overstuffed couch. Her blond head contrasted starkly with the brown and orange flowery fabric covering it. "So you're interested in healin'?"

"I'm interested in the various plants and herbs used in the process."

Truman studied her with cornflower blue eyes. "Since you don't strike me as a holistic believer, I assume this has somethin' to do with the death of that poor girl they found a couple weeks ago." She held up a hand to stem any response Ramsey might have made. "I know you can't talk about it. Don't want to hear it, truth be told. I shudder just thinkin' of somethin' like that happenin' so close to here."

"I'm not lookin' for any plant derivatives that might act as intoxicants." Ramsey knew she had to choose her words carefully. The presence of the plant root in the victim's stomach hadn't been released to the press, and if she had anything to say about it, wouldn't be. By holding the detail back, they'd have a fact only the killer would know, which would be important when they got a suspect in custody. "What I mostly need to know 'bout is things 'round here that would be easily accessed for medicinal purposes."

Cora Beth tipped some more tea in Dev's cup, which was miraculously empty. Ramsey made a mental note to ask him later if he really liked the brew. She'd start to worry about him if he did. She'd rate the taste just slightly above that of swamp water.

"I have my own medicinal herb garden," the woman started, tucking both ankles neatly to the side in a gesture that managed to look feminine and uncomfortable at once. "Most healers do. Mix my own healin' agents for various ailments according to whatever complaint my patient has."

"Such as?"

The woman wrinkled up her brow. "Oh, for instance the leaves of aloe vera can be used as a gel for burns, cuts, and abrasions. Ginger can be helpful for anythin' from migraines to calmin' nausea or fussy bowels. Valerian root can assist with insomnia or anxiety. Dandelion leaves can be used as a diuretic, and its root can stimulate liver function. Even Queen

Anne's Lace, a wildflower, has many uses." Her expression turned mischievous. "Its seeds can treat a hangover."

"Good to know," Dev murmured.

But Ramsey had picked up on one of the woman's earlier examples. "What other roots have healin' powers?"

"Oh, there's kava. The word refers to the plant and to a beverage made from its roots. It's not indigenous to our country, although I know healers who grow it. Chewin' on the root or drinkin' the beverage made from it has strong intoxicant effects. It acts as a tranquilizer. The roots of Queen Anne's Lace contain vitamin C and carotene. The bark from tree roots are often used in healin', but I tend to steer clear from harvestin' them, since it's difficult to do so without injuring the healthy tree in the process."

Cora Beth rose suddenly. "I think I have somethin' that might help you." She hurried to the back of the house, where Ramsey could see rows of planters on top of tables beneath the large window.

She came back holding a pamphlet in her hand, which she thrust toward Ramsey. "This brochure is put out by Natural Herbal Healing and lists several plant roots used. Many of them are also used by hoodoos."

Ramsey and Dev shared a glance. "Hoodoos?"

Cora Beth's smile showed a dimple that made her face look more youthful. "Sorry. Hoodoos are root doctors who use plants, especially roots, for their magical, healin', and spiritual powers. Some of them prepare sachets from herbs for protection, or good luck. Others use plants with mind-alterin' effects for their ceremonies, as well."

"Would you consider sellin' any of your plants outright?" Ramsey asked. Maybe if she could take some samples back to Jonesy, he could use the roots for comparisons to the substance taken from Cassie Frost's body.

But Cora Beth's negative response was emphatic, and even Dev's wheedling couldn't sway her.

"I have to save my plants for people who need 'em," she said firmly. "I just can't grow replacements fast enough to be sure I have everythin' I use for my patients."

Armed with the brochure the woman had given her, Ramsey stood. "Do you know any hoodoos in the area?" she said, as the woman was leading them to the door.

After a long hesitation, she responded, "I don't. Katie Patterson used to mix potions and such for anyone silly enough to approach her, but she ran off years ago with Eleanor Perkins's husband. Neither of them have been back since."

Her gaze shifted back to Dev then, and warmed. "You stop back anytime, now, hear?"

He took her hand in his, holding it a moment. "Tell Sam I said hey, will you?"

"You can be sure I will."

Ramsey's mind was racing as the two of them descended the steps and headed toward the car. Maybe the root Cassie Frost had ingested wasn't meant to be herbal or medicinal in nature at all. Maybe it was symbolic in some way. She'd worked cases before that skirted the occult. Had put away a woman claiming to be a witch, Satan's own handmaiden. Since she'd managed to kill two men before she was stopped, Ramsey tended to agree with the description, figuratively at least.

Because Dev knew his way around these parts, Ramsey reluctantly allowed him to drive while she took his place in the passenger's seat.

"I don't pretend to know what's behind your interest in plant roots, but Cora Beth's mention of hoodoos did bring about a thought. You might consider people dabblin' with the occult. Various plants and herbs are used for protection circles, for example. Others to ward off evil."

"So you think I should be looking for Satan worshippers frolicking around at midnight, burning devil circles in the ground while swilling a concoction they've made from plants?"

Ignoring her flippancy, he continued, "That, or by association, a religious organization."

She stared at him blankly. "Religion? The last time I checked, it wasn't associated with the occult, except in the most hardened zealot's ranting."

Managing a turn in the drive, he headed toward the road,

using far less care than she had to avoid the ruts and potholes. "Witchcraft, for want of a better word, and religion aren't that far apart, at least in terms of origin and followers. You'll find some of the same symbols, some of the same characters, integral to each. Different interpretations, of course, but consider the practice of voodoo, for an example. Elements from Catholicism are intricately interwoven into the practice, probably because missionaries were converting the natives and elements of the faith intermixed with the native beliefs."

He'd given her something to consider. The substance found in Cassie Frost's stomach had to have been ingested after her capture. Which likely meant it had been forced on her by her attacker. Even if Powell was right, and it was the act of power rather than the substance itself that was important to the UNSUB's ritual, Ramsey had to believe there was a reason for the attacker to choose that particular material. Either it produced a desired effect—intoxication, sedation, elevated libido—or it symbolized something to the offender.

And if she could figure out exactly what it symbolized, she would have drastically narrowed the search for the perp.

The hour spent at Nellie Rodemaker's was, in Ramsey's estimation, a total waste of time. The apple-cheeked woman welcomed Dev with an exuberant hug and a good-natured scolding for not stopping in sooner. From the occasional question Ramsey could manage in between all the gossip about relatives between her and Dev, it appeared that Jenny Callison had been right. Nellie was more midwife than herbalist, although she appeared to have a handy collection of natural remedies for everything from morning sickness to contractions.

It took some less than polite insistence, but she eventually managed to extract Dev from the woman's home, and they headed in the opposite direction to Raelynn Urdall's house.

Slanting him a glance as he drove, Ramsey looked for signs of upset in his expression but didn't find it. "She wasn't exactly complimentary about your mother."

He gave a nod, his handsome face pensive. "Blames her for goin' off and remarryin' so quick, sounded like. I've never gotten that impression from any of my other relatives. Most folks would understand a young widow wantin' to put the past behind her, 'specially with all that had happened with my daddy." Checking his mirrors, he passed a battered pickup hauling a teetering load of brush. "'Course I seem to recall my granddaddy sayin' once that Nellie was sweet on my daddy at one time, so I'll just consider the source."

His words brought back some of the questions she still had regarding that old police report he'd shown her. Resigned to the fact that she wasn't going to be able to put them out of her mind, she asked, "Is the man who served as chief of police back then . . ." Searching her memory, she plucked out the name. "John Kenner . . . still around?"

"As far as I know, he still lives over on Hazlewood. He must be . . . I'd guess mid-seventies by now. He and Doc Theisen are fiends at checkers. Used to play every Thursday night."

She mulled over the information as Dev pulled into a recently regraveled drive and nosed the car up the wind of it to the house perched above. There was absolutely no reason to believe a link existed between Jessalyn Porter's death and that of Cassie Frost. No reason to think a nearly thirty-year-old closed homicide case had any connection to the one she was hired to investigate.

So she didn't even want to contemplate Adam Raiker's reaction if he discovered she was considering poking around in that old case for reasons that weren't, by any stretch of the imagination, professional.

She was working sixteen-hour-days, she rationalized, getting out of the car when Dev pulled to a stop before a small clapboard house desperately in need of some tending. If she wanted to take an extra hour and get a few questions answered, it was hardly detracting from her devotion to this investigation. It wasn't as if she slept a full night.

The new front porch on the house managed to make the rest of the structure look seedier. There was a woman bent over in a garden at its side who'd risen at their arrival, slipping off gardening gloves and raising a hand to shield her gaze as she studied the visitors.

"Hey there, Mrs. Urdall. It's Devlin Stryker." His gait as lazy as a nap in a hammock, Dev ambled over to the woman, an easy smile on his face. "Maybe you don't remember me, but I roomed next to Tad our first year at the university."

"I recall." With no answering smile on her face, the woman jerked her head to Ramsey. "'Member you, too. Told you yesterday I had nothin' to say to you. That hasn't changed."

There was more here, much more, than a wariness with strangers. The woman's dislike was almost palpable. Sifting through the possibilities, Ramsey quickly settled on one. For whatever reason, Raelynn Urdall didn't like cops.

"Haven't seen Tad for . . . shoot." Dev scratched his jaw, eyes narrowed against the sunlight. "Two years now, I guess."

Raelynn's face, tanned and creased from the sun, registered surprise. "You saw Tad two years ago?"

"I look him up regular when I'm in New York seein' my editor. Never did answer my calls last spring when I was there. I was sorry to miss him."

The wave of grief that washed over the woman's face was as immediate as it was tragic. "You must not have heard the news. I'm surprised, since the town buzzed about it for months. He's in prison." The bitterness was directed at Ramsey. "Cops in New York set him up. Wanted him to inform on some of his friends, and when he refused, one of them planted drugs on him. Enough to get him sent away for intent to deliver."

Ramsey was silent while Stryker commiserated with the woman. Urdall's accounting of the events was possible. There were crooked cops in every department. But it was even more probable that Tad had been a dealer who'd refused to give up the bigger fish in the chain and had taken a fall because of it.

Stryker had his arm around the woman's shoulders now, his head bent closer to hers, as Raelynn dabbed at her eyes.

"I am purely sorry to hear 'bout Tad's problems, ma'am. You tell him hey for me the next time you talk to him. It's got to be a hard thing for you. How've you been holdin' up?"

Ramsey caught a note of genuine concern in his voice, and she slanted a glance at him. It had been easier to resist that charm when she could dismiss him as no more than a small town Romeo used to conquering women with his slow-as-molasses drawl and affable smile.

But there was more. *He* was more. She shifted uneasily. And the unexpected depths of him shook her long-held defenses. Made her question hard-learned lessons. And that was alarming enough to make him a very dangerous man.

Certainly Urdall was responding to him. But then Ramsey was beginning to believe that anyone with two X chromosomes would. With the exception of Hannah Ashton this morning, he seemed capable of turning anything female into fluttering eyelashes and cooing responses in a matter of seconds. Even Ashton had thawed in his presence, which she'd be willing to bet represented a notable response for the woman.

"Sounds like Tad didn't get justice," Dev was saying as he walked the woman slowly up to the porch, his arm still around her shoulders. "I can't tell you how sorry I am 'bout that. But the fact is, too many people don't these days. Take that young lady they found dead a coupla weeks ago. They still don't know who did it or why."

Tears dried now, Raelynn fixed Ramsey with a stare. But it wasn't quite as hard as it had been earlier. "Thought that was your job."

Giving a slow nod, Ramsey said, "It is. But people 'round here aren't always willin' to speak to an outsider, especially one workin' with the law. Gettin' answers can be slow." It was easier than she'd like to don the drawl at will. She'd much rather believe she'd lost it years ago. Certainly she'd worked at it.

Dev took a perch on the top step of the porch, and Rae-lynn sank down next to him. "We all have our reasons, I guess. But I s'pose it wouldn't hurt to give you the information you was askin' for yesterday. Don't know what it has to do with that poor girl's murder. You wanted to know about plants used in healin', you said."

"That's right." Sensing capitulation, Ramsey pulled a notebook out of her jacket pocket, jotting notes as the woman rattled off more examples than even Cora Beth had given them.

"'Course herbs are used for more reasons than healin,'" the woman said as she wound down.

Interest sharpening, Ramsey flicked her a glance. "Such as?"

"Flowers each have an associated meanin'. Like the magnolia stands for nobility, and the daffodil for unrequited love." Raelynn shrugged, as if the matter were inconsequential. "I don't hold with all that, you understand, but there are some who do."

"What if I wanted to buy a sample of everything you grow?" Ramsey asked, forgetting her drawl in her rising excitement. "What would that cost me?"

The woman hesitated, glancing at Dev and back. "I don't know . . ."

To help the woman make up her mind, Ramsey named a price that would have her checking account bleeding. Urdall's eyes widened.

"Just one of each, you said?"

"I'll want the entire plant. Root, stem, leaf." Were there other parts? She thought that should cover it. "If you could put each in a clear plastic bag and label it, that would be a help."

"I can have them ready by tomorrow mornin'. Will that be soon enough?" Urdall's sudden metamorphosis into businesswoman was hardly surprising, given the look of her property. Ramsey imagined the amount she'd promised was more than the woman saw in a month.

Taking a card out of her pocket, she scribbled the name of the motel she was staying at, and the cabin number. "When you deliver them, you'll get paid in full."

"You'll be doin' Ms. Clark a huge favor with your generosity," Dev put in.

Recognizing the glint in his eye, she mentally sighed. Too often she forgot the niceties considered so important in social discourse. Manufacturing a smile, she stuck out her hand. "You certainly are. I appreciate all your help. And I'm sincerely sorry to hear about your son."

Visibly cloaking herself with dignity, the woman inclined her head. "Life ain't always fair, and that's a fact."

They exchanged a look, a thread of understanding passing between them. Life sure as hell wasn't fair, Ramsey agreed silently. But she'd spent the last several years of her life trying to even that score.

Some days it even felt like enough.

Chapter 13

"If it's all the same to you, I'd like to put off stoppin' to see Rose Thornton until later on this evenin'."

Ramsey shot Dev a look. "We can't wait until too late. She was probably in bed by the time I stopped in last night, and it was barely nine thirty." At least she'd figured the woman had turned in. The more she considered her age, the more Ramsey was convinced the woman hadn't been the one tromping around the woods with a flashlight.

Which meant someone else had been.

"Agreed. How 'bout I pick you up at seven or so? Better yet, we'll make it six. You can pay me that dinner you owe me, then we can head out to the Thornton place."

The idea wasn't as unwelcome as it should have been. She blamed that on the spotty breakfast she'd had. It was dinner that beckoned, not more of Stryker's companionship.

She had the thought, tried to believe it.

"All right." She could use the time this afternoon to return to the motel and follow up on those ViCAP hits. And if there was any time left, she'd drop in to nag Jonesy and do a little research on plant roots and their effects. "What will you be doing this afternoon?"

He leaned forward to fiddle with the radio. A moment later, some sixties rock filled the interior of the vehicle. "Haven't been to see my granddaddy for a coupla days. Just might drop in to have lunch with him." His mouth quirked. "Don't want to cramp his style, though. He's got a full stable of interested ladies that seem to be hangin' 'round every time I'm there."

"Somehow that doesn't surprise me," she said drily. The

apple certainly hadn't fallen far from their particular family tree.

She went silent for a time, watching blindly as the scenery whipped by the window, emulating the thoughts crashing and colliding in her mind. Herbs for medicine, healing, and for magic spells. And then there were flowers, trees, and shrubs related to the same. A dull throb began in her temples. She needed a list. A clearly labeled diagram that cross-referenced plants indigenous to the region.

But wait. She raised a hand to rub at the ache. Even if a plant wasn't natural in this setting, it could be grown inside, couldn't it? People had greenhouses these days. She'd once busted a guy outside Memphis who had turned his entire basement into a pot garden. Given the right incentive, a person could grow any damn thing they wanted.

So she needed more information from Jonesy. And possibly from the medical examiner, regarding the rootlike substance in the victim's stomach. If one could estimate how much mass the root had, she might be able to eliminate some of those Urdall would be delivering.

Because it was damn certain that she couldn't expect the scientist to compare a sample found in the stomach contents with every known plant root in the area.

"Thinkin' 'bout what you're gonna wear on our date tonight?"

"What?" Her head swiveled to face him. "Why would I do that?"

"Because you want to dazzle my eye and befuddle my senses?"

Settling back into her seat, she said with a smirk, "Something tells me you're easily dazzled, and befuddlement is too effortlessly accomplished to be considered much of a feat."

"I've been befuddled since meetin' you, and that's a fact." He made the turn that would lead them into town again. "Spent more time than I'd like to admit wonderin' all sorts of stuff 'bout you."

Her guard skated up and clanged shut with a decided slam. "Like what?"

"Oh, li'l things. Important things." He raised a hand to the couple walking along the side of the road. "Like whether you prefer *The Munsters* or *The Addams Family*. Personally I find *The Munsters* more entertainin', but *The Addams Family* had Thing, which was sorta creepy."

Ramsey could feel the tension easing out of her body, bit by bit. "Yeah, those old Nick at Nite reruns are pretty vital, all right."

The Boss came on the radio then, singing the merits of being born in the USA. "There's other things I think 'bout. What kind of music you like. How you manage to turn that drawl on and off at will. How many of those suits you own. And what sort of lingerie you just may wear under them."

"Springsteen's always a good . . ." His last statement registered belatedly, and she sent a jab to his shoulder, satisfied when he flinched. "At the rate you're going, you'll never find out."

"Never say never, Ms. Clark." There was a look of pure masculine amusement on his face. "Admit it. A few days ago you'd never have considered you'd be ridin' down the road with me and contemplatin' dinner together."

Because his words were true enough, she remained silent. And tried not to worry about the way they resonated. Maybe she had more in common with every other woman in Buffalo Springs than she wanted to admit. The thought made her squirm. But there was no denying he elicited a response from her, one she was usually careful to deny.

One she was becoming less and less certain she *wanted* to deny.

Since she left Cripolo—although escaped seemed a more accurate word—she'd had one brief disastrous marriage before she figured out the obvious: she wasn't made for hearts and flowers. Wouldn't know what to do with that kind of relationship if it appeared. She had, however, perfected the no-strings, no-backward-glance hookup with none of the sticky entanglements other women seemed to relish.

She'd never met a man yet who wasn't happy with just that sort of encounter. Shoving aside the thread of doubt that

threatened, she settled more comfortably in her seat. If she
did decide to try the man on for size, there was no reason to
believe that Devlin Stryker would be any different.

When Ramsey returned to the cabin they used as an
office, Powell was as animated as she'd ever seen him. For a
moment, she suspected the man had broken down and gone
off his bland diet. Maybe eaten some BBQ ribs or fried
chicken.

But apparently a break in the case had a similar effect on
him.

"Quinn Sanders," the agent informed her with a hard glint
in his eyes, "is a lyin'-ass dog."

"What've you got?" she asked as she shut the door behind
her and walked to the table where he was working. Her gaze
dropped to the pages strewn across its surface. "Frost's LUDs?"

"Damn straight." Powell stabbed a finger at the circled
numbers on the top sheet before flipping through the pages to
show several others similarly marked. "Son of a bitch didn't
call her from his cell phone. Probably figured the sister would
be checkin' that. He cheated with her on the first one, right?
Bastard can't be trusted. But this number corresponds to that
of the health club he owns, a 24 Hour Fitness. Thirty-seven
calls to the vic's cell phone since she left town. At least," he
amended, "since the date her sister says she left."

Intrigued, Ramsey crowded in next to him, scanning the
pages in question. "Looks like she called him a few times,
too." Pulse quickening, she quickly counted up the number of
calls to the club from the victim's cell phone. An even dozen.

"Who else works there? Any chance she might have been
talking to a friend there, another worker?"

"Not unless she was a friend with the custodian or book-
keeper." Powell linked his fingers, cracked his knuckles.
"The custodian only works nights and the bookkeeper comes
in once a week, so neither could account for all those calls.
It's the type of place that can be accessed around the clock.
Every client has a fob to unlock the door. According to Mat-

thews, the phone is in the office, which is locked by a separate key whenever Sanders isn't there. Not much doubt that he made them."

The question, Ramsey mused, was *why* he'd made them. "Do we have Frost's financials yet?"

As an answer, Powell reached for a separate file folder and handed it to her. Flipping it open, she quickly skimmed over the bank statements. "Doesn't look like blackmail," she murmured. Up until the time the woman left her home, there had been twice monthly deposits from her bank job. Since then, the deposits had been spotty and less than half what she'd made earlier. Ramsey checked the savings records. It appeared as though Frost had been hitting her savings regularly to supplement her income.

Not for the first time, a stab of sympathy pierced her. She understood the need to run from the past. But from the looks of the phone records, Frost's past hadn't been willing to let go of her.

"Be nice to get a look at Sanders's LUDs and financials," she muttered.

Powell was matter-of-fact. "Not even close to that yet. But I told Matthews to stay put in Memphis. I want you to join him there tomorrow for another run at Sanders. A little harder this time." They exchanged a glance. "Man flat out lied about havin' any contact with the victim since she left."

"So he's either stupid, or thinks we are."

"He's got somethin' to hide. I want to know what it is. Either he's a slime-suckin' slug trying to work it with two women, or he's got reason to stay in contact. Find out which."

"How hard do you want me to push?"

"As hard as it takes."

Ramsey nodded, satisfied. "I'll take off early tomorrow. I'm expecting a delivery in the morning." Briefly she filled the man in on the events of the day and her suppositions.

Powell looked unexcited. "Tryin' to match the roots seems like a needle in a haystack at this point."

"Maybe," she admitted. "But I still think it's an integral part of the ritual. No reason Jonesy can't be checking it out while I'm running down detectives from the ViCAP hits on similar homicides."

The other agent lifted a shoulder as he began to shuffle the phone records into a file folder. "I'm due to meet Rollins at the sheriff's office to bring him up to date. When you get back from Memphis, you should probably talk to him more in-depth about the lead you're followin' on the root. Always need to be careful about extendin' professional courtesies when we're called to a case. Even more important when dealin' with a small-town department."

She nodded, although she didn't need the reminder. Hopefully she'd have more to tell the sheriff by the time they discussed it. Maybe she'd get lucky on one of the calls she was about to make to—she mentally calculated—six detectives across the country who had worked a homicide with similar elements to this one.

Riffling through the contents on the table, Ramsey came up with the ViCAP responses. She said good-bye absently as Powell left, her mind already on the upcoming phone calls. Given the time change, she'd start with the hit from the east coast first. She knew she'd be lucky to catch any of the cops at their desks.

Stealing a quick look at her watch, she dialed the first number. There'd probably be plenty of time before dinner to harass Jonesy, as well. Depending on how these calls went, that might prove to be the highlight of the afternoon.

———

"Vickers, you damn thief! Keep your arthritic fingers out of my candy drawer!"

Dev halted outside Benjamin Gorder's assisted living apartment and turned to look at the man his granddaddy was shouting at. The accused, a stooped bald man who appeared to be about ninety, cupped a hand to his ear quizzically as he hurried away down the drive.

Although "hurried" might not be an appropriate description for a man using a walker and tottering along at a speed a snail wouldn't find challenging.

Dev waited for his granddad's attention to settle on him before observing blandly, "Looks like quite a desperado. Has he made FBI's most wanted list yet?"

Benjamin glowered at him. "Don't be a smart-ass, Devlin. Vickers just looks harmless. Comes and goes in everyone's unit any time we step out for a moment. Can't keep lemon drops in the place 'cause of him. I swear, he's worse than an army of ants."

"Some might think that reason enough to lock their doors." Dev handed his granddaddy a bag containing several bags of the man's favorite candies. Including lemon drops.

Peeking inside, the man's expression lightened. "You're right. I know you're right. But he must sit with a pair of binoculars and time it the moment I slip out to water flowers or talk to the neighbor. Don't let that walker fool you. He's as quick as a snake when he wants to be."

Casting another look at the "thief" who had barely made it out of the drive in the intervening time, Dev said doubtfully, "If you say so." He followed his granddaddy into the small apartment and sat down on the couch. And studied the man who'd mostly raised him, trying not to be obvious about it.

He looked fit if a little tired, Dev decided with a flicker of relief. The stroke had left one side of his face partially paralyzed, but other than that and the shock of hair that had long-since gone white, he looked very much the way he had all Dev's life. Still close to six feet, with a rangy build that maybe was looking just a bit bonier. He made a note to talk to the facility's head cook to ensure the man was eating more than his favorite candy.

"Where you been?" Benjamin sat down in his recliner facing Dev. "Haven't seen you for a coupla days."

"Here and there. Takin' care of some business."

The older man leveled a pointed look at him. "Business that included gettin' copies of old police reports, I hear."

"The town's grapevine seems to be in workin' order."

Benjamin snorted. "Never known it to fail yet. What's goin' on with you, Dev? Figured if you had questions, you'd come to me with them."

"I don't know what questions I have yet," he admitted. Or even if there were questions remaining unanswered. "Just tryin' to get a picture of events from that night."

The explanation didn't seem to lessen the man's worry. "No reason why you wouldn't wonder. And I've never been one to hide the facts from you. Did you call your mama with any of these questions that aren't questions?"

"Yes." And the memory of that particular conversation still rankled. "She didn't want to talk 'bout it."

Why, Devlin? Celia Ann Stryker's voice had taken on that disapproving note that sounded in it too often when they spoke. *What's the point of dredgin' all that ugliness up now? That's the problem with you, you've never learned to just get along, to just let things be.*

The statement had burned. Seemed like he'd been *gettin' along* for most of his life. But he'd let the subject drop. He'd long-since accepted his mama's methods of coping. They all made their own choices in life. He was just grateful he no longer had to live with hers.

Benjamin sighed. "Well, I'm not surprised. Celia Ann went to pieces over the whole thing. She never was one to deal well with any sort of unpleasantness." He stared at his grandson, his expression torn. "Gettin' on with her life the way she did doesn't make her a bad person, son. Just maybe a weak one. Fact is, most folks thought she coulda done more to stand by Lucas. Whatever happened that night, your daddy wasn't in his right mind. You get your nature from him. Took a lot to rile him, just like it does you."

"So what could Jessalyn Porter have said or done to rile him enough to wrap his fingers around her throat and choke the life out of her?"

Benjamin's wince made him regret his blunt words. "When a body gets filled with more liquor than sense, there's no end of heartbreak that can happen. Your daddy wasn't a big drinker—your mama never woulda allowed it—but he was known to tip a few with his buddies time to time. He'd been out with one of them before goin' on over to Jessalyn's house."

After weighing the decision for a few moments, Dev asked the question uppermost on his mind since showing the report to Ramsey. "The police report said he'd had two beers prior to visitin' Jessalyn that first time. But his blood alcohol was through the roof the mornin' they'd found him next to her body. Where was he drinkin' in the meantime?"

His granddaddy opened his mouth. Closed it again. Finally he scratched his ear. "Well, I don't rightly recollect. Fella he'd been drinkin' with earlier spent the rest of the evenin' with his family, I recall that. All I can be certain of was your daddy didn't go on home. Celia Ann didn't see him at all that night. I remember her bringin' you on over and spendin' the night. She never did like to stay in an empty house. Near out of her head with worry by then, she was."

"And you never heard any talk 'bout where he might've been in the meantime? Who he might've been drinkin' with?"

Benjamin looked suddenly fatigued, as if the conversation had aged him. "Son, there's always talk, you know that. There were some who claimed he never left Jessalyn's a'tall, that there was somethin' romantic goin' on between them. Not to speak ill of the dead, but knowin' Jessalyn, that's hardly likely. She'd have been a good twenty years older than your daddy at the time. I do know no one ever stepped forward to say he'd been with Lucas drinkin' that night. But that don't mean the fella isn't out there. Just that he didn't want to get dragged into the mess. People bein' what they are, that's hardly surprisin'."

"No. Not surprisin' at all." The police had had a dead body and a murder weapon with prints matching the drunken man lying next to it. What had it mattered that no one had seen the murder suspect drinkin' himself into a stupor? Some answers had gone to the grave with Jessalyn Porter and Lucas Rollins.

Dev was beginning to believe this might just be one of them.

Because he could see the concern etched into his granddaddy's face, he deliberately lightened his voice. "So what's a fella gotta do to be offered some of that candy stash you're hoarding?"

Benjamin stared at him a moment longer, his gaze shrewd. He'd recognize the diversion for what it was. But the man had always been a master at knowing when to push and when to let things go. "Fella just has to ask. That's what that damn Vickers can't get through his head." He rummaged through the sack he still held, came up with the package of red licorice that had always been Dev's favorite. "Of course, if the fella also was in the mood to talk 'bout the woman he's been seen with 'round town, well, I reckon he might get first dibs on the licorice."

"I've never been able to resist a bribe." Dev stretched his legs out and crossed them at the ankle. He held his hands out to catch the strands his granddaddy tossed to him. But already he was at a loss as to where to start. Ramsey Clark was even more of a puzzle than the events surroundin' his daddy's arrest.

But damned if she wasn't a pleasure to contemplate.

———

"This is stupid," Ramsey muttered under her breath. What in God's name had caused her to venture into a shop with the ridiculous name of Sumpin' Special?

It was that damn dinner with Stryker, she thought aggrievedly, darting a glance around the shop's crammed interior. Not that she had any intention of dressing up for him. God no. But the luggage Ryne and Abbie had dropped off for her contained little more than the pantsuits and blouses he'd already commented on. She hadn't yet laundered anything— when the hell would she have had time? That was something else she was going to have to take care of before much longer.

But she still had a few outfits unworn. Mentally calculating the contents of the motel room's closet, she began edging backward toward the door. Listening to Stryker's snide comments when she wore yet another suit was infinitely preferable to plunging into the baffling process of mixing and matching clothes that inevitably had to be tried on.

She was within reach of the door now. With a sense of relief, she turned to grasp the handle and push it open.

And cringed, when a familiar voice called, "Well, Ramsey Clark. I never would've expected to see you here."

Manners battled with self-preservation and only narrowly won. Squaring her shoulders, Ramsey turned, returning the greeting. "Hi, Leanne."

The other woman was standing in front of a three-way mirror, wearing a short black cocktail dress with a plunging neckline and a friendly smile. "I was wonderin' when I'd see you again. Never figured it to be in here."

"Actually, I was just leaving . . ."

"Oh, fiddlesticks, you just got here. What do you think of this dress?" The woman cocked her head, studied her reflection critically.

Ramsey felt hunted. "It . . . seems to fit." Although there didn't look to be quite enough fabric to cover the woman's chest completely. But that was probably the style, wasn't it?

"I have a date this weekend with someone new, and we're goin' to a friend's party in Knoxville. My ex-boyfriend will be there, not that I give a whit one way or 'nother. That ship sailed long ago, if you know what I mean."

Although she was uncertain she did know, Ramsey nodded politely.

Leanne chattered on as she strolled to a rack of dresses and flipped through the hangers casually. "But since the opportunity arises, I just thought it wouldn't hurt to look my nicest."

"Let him see what he's missing."

The other woman nodded. "Exactly. I want to wear somethin' that will make him bleed."

The words surprised a laugh from Ramsey. "I think that dress might be the perfect weapon."

"You think?" Leanne turned to face the mirror again. "I'm gonna get it then. 'Cuz that man surely does deserve to be wounded. Just a little." She whirled around, clapping her hands in delight. "So now we can take care of you."

The words shot Ramsey with stark terror. "I'm not . . . I don't need . . ."

"Nonsense." Leanne walked determinedly to a rack of more casual clothing and started flicking through it. "Lookin' for somethin' for dinner with Dev?"

"Absolutely not."

Laughing gaily, Leanne pulled out a sleeveless cherry-colored top with buttons down the front. "Too matronly," she decided, and shoved it back into the rack of clothes. Seamlessly, she returned to the earlier conversation. "Mama said he'd told her when they had lunch that you had to bow out. Knowin' him, he extracted dinner in exchange."

"You seem to know him well."

"Better than most 'round these parts do." With a dismissive gesture Leanne waved away the clerk who was hovering and continued speaking as she pulled out clothes, holding them up to survey before shaking her head and returning them to the rack. "Most see only what Dev shows on the outside, y'know? He's so agreeable and, let's face it, so damn good-lookin', not everyone thinks to look deeper."

Her words underscored a suspicion Ramsey had had about the man all along. Everybody devised defenses. And living down his father's past in this town couldn't have been easy.

The other woman barely took a breath. "But I know him well 'nough to recognize when he's smitten. He's taken with you, there's no denyin' it. Can't say you're his usual type, either. You should try this on." Quick reflexes had Ramsey catching a jade green top in a slinky material, hanger and all, as Leanne tossed it to her. "It'll make your eyes look more green than hazel."

Ramsey couldn't say which she found more baffling, the fashion advice or Leanne's casual talk of Dev's feelings toward her. "I'm not . . . neither of us are looking for anything serious."

Leanne gave her a droll look before heading over to another rack. "Honey, no man is ever *lookin'* for it. 'Serious' sort of has to sneak up on 'em. Whack 'em over the head before they know what hit 'em."

"Now *that's* a sentiment I've often had around Stryker."

"That's why you'll be good for him." Leanne's voice was

muffled as she flipped rapidly through a rack of shorts and pants. "You're not wantin' to hogtie him and drag him to the altar. That novelty alone was sure to intrigue him. Did you ever shoot anybody with that gun you wear?"

The non sequiturs were enough to make her head spin. But she didn't bother to dissemble. "Yes."

Rather than shocking the other woman, Ramsey's answer seemed to satisfy her. "I knew it. I told Dev I saw a piece on The Mindhunters last year on TV. What's Adam Raiker like to work for?"

"Intimidating. Demanding. Brilliant." Brutally honest with a keen insight that Ramsey found nothing less than terrifying when it was turned on her. Failure was more than just difficult to contemplate knowing it would have to be explained to Raiker. It wasn't an option.

"He half scared me to death just watching the interview. He's so . . ." The woman cocked her head for a moment, searching for the word. ". . . *intense.*"

"He is that." Surreptitiously, Ramsey tried to shove the shirt she was holding onto the rack before her, but Leanne turned at that moment and held up a pair of pencil-slim long black shorts. "Try these with the top. By sticking with black, you probably can wear shoes you already have. The dressing room is right over there." She practically shooed Ramsey into it, whisking the curtain shut behind her.

It was a bit like getting caught in a hurricane, Ramsey considered, stripping off her clothes with grim purpose. Getting blown this way and that only to find herself landing in a foreign place wondering what the hell just happened.

She heard Leanne speaking with the clerk outside the dressing room. Something about chunky jewelry, whatever that was. Dragging on the clothes and straightening them, Ramsey was struck when she looked in the mirror that the woman outside the room, blast her, had been right. The outfit looked like something Ramsey would pick out, and it fit her exactly.

Without taking much time to consider her reflection, she stripped swiftly again. It wasn't as if she didn't have similar outfits in her closet at home, she reminded herself. Regardless of Dev's cracks about her wardrobe, she did have regular clothes.

Even if she didn't want to think about how long it had been since she'd worn anything that wasn't work-related.

And there was no way to blame Stryker for that.

Scooping up the garments, she opened the curtain to the dressing room again. She may be buying the things Leanne had picked out, but only because she had nothing else appropriate to wear. It certainly wasn't because she was dressing up for the man.

"I picked out a necklace and earrings that will be just the thing for . . ." Leanne looked up at Ramsey's re-entry disappointedly. "Didn't the outfit work?"

"It's fine." Ramsey lifted her arm, which she had the clothes draped over. "I'm getting it."

"I knew it." Satisfaction laced her words. "You're goin' to have him trippin' over his tongue. Serve him right, too. That man is entirely too sure of himself when it comes to women. Don't know one personally he can't wrap 'round his finger, with the exception of his mama. But that woman's got glaciers in her veins, so she doesn't count."

She shouldn't ask. Ramsey definitely didn't want to get any further entwined in Devlin Stryker's life. But her tongue worked at odds with her brain.

"He and his mother aren't close?"

Leanne tilted her head, with its dark cap of hair, and sent Ramsey a sly look. "If I tell you, will you tell me who you shot and why?"

"No."

The other woman made a moue of disappointment. "Well, it's more ancient history than gossip, but it's no secret in these parts that Celia Ann Stryker couldn't wait to put road between her and Buffalo Springs after Dev's daddy was accused of murder. Got rid of his last name mighty quick, too. Guess I can see how hard it would have been on her," she allowed, as she trailed behind Ramsey to the counter. Laying the jewelry on top of the clothes, she continued, "From all accounts, Lucas Rollins was a lot like Dev. Easy to get along with and not much for gettin' liquored up and carousin'. Which seems sorta ironic. Woman like that would drive most men to drink."

Ramsey listened with half an ear while contemplating the jewelry—which was definitely chunky, and the same jade green as the top. It was unlike anything she'd choose, but she'd be the first to admit that her taste tended toward the functional.

"Listen to me rattle on." Leanne's rueful tone had Ramsey's attention jerking back to the woman. "You're goin' to think I'm a terrible tongue wagger. I'm biased, I'll admit it. I just think there's a special place in hell for a woman who puts her second husband before the welfare her own child, don't you?"

"Some women weren't meant to be mothers," Ramsey agreed as she handed the clerk her charge card. Although as mothers went, she figured her own would make Celia Ann look like Mother of the Year.

But she'd survived Hilda Hawkins. Had, in fact, survived her childhood, and Cripolo, Mississippi. No one passed through life completely unscathed. She was honest enough to admit snippets from her past still had the power to haunt her.

Ramsey couldn't help wondering just how much his past haunted Dev.

———

Behind the gag, her breath came in sharp muffled gasps. Her bound wrists were slick with blood. But Kathleen Sebern continued to rub them against the sharp edge of stone her naked body was propped against, terror fueling her desperation.

The pain from her wrists paled in comparison to what she'd already been subjected to. What awaited her still, if she didn't find a way to escape.

Had she been here one day? Two? Time had ceased to exist. There had only been the hours *before*, when *he* had been here. And the hours since, shrouded in darkness. Praying that somehow she could get away before he came back.

A shudder racked her body and her efforts redoubled. Were the binds loosening? She worked her wrists more furiously, uncaring of the searing pain as stone tore at flesh.

In the next moment she was free.

Disoriented, she clawed at the tape over her mouth first. The need for air, to fill her lungs and scream her fear and anguish, rose up inside her in a powerful surge. Her fingers were numb, though. Clumsy. The seconds ticked by interminably before she could tear the tape from her mouth, from lips already cracked and swollen.

The first inhalation of air was sweet, a greedy swallow. With the second came a small sound. Everything inside her stilled.

She heard the footstep first. Boot scraping against stone. Panic sprinted up her spine, fueled by desperation. She tried to rise, but her bound feet were numb, and she stumbled forward only a few steps before falling to her knees. Then she crawled. Blindly. Into the shadows, uncaring of obstacles she hit in her path. She had to get away. Had to. Had to. Had to . . .

A sliver of light stabbed through the shadows, and the wail of despair welled up in her and burst out, a wild piercing note of desolation.

"Well, well. You've been busy, haven't you?"

That voice. That hated voice. Kathleen scrabbled farther, not even trying to rise, heading for the darkest corners. No longer even thinking of escape. Her instinct was to hide.

"Do you read the Bible, Kathleen?" The light shone around the dark cavelike area, catching her in its gleam like a spotlight.

She crawled rapidly out of its beam, struck her head on something solid with enough force to have stars dancing before her eyes. A moment later he was there, above her, his hand in her hair, yanking her head back.

"Of course you don't. That's why you're here. 'And if ye will not yet for all this hearken unto me, then I will punish you seven times more for your sins.' Leviticus chapter twenty-six, verse eighteen."

She tried to swing at him, but he was crouched behind her now, one hand forcing her head nearly to the ground. He slipped some sort of thin noose over her head. Tightened it around her throat.

"You've more penance to do. And you're in the perfect position already."

Her scream was strangled as he rammed himself into her from behind, the sound ricocheting off the stone walls. Shrieking through her brain. The agony knifed through her, pain and fear colliding, engulfing her. The noose tightened, and spots danced before her eyes as her lungs heaved for oxygen. Then it loosened, allowed her a short gasping breath. Then tightened again. Over and over.

But through it all there was still his voice. In her ear. In her head. Ragged and panting as he thrust.

"Atonement is your path to salvation, Kathleen. Because the wages of sin are death."

Chapter 14

It was ten minutes to six when Ramsey checked the caller ID on her ringing cell phone. A moment later, she considered not responding. A Mississippi area code. She almost always let calls from home go right to voice mail. Then tortured herself for hours or days afterward until she worked up the fortitude to return the call.

But this number, though originating in Cripolo, was unfamiliar.

Even knowing she'd regret it, she hit connect and answered with a short, "Ramsey Clark."

There was a moment of silence. Then tentatively, "Ms. Clark?"

"Who is this?" She could see Dev pulling in to one of the slots outside her cabin. Of course he'd be early. No surprise there.

"Ms. Clark, this is Curtis Feckler, of Feckler Realty in Cripolo, Mississippi." A nervous laugh. "I admit, I wasn't 'spectin' you to answer. You must be feelin' a whole lot better. Congratulations on your recovery."

She went to the door and opened it, waving Dev inside. "I think you've been misinformed," she told the Realtor. "I haven't had any health issues. What's the purpose of your call?"

Another hesitation, during which her attention was diverted by Dev's low wolf whistle. Ridiculous to feel a flush of pleasure by the admiration in his expression as he gave her a long once over. So she was wearing different clothes.

Clothes were clothes, weren't they? And these gave her nowhere to hide her weapon. She felt naked without it.

"I'm sorry, I'm not sure what's goin' on here." Feckler's voice was confused. "Your brother brought me a notarized statement that you were at death's door. He said you needed to sell your house in Cripolo to pay the medical costs, and I've found a buyer. Your number was on the copy of the deed he showed me, but this contact was mostly a formality. We're required to follow up on things like this. I'm afraid I don't understand. Your brother assured me . . ."

A familiar sense of fatality filled her. "I'm sure he did. Unfortunately my brother is an ex-con precisely because he's a conscienceless liar and thief. The house isn't his to sell, Mr. Feckler, and since I'm not interested in unloading it, you've narrowly avoided landing yourself in a lawsuit. Next time, you'd best get a better idea of who you're dealing with before you take them on as a client."

The man began to sputter. "Well . . . I've never seen such a thing. I assure you, Ms. Clark, I'm an honest businessman. I just moved to Cripolo a few months ago to open a new branch of my realty company. Granted, I don't know the townspeople well yet, but . . ."

She gave a humorless laugh. "That explains it then. When you do, you won't make a mistake like that again. Good-bye, Mr. Feckler." She disconnected the call, dropped the phone into her purse. "Ready to go?"

Dev surveyed her carefully as she walked by him. "Trouble at home?"

"Nothing out of the ordinary." For the first time that day, she was glad she had plans this evening. When it came to diversions, Devlin Stryker excelled. And she welcomed any distraction that gave her an excuse to delay dealing with her brother.

She heard the door close behind her as she headed to his car. No way to know for sure if Luverne had been acting alone or if their mother had put him up to it. Eventually she'd have to call home, immerse herself in the genetic jungle that was her family.

But for now . . . she looked up, startled to find Dev leaning in to open the car door. She slid into the passenger seat and he shut the door after her.

For now, she'd spend a few hours engaged in what passed as normal for most people. And forget for a while that her life had never shared more than a passing acquaintance with "normal."

"Given our plans for later this evenin', there wasn't time to drive out of town for dinner." Dev caught the quick suspicious glance Ramsey slanted his way, and amusement filled him. "On account of your wantin' to go by Rose Thornton's tonight."

"Right."

He was careful to hide his grin when she passed him to enter the Half Moon restaurant. It wouldn't do to let her see that he'd accurately guessed her first interpretation of his words. He figured he ought to be grateful her mind was running along the same lines as his. Damned if persistently carnal thoughts involving her hadn't about worn a path through his brain.

He caught Molly Fenton's eye, and the waitress whisked off to find them a table. The interior of the restaurant was already crowded but not nearly as packed as it would be in another few hours when it filled with more drinkers than diners.

"I suppose you know everybody in here," Ramsey muttered.

He scanned the interior, saw nothing but familiar faces. "All the locals, anyway. And I'm noddin' acquaintance with most of the others." He sent a friendly wave to Donnelle and Steve sitting in the corner. Felt a flash of annoyance when he saw Banty Whipple and a couple of his equally thick-headed buddies turn around to survey him from their stance at the bar.

"We're not going to be surrounded by more of your adoring fan club while we eat, are we?"

He thought, he was almost sure, that Ramsey was joking.

When Molly gestured toward them, he placed a hand at the base of Ramsey's narrow back and nudged her forward. "Fact is, not everyone in these parts is a fan."

Her quick look this time held uncertainty. "Because of your father?"

"There's that. And others who just don't find my winnin' personality irresistible."

There was a definite smirk on her lips as she sat in the chair held out for her. "Go figure."

That curve of her lips held him transfixed for a moment. He'd never seen them glossed with lipstick before had he? As a matter of fact, he wasn't sure he'd ever seen Ramsey wear makeup at all. But she was wearing some now, though he'd been too interested in the curves and uncovered skin she was revealing to have noticed it earlier.

He took his seat across the table and studied her as she looked around at the other occupants. He gave high marks to the manufacturer of that slinky green top she had on. It left her arms bare and dipped low enough in front to hint at cleavage. He'd already noted that the long shorts she wore were trim enough to show off her very fine ass.

She turned back to him, caught him staring. One eyebrow winged up in question.

He grinned, unabashed. "Just admirin' the scenery."

To his delight, she looked discomfited. He wondered how much time Ramsey Clark set aside for a social life. Not much, he figured, giving a nod to Digger Lawton, who had shouted his name from his stance at the juke box. She struck him as someone whose life revolved around her work.

She struck him as someone who had reasons to keep it that way.

"What'll ya have?" Molly skidded to a stop beside them, flipping open her order pad.

"Lemonade," Ramsey said without hesitation.

"Bring me a Bud Lite," Dev told the woman, who nodded as she scribbled the order even as she moved on to the next table.

"Who's the sawed off little shrimp at the bar glaring daggers our way?"

Surprised, he looked over her shoulder, saw Banty giving him the evil eye. "You've had your back to him since we walked in. How'd you notice Banty Whipple?"

"I notice everybody."

He looked at her with renewed respect. He'd just bet she did. Probably took stock of the place and everyone in it upon the first few seconds of entering. Sometimes it still took him aback, those qualities of hers that must be embedded from years doing her job.

"Well, he's not the president of my fan club. Although he's probably contemplatin' bringin' a club if he ever drops by my place again."

Molly came by and dropped off their drinks then, and he paused to take a pull of the beer while returning a long level stare back at the man. It satisfied Dev to see the mark on Banty's jaw. He hoped like hell it was one he'd put there.

Setting down his bottle, he continued, "Mostly we just can't abide each other. It so happens his son was one of the kids who found the body."

A cell rang then, the muffled sound loud enough to have him automatically checking his pocket even as he realized the ring was unfamiliar. In the next instant he looked at her purse, sitting on the chair between them. "Is that your phone?"

Ramsey took a long drink of lemonade, avoiding his gaze until the ringing stopped. Only then did she reach into her purse to check the caller ID. Nothing flickered in her expression when she slipped it back inside. "It can wait until later."

Which meant it didn't concern the case she was investigating. She was too much of a professional to ignore it if it did.

Recalling the conversation she'd been having when he'd gone to pick her up he guessed, "Your brother?" And by her arrested expression, knew he was correct.

She toyed with the straw in her glass, the gesture strangely diffident. "He'll be put out that his latest get-rich-quick scheme has been thwarted. It's best to wait until he's a bit more rational before verbally kicking his ass."

He didn't smile at the words. Couldn't, not when they were accompanied by that flash of pain in her eyes. He hadn't grown up with siblings himself, but knew enough of family to recognize the emotion they engendered wasn't always positive. Not by a long shot. "If he's tryin' to steal your house, the ass kickin' might need to be more than just verbal."

"I know how to handle Luverne." Then, catching his gaze on her, she blew out a breath. "I bought the house long ago for my mother to live in." One bare shoulder lifted in a shrug. "She never did move out of that tin can of a trailer we were raised in. Saw an opportunity to get some extra cash monthly by renting it out instead. I let that go, but it was only a matter of time until one of them came up with this idea." Her smile was little more than a grimace. "We're not close."

He had a feeling that was an understatement. One he could fully appreciate. His occasional calls home were fueled more by duty than familial devotion. He could mourn the lack of emotion even while realizing there was no other way. It was hard saying who had been more relieved when Dev had stopped making infrequent trips home. His mama, his stepdaddy, or him.

"Looks like Doc Thiesen has some company tonight."

Dev recognized the change of topic for what it was, and followed the direction of Ramsey's nod to a corner of the room. Although the older man had his back to them, there was no mistaking his identity. Especially when he saw the man's dining companion.

Dev lifted a hand in greeting in response to the woman's wave and turned back to Ramsey. "That's his daughter, Martha Jane. She lives in Knoxville but gets back here regular to see her dad. She and Doc have always been tight. He raised her alone after his wife left them years ago. He never remarried."

Which was a far cry from his mama, who'd had someone new lined up less than a year after his daddy's death. Dev reached for his beer again, tipping it back for a swallow. He wasn't sure what to make of that, but he thought there should be a happy medium between pining for decades and a too-quick plunge back into the matrimony pool.

Because the mood had grown too serious, he deliberately sought to lighten it. He let his gaze linger on her until that heat was back in her eyes.

"You're staring, Stryker."

"Just wonderin' where you're packin' your gun."

"Armed or not, I can still handle the likes of you."

He relished the half-serious challenge in her voice, raised his bottle to her in salute. "And I'm lookin' forward to bein' 'handled.'"

She shook her head, a slight smile curving her lips. And he fancied he could see the tension easing from her muscles. "You've got disgracefully low standards. I refuse to find that appealing."

He gave her a slow wink as the waitress returned to take their order. "You've appealed to me since the first time I laid eyes on you, sugar. Only seems fair that the feelin' be returned."

"So tell me about Rose Thornton."

Dusk had already settled over the road to the woman's cabin. They'd gotten a later start than Ramsey had wanted due to the slow service at the restaurant. Dev refused to feel guilty about that. She'd been as relaxed as he'd ever seen her over dinner, and despite her fears, he had no doubt they'd find the old woman at home. There was simply nowhere else for her to be.

"Not much to tell. I always heard she'd been married for a long time, but her husband was dead long before I was runnin' 'round these parts. Always been as cranky as a cat with its tail in a crack, that's for sure. Caught some of her buckshot in my—ahem—nether regions once when Matt and I were hangin' out on her property drinkin' beer he'd stolen from his daddy's fridge."

He felt rather than saw her look at him. "Your . . . nether regions?"

"The scarring," he informed her with great dignity, "was more emotional than physical."

"I'll bet."

The road narrowed past the cemetery as they got closer to her place, and he slowed accordingly. "She's not much for people, I'd say, although she always treated those in need of medical assistance. At least those who didn't hold with doctors and hospitals. I s'pose that's how she's made ends meet, although she's lived pretty simply all these years. Only goes to town every month or so to pick up what she can't grow or hunt."

"Sounds like there's some bad blood between the two of you," Ramsey observed, looking out the window. "I'm not sure you'll be much help in getting her to talk to me."

"She wouldn't talk to a stranger," he corrected her. "And even if she isn't in the mood to chat with me there, at least I present a bigger target if she's totin' a rifle."

"There is that." There was amusement in Ramsey's voice. "But since my medical knowledge tends to be pretty rudimentary, you may want to be careful about catching any more buckshot."

He pulled over to the shoulder of the road alongside Rose's property, hugging the ditch. "She doesn't have much in the way of a driveway, and I think it's safer all around to walk up to the house and knock." The twin bare tire trails leading from the road made a wide swoop around the cabin to the ramshackle lean-to to the rear of the structure. There was no telling from here what kind of shape the "drive" was in, and he wasn't anxious to scrape off vital parts of his car finding out.

Turning off the ignition, he said, "Better slide across this way. Don't want you tumblin' into the ditch on your side."

Dev waited for her to follow him out before closing the door and locking the car. Shoving the keys in his pants pocket, he took her hand and headed toward the tire tracks leading to the house. He felt the immediate tension that shot through her at the gesture.

"Ground's gonna be uneven," he observed casually. "Don't know what Rose is drivin' these days, but figure it's still that big ol' barge of a Buick she's had since the sixties. She doesn't use it enough to keep the drive level."

As they strode closer to the cabin, he was struck by the tranquility of the scene. Already the locusts were tuning up, and fireflies blinked as they darted about. The property boasted a large clearing, mostly filled with knee-high weeds, and was fringed on two sides by woods. "Pretty place."

"If you like nature."

Humor flashed. "If you like nature," he agreed. "I 'spect Rose mostly likes the privacy."

"There are no lights on," Ramsey pointed out. She stumbled then, just a little, and he paused to support her.

"I can still recall when Rose had this place outfitted with electricity. I doubt she'd be one to waste it." They were standing in front of the steps now, and the dark windows didn't have him lessening his guard. It was the old woman's penchant for shooting first and asking questions later that had him wary. "Be best for you to wait here, and I'll go up and knock. Get an idea what our welcome will be." Although with Rose, welcome was a relative term.

"Nice try." Ramsey began striding to the house ahead of him. He caught up with her at the steps of the porch. "But I don't need protecting."

"You've never met Rose," he muttered. But rather than arguing, he inserted himself in front of her so he'd be first at the door. And hoped Rose hadn't exchanged buckshot for bullets in the years since he'd seen her.

But knocking for a full five minutes failed to rouse anyone. "Odd." He looked at Ramsey, who was trying to peer into the curtained windows. "Haven't heard anythin' in town 'bout her health. But I s'pose she could have gone to visit those relatives of hers." He had a hard time imagining it, though. He doubted she was any closer to them than she was to her neighbors.

"Even if she's sleeping, you'd think the knocking would have wakened her."

"Not if she's in the habit of takin' something to sleep." Who knew—the woman might even be self-dosing with something holistic for some age-related ailment. "Probably the best thing to do would be to come by sometime in the daytime, since you've missed her twice in the evening."

"I suppose." Disappointment tinged Ramsey's tone as they made their way back down the steps. "I'll be out of town for a day or two, so it'll be a while before I have an opportunity."

It was on the tip of his tongue to question her about that, although he assumed her trip had something to do with the case, meaning she wouldn't tell him much. But as they rounded the edge of the cabin to head back to the road, his mind was wiped clean by the sight of a shotgun pointed at them.

"Jesus!" Dev shoved Ramsey aside and stepped to place himself between her and the woman wielding the gun. "Ms. Thornton. It's Devlin Stryker. Good to see you again."

Surprisingly, she looked much as she had when he'd last seen her, although that had to have been five or six years ago. He recognized the tattered wide-brimmed straw hat she wore, with the spiky iron gray tufts of hair poking out beneath it. The shapeless man's coat, flannel shirt, suspenders and jeans also looked familiar.

But damned if the gun wasn't even more memorable.

"Stryker." Her voice was the same raspy croak he remembered. "You haven't outgrown your habit of sneakin' round where you ain't wanted."

"Actually, we came to see you." He shifted just enough so she could glimpse Ramsey but hopefully not enough to provide her with a clear target. "This is Ramsey Clark. She's interested in talkin' to you 'bout your healin' work."

The weapon lowered as the woman eyed them both suspiciously. "She don't look sick."

"I'm not sick."

Too late Dev recognized that Ramsey had stepped out from behind him to face the woman. "I'm working with TBI on a homicide case. I understand you're very knowledgeable about healing herbs and plants."

"Not much I don't know 'bout 'em," the woman agreed, the weapon lowering enough to have Dev breathing easier. "But I don't hold with people trampin' 'round my property without permission." Her glare, which swept the both of them, was fierce. "'Specially the law."

"We're here only to see you," Ramsey emphasized. "I have just a few questions, and then we'll be on our way."

Seemingly mollified, the older woman cradled the shotgun in her arms, surveying them. The shadows cast by the cabin in the dwindling light shrouded her face.

"I'm especially interested in reasons a specific plant root would be ingested," Ramsey put in.

"Lots of reasons people might take such a thing. Like if'n they're ailin'." Rose's words were grudging. "Or wardin' off gettin' sick. Lots more reasons that have nuthin' to do with health."

"What would those be?"

"Not much some won't do to get their head buzzin'." She used the rifle barrel to gesture in Dev's direction, a gesture that caused him a moment of nerves. "This'a one here is proof of that. Used to lay out of school regular to lurk down here with his no-account cousin gettin' liquored up."

He felt compelled to come to his own defense. "Actually, it was only that one time."

Both women ignored him. "So other than medicinal purposes, some plants are used as an intoxicant," Ramsey noted.

"And there's them used in ceremonies of a sort."

"Like hoodoo? Witchcraft or dabblers with the occult?"

"Witchcraft and religion." Rose's face screwed up in an expression of disgust. "Difference 'tween the two don't 'mount to a bucket of warm spit."

Dev slid a gaze toward Ramsey. He'd mentioned as much—a great deal less colorfully—earlier today.

But if she recalled it, there was no sign in her expression. She was studying Rose intently. "Do you still practice healing?"

"Slowed down some. Can't keep up the garden all on my own."

His attention jerked back to Rose. In all the time he'd known her, he'd never heard her admit to physical weakness. "If you need some help, Rose, I'm sure I can . . ."

"Din't ask for help, now, did I?" The snap in the woman's tone was all too familiar. "Don't need you out back diggin' holes all willy-nilly. Got folks laid to rest on this property, and I won't have 'em disturbed."

"Is your husband buried here?" Ramsey asked in a voice softer than he'd ever heard from her.

"He is. Buried him myself, and din't need no preacher from town sayin' words over 'em, neither."

No doubt there were ordinances prohibiting that these days, but Dev figured the powers that be in town had turned a blind eye. Few would have been willing to take on Rose, even less so years ago than now.

Another thought struck him then, and he arrowed a look at the older woman. "Learned just recently that this cabin might've been the first structure in these parts. That it was built by Rufus Ashton, the town's founder."

"I wouldn't be knowin' 'bout that." She took a step back. "You two get on outta here now. A body's got a right to turn in at night without worryin' 'bout nosybodies pokin' 'round." She leveled a stare at Ramsey. "You need to keep your watch up, missy. Hornin' in 'round these parts is baitin' trouble. Wouldn't be a bit surprised if'n you found it."

"What do you . . ." But Ramsey's question was leveled at the woman's back. Rose walked, surprisingly briskly, toward the back of the cabin, rounded the corner, and moved out of sight.

The two of them blinked after her. "Was she actually threatening me?" Ramsey asked, clearly nonplussed.

"Warnin' you, most likely." With a hand to her elbow, Dev turned her toward the car. The conversation had been surprisingly civil for Rose. He wasn't anxious to push their luck. "It's not like you haven't heard over and over that murder 'round these parts gets some folks antsy 'bout talkin' to outsiders."

"I wasn't talking to her about murder," she pointed out.

She began to move, slowly, in the direction of the vehicle. "At least, not directly."

"Close enough. Her talkin' 'bout buryin' her husband on the property put me in mind of somethin' though."

"Don't tell me." It was too dark to see her roll her eyes, but he could hear the emotion in her voice. "Not another graveyard outing. What would Jim Thornton have to do with the legend?"

"Not Jim Thornton." Headlights speared through the approaching darkness as a lone car rolled down the road before them. "I'm wonderin' about Rufus Ashton. Goes to figure that the earliest settlers here wouldn't have a graveyard, that they'd bury their dead on their property, much the way Kuempers did. And given the lights you saw yesterday, that gives me one more reason to want to check this property out further."

"You might want to consider a little thing called trespassing," she said caustically as they started up the incline toward the road. "Rose looked pretty serious with that shotgun. She'd be well within her rights to use it if she finds you on her property again without permission."

"I was gonna ask her 'bout it when she up and left." Although in this instance it just might be better to beg forgiveness than to ask permission. Rose likely wouldn't even know he was there.

"You're wasting your time." Back at the car now, Ramsey followed him to his side to get in. Once she'd slid across the seat, she waited for him to get in before continuing. "I know what I saw, and it wasn't in the least ghostly. It was just . . ."

When her words halted abruptly, he shot her a look and found her staring out the window toward the Thornton place. Following the direction of her gaze, he felt a spurt of adrenaline rocket through his body.

The lights were clear from the road. Bouncing, dancing balls of illumination along the edge of the woods. They skipped and slid from side to side before darting in the opposite direction. He stared for a moment in fascination before the scientist in him clicked into place.

He was reminded of his reason for waiting until near dark to come here tonight. There was no way in hell he was leaving here without getting a closer look.

"You can stay in the car. I won't be put out if you do." He popped the trunk and was out the door before Ramsey could fashion a response. He grabbed the baseball cap he'd fitted with the camp light and donned it, his mind whirring.

It would be good to take the motion detector. Determine once and for all if someone was 'round to cause those lights. He grabbed the thermal scanner and EMF meter. He'd need the infrared digital thermometer with laser pointer, but he left the ion detector and gaussometer. He could always come back and get those if he needed to.

"What the hell?" He hadn't even heard Ramsey's approach. She stood by his side gaping down into his trunk. "You can't tell me you're going to . . . Dev!"

He headed back toward the Thornton property. "If you're comin', bring that big Mag-Lite, will you?"

"I'm not coming because I don't want to give you a reason to play doctor picking buckshot out of my butt. Dammit!"

Her voice, he noted as he jogged toward where those lights still bounced and skated about, got a little meaner when she didn't get her way. He was willing to bet it didn't happen often enough for her to get used to it.

And then all his focus shifted to the lights ahead of him. They could be some sort of reflection, he considered, shifting the strap of one bag to reposition it on his shoulder. But from what? He sent a look up and down the road over his shoulder, looking for cars. All he saw was a light on low beam heading toward him.

His mouth kicked up. So Ramsey was coming after all. Disgruntled without a doubt, but still joining him.

Rose's house as he passed by it was dark. No lights shone from within. The woman had indicated she was going to bed. Had she just been trying to get rid of them? Was she in the woods doing . . . something . . . that would account for the lights up ahead? He found it hard to fathom.

Which didn't mean someone else wasn't in those woods.

One moment the lights were there. The next they'd vanished, as if someone had turned off a switch. "Shit," he muttered, breaking into a run. But when he'd reached the edge of the woods, there was still no sign of them.

He set the bags on the ground and went down on one knee, rummaging through them for the infrared digital thermometer. He aimed the laser pointer in the direction the lights had been, but he didn't need a reading to recognize the change. Nights cooled down this time of year. But the surrounding air was frigid.

Looking down, he checked the temperature readout. Forty-five degrees. His brows rose. Definitely intriguing.

"Whoever was here, you must have scared them away."

He'd barely noticed Ramsey's approach. Dev was moving slowly around the area where those lights had been skipping and dancing in the air. There must be another explanation. He'd debunked every orb photo he'd ever been presented with, although there were a few videos that still had him wondering.

But he'd never seen orbs for himself. Was a long way from admitting that he'd seen them this time.

But he damn well had seen *something*.

"It's freezing this close to the woods. Since there's nothing to see here, let's *go*."

"Step back 'bout ten feet and you'll be a lot warmer," he instructed absently. He went down on one knee to pull his notebook out of one pack, used the illumination from the camp light on his cap to jot down some notes.

Forty-five degrees. Six inches to the right. Forty-eight degrees.

He swept the area slowly, taking frequent measurements and making notations. The contrast was stark. There was at least a twenty-degree difference between the area he thought the lights had emanated from and the space several feet away from it.

Next he set the EMF meter down and flipped it on, watched

the needle sway wildly before settling well into the elevated range.

"Stryker."

He looked up absently from the notes he was scribbling to be practically blinded by Ramsey's light. "What?"

"What are you doing?"

"Checking for elevated levels in the electromagnetic fields. Need to come back here tomorrow for a control check," he muttered, scribbling another note. He'd also have to look at the proximity of any electrical wires, which could play havoc with the EMF meter. But they were a good distance away from the cabin. And he didn't see any poles in the vicinity.

"You know there are a dozen possible explanations for those lights, right?"

"At least," he agreed. He made a mental note to check how close the nearest airport or radio tower was. Although the lights had seemed to skip rather than sweep, he needed to be thorough. "What color would you say they were?"

"The lights?"

"Yeah."

"White."

He looked up then, his gaze direct. "Did they look totally white to you?"

She hesitated. "From a distance, they appeared to have a purple haze around the rims. But what possible difference does that make? They're reflections from something or someone inside the woods."

"So they're the same thing you saw here last night?"

This time her pause was longer. "I couldn't swear to it, but yeah. Seemed like it."

"At least we can be fairly certain they don't have anything to do with Rose. At her age, there's no way she could have gotten to the woods in the time it took us to walk to the car. And she wasn't carrying a flashlight."

He rose. "I'm goin' back to the car to get the gaussometer. And I really want to measure the ion activity in the area."

"Stryker."

Moving toward her, he continued, "You better come with me. I don't want you waitin' down here alone in the dark."

"Stryker."

He tried for a note of humor. "I know it's probably not the most romantic date you've been on, but you have to give me marks for originality, right?"

"Stryker!"

Close enough now to see her outstretched hand, he turned, baffled, in the direction she was pointing. Felt a spike of pure exhilaration when he saw the lights again, this time glowing from a spot deeper in the interior of the woods.

"C'mon. Let's check it out." He grabbed her arm and started toward the trees. Felt her dig in her heels like a lamb being led to slaughter.

"Not a chance."

"Well, there's no way I'm leavin' you out here alone," he countered. Dev had no way of knowing what the hell was going on here, but there weren't any scenarios that had him comfortable with stranding Ramsey while he ran ahead into the woods.

Curiosity got the better of chivalry. Grabbing her arm more firmly, he fairly dragged her into the woods alongside him, his eyes on the lights that danced ahead.

Chapter 15

For an instant, past and present collided with enough force to make the two all but indistinguishable. Ramsey fought wildly against Dev's careless grip as he urged her into the trees. As if by breaking free she could divest herself of the hold the past had upon her, as well.

The fronds and scrub brush scraped at her naked skin as she crouched low behind the huge pine. The surrounding trees hemmed her in. The darkness wrapped around her like an inky smothering beast. She was afraid to breathe. Afraid the sound of it would give away her hiding place.

He was close enough to reach out and touch. And the thought of what awaited her if she failed turned her blood to ice. Her skin frigid.

"I know you're 'round here somewheres. I can smell yer cunny. Why doncha just come on out and you and me can have ourselves a time afore them other assholes find us. Ain't settlin' for sloppy seconds this time. C'mon, bitch, you know you want it. Quit wastin' time."

She came out. Swinging the tree branch at his head with all her might.

"There now, I've let go of you, see? Damned idiocy to go barrelin' into the woods this time of night, anyway. C'mon, now, Ramsey. We'll just walk out and get on back to the car, shall we?"

It took a minute for Dev's low soothing voice to reach her. Another before his words registered. When they did, when her wooden muscles would respond, she swung the flashlight in his direction. And what she saw in his expression had mortification firing through her.

Pity. Mingled with wariness. And why wouldn't he be wary? She'd acted like a certifiable crazy woman on her way to being fitted for a straitjacket.

Jesus. She hauled in a deep shuddering breath. Wished she could still the rocketing of her pulse. Based on her reaction, she wasn't so sure she wasn't straitjacket material. Damned if there weren't still shudders chasing up her spine, racking her body.

"I'm okay." *She was.* Anger finally chugged through her system, battled with the remnants of fear.

"Sure you are." Dev began edging toward the direction they'd come. "But all of a sudden, I'm not crazy 'bout chasin' through the woods. Can't do a damn thing tonight that I couldn't do in the daylight. Why don't we head back to town?"

There was an instant when everything inside her leaped at the chance to take the easy out he was offering. To allow him to pretend that it was he who'd changed his mind. He who couldn't face the thought of running deeper into the shadowy woods after night had fallen.

And the strength of that longing stiffened her resolve. Even if it failed to batten down the trembling that still shook her limbs.

She shook her head violently. "It's okay. I'm fine now."

"But I'm not." Dev looped an arm loosely around her waist to guide her gently back to the clearing. With her teeth firmly clenched, she ducked away from his touch and took a step deeper into the woods.

"The lights are still there." Did they seem dimmer now? Farther away? Her body quaked at the thought of following them.

"Ramsey." Dev's voice at her side was as gentle as she'd ever heard it. And the sound of it made something inside her wither in shame. "You don't have to do this. Neither of us do."

"Are you coming?" Her foot felt like it was encased in

lead as she lifted it for a step forward. Her breathing shallow, she forced herself to take a second step. And then another.

It took everything she had not to flinch at the slight noise he made coming up slightly behind her. To not cringe away when he slid his arm through the crook of hers. This was Tennessee, not Mississippi. It was Dev, not . . . *them*.

And she was no longer fifteen.

"The lights are drawing away," he muttered, his stride beginning to quicken.

"Almost like whoever is holding them is running away."

Dev reached up to push a low-hanging branch out of the way. "Doesn't make sense. If the lights are from some man-made illumination, they'd have to be on a person's back to be visible if they're running."

There was a low croak from somewhere to their side, and her flesh prickled. There wasn't a swamp in the area, she assured herself. And they were a good distance from Ashton's Pond.

"Maybe it's clothing with some sort of reflective strip attached," Ramsey suggested. It was a fraction easier to keep placing one foot in front of the other when she was distracted from where she was. What she was doing. She couldn't imagine what someone could wear that would cause the lights either, unless . . .

"Or fiber optics." She gave Dev's arm a jerk where it was linked with hers. It helped to focus her attention elsewhere. Eased nerves a bit that were already raw. "Like those Christmas trees that have different-colored lights fading in and out. Or what about those novelty sweatshirts that have little light-bulbs flashing on them? How do they work? Watch batteries or something?"

The screech that sounded behind them then was inhuman. The echo of prey meeting predator. And it was so close that Ramsey all but jumped in Dev's arms, startled obscenities tumbling from her lips.

"Shit, they're gone. God dammit!" Dev swung his head from one direction to another, temper emanating from him like steam off a boiling pot. "Do you see them anywhere?"

Ramsey shook her head, clenching her teeth to keep them from chattering. The only illumination came from Dev's camper's light on his cap and the beam of her flashlight. She swept the area in front of them with its beam slowly. Once. Back again.

And barely caught the swift movement of long shadow joining with shadow. For an instant, everything inside her froze as she beat back fears that had been born well over a decade earlier.

"Ezra T., c'mon outta there." Dev's voice as he reached for her flashlight was firm. "I know it's you. Heard the animal noises you've been making for the last little while. C'mon now. We're not gonna hurt you."

Ramsey held herself stock-still, her limbs thick with tension. She felt like if she eased them, she'd fly into a million pieces.

There was a drawn-out silence. Then finally a voice sounded. "Ain't Ezra T."

"Yes, you are. Now come on out. I'm not foolin' 'round with you."

Even in the shadows, Ramsey immediately recognized the man who slipped from behind a tree trunk to sidle a bit closer to them before taking cover behind another stout oak. If she didn't miss her bet, he was dressed exactly as he'd been the first time she'd caught a glimpse of him behind the Tibbitts' house. His brown hair was stringy and matted and stuck up in odd tufts over his head. With his several days' growth of whiskers, he looked older than his years.

"You din't know it was me."

"I've seen you before. You were watchin' me down at Ashton's Pond a few days ago, weren't you? Those bird calls of yours sound just like the real thing."

"Yer Stryker. Duane told me all 'bout you." Ramsey could feel the man peering at her in the darkness. "You been bad, missy?"

Despite the chills still skating over her flesh, she stepped forward. She'd been wanting to talk to this man since she'd first heard about him. "My name's Ramsey, Ezra T. You know these woods pretty well, don't you?"

"Gonna get butt sex if you're bad," he babbled. Dodging around the other side of the tree, he disappeared from sight for a moment. "Yessiree."

"Have you seen anyone in these woods lately, Ezra T.?" Dev had warned her about the man's intellectual capacity. Rollins, too, when she'd asked him whether he'd questioned the man. But even a child could give valuable information if it was extracted properly.

The other man didn't appear, but he stabbed a finger around the trunk in Dev's direction.

"So you saw Devlin when he was at the pond. Did you see anyone else before you saw him?"

"Saw the cops." The voice seemed disembodied, floating as it did from his hiding place.

"I'll bet there were a lot of them at the scene." Without conscious thought Ramsey moved closer to the tree trunk he was hiding behind. "How about before the cops were there?"

"Dead is dead. She be dead. She bad."

Ramsey stilled. "Who, Ezra T.? Who was bad?"

"But now she back. All the time screamin'. Can't you hear her screamin'?"

Dev's voice was low. "Ramsey, he can't help."

But she was unconvinced. Keeping the flashlight pointed at the ground, she moved around the tree until she had the other man in her sight. "Did you see the woman dumped in Ashton's Pond, Ezra T.? Did you see who put her there?"

"Make her stop screamin'." His voice was growing shrill, both hands clapped over his ears. "Make her stop."

"You heard her screaming? Was she crying for help? Who was hurting her, Ezra T.? Did you see who put her in the pond?"

"Only one way to make her quit screamin'. Make her dead. Make her stop." His words were coming faster, more frenzied. And the expression on his face had the ice forming anew in Ramsey's veins.

"Did someone make her stop screaming, Ezra T.? Did you see who it was? Did you . . ."

Suddenly, he lunged for her. She dodged too late. Stumbling backward, Ramsey caught her foot on her tree root and nearly fell. His arm was around her throat in an instant, hauling her back against his chest with a surprisingly strong grip.

"Yer bad, too!" He smelled of body odor and the faint scent of decay found in the woods. Grimacing, Ramsey fought to break his hold without hurting the man. "Yessiree. You gonna get dead. But don't you start screamin', hear? No more screamin'."

Dimly she was aware of Dev at her side, shouting, trying to break Ezra T.'s grip. But spots were beginning to dance in front of her eyes as he pressed more tightly against her windpipe. And any remaining concern about the man abruptly vanished.

She jabbed her elbow into his gut with all the force she could muster. He gave a surprised mewl, the sound oddly childlike, and his grasp loosened. Dev wrested Ezra's arm from around Ramsey and pushed her farther away.

"What the hell's wrong with you, Ezra T.? You know better than that!"

"She bad, she bad," he jabbered, his finger pointing in Ramsey's direction. "She gonna get dead."

"Ezra T. . . ."

The other man bolted then, his movement as swift and sudden as a bird taking flight. And when Dev started after him, Ramsey said, "Let him go."

He glanced back at her, his expression as grim as she'd ever seen it. "You were right. He's got some explainin' to do. Now more than ever."

Wearily, she shook her head. "No, *you* were right. You and Rollins both said he was useless to question. He can't help. Let's go."

His reluctance clearly showed as he moved back toward her. But then he paused in front of her, his fingers gentle as they brushed her neck. "Did he hurt you?"

His tenderness, on top of the other blows tonight, turned her bones weak. To stiffen them, she shrugged. "I've had worse than this chasing down a pissed-off crack whore."

"A vivid mental image." Placing an arm around her waist, he headed with her toward the clearing. It occurred to Ramsey that the events with Ezra T. had completely distracted her from her reaction to the woods.

Somehow she couldn't feel it in her heart to be grateful to the man for that.

"I've told you, I'm fine. And as . . . unforgettable as this date has been, I need to get back to work."

Imperturbably Dev waited for the microwave to ding and then opened it to extract the mug. "Marshmallows?"

"I said . . ." She stopped to look harder at him. "Marshmallows?"

"As a kid, I never did think hot cocoa quite hit the spot without a few marshmallows melted on top."

"I'm not six, Stryker."

Taking that as a no, he picked up the Bailey's, gave the contents in the mug a stiff shot, then stirred the concoction before setting it in front of Ramsey.

She eyed it suspiciously before transferring her jaundiced gaze to him. "What'd you put in it?"

His mouth kicked up. "As an adult, I never did think hot cocoa quite hit the spot without a belt of a li'l hundred proof." To allay her fears, he reached for the mug and sipped from it before setting it back down in front of her. "Drink." Her fingers clenched around it, as if soaking up its warmth. Given the chilliness of her skin, she still needed it.

"And I thought Cripolo had some colorful characters."

"I'm sure they do. We've got our share here, too." Because she seemed to need the reminder, he nudged her hand until she brought the mug to her lips for a swallow. "I never expected Ezra T. to go off like that. I'm sorry he hurt you."

"I'm embarrassed he got the chance." Her tone was disgusted but stronger than it had been before. She took another drink. "It was just sheer stupidity on my part to let my guard down like that."

He'd be willing to bet it didn't happen often. Her guard was as much emotional as physical. Both were equally daunting. "You were distracted."

"All around, not one of my finer nights."

"You don't have to be invincible all the time, Ramsey. Leastways, not 'round me. Bein' vulnerable once in a while doesn't make you weak." The sight of her vulnerability, though, had weakened *him*, and he wasn't ashamed to admit it. His gut still twisted when he recalled the panic that had filled her. He couldn't help wondering about it. Couldn't help feeling protective.

Which made him short a couple screws, because until tonight, he couldn't imagine anyone in less need of protecting than Ramsey Clark.

She sipped in a contemplative silence for while. When she finally spoke, her voice was low. "Once you've been at another's mercy, you swear to yourself it will never happen again. That you'll get stronger. Smarter. And history will never repeat itself because you've grown and changed and you're not the same person anymore."

Dev nodded, reaching for her mug. He took a long swallow before handing it back to her. Her words resonated deep inside him, where memories of himself as a young preteen still lingered. His stepdaddy's idea of teaching him to box had just been a semi-civilized excuse for beating the hell out of him whenever he took a mind to. He could still recall the vicious burn of bitterness as he'd lie across his bed, nursing his latest bruises. He'd worked out twice as hard. Practiced every spare minute he had. Just for the moment he could lay that bastard out for the first time.

"They have a saying in Cripolo, Mississippi. If you're born in the gutter, you grow up smelling like shit. I guess I've spent most of my life trying to get rid of the stench. Even ran off and got married when I was seventeen, determined to leave Cripolo and the Hawkins name behind."

Her smile was self-mocking. "In our three months of wedded bliss, he punctured one of my eardrums, broke my nose and two ribs, and knocked out my top right bicuspid.

When I walked out on Marlin Clark, it was with the intention of never seeing him again. But I kept his last name, because even the name of a lying, cheating, wife-beating lowlife scum was better than being Ramsey Hawkins." She brought the mug to her lips again. "So, yeah. Invincible is good."

He didn't respond right away. Couldn't. Not with this boulder-sized knot of rage lodged in his throat. His fingers clenched and unclenched while he battled back a primitive wall of fury that was as unexpected as it was overwhelming.

Long minutes passed before he could speak. His voice was tight. "It'd be easy 'nough to find out where the guy is these days." His smile was feral. "Maybe pay him a li'l visit." Discuss old times. Settle old scores on her behalf.

She looked at him over the rim of the mug, her gaze puzzled. "What for?" Something in his face must have alerted her then, because astonishment quickly followed. "You don't even know him."

"I know you."

It was, he thought, one of the only times he'd seen her at a loss for words. Their gazes held for long moments before hers softened imperceptibly.

"He's dead. In a bar fight several years ago. He's not worth wasting time thinking about. I rarely do."

But Dev knew he would. Knew he'd mourn the opportunity to make the son of a bitch bleed, just a little, for what he'd put Ramsey through all those years ago.

Just as he knew that whatever had shaped her, her ex-husband was only part of it.

She pushed the mug aside and rose. She'd want to leave now, and he couldn't think of a single way to stop her. Wasn't sure it would be wise to try. Not with all this emotion crashing and wheeling inside him.

He stood, too. Made to turn away. But then Ramsey was there, her hand on his arm. Her manner more tentative than he'd ever seen from her.

"I don't know that I've ever had someone come to my defense before." The wonderment of it still showed in her expression. She came up on tiptoe and brushed her mouth over his, first lightly, before returning to press more firmly. His arms went around her of their own accord, and he returned the kiss without any of the restraint he'd shown to date.

There was no holding back at any rate. The events of the evening, the revelations Ramsey had made, unleashed something primal that Dev had no idea how to contain. He could no longer recall why he wanted to.

Cupping the back of her head with one hand, he returned the kiss with all the hunger that had been building inside him for days. Every last bit of self-discipline he possessed abruptly went up in smoke.

The taste of her whipped through his system, amped up his heart rate. Created havoc with hormones that had been under "down boy" command since meeting her.

A command that was currently being ignored.

Without releasing her, Dev moved her backward until her back was against the fridge. His mouth eating at hers, he ran his free hand over the rounded curve of her bare shoulder. Traced her arm, firm with muscle beneath the sleek skin. Slid his hand inside the slinky material of her top to cup warm soft flesh.

Her nipple was a tight knot, and he rolled it between his thumb and forefinger. Felt her fingers tunnel into his hair as she pressed closer. Heard the hum of pleasure she made in response.

He'd spent some time thinking about just this moment. Thought about every inch he wanted to taste. The way he'd take his time to touch and stroke until he'd explored every part of her body. But his desire was an uncaged beast, recklessly lunging forth, and it made a mockery of any efforts at control. *Slow* wasn't going to be an option.

Their mouths did battle, lips and tongues and teeth clashing as the kiss deepened. Took on an edge of frantic.

His brain fogged with lust. But he could still register a vague sense of alarm at how quickly the taste of her rocketed through him. Left every part of him quivering and straining.

His lips cruised a path up her jawline before closing, not

quite gently, on her earlobe. "If this is only about gratitude, better tell me now." Every muscle in his body clenched in anticipation of her answer. Made a mockery of his unspoken intention of bringing a halt to this.

Her eyes opened slowly, the eyelids heavy. And what he saw in their depths had his gut tightening into a hot ball of need. "I'm not *that* grateful." She tugged his shirt loose to skate her palms up his sides.

His hands lacked their usual finesse as he dragged the straps of her top down her arms to free her breasts. Then he swallowed hard at the sight of them, high and firm, smooth white globes tipped with pink nipples. And need clenched in his gut like a fist.

He'd never been a man to take intimacy lightly, but he couldn't recall ever feeling this urgency before. His blood was churning with it. A more sensible man would take a step back, just long enough to calm his pulse. Regain a measure of reason.

But he'd never felt less sensible. In a primitive quest for the taste of flesh, he lowered his head to take one nipple in his mouth even as he continued to tease the other.

Dev lashed the taut bud with his tongue before sucking strongly from her. Her hands grew just a little frantic as she slid them up his chest, her nails scraping lightly before her fingers clenched on his shoulders. Dimly he heard something clatter to the floor before he felt her knee bend to tighten around his thigh. And he knew that this time, Ramsey wasn't going to stop him. Wasn't going to draw away. For some reason, the knowledge helped him regain a measure of control.

He lifted his head, his eyes opening to see her nipple, tight and moist from his mouth. The carnal image pleased him even as it whetted his appetite for more. He wanted her naked. Flesh against flesh. He wanted to see her aroused and demanding, sated and satisfied. And every emotion in between. Whatever he could get from her. Whatever those stalwart defenses of hers would allow.

And then he wanted more: all the secrets she hid from the world; all the emotion she denied herself. He wanted to smash the walls she used to protect herself until he could steep himself in every scent, every whisper and sigh. And tell himself, finally, he'd had it all.

Knowing it was impossible only fanned the flames of need hotter.

She pushed his shirt up his chest, and obligingly, he lifted his arms so she could drag it over his head. Then he snaked an arm around her waist and hauled her closer so skin kissed skin. The sensation had them both hissing in a breath.

"I think we need to move this out of the kitchen."

"Really?" With the nail of her index finger, she traced the seam of his chest where it met her torso. "What's your hurry?"

"No hurry." He leaned forward to worry the cord of her neck, nipping gently at it. "I got all the time in the world. And I find myself curiously turned on at the thought of strippin' you bare and stretchin' you out on the table." A smile curved his lips at the thought, and he flicked one nipple with the edge of his fingernail. Felt her shudder. "I'd be lyin' if I said I haven't been thinkin' of feastin' on you pretty much since the first time I laid eyes on you."

As if in response to his words, she placed her hands on his chest, gave him a light push. Obligingly he moved away a fraction. When her hands dropped to the hem of her top, his heart stuttered hard once before settling into a heavy thud.

Her eyes on his, she worked the material up her waist and over her head before discarding it. And the sight of her bare torso compelled him to touch.

He dipped to trace the hollow at the base of her throat with the tip of his tongue. Smoothed a hand over the satiny skin of her waist. Cupped her breast. The stark contrast between the softness beneath his hands and her inner toughness was endlessly fascinating. One he wasn't sure he'd ever get tired of exploring.

The thought had him mentally backpedaling. Women didn't come any more complicated than Ramsey Clark. It wouldn't do to be thinking of more. This, now was likely all there'd be. All there could be.

Distracting himself from the stab of regret that observation brought, he cupped her butt, flexing his fingers over the firmness there. And drove himself a little mad just thinking of stripping the slim shorts down her long legs. Following each inch of bared skin with his mouth.

But Ramsey took that decision out of his hands the next moment when her fingers went to the fastening of her shorts and unbuttoned them.

His throat grew thick. The little smile on her lips was knowing. And he recognized that she'd just taken control of the moment. Because he wasn't a man to miss an opportunity, he stepped back and let her. For now.

Her zipper was worked down with excruciating slowness. Dev could feel perspiration beading on his forehead. His gaze was arrowed on each inch of pale flesh revealed during the zipper's descent. Whatever the outcome, he knew he'd remember this moment, Ramsey's eyes dark and knowing, a seductive curve to her lips. Breasts bared and flushed. Nipples beaded with desire.

He curled his fingers into his palms to curb the need to reach for her. Instead, he backed up a few steps and propped his hips against the edge of the table, his gaze never leaving her figure.

She hooked her thumbs in the sides of the waistband and began to work the shorts slowly over her hips. It seemed to take an inordinate amount of time. "Need some help with that, sugar?" When she stilled, it was all he could do not to throw back his head and howl.

"Been undressing myself for a long time now."

"Honey, if you've been doin' it like that, I'm surprised you ever got another blessed thing done."

She eyed him knowingly. "Criticizing my technique?"

He shook his head, willed her hands to start moving again. "Just makin' an observation."

"It occurs to me that this is the first time I've ever seen you in such a rush."

"No rush." Folding his arms across his chest, he willed the words to reach his brain. And lower. "Got all the time in the world here."

After a pause that could only be considered cruel, she started inching the shorts down again. Low enough to reveal her flat belly. To show a scrap of lacy black panties he never would have guessed to find in Ramsey's wardrobe.

Sending up a prayer of thanks to a gracious god, he swallowed hard and tried to call upon his flagging self-discipline. The shorts were to her upper thighs now. It seemed only gentlemanly to reach out and peel them down her legs before taking a long look at the picture she made clad only in the wisp of lingerie.

His blood pooled in his groin.

"You've got a streak of mean, sugar." He nibbled her neck while sliding his hands over her silk-encased bottom. "But you have superb taste in underwear."

His fingers skimmed under the elastic to touch the smooth rounded cheeks beneath. But when her hands dipped to his waistband, he thwarted her move by going down on his knees in front of her.

He used his grip on her butt to draw her nearer. Felt her hips jerk helplessly as his breath hit her behind the lace. And then he placed his mouth on the thin fabric shielding her moist heat from him. He dampened it with his tongue, his fingers stroking along the crease of her thigh.

Hooking a finger into the side of the panties, he drew them down her legs and pressed his mouth to the slick flesh he'd revealed. Felt her body shudder.

There was a rollicking in his system. A roaring in his ears. The taste of her, the feel, had nerve endings firing. His heart was leaping in his chest. And when he parted her slick flesh to send a finger deep inside her moist center, the broken cry she uttered had primitive satisfaction surging through him.

His tongue stabbed at her clit in rhythm to his stroking fingers. Her fingernails bit into his shoulders, and the sting of pain whipped his hunger to fever pitch. She'd seek to keep a part of herself back. Somewhere deep in the recesses of his mind, he knew that. Her hips began to move, faster and faster, to match the rhythm of his mouth. And when she shattered, the cry she made was drenched in shocked pleasure.

The sound of it sent razor-edged desire sawing through him. Her body was boneless, and he rose, supporting her with one arm around her back. Her eyes fluttered to half-mast, looking drowsy and drugged. And the sight of her had his control fraying dangerously.

Desperation raced through him. He toed off his sandals and shucked his pants, his movements jerky with tension. At the last moment, he remembered to retrieve a condom from his pocket. Then all conscious thought drained out of his head when Ramsey shoved down his briefs and took him in her hands.

Her touch was sure and knowing as she stroked him. Her eyes were slumberous and aroused as she watched him try to summon his rapidly diminishing restraint. He clenched his jaw against the pleasure roaring through him. Every clever clutch and slide of her fingers drew him closer to a shattering response. One that was going to have him embarrassing himself if he didn't end this soon.

He pushed her hands aside and sheathed himself in the condom with more haste than grace. Then he reached for her, his heart hammering so loud he was certain she could hear it, and turned her to lift her to the table's edge. Nudging her knees apart, he stepped between them, and her legs climbed to his waist.

"I thought you were kidding about the—" she gasped as he worked the tip of his cock just inside her opening—"table."

"Next time, I offer you a bed . . ." He entered her with one long stroke, stopping only when he was buried deep inside her. Conscious thought fragmented. He could feel the delicate pulsations of her inner muscles working against him. His vision graying, he withdrew almost completely, only to seat himself inside her again, in a movement that had them both groaning.

The hunger burst through him then, a fierce savage beast intent on release. Her arms twined around his neck, and he gripped her hips as he thrust into her with a brutal greed that wouldn't be denied. There was no thought of control, no thought of holding back. Sensation slammed into sensation in a blinding kaleidoscope of pleasure. He heard her moan as she crested, and need turned to madness. His face buried in her hair, he thrust harder and deeper inside her until he felt surrounded by her. Entwined in her.

And when his own climax ripped through him, catapulting him over the edge, he thought of nothing but her.

———————

The mattress moved, and Dev came instantly awake to see Ramsey heading for the bedroom door. "Where you goin'?"

"I told you, I have an early day tomorrow. Make that today. Go back to sleep."

Like hell. He rolled from the bed to follow her out the door, down the hall, and to the kitchen, where she was gathering up her clothes and quickly pulling them on in the dark.

Dev backed up, rested his bare ass against the oven door, and folded his arms across his chest. "C'mon, honey, let's go back to bed."

"Uh-uh." She held up a warning hand. "That only works once. Okay, twice. But now I really have to go."

He flicked a glance at the clock face on the stove. Three A.M. Dev couldn't think of a blessed reason she needed to leave at this time of night, regardless of how busy her day might be.

But he suspected a woman as guarded as she might want to regain a bit of distance after spending the last several hours wrapped around a man. Or, to be more exact, over him, under him, and several positions in between.

Ramsey wasn't leaving on account of work. She was *running*.

"You should try sleepin' sometime," he suggested blandly. Reaching down, he scooped up one of her sandals near his bare foot and held it out by its strap, letting it dangle from one finger. "That's what most folks do this time of night." He couldn't shake the suspicion that had he not wakened, she'd have snuck out like a thief.

"I sleep." She grabbed for her shoe. Slipping it on, she looked around the room. He wondered if it was his imagination that her gaze skirted the table. "Do you remember where I left my purse?"

"In the car. Do you remember how you got here?"

Given her stricken expression, he figured she'd forgotten. "If you're that intent on run—goin' home," he amended, "give me a second to get dressed. I'll drive you."

"Shit. Now I feel guilty."

"I sincerely hope so." He began searching for his own clothes on the kitchen floor. It was doubtful that guilt was the primary emotion she was experiencing. It was panic.

The sort of panic a person like Ramsey would feel from letting someone too close, too fast. Understanding that almost made it easier to allow the night to end like this.

Almost.

Chapter 16

Matthews strode alongside Ramsey toward the front of 24 Hour Fitness, a decidedly sullen expression on his face. "How come you get to play bad cop?"

"Because I'm not playing."

"You're also not a cop. Not anymore."

She stopped, one foot on the first step, and looked at him. "If you've got a problem with the strategy, take it up with Powell. This is how he laid it out." Digging her cell from her navy suit jacket pocket, she extended it to him.

He glanced at it, then away. "I'm the one who's been busting my ass running all over the state getting these interviews."

When he made no move toward the cell, she put it away. He had a legitimate complaint, so she nodded. "But in doing so, you're familiar to all the interviewees. It's better to bring in a stranger, one Sanders has no rapport with, when we hit him with what we've got."

"Yeah. Still . . ."

"I haven't exactly been vacationing in the Jamaican isles in your absence." She restarted her ascent up the steps.

"Jamaica's an isle. I don't think it has other ones."

"Whatever. Sanders has been lying through his teeth about this whole thing." And why would anyone be surprised at that, since his lying started while he was still engaged to Cassie Frost? Ramsey looked at the TBI agent, her hand resting on the front door's handle. "So let's go nail his ass to the wall."

Quinn Sanders had piercing blue eyes, thick light brown hair that would make Leanne beg to touch it, and a body that looked like an advertisement for his health club. He wore a tight sleeveless T-shirt and shorts, an incessant smile, and an edge of nerves that showed every time he glanced in Ramsey's unsmiling direction.

She could smell fear on the man. She figured it was there for a reason.

After the introductions and pleasantries were out of the way, Sanders spread his hands. "I'll admit I'm surprised to see you again, Agent Matthews. I told you everythin' I knew the last time we talked. Unless . . ." His voice trailed off, inviting one of them to pick up the conversational gambit. When neither of them did, he continued, "Did somethin' new come to light in Cassie's case?" He looked from one of them to the other, his expression hopeful. "Did you catch her killer?"

"I'm afraid not, Mr. Sanders." Matthews was playing it just right. Professional. Courteous. With just the right note of friendliness. "There were a few more questions that came up. Figured it'd be easier to take care of them now before I head back to Buffalo Springs."

Ramsey got out of her chair while they were speaking. Roaming the office, she paused before a framed diploma certifying that Quinn Sanders had graduated from the University of Tennessee with a degree in exercise science. Since when was exercise considered a science? Shaking her head, she turned to look at Sanders over her shoulder. "So this place has been open . . . what? Two years?"

"Twenty-six months." He gave a boyish grin she immediately distrusted. "I sank everythin' I had into it, and haven't even drawn a salary yet. But it's startin' to show a profit. Better every month, in fact."

She didn't return his smile. "Did Cassie Frost put any money into this place?"

"Cassie?" He looked nonplussed. "No, of course not. She

didn't have any money. I mean she made a good salary when she was working in a bank here in Memphis. But she bought a town house a while back and tied up her savings in that. No, this is all mine. Mine and the bank's."

She'd already seen a copy of the deed to this place that Matthews had uncovered at the courthouse. Sanders had financed rather than rented the building. Given his previous job and the fact he wasn't independently wealthy, he had to be in hock up to his eyeballs.

"That must have been tough. Before you opened up, you were, what? An accountant? They must rake in serious dough for you to have enough stashed away to live on while you wait for this place to make it."

He was plainly taken aback by the derision in her tone. Appearing to choose his words carefully, he said, "I've continued workin' with my tax clients to supplement my income, of course."

Matthews gave him an approving nod. As an aside to Ramsey, he said, "There will be tax records of that."

Sanders's gaze bounced between Matthews and Ramsey. "What's goin' on here, anyway?"

"Routine follow-up," she replied, making no effort to insert sincerity into her voice. "Matthews is convinced you're the real deal. A good guy. Me?" She strolled over to place her palms on his desktop. Leaned forward. "I'm still waiting to be convinced."

"Well . . . hell. Do I need a lawyer?"

"I don't know. Do you?"

Sander's gaze widened. "I haven't done anythin' wrong!"

"So why would you need a lawyer?"

"C'mon, Clark, back off." Ramsey thought—she was almost certain—the agent's words were part of the routine. "He's been nothing but cooperative through this thing."

"Cooperative?" She drilled a look into Sanders.

"Yeah, totally." He gestured to the agent. "I've answered every question Agent Matthews asked me."

"Yeah, but see, the thing is, Quinn, when you answered those questions of his, you lied like a dog." Ramsey slammed her palms on the desk in emphasis. "That doesn't look like cooperation to me. That looks like someone with something to hide."

"That's bullshit!"

Yeah, the fear was unleashed now, Ramsey noted with a degree of satisfaction. There was a muscle twitching under one eye, and his Ken doll perfect manner had slipped several notches.

"Oh, so you *didn't* tell Agent Matthews you hadn't spoken to Cassie since the breakup?"

"I . . ." Looking hunted, Sanders shot a glance at the TBI agent, then back to Ramsey. "I didn't mean not at all."

"Oh, so the agent misunderstood you? He specifically asked, and I quote, 'Can you tell me when the last time was that you had any sort of communication with Cassie Frost?' And you said—still quoting here—'That would have been the night we broke our engagement, Wednesday, March eighth, last year, when we . . .'"

Her recitation of his statement was interrupted by the younger man. "Okay, I'll admit I wasn't totally truthful about that."

Matthews managed to look shocked. Ramsey thought he might have a frustrated actor gene buried somewhere inside him. "Quinn, are you saying now that you did have further communication with the murder victim after the breakup?"

"It's complicated." The man ran his hand through his hair. "Okay, I talked to her a few times. What's the big deal? I never saw her once she left here. There were a few things to iron out, like some items I'd left at her town house. A tie I was missin'. Stuff like that."

Ramsey reached into her jacket's inner pocket to retrieve a copy of Frost's cell phone LUDs. "Well let's count those calls. Between March eighth and the week before her death, I come up with . . ." She pretended to tally, as if she didn't have the exact number branded on her mind. "Thirty-seven. Over three dozen times you had to talk to Cassie about 'stuff.'" She paused a beat. "That's a lot of ties."

Sanders sent a wild look in Matthews's direction, but the

agent was surveying him expressionlessly. "I couldn't admit that I'd talked to her," he pled. "If Sarah found out Cassie and I were still in touch, she would have hit the roof."

"What happened, Quinn?" Ramsey asked rancorously. "Couldn't decide which sister you wanted after all? Or did all the excitement of the chase sort of disappear once Cassie removed herself from the mix?"

"Yeah—no!" The man sank into his desk chair. "I mean, I thought I wanted Sarah. But later . . . I couldn't stop thinkin' about Cassie, y'know? And everythin' we'd meant to each other."

"And you started to think maybe you'd made a mistake breaking things off with her. Sarah's rushing you to the altar, and you stop and think, hey, is this really what I want?" The sympathy was back in Matthews's voice. "That's understandable."

"And maybe Cassie wanted to use you to get back at her sister."

"No." Sanders looked at Ramsey with dislike. "Maybe we talked about gettin' back together at first, but when I didn't break things off with Sarah right away, Cassie wouldn't discuss it anymore. It was just . . . I missed her, y'know?" He hunched his shoulders, managing to look miserable. "And I think she missed me, too. Or at least, she missed havin' someone she knew to talk to. So we'd talk, that's all. Totally innocent."

"So innocent that you called her from this number instead of your cell phone, so your current fiancée wouldn't find out."

Sanders swallowed hard. "She wouldn't have understood."

Ramsey gave a feral smile. "See, now I think you've underestimated Sarah. I'll bet she would have understood *perfectly*."

"You can see how this looks, Quinn." It was Matthews's turn to work the man, his voice persuasive. "If there's more you haven't told us, now's the time to come clean. The more you try to hide, the worse it is for you in the long run."

Sanders slumped in his chair, scrubbing his eyes with one

hand. "I know this looks bad, but you have to believe me. One of the reasons we kept talkin' is because she was spooked. She thought someone might be followin' her."

Her derisive snort couldn't be contained. The younger man's head came up, and he glared at her. "See I knew you'd blow it off, but it's true. And she was really creeped out by it."

"Couple problems with that, Quinn." Ramsey hooked a straight-backed chair with her foot and dragged it close enough to sit in. "One is you never mentioned this mysterious stalker until your neck's in a vise. And two, no one who knew her in Kordoba can back you up. She never mentioned being afraid to anyone there."

"But she did in Lisbon." He was eager now to make them believe him. "I couldn't mention it earlier because I'd have to admit we had kept in touch. She moved to Lisbon from here after we broke up. And about a month after she got there, she said some guy tried to pick her up at a restaurant. She gave him the brush-off but said she'd see him around at random times, watchin' her. And after she'd been in town a couple months, she woke up and saw someone trying to break in through her bedroom window."

A tight frisson of rage fired through Ramsey's veins. "Convenient that your memory cleared up once we've caught you in a pile of lies."

"I didn't tell you before because there wasn't really anythin' she told me that would help, you know? And if Sarah found out we were speakin' . . ."

"Yeah, you said. She wouldn't understand." Ramsey regarded him with disgust.

"I can prove there was someone she was afraid of. She reported that window peepin' incident to the police." He looked from one of them to the other. "There'd be a record of that, wouldn't there?"

Ramsey easily kept up with Matthews's stride as they made their way to their respective cars. "Powell was right. He's a lying-ass dog."

"Just because he lied about not talking to her doesn't mean he's lying about everything." The agent sent her a pointed look. "Easy enough to check out. If she filed a complaint, there'd be a record of it."

"Wouldn't prove a damn thing." But she was already thinking about it. Worrying at the ramifications like a dog with a bone. They'd gone through Frost's life in Kordoba thoroughly. And once they'd traced her to Memphis, Matthews had been similarly methodical there.

But had they missed something important by not being as painstaking with the places she'd lived in between the two towns?

"I'll let Powell know I'm sticking around here with you," she said. "Maybe if we go at Sanders again tomorrow, we might be able to convince him to voluntarily let us look at his financials as a show of good faith."

"More likely he'll lawyer up if we hit him too hard," Matthews warned.

"Possibly. Which makes it all the more critical to get info from him before then. Maybe if he thinks we're going to let Sarah know about his continued interest in Cassie, he might be more forthcoming." They'd have to tread gently there. Matthews was right. They'd pushed Sanders to his limit today.

"I'm heading back to the motel." The agent stopped by his car, a black four-door Crown Vic. "If the report exists, we can always get a copy by fax."

"Let me see what Powell has to say. Once we finish up here, I wouldn't mind swinging through Lisbon on my way back to Buffalo Springs."

"Really?" Matthews looked considerably more cheerful. Ramsey figured he thought he was going to get stuck with that duty, too.

"Yeah, I'd like to poke around." From the victim's financials, she could glean her old employer, her landlord, even her former hair stylist and nail salon.

"Fine by me. I'll catch you later."

Ramsey got in the Ford, sending the TBI agent an ab-

sentminded wave. She was ninety-eight percent certain that
Sanders was sending them on a wild-goose chase. He wasn't
exactly racking up points for honesty.

Inserting the key, she started the ignition. She wasn't going to overlook anything that might bring them closer to the
killer, no matter how remote the chance might be. Grimly,
she checked her mirrors and headed off the lot.

Cassie Frost had been let down by those who were supposed to love her most. Ramsey figured she owed the woman
at least this much.

———

The sun was almost straight overhead by the time Dev
made it back to Rose Thornton's place. He gathered the equipment he'd need from the trunk of his car, and with a sense of
déjà vu, headed off toward the woods fringing the old lady's
property.

All the while, he kept a wary eye on the door of her cabin.
Although there were some experiences he wouldn't mind
repeating, having buckshot removed from his ass wasn't one
of them.

The late start was courtesy of his lack of sleep the night
before. Dev was normally not a late riser, but once he'd returned Ramsey back to her place, he'd laid sleepless for a
long time, wondering if he could have played it any differently.

The answer to that had been evasive, so he'd fallen into a
restless sleep about the time the birds had started waking.
And had woken surly and out of sorts as a result.

There was nothing that cured surliness like buckling down
to work.

So he spent a couple hours setting up and getting those
control measures to compare to last night's readings. And
then sat contemplating the results, his mind racing.

Because the readings today were well within the normal
range.

The outdoor temperature would be expected to be warmer,

of course. He'd need to take another reading tonight at the same time he and Ramsey had been here. But the EMF meter should read the same today as it did last night if the previous elevated reading were due to power lines. Trouble was, they were in the normal range, too.

Intrigued, Dev rocked back on his heels. He'd need to do a bit more investigation, but his attention was caught, no denying it.

He shot a considering look at Rose's cabin. It looked quiet. If she were up and around, he hadn't seen her. Hopefully his luck would continue to hold. Because come dark, he was going to be back here to see if the readings compared to last night's.

In the meantime, he had some local history to bone up on. It would, he hoped, as he placed his equipment carefully back into their bags, take his mind off the woman who had hovered at the edge of it for most of the day.

He was slamming the lid of his car's trunk when his cousin pulled up beside him in the department-issued Jeep. Rounding the car, he went to the passenger side of the other vehicle. Mark buzzed down the window.

"Hey." Dev bent down to rest his forearms on the opened window, peering inside. "I'm gonna get me a job like this someday. Spend my days ridin' 'round the county, duckin' out of my responsibilities at the office."

"Bite me," Mark suggested pleasantly. "You haven't punched a clock since you worked for old man Hanly at the soda fountain back in high school. And all you did then was give free ice cream to all the pretty girls that came in."

The memory had Dev smiling. "Hanly took it out regular from my paycheck, too. Finally had to quit when it got to where I owed him more than he paid me." He'd held other jobs since then, of course. But all had lacked the appeal that came from the research and writing he did now.

Mark looked past him toward Rose's cabin. "You always did like to live dangerously. Does Rose know you're out trompin' 'round her property?"

"Haven't seen her this mornin', but Ramsey and I spoke

to her last night." He neatly sidestepped the question. "Can't say that she's changed much."

"You talked to her? Well, that's one thing off my list for today. I was gonna check on her. Folks have mentioned she hasn't been to town lately."

"She'll probably outlast us all."

Mark eyed him shrewdly. "What were you doin' with Ramsey out here anyway?"

"She saw some lights near the woods night before last, and we came to check them out. Saw them again last night and went to follow them. Had a run-in with Ezra T." Dev recounted the incident, finishing with, "Have to say, I was pretty surprised. Didn't figure on him bein' the violent sort."

The sheriff frowned. "Can't say as I like the sounds of that." He appeared to mull it over for a few moments. "Makes me wonder if Duane and Mary are seein' to it that he takes his medication regular. That's one of the conditions of them keepin' him at home, I know. I'll make it up there sometime today and have a talk with them."

"Probably wouldn't hurt." But Dev's mind was somewhere else. "You get a lot of poachers in these parts?"

Mark gave a shrug. "Always have some. More trappers than anythin' else. That might account for the lights you saw. Some guys settin' or checkin' their traps for the evenin'."

"Probably was," Dev agreed. He wasn't near ready to discuss what he thought the lights could be. There was a lot more evidence to collect before then.

He knew his cousin. He wasn't any more open than Ramsey to "evidence" he couldn't see or hear or touch.

But Dev was beginning to believe that he just might have stumbled on a site of genuine paranormal activity.

———

"Sonofabitch."

Catching the curious looks from nearby diners, Ramsey lowered her voice as she continued the cell phone conversation with Agent Powell. "How much is the policy worth?"

"A hundred grand. The insurance company in Memphis

contacted the local police when they heard of Frost's murder. We just got word. Looks like Sanders took the policy out on Frost a year ago last fall."

Well before their breakup. She thought of Sanders's business and wondered if it was doing as well as the man would have them believe. "Smells like motive to me."

"Damn straight. Since it's the weekend, I had Jeffries contact a judge in Memphis. When I get there, I'll swing by and pick up the signed warrant. I've already talked to Matthews and told him to wait for me."

"I'm still here, too. I'll stay until you . . ."

"No, I want you to head to Lisbon and check out Sanders's story about the police report Frost made. See if you can line up any other verification. People she might have confided in. If this turns out to be another hole in his story, we can use it to nail him."

More than a little deflated, Ramsey agreed. "I'll let you know what I find out."

"This doesn't shake his alibi, of course." Powell sounded as revved as she'd ever heard him. "But Sanders wouldn't be the first to hire someone to off a loved one for that kind of money. We'll know a lot more when we get hold of his financials."

"Speaking of financials, can you check the log of Frost's transactions? I'm looking for names that might be a landlord, salon, favorite restaurants." She got a pen and paper from her purse and wrote down the information Powell read off for her on the back of her napkin.

The call ended moments later, and Ramsey put the list she'd made in her purse. Looking at the half-eaten sandwich on her plate without interest, she signaled the waitress for the check.

Her enthusiasm for the task ahead had waned considerably in light of the recent news. It would be cynical to think that the TBI agents were rushing to take control of what could only be construed as their best lead yet in the case.

But Ramsey had been born cynical. She'd also worked enough investigative teams to know how the politics worked.

If there was a break in the case, the local law enforcement would close ranks. That way they could bask in the resulting glory of successful resolution of a high-profile investigation.

Being used to it, though, didn't mean it didn't suck.

―――――――

When Dev arrived at the Historical Museum and found Shirley Pierson working as the day's volunteer, he was tempted to skip this leg of the research and head straight to the library.

The woman hadn't been friendly since he'd bloodied her son's nose for him in the summer he'd been ten for calling him Killer's Kid. In those days, he'd had more temper than restraint, and the woman had never forgotten it. There'd been a loud phone conversation with his granddaddy as a result, and then a lecture from Benjamin on the virtues of turning the other cheek.

He didn't have enough cheeks to pacify Shirley. Based on a few things he'd heard over the years, Ira Pierson had only been repeating what he'd heard at home.

"Well, bless your heart, I can't imagine what the likes of you would be wantin' here, Devlin." With the skill of a true southern gentlewoman, Shirley covered the insult with enough sugar to almost obscure the sting.

"Ms. Pierson." Mindful to this day of his granddaddy's lecture, he kept his tone pleasant. "How's the family?"

"Fine. You might be interested to know that Ira is a writer, too. A real writer," she stressed. "Just last month he had a short story published in *Country Home and Heart* magazine."

He offered a bland smile. "I'll bet you're real proud. Tell him I said hey."

Her mouth pinched together tightly. "I'm afraid I'm terribly busy. Perhaps you could come back another day."

Since the place was empty, and it didn't look as though the woman had been doing anything more strenuous than dusting the exhibits, he knew he was getting the brush-off. And had a fleeting moment to understand how Ramsey had felt when Donnelle had treated her similarly.

Undeterred, he held his ground. Sending a glance around the place, he said, "That's fine, I won't be a bother. Just point me in the direction of any information regardin' the town's foundin' father, and I'll be out of your way." If her lips tightened any further, he observed, they'd disappear completely.

"I'm afraid I can't help you."

"Okay." He headed into the next room. "Don't mind me. I'll just poke 'round on my own."

"I really can't have you touchin' anythin'." He heard her scurrying after him. "The guidelines here are quite strict. Visitors aren't to handle any items without supervision."

He halted and turned to face her, irritation bubbling. "What do the guidelines say about volunteers who refuse to help town residents when they come in here?"

Her tone went regal. "I swear, Devlin Stryker, you didn't learn those manners from your mama."

The inference was clear. "No, ma'am, I didn't. Turns out I learned very little from her over the years." He didn't bother to keep the edge from his words. "Now 'bout that information . . ."

With a sniff, Shirley swept by him, leaving him awash in the unmistakable scent of Chanel No. 5. It'd be difficult to say which of them was more out of sorts over the exchange.

———————

Two hours of poring over the cramped writing in century-old journals was enough to have his eyes burning. He hadn't brought his glasses, and he really required them to read. As a result, his eyes felt like he'd spent the last couple hours in a sandstorm.

With a harridan at his back.

Shirley hadn't grown any more accommodating as the time went on, but she had eventually stopped hovering and had attended to her other duties, leaving him alone for stretches of time. He found himself skimming large parts of text that recorded in painstaking detail daily life in these parts a century ago. Making candles and soap. Tanning animal hides. Curing meat.

And prayer. There was lots and lots written regarding prayer services and "daily devotions," whatever the heck that meant.

Dev leaned back in his chair and consulted the notes he'd written. He'd thought about using his microrecorder, but with Shirley fluttering around, he'd decided to handwrite the notes.

From everything he'd read so far, Rufus Ashton had been regarded with near godlike status from the writers of the journals. However, given that each of the journal authors had shared the Ashton name, he had to figure in a certain amount of familial bias.

Among the man's accomplishments noted were the start of the first church, the quarry, the original bank in town, and the first general store. Even in these days, he'd be regarded as something of an entrepreneur. He couldn't find any reference to the man's original home or what had brought him to Buffalo Springs, but he did find the date of his death. That gave him a place to start.

"We close at three o'clock sharp on Saturdays." Shirley's voice behind him was crisp. "It's fifteen minutes to, and I really need to get these journals back into place before I lock up."

"Okay." He pushed back from the small table he was sitting at and stood, working his shoulders. "I think I've read enough for a start."

The woman's gaze traveled between him and the stack of journals on the table and back again. Curiosity apparently getting the better of her, she blurted, "Whatever has someone like you so interested in that old history?"

He stilled. "Someone like me?"

She had the grace to flush. "I mean, given your interest in ghosts and such, I can't imagine what you hope to find by looking up our foundin' father. I just hope you aren't going to write somethin' unkind about him. There are still Ashtons in these parts, and they wouldn't appreciate their ancestors bein' slandered."

His smile revealed none of the emotion twisting inside

him. "You've always been an expert on slander, so I'm gonna take your word on that." He moved toward the door, leaving her with her mouth agape at his rudeness. "My regards to your family."

Chapter 17

"You're one of them Mindhunters, ain't ya?"

Ramsey looked up from the copy of Cassie Frost's police report to the young Lisbon police officer on the other side of the counter. His nametag identified him as Joseph Redmond. She'd bet her next paycheck he went by Joey. Although she'd have pegged him for late teens, the fact that he was on the force meant he was probably at least twenty. Maybe even a couple years older. "I work for Raiker Forensics, yes."

"I thought so." With a practiced move, the officer raked his limp blond hair back from his forehead before propping his forearms on the counter. "I've been followin' that story on the Spring County murder. Heard the TBI was bringin' in a special consultant." He paused expectantly, but Ramsey had gone back to skimming the police report.

"So how'd you get in to that line of work?"

Without looking up, she responded, "I used to be with TBI before Raiker contacted me for an interview." She noted the signature on the report. "This statement was taken by an Officer Elwin Uetz. Is he around? I'd like to talk to him."

"Naw, Elwin retired eighteen months ago. He and his wife moved to the Ozarks so's he could fish all year round. I recall hearin' 'bout the case, though."

It had hardly qualified as a "case," since it appeared from the information in her hand that the incident had consisted of little beyond taking Cassie Frost's statement. Still, she looked up at the officer's earnest expression quizzically.

"Frost was pretty spooked by the time Elwin got there. She seemed to think the man lookin' in her window was the same as one she'd seen 'bout town a few times." Redmond paused for a breath, his protruding Adam's apple bobbing. "Ol' Elwin figured she was just more scared than accurate. Her description wasn't much help. Tall guy, 'bout sixty, with gray hair. Jeans and dark shirt." The young man shrugged. "Fact is, there's probably no way to be sure, 'cuz the man tryin' to break in her window wore a face mask. Plus she woke up from a dead sleep, and it was dark out and all."

"So Uetz thought . . . what? That she'd dreamt it? That it was just a window peeper?"

The edge of impatience in her tone had the young officer rearing back a bit, eyeing her more carefully. "No ma'am, she didn't dream it. There were fresh scrapin's on the window. If'n Frost hadn't woken and called 911, whoever was out there would have gotten in that window, no doubt 'bout it. Looked like he was takin' the screen off to gain entry. She had the inside window cracked, and it would have been easy 'nough for him to pull it open farther, climb inside."

Ramsey's skin prickled. Frost had been asleep. Vulnerable. But not defenseless. She'd had the foresight to put a call in to the police.

Which bore out at least part of the story Sanders had run by them.

"What exactly did Uetz do about it?"

Redmond scratched at his smooth jaw, which probably didn't need shaving more than once a week. "Well, he checked 'round, I 'member that. We've got a couple no-goods in town who aren't above a free peepshow, if'n they can get one. Neither have ever done more than look, near as I've heard, but Elwin, he spoke to both of 'em. Followed up real thorough. Nothin' ever came of it, though. Middle of the night, no one can dispute if a fella claims he was home in bed. Elwin figured one of 'em got brave when he saw the window cracked open and tried to get in. That happens sometimes you know." The officer's voice went solemn. "People think peepers are harmless, but there was an article in *Officer's Quarterly* last year that said some rapists start out that way, so could be one of them peepers was escalatin'. Got scared off when Frost woke up."

"Have there been similar reports since?" At Redmond's furrowed brow, she went on. "Seems like if one of them was escalating, they would have made another attempt."

That gave Redmond pause. "No-o-o," he admitted slowly. "Can't say that there has been. But Uetz didn't get nowhere checkin' on the stranger Frost claimed she saw 'round a few times, neither. And she moved a few weeks later, so there wasn't much follow-up."

Ramsey digested the information silently. No way to tell if the incident was connected to the victim's murder a couple weeks later. But it seemed coincidental, to say the least. She'd never been fond of coincidences.

On the other hand, the description she'd given sure hadn't matched Quinn Sanders. If the man had hired someone to off Frost, would that person be dumb enough to speak to her first? Be caught watching her? And what connection did the man have with Spring County? Because whoever had killed Cassie Frost had been thoroughly familiar with the woods and Ashton's Pond.

Since there would be no answers to those particular questions to be found here, Ramsey rolled the copy of the report up loosely and used it to gesture to the man. "Thanks for this. I have a few other stops to make, so I'll be moving on." She turned for the door. Was stopped by Redmond's voice before she took more than a couple steps.

"Miz Clark?"

She turned to aim an impatient glance over her shoulder. Officer Redmond shot a look to either side of him, as if to check for interested ears in the empty office. "Maybe you could tell a fella just how to get on with Adam Raiker." A sheepish grin lit up his face. "I been readin' up on him since I was knee high to a tadpole. Memorized crime details the way most boys collected baseball stats." His expression went hopeful. "Always been my dream that someday I'd end up workin' with one of the best, just the way you do."

"You don't apply to work with Raiker," she told him bluntly. "He doesn't accept resumes. He handpicks his people." And she was still bemused that she'd come to his attention to warrant an interview, much less to be deemed worthy of joining his team. Raiker's standards were as legendary as his background.

Taking in Redmond's crestfallen face, she hesitated for a moment. Then, with a kindness that usually eluded her, she added, "The best way to attract his notice is be outstanding in your field. Flawless police work. An exceptional reputation. That's what catches his eye." That, and an uncanny intuition that seemed to allow the man insight into his operatives' deepest darkest secrets. An insight that never failed to leave her feeling raw and exposed in his presence.

The young officer was beaming again. "That's real good advice, Miz Clark. Thank you for that. I'm gonna take it, too. Gonna make somethin' of myself here, and who knows? I may be workin' with you one of these days."

"Good luck," she said, and headed out the door. Although truthfully, the best luck he could have was to not come to the legendary ex-FBI agent's notice at all.

Raiker would eat him alive.

"Devlin Stryker, you old dog. You still chasing ghosts and goblins and whatnot?"

Dev grinned and settled more comfortably into the worn leather recliner at his granddaddy's house. The sound of Denny Pruett's voice was so welcome, he was kicking himself for not calling his friend more regularly.

It didn't take much imagination to picture the man on the other end of the phone. With dark geeky glasses and thinning black hair, he'd be sitting behind a desk that would be piled with research books, his students' essays, and at least two computers. Wouldn't matter that it was the weekend. From his recollection, Denny's home office was nearly identical to the one he kept in his ivory tower on the NYU campus. He'd be in one office or the other.

"Are you still looking for God 'round every corner?"

Denny's laugh was hearty. "That's no way to talk to the head professor of theology, son. Matter of fact, it's downright blasphemous."

"Head professor?" Pure delight ran through Dev. "Congratulations. I'll bet Patti's proud, too."

"She is. She just got a grant to do a longitudinal study on the effect of group prayer on terminally ill patients, and . . ." The man trailed off abruptly. "And that isn't why you're calling, so I'll shut up and let you get to it."

"It's not, but that doesn't mean I'm not interested. Got a little research to do on one of the foundin' fathers of the town down here. Looks like he was heavy into religion, and I thought of you."

"How old?"

Dev could hear the clacking of computer keys on the other end. "A bit before the turn of the century—1892 or thereabouts. What I have been able to uncover is a man by the name of Rufus Ashton came down from Pennsylvania and settled Buffalo Springs, Tennessee, in what's now Spring County." He checked the notes he'd taken today at the museum and library. "Among other things, he started the first church down here, which is still standin'. It serves the Methodist congregation now. But that doesn't seem to match up with old records regardin' their faith. I was wonderin' 'bout the man's beliefs back in the time he began it."

"I'll check into it for you. But only because I like having you in my debt."

Dev toed off his shoes and slouched down, preparing for a long catch-up with his old college buddy. He hadn't had dinner yet, and dusk was already falling, but it had been too long since he'd heard the other man's voice. "Shoot, the way I figure it, we're even. I did rid your office of the ghost that was hauntin' it."

"Rigging up a camera to catch Professor Hammond on tape using my office to diddle his grad students hardly qualifies as an exorcism."

"It does if it . . ." The crash that sounded then had Dev

bolting upright in his chair. Had the man on the other end of the line halting midsentence.

"What the hell was that?"

"I'm gonna have to call you back, Denny." Unmindful of the glass scattered on the floor, Dev flipped the cell phone shut and ran to the shattered front window and peered out. Just in time to see a dark rusted-out pickup tear around the corner and out of sight.

His gaze turned to the room. Seeing the brick that had been thrown through the window had his mouth flattening. There was no note tied around it. Nothing that dramatic. The brick was message enough.

Someone around these parts wasn't any too fond of him. And although he hadn't recognized the truck wheeling around the corner, this had Banty Whipple's name written all over it.

Something pricked the bottom of his stockinged foot, and Dev absently turned his foot over to pick a piece of glass out of it. Carefully he stepped around the mess to go in search of a vacuum. Someone on the police department might have an idea of whom the truck belonged to, but he knew his chances of proving anything were slim.

He pulled the vacuum from the back closet and headed to the living room to clean up the mess. Hopefully this little incident had evened the score in Banty's mind. But in case it hadn't, it'd pay to keep his guard up.

Maybe, if Banty were lucky, by the time Dev caught up with him, he'd have lost the urge to pound the cotton out of the man.

———

"Thought you were going to be gone for a while." From Jonesy's decidedly unenthusiastic tone, Ramsey had a hunch the man had been counting on it.

She'd donned the protective clothing before stepping into the lab, immediately noting the bagged and tagged evidence bags pinned neatly to a white board. They were the samples they'd collected from Frost's apartment and car.

"I was gone. Now I'm back." She strolled over to the board to peer more closely. "Did you come up with anything?"

"Came up with a lot of stuff." Jonesy glanced at his watch before joining her at the board with a long-suffering air. "As far as matching the fibers and hair to anybody or thing . . . that's going to be your job."

Ramsey studied the board. He'd attached a note card specifying where each sample had been found, and had included another of his own findings—printed in handwriting that would shame a third grader—below each.

"I've got several samples of hair matching the victim. A couple other samples matching an elderly woman who uses blue dye on it."

"Probably the landlady's," she murmured.

". . . and one gray strand dyed by a different product, most likely coming from a wig. Human hair wigs are treated with an acid bath to remove cuticles, and the chemicals used were detectable in the tests."

"Could you identify race or gender?"

"I can tell you they're all human and Caucasian. Each strand originated from the head. But without roots on any of them there's no DNA testing to be done."

She nodded, wondering about Frost's landlady. Would she be the source of the gray wig? Ramsey remembered a couple older women in Cripolo who came to her mother's hair-styling shop in their trailer for a color and set once every six weeks. Rather than paying to come more frequently, in between appointments they'd wear wigs when their hair no longer looked "presentable." She made a mental note to call Phyllis Trammel later and ask her.

Jonesy went on, talking faster now. "I've got stray carpet fibers everywhere. That carpet is circa 1980s and sheds like a diseased Siamese. A couple threads that match clothes from her closet. Some other fibers that match the carpet in her car. Food particles. Like I say. A whole lot of nothing."

He glanced at his watch again, and noting his tension, Ramsey eyed him anew. Observed for the first time that, for Jonesy, he was dressed up.

Still decked out in black, of course. But instead of his usual T-shirt and black jeans, beneath his lab coat, he wore a button-down ebony shirt with matching dress slacks.

Her brows skated upward as she raked his skinny figure with her gaze. Nary a chain in sight. His Mohawk was slicked up bristle straight. She couldn't be exactly sure, but she thought she counted less piercings than usual.

"You going somewhere?"

He struck a bored pose, ruined it by sneaking a look at the clock on the wall behind her. "Got a date."

She felt like she'd been poleaxed. "With a person?"

He glared at her. "No, with a three-legged pygmy goat. Hell yeah, with a person. With a *woman*, you smartass."

"Oh." Since diplomacy seemed beyond her, she didn't bother to hide her shock. "Where'd you meet her?"

"I haven't been slacking off, if that's what you're thinking." His glare was murderous. "I work ten, twelve hour days. Even started running some of those plant samples you left this morning, though I'm not near done yet, and dammit, I don't have to account for my free time with you!"

"Did I say you did? Jesus, you're touchy. I just wondered . . . given the hours you keep, where you met someone, is all."

Jonesy stared suspiciously at her, but something in her expression must have mollified him. "Met her down at The Henhouse this morning when I went in for breakfast. You woke me up at the butt crack of dawn with those damn plants, so I headed downtown to get some more of those biscuits and gravy. That's where I met Vicki."

"The waitress?"

"That's right."

By Ramsey's estimation, the woman had a good fifteen years on Jonesy, but that didn't seem to be dampening his enthusiasm.

"Well . . ." What the hell was she supposed to say? "Uh . . . have a good time."

"You know, Ramsey, it wouldn't hurt you to get out more."

She narrowed her eyes at him in warning, but Jonesy seemed oblivious.

"Sex loosens up the muscles. Releases endorphins that increase brain productivity."

"I'm plenty loose." If there was any truth to his words, after those few hours with Stryker last night, she ought to be a proverbial rag doll.

And where the hell had that thought come from? She'd done her damnedest to sweep thoughts of him from her mind every time his image had horned in today, and that had been fairly often. He was as difficult to banish mentally as he was in person.

Jonesy, damn him, managed to look doubtful. "Uh-huh. All I'm saying is, you could use a few more endorphins to take the . . . ah . . . edge off."

She bared her teeth at him. "I happen to like my edge. And didn't I tell you once before I did not want to discuss sex with you?" She was going clammy all over just thinking about the man—she suppressed a shudder—*doing it*. It was enough to have that slice of pizza and soda she'd consumed in the car congealing in her stomach.

"Well, I'm going to be late." He inched toward the door before turning back hopefully. "I don't suppose I could use your rental?"

It was on the tip of her tongue to refuse, but that seemed churlish. Digging the keys out of her purse, she tossed them to him. "Get naked in it, and I will hold you down and tear out every one of your piercings with needle-nose pliers."

He grinned. "That'd be a shame. Because Vicki seemed especially interested in at least one piercing I told her about."

"Please." Ramsey squeezed her eyes closed against the mental image that threatened. "Stop talking."

"Lock up, will you?" Without another word, the man hastened out the door to the parking lot where she'd left her SUV. Leaving Ramsey thinking about sex and endorphins and loose muscles.

And how all those things related to Stryker.

She scowled. It had taken some doing, but she'd managed to shove the man's specter aside every time it popped in her mind today. She wasn't quite as successful at shrugging off the guilt she felt at forcing him to drive her home in the middle of the night.

Guilt that she'd just have to get over. Sex was one thing, but the thought of *sleeping* with another person—any person—had her palms going damp. She'd exposed quite enough vulnerability to the man earlier yesterday evening. The last thing she'd wanted was to treat him to a front-row seat if she had one of her nightmares. He probably already thought she was a few bricks shy of a full load after the incident in the woods.

Muttering a curse, she headed out the door and secured it after her before setting the alarm. What did she care what Devlin Stryker thought about her, anyway? They'd had sex. Amazing, mind-numbing sex. It wasn't like they were planning to ride off into the sunset together.

The thought had her throat easing. With neither of them racing to throw ties on the other, there was no harm in indulging the attraction, was there? It's not like Dev was directly involved in the case.

And Jesus, the man *was* talented in bed.

She got to the parking lot in time to see Jonesy spraying gravel as he pulled out onto the road. For the first time, she considered just what it meant to be without her vehicle.

Pulling out her cell, she dialed the sheriff's number. If he was still on duty, he could swing by and speak to her here. If she ended up having to walk into town to talk to him, she'd have only herself to blame.

Being nice usually proved to be a pain in the ass.

"So you're sayin' Frost might have been a hit? That her ex-boyfriend hired someone to off her for the insurance money?" Mark Rollins's pleasantly homely face was alight with interest.

Ramsey chose her words carefully. "Powell and Matthews are following up on the possibility. They'll be out of town for a few days while they comb through Sanders's financials and whatever the warrant turns up."

"I'll be damned." Mark leaned back in his chair and

squinted at the ceiling. "Man would have to be ice cold to hire someone to do Frost that way. Can't say as I like the idea of a hired killer familiar enough with the area to use the county for his dump site. But I'd be lyin' if I claimed it wouldn't serve to settle down the notion of that blasted legend." Catching Ramsey's eye, he shifted uncomfortably. "I'm not bein' unfeelin' here; I'm lookin' out for my people."

"There's a possibility she was stalked prior to the kill." Ramsey gave him an abbreviated version of the man Cassie Frost had reported watching her. The same one she'd identified trying to break into her window. "No way to tell at this point, of course, if the man she saw is the one we should be looking for."

"Lisbon is a town of 'bout fifteen thousand, right?" Mark sucked in his lip, considering. "Small place like this, a stranger gets noticed. Not so much in a town that size. I don't s'pose the investigation turned up anyone who could back up her description of the guy."

Ramsey shook her head. "Not that I could find." And she'd spoken to the woman's employer. Her coworkers, neighbors, and landlord. Even the gals who had done her hair and nails. All had described a woman who was friendly but quiet. Cassie Frost hadn't made any close friends in that town, either. At least not anyone close enough that she had been comfortable sharing her fears with. And Ramsey couldn't help feeling sad about that.

"Wouldn't hurt to start pokin' at Sanders's background. See if he has some distant connection to these parts. Even if he didn't do the deed, the killer was likely familiar with the woods and Ashton's Pond."

"It's possible," she allowed. "I still think even if we do discover Sanders was behind it, the killer added some personal touches, and the dump site probably was one of them."

"Like what?" Mark stretched his long legs out before him and slouched more comfortably in his seat. He'd agreed to swing by the motel for a conference when she'd called, even though she had been able to tell from the noise in the background that she'd interrupted family time at his place. There had been earsplitting screams of childish laughter, emanating, he'd explained, from bath time for his kids. Ramsey didn't remember baths being anywhere near that fun-filled. In the trailer she grew up in, hot water—and privacy—had been rare luxuries.

"Don't forget the plant he had Frost ingest. There had to be a reason for that." Ramsey let her gaze wander for a few seconds over the photos of the victim tacked on their murder board. "Likely the reason stemmed from him. It means something only to the killer. It's just as likely the location of the dump site does, too."

Rollins looked doubtful. "It's also possible that Frost ate that plant or whatever on her own. It might be a clue to where she was being kept, ever think of that? One of the first cases I worked in TBI was a suspicious death. Husband swore up and down his wife had committed suicide. Swallowed a bunch of pills and booze. Autopsy found a key in her stomach. Turned out she'd found a strong box he kept with photos of him and young—very young—male prostitutes. He walked in on her before she could put things away, but she managed to swallow the key without him knowin'. Helped us crack the case wide open."

"Well, until we get a lead on the identity of the plant, we're just spinning our wheels." But somehow she doubted Cassie Frost had been free to pick a plant and eat it shortly before her death, especially given what she'd endured in the time prior to her murder. "Can't say I've gotten lucky on any of the ViCAP hits regarding that similarity in homicides."

Looking surprised, Rollins said, "Why, how many hits did you get?"

A yawn ambushed her then, and Ramsey was reminded of just how little sleep she'd gotten the night before. "Six. But I heard from four of the detectives today, and none of the foreign objects ingested were plant substances." Fecal matter, shell casings, and in one instance, shoe leather . . . the cases had ranged from the gross to the bizarre. But none had matched this case.

Rubbing his chin, Rollins glanced at his watch. "If Sanders hired someone, it was a rank amateur. No other word for someone dumb-ass enough to hang 'round and let her see him."

"If those incidents are related, yeah."

"Seems a bit too coincidental to believe she came to the attention of a stalker *and* a killer, doesn't it?"

She nodded. His words closely aligned with her own thoughts. "But the thing that gets me is, after talking to Sanders, I'm convinced he's a scumbag. Maybe he wanted Cassie dead for the money. But as much as I dislike the guy, I find it difficult to imagine him ordering his ex-girlfriend to be brutalized the way she was prior to death." To hear him tell it, he'd still had feelings for the woman. A bullet would be more his speed. Something quick and easy, over in a few seconds. He'd tell himself she hadn't suffered a bit, wait a few weeks and collect the insurance money without too many pangs of conscience.

Rollins snorted. "Yeah, well that's the breaks when you hire a hit. Especially an amateur who decides to vary from the plan a little. Probably figured to get his jollies prior to doing the job and no one would be the wiser. It'll be interestin' to see if somethin' shows up in Sanders's financials pointin' to him payin' someone for the job."

And how much, she added silently, Sanders would have been able to afford to pay to make it happen.

Rollins got to his feet. "Meant to talk to you, too, 'bout Ezra T. takin' after you that way last night. Dev told me 'bout it today. You'd be within your right to press charges. Figured you wouldn't be wantin' to but needed to ask formally."

A flush of embarrassment warmed her cheeks. "No, forget it. You were right. He's not a reliable source of information."

Mark looked grim. "He's not, but he needs more lookin' after than it 'pears he's gettin'. I went up to the Tibbitts's place this afternoon to tell 'em as much, too. Thought I'd swing by again tonight. Be sure they're keepin' him home and givin' him his medication the way they're supposed to."

Uneasy with the topic, she merely nodded.

"Never heard 'bout him goin' after someone that way before." Rollins started moving toward the door. "Didn't want you to think I was takin' it lightly."

"Dev says he's harmless."

"Usually I'd agree. But I can't allow him to be attackin' people without provocation, either. Next time he might pick someone not as capable of defendin' themselves, and we could have an injury on our hands."

Her cell rang then and he turned to go. "I'll just let myself out. Appreciate you bringin' me up to date on the case."

She pulled out the phone. Saw the Cripolo number and felt her stomach clench into a tight knot. "I'll keep in touch." But even as the man pulled the door open and walked through it, she made no move to answer the call. It rang until the phone automatically went to voice mail. She could only imagine her brother was leaving another profanity-laced threat to join the other half dozen that had accumulated since last night.

Ramsey needed to deal with him, deal with the whole mess he was trying to embroil her in, but she couldn't bring herself to do it tonight. Tomorrow would be soon enough, after she got a good night's sleep and her mind was clear.

She definitely needed a clear head to deal with her brother, with his victim mentality and circular thinking.

The phone started ringing again, and after seeing the same number show up on the screen, she dropped it back into her pocket. Closing and locking the door behind her, she headed toward her cabin. First she needed sleep. Maybe by morning she'd have arrived at a plan to deal with her family.

Ignoring them was the best way she'd found to date, but that wasn't always possible. Ramsey doubted that a few hours of unconsciousness was going to make the feat any easier, but she could always hope.

"I was out walkin' Mr. Biscuits and saw the whole thing." Bunny Franzen bobbed her head, sending the tiny spirals of white hair covering it swaying. "Meant to call you, but I swear, the thought went clear out of my head the moment I got home. Didn't think of it again until Mr. Biscuits needed walkin' again and I saw you sittin' up here on your grand-daddy's porch."

Dev nodded politely when the woman stopped to take a breath. She'd lived down the street from Benjamin as long as he could remember. Mr. Biscuits, a nasty-tempered bichon frise was currently relieving himself on Benjamin's azaleas, a detail he wouldn't be sharing with the man, given his grand-daddy's intense dislike for the animal.

"Didn't happen to get the license plate number of the truck, did you?" He'd cleaned up the broken glass and patched the window as best he could. He'd call the hardware store to-morrow to see if Beau—

Too late he recalled that Beau Simpson wouldn't be order-ing him some replacement glass. He'd have to mosey by the store in the morning and see if Marvella had it open. Other-wise he'd have to check around for another place to order it.

"I didn't need to get the license plate. I recognized the driver. There, there, Mr. Biscuits," Bunny cooed as the dog started barking crazily. "We'll continue our walk in just a minute." Her voice normal again, she continued to Dev. "It was that youngest Harris boy. Zachary. I see him drivin' that truck of his all the time, devil's music blastin' all the while. I've called the police a time or two, but if they bother to talk to him, it doesn't do a whit of good."

"Zach Harris?" Dev recognized the name. The man was a buddy of Banty Whipple's—no surprise there. Matter of fact, he'd been one of those drinking with Banty last night when he'd taken Ramsey to dinner at the Half Moon.

"That one's never going to 'mount to a hill of beans, mark my words." Bunny nodded again, and when he saw her tight curls bobbing this time, he had a sudden, completely inap-propriate thought that the woman bore more than a passing resemblance to her dog. "Oh, he's got a job at the mill and all, but the way I hear it, he drinks up his paycheck just 'bout as fast as he can cash it. Do you want me to tell the police what I saw?"

He considered for a moment. He hadn't called in the incident yet. Had, in fact, been lounging on the porch with a beer while he thought about the best route to take. But since he had an eyewitness account to it, he may go ahead and make a report.

Might be interesting to see what Banty would come up with next. Because it wouldn't surprise Dev at all that this incident was hatched between the men last night. He'd never had any run-ins with Harris before.

"I'll call them in the mornin' and have them contact you," he responded and turned a jaundiced eye on the dog who was now chewing on the edge of the bottom step. "I appreciate you stoppin' by and lettin' me know, Miz Franzen."

"Well, I'm just doin' my neighborly duty, and that's a fact." Bunny made to leave before turning midway down the walk. "You tell that granddaddy of yours hello for me. I have half a mind to take him a fresh peach cobbler in the mornin'. He always did take a shine to my peach cobbler."

With a hint of wickedness flickering through him, Dev said, "I know he'd enjoy that, ma'am."

"I'm goin' to do that very thing. Take him a warm peach cobbler and have a nice long chat. Probably take Mr. Biscuits with me. I know how your granddaddy loves animals." With another firm nod that sent her curls jostling, she turned and marched down the walk, the picture of a woman with a plan.

"Thanks again," Dev called after her. Reaching for the bottle he'd sat on the floor next to his chair, he tipped it to his mouth for a sip, unable to prevent a grin. He couldn't wait to hear his granddaddy moan about having to sit through a morning chat with Bunny Franzen, who'd never made any secret of the fact that she found Benjamin Gorder extremely eligible.

Thinking about his granddaddy's reaction when he admitted he'd encouraged Bunny's intention, Dev's lips curved again. The man could probably stand some company, but he'd have plenty to say about the choice of companions.

A pang hit him then and had the smile dissipating from

his lips. He took another swallow of beer. He'd never been a man to be uncomfortable in solitude, but he'd be lying if he denied the longing to hear one particular voice now.

Digging his cell out of his jeans pocket, he propped his legs up on the porch railing and dialed a familiar number.

The voice on the other end of the line sounded sleepy, surly, and lethal. "Dammit, Luverne, you're lucky I can't spare the time to come down there and kick your ass."

His brows rising, Dev settled more comfortably into the cushion of the old wicker rocker. "Ramsey. I woke you." It was barely ten o'clock. And where had he gotten the idea the woman never slept? "I'm sorry."

"Dev?" Alertness had returned to her voice. He could picture her sitting up in bed, shaking the cobwebs of sleep from her mind. "Sorry. I thought you were . . . someone else."

He watched the fireflies flicker and dance across the yard. "Have you talked to your brother yet?"

There was a long pause. "Not yet."

"Figure you know best how to handle him," he said mildly. And waited a beat before going on. "But if you need any help in that direction, I'd be glad to join in the ass kickin'."

"Thanks for the offer," she said around a yawn. "But I'll handle it."

"When you comin' back? We never did get 'round to havin' dessert last night." He tipped his head back to study the stars while thoughts of her filled his mind. "I never do consider a dinner complete without dessert."

"And somehow I'm not surprised to hear you trying to attach new conditions to a deal that's already been met." Humor sounded in the words. "I'm here at the motel, actually. Got back this evening."

This evening. Dev stared at the streetlight across the street without really seeing it. Because he wasn't a damn fourteen-year-old girl with her first crush, that absolutely was not disappointment stabbing through him. No reason at all that she would have let him know about her change in plans. Sex didn't change the parameters of their relationship. Ramsey wouldn't allow it to. A normal man would be doing cartwheels over the knowledge.

"Your day must have been successful if you were able to cut the travel short."

There was a hesitation. Then, "There's a new lead in the case. No telling where it will go, but Powell and Matthews will follow up from that end. I've got plenty to check on here."

"Well, you could come to my place. Check on me." The scent of magnolias stung the air, drifting over from his neighbor's garden. "Can't remember the last time I had a good checkin' over."

"Really?" Her tone was dry. "Then you have a remarkably short memory."

He grinned into the darkness. "I do. That's what I'm sayin'. Maybe you should come on over and jog it."

"As much as I'd enjoy 'jogging' you, I'm going to pass. I didn't get much sleep last night."

"That's a fact. And I'll let you go back to sleep if you answer one li'l question for me."

"Which is?"

"What are you wearin'?"

"What makes you think I'm wearing anything?" she countered.

His lips curved. "Now you're just bein' mean."

"I thought you liked that about me."

"Can't deny it. I'm gonna let you go back to sleep while I sit here all night contemplatin' you in that cabin room stark naked. Gonna figure out a way for you to make that up to me, too."

"I don't doubt it."

He started to say good-bye but was interrupted by her next word, uttered in a softer voice.

"Dev?"

"Yeah?"

She paused a long moment. Then in a rush, she said, "It's good to hear your voice."

The connection ended, eliminating his chance to respond, even if he'd been able to.

He sat in the darkness long after his beer had been emptied. Watched the moths do their fluttering death dives around the street lamp.

And contemplated why it was that such a difficult woman should hold such a fascination for him.

Chapter 18

He swept the area with the beam of his high-powered flashlight. Found the woman still bound in the corner.

Her head reared up like a frightened animal, her eyes blinking in the illumination. Satisfaction seared through him at the sight. She was waiting for him. Awaiting the tutelage that would be her redemption.

Did she understand that yet? Had he banished the demons that possessed her body, the ones that made her fight and kick and scream against her salvation? Evil could be difficult to expel from a person once it took hold. The enjoyment he took in banishing it owed nothing to the physical. No, that came from knowing he was doing God's will.

He took another step closer, enjoying the way she strained against her bonds. Acting alone to cast out her demons had proved to be as rewarding as he'd remembered.

The stone floor was cool against his bare feet. He'd shucked his clothes inside the door. In his free hand, he carried the bag of necessary equipment. He still had plans for Kathleen Sebern. So many plans to drive out the devil.

But when he drew closer to her, she just huddled in a ball at his feet, the fight seemingly gone from her. He gave her a light kick and got nothing more than a whimper. Was this another trick? Was she waiting until he got nearer to loosen her bonds before striking at him again, kicking and biting like a wild thing? Anticipation eddied inside him at the thought.

He reached down and grabbed her hair, dragging her upward, bracing for a battle. Eager for it. Her body remained limp. Her eyes closed. He twisted her nipple cruelly and got barely a flinch in response.

Disappointment raged through him. He'd had such plans for her. Plans to pit himself against the evil that possessed her and conquer it. Cast it out with the purity of his intent. He shoved her away forcefully, and she fell to the ground. Lay still.

He drew a deep calming breath. And then another. And when his head cleared, disappointment had been replaced with understanding. His own needs couldn't supersede God's will. Goodness had already triumphed. It was time to finish it.

He strode over, hauled her up by the binds on her wrists, and dragged her over to the stone altar in the center of the space. From the basket there, he took out a root and, ripping the tape from her lips, pried open her mouth to shove it inside. He had to manually work her jaws to chew it.

"Swallow," he commanded. He picked up the water bottle from the basket and squirted water down her throat until she gagged, choked, then swallowed.

"It is by the spirit of God that I cast out demons, Kathleen." He shoved her back on the altar, climbed on top of her, and spread her legs. Ramming himself inside her, his hands closed around her neck as he began to thrust.

"Surrender to the spirit all the evil in your past," he panted. His hips pounded against hers, his gaze fixed on her eyes as they began to bulge. Finally she began to struggle a little as the life was slowly squeezed out of her.

And when death took her, he came with a power that could only be described as holy.

When it was over, after he'd dressed, there were the usual preparations to be made. Her body to be washed down. Her nails scrubbed. He worked swiftly in near silence, his only light coming from the flashlight he'd set nearby. The heavy chain he wrapped around her body added thirty pounds to her weight, but it was necessary.

There couldn't be another mistake.

He'd return later for her clothes and purse. They'd be disposed of far away from here. But first Kathleen would find her final resting place. A fitting burial.

At the bottom of Ashton's Pond.

———

Ramsey rolled to a stop before the 1960s ranch-style home and returned the wave of the man riding the lawnmower in diagonal patterns across the yard. Apparently John Kenner, ex–chief of police, was an early riser. It was barely seven-thirty.

She got out of the car, walked up to the gate, and took a good long look at the man who'd signed the police report for Dev's father's arrest. Midseventies, she estimated, as he jostled over the velvety grass, with a build more beefy than fat. He rounded a tree, saw her standing there, and cut the power on the machine. Ramsey took that as an invitation.

The wide expanse of grass was still damp with dew. But Kenner had considerately caught the grass clippings in a bag attached to the mower, so she didn't have to worry about leaving here smelling like a haymow.

"Mornin' to you."

"Mr. Kenner." Having left her sunglasses in the SUV, Ramsey shielded her eyes from the early morning glare. "I'm Ramsey Clark, special consultant working with the TBI."

"Figured who you were." Kenner made no move to dismount, but his expression was friendly enough. His skin was ruddy, the color of a naturally light-complected man who'd spent too much time in the sun. "I know most folks in this town. And of course I'd heard 'bout you joinin' the team investigatin' the murder."

"I didn't really come to see you in an official capacity," she admitted. And now that she had, she was feeling a small modicum of embarrassment. But this was important to Dev, and if she was truthful, a few questions kept nagging her about that report all those years ago. "Actually I came to talk to you about the last arrest you made for a murder here.

The last time the red mist was sighted, nearly thirty years ago."

The smile had vanished from his lips. And she recognized the flash of pure cop in his eyes. "You mean Lucas Rollins."

"I do."

He scratched his jaw, not bothering to hide the speculation in his gaze. "Can't see what that has to do with the poor girl they found in the pond."

Ramsey shifted so the sun was at her back so she wouldn't have to squint at the man. "Probably nothing. But it's my job to make sure we aren't overlooking a pattern of some type."

He snorted. "You mean the legend? Shoot, that's all a bunch of bunk. Never has served more than to rile people up and set tongues to waggin'. Lucas Rollins wasn't in his right mind to do what he did. Doesn't make him part of the local superstition, just makes the whole sorry mess sadder."

"He wasn't in his right mind. Because of the alcohol he'd had to drink that night." Ramsey slipped her hands in the pocket of her suit jacket. It was the last fresh set of clothes she had with her, she recalled with a mental sigh. When she left here, she needed to hunt down the nearest Laundromat and make note of its hours.

"That's right."

"Were you used to seeing him that way? Was he a big drinker?"

"Can't say that he was." The ex-chief's manner was still polite, if not especially forthcoming.

"That's what I've heard, too. So that's what keeps me wondering. A guy with no reputation for getting shit-faced goes off and drinks so much he commits murder and doesn't recall it the next day." She paused, but the man said nothing. "There wasn't anything in the police report about where Lucas had been during the intervening time. Whom he might have been with."

Kenner's mouth twisted. "So seein' that you figured maybe we're that slow down here, just yokels who don't know how to do real police work."

Her gaze never left his. "Or that you had a reason for not

including your findings in the police report. Now that I've met you, I'm betting on the latter."

There was a flicker in his eyes, but his expression remained impassive. It was enough to solidify her opinion. This man had known how to do his job.

Which meant he'd been keeping a secret for over thirty years.

When he spoke again, his voice was pitched low enough to be barely audible over the sound of the idling mower. "I done a bit of research on you. 'Nough to know you started out with TBI. Probably used to big-city crime and a big-city pace. Not sayin' one type of experience is better than t'other, but they're different, know what I'm sayin'?"

Ramsey nodded. Found herself leaning forward a little so as not to miss a word.

"Another difference 'tween your sorta work and bein' a local law enforcement officer is the local part. Whatever happens, wherever my investigations took me, at the end of the day, I still lived here. Still ran into the same people day after day. Still lived by the same neighbors. Still churched with the same congregation. Not sayin' that changes the job, but it changes the way we *do* our job. That means not embarrassin' people unnecessarily. Not makin' public things that don't change the outcome of a case. Not feedin' the local grapevine with details that are no one's business. That's part of bein' a small-town cop."

"So you're saying the missing information—where Lucas was drinking and with whom—you covered that in your investigation but didn't include it in the police report for fear of embarrassing him?" It was hard to imagine what could have seemed more embarrassing at the time than being charged with murder. Unless . . .

Even as comprehension hit her, Kenner was leaning forward to rev up the mower's engine, preparing to resume his task. "The missin' details have nothin' to do with this recent murder case, I can tell you that. Other than that, they aren't your affair, so as far as I'm concerned, this conversation is over."

He turned the mower and effortlessly got back on track to begin again those regimented diagonals in the lawn. But Ramsey wasn't satisfied yet. She trotted beside the machine, uncaring for the moment that the wet grass was dampening her shoes.

She raised her voice to be heard over the motor. "And if I'm not asking for myself, Chief Kenner? If I'm not asking for this case, just whose business would those details be?"

She knew her question had struck home by the quick sideways glance he threw her. Knew he'd probably heard she and Stryker had been seen together around town.

His answer could barely be heard above the revving of the motor. "If Dev Stryker takes a notion to follow up on that line of questionin', he'd be the one to take up those answers with his mama. No one else's business. Not then. Not now."

———

Ramsey took her time driving back to the motel, first placing a call to Phyllis Trammel, Cassie Frost's landlady in Kordoba, before checking in with Agent Powell. From the tone in Powell's voice, she recognized her conversation with him might be as fruitless as her words with Trammel.

"We got in one interview with Sanders this morning before he lawyered up, and he didn't give us jack when it comes to new information." The older man's voice was frustrated. "Workin' out a deal now where we'll allow him supervised access to his computer files so he can still run his business, in exchange for his cooperation. 'Course what he and his high-priced attorney consider cooperation isn't likely to jibe with our interpretation."

"Rollins is going through his background to see if he can establish a link with a relative in the Buffalo Springs area."

Powell grunted on the other end of the line. "Has to be done, but it's just as likely that the killer is the source of the local link, rather than Sanders. I've got Matthews runnin' old college classmates, high school friends, and neighbors through the databases for criminal records. With Sanders alibied, it's doubtful he brought a middleman in on the plot. I don't see him wantin' to cut someone else in on the money. He'll be the link to the killer. We just have to work through his past to find it."

She brought him up to date on Jonesy's findings on the fibers. "I'll be sending one of the deputies back to Kordoba to get a sample of Trammel's hair to compare to two strands included in the initial evidence inventory." Injecting a note of humor into her words, she added, "Trammel was rather unhappy with my suggestion that she owned a wig, so the other gray strand is unaccounted for." It was hardly a rarity for them to be unable to match every fiber, stain, or particle of evidence with its source. But she thought Jonesy had done remarkably well doing what he had.

"Anythin' show up on those ViCAP matches yet?"

Briefly, she recounted the conversations she'd had so far with four of the detectives. "I'll follow up on the other two today." But she remembered how returning phone calls like hers were at the bottom of the list of things for a busy detective to do when there were eight or nine active cases being worked at any given time.

"We'll be turnin' Sanders's financials and computer over to forensic accountin' and computer techs at the TBI labs. Jeffries has assured me it'll be given top priority."

About to sign off, Ramsey was struck by a thought. "Oh, Ward, if you get a chance . . . Frost didn't give much of a description of the man she thought was watching her in Lisbon. Tall, thin, gray hair. I wondered if she'd said more to Sanders. He'd indicated also that someone had asked her out at a restaurant. Seems like she would have mentioned it to the police if it were the same guy, but I wondered about it."

"Like I say, Sanders has been pretty useless today. Matthews followed up on that, though, and all he said was that she'd mentioned an older distinguished-lookin' gentleman asking her out right after she'd hit town in Lisbon. Sanders seemed to think she'd mentioned it just to make him jealous, but then his type would think that."

Maybe, Ramsey mused, as they disconnected the call. And maybe she'd succeeded beyond her wildest dreams.

Cassie might have made Sanders so jealous he began to think about getting rid of her altogether.

———————

"Are you busy? Can you talk?"

Dev was squatted among the equipment spread out around him with the open notebooks for his readings. "Never too busy to talk, Denny, you know that. Especially when I'm hopin' you have some answers for me."

From the corner of his eye, he could see the oldest of the Landish girls, Sissy, he thought it was, peering at him from around the corner of the porch. The old Kuemper place had changed hands dozens of times since Lora Kuemper had met her untimely demise in the well on this property. Fortunately for him, Stella and Eldin Landish were intrigued enough by his work to offer him free access to their property.

Their three girls were curious enough to be watching him with a pair of binoculars the entire time, a fact that would likely have their very proper mother faint of mortification if she caught them at it.

"Well, I don't know that my news is as exciting as having someone heave a brick through your window, but hopefully it's more helpful."

Dev had called Denny back after he'd cleaned up the mess last night and given him an abbreviated version of the events that had interrupted their call. "What d'ya got for me?"

"More than I should have in this time frame, luckily for you. Turns out there was a thread about your Rufus Ashton in an honor's thesis written by one of my undergrad research assistants last year. 'The Spread of Religious Methodology in Early America.' Seems your Rufus Ashton was more than the founder of the first church in Buffalo Springs. He founded the religion called Sancrosanctity, an offshoot from the Church of Elders."

Feeling a familiar thread of impatience, Dev interrupted, as pleasantly as possible, "Got anythin' good from this paper?"

"Well, at the very least, we've got another living case of how striving for religious acceptance can morph into intoler-

ance. At the most . . . we just might have a case where religion is a guise for church-condoned serial torture, rape, and
murder."

The words had Dev sinking to a sitting position, juggling
his cell phone with the notebook and pen he snatched up. He
was only half aware of the wrestling match going on some
distance away on the Landish porch between two of the daugh-
ters struggling for possession of the binoculars.

"You've got my attention, Denny."

"Somehow I thought that would do it."

"Detective Hopwood? I'm glad I caught you. I've left a
couple messages regarding a ViCAP hit linking elements of
one of your cases to a current homicide I'm working."

"Yeah, I've been meaning to get back to you," was the reply on the other end of the line. Ramsey interpreted that to
mean that the DC detective had placed her on the bottom of a
very long list of things to do. She didn't harbor a grudge.
Working for Raiker gave her the unheard-of luxury of working one case at a time, compared to juggling a dozen or more
active cases as she had for the TBI. Real police work was often
a simple case of luck and perseverance, because law enforcement agencies were notoriously understaffed and under-
funded.

"The case I'm interested in would have been from four
years ago. Victim's name was Cordell. She'd been raped and
strangled and had ingested a foreign object prior to her
death."

"Right, I remember. Some sort of plant or something. Can't
say I spent much time figuring out exactly what it was."

For a moment, Ramsey was speechless. She'd been half
convinced that she was going to strike out with Hopwood,
the last detective she had to contact regarding the ViCAP
hits, the same way she had all the others. "You're saying the
foreign object was a plant?"

"Likely a root, our lab guy said. Hey, I'm on my way out
on a call, so I'm gonna walk and talk, that okay with you?"

"It's fine."

"'Course I didn't get the lab work back for about six months, and the case had landed in the unsolved file by then." Ramsey could hear traffic on the other end of the line and assumed the detective had walked outside of the precinct house. "It wasn't an intoxicant, the tech could tell me that, so that blew my theory that it was some sort of weird drug use gone bad. Near as I recall, I figured she was raped and killed outside, and he forced her to eat whatever was available. Like a control thing."

"Where'd you discover her?"

"Almost didn't find the body. It'd been weighted down with rocks and ropes and tossed in the Potomac. A fisherman hooked something and waded out to see what his line had caught on."

"So, no physical evidence." A feeling of frustration swept over Ramsey. A watery dump site was another similarity in the two cases, but it was difficult to get too excited in lieu of physical evidence that was going to help solve the case. Either of them.

"Well the rope was clothesline that could be bought at any discount store. There were a couple gray hairs twined in the knots but difficult to tell if it could have come from the killer or a worker on the assembly line packaging it."

The words had a spark of interest flaring. "Gray hair?"

"I know what you're thinking." The detective's voice was heavy with irony. "Forget DNA. It was human hair, but came from a wig. Useless any way you look at it. Look, I'm en route to a crime scene. I'm not sure there's much else I can tell you, so if you don't have other questions . . ."

"Just one. Is the evidence still intact if we wanted to send someone over to collect that hair to compare to a couple we found on my case?"

"Should be, but I'd have to find out. Stuff disappears sometimes."

After eliciting his promise to check on the evidence in the morning, Ramsey disconnected the call. But her mind was still racing. She went to the evidence board that she'd had

Jonesy move from the mobile lab to the cabin. Stared at the individual gray hairs bagged and tagged neatly on the board. Those with the decidedly blue tint would no doubt match the sample the deputy was bringing back from Phyllis Trammel.

That left those from a wig, the mere mention of which had caused Ms. Trammel to take all sorts of offense. If the woman could be believed, she didn't own one.

Don't need no false hair, thank you very much! I got plenty of my own, and I don't 'preciate you sayin' any different!

She stared at the board blindly, tapping her closed cell phone on her palm. And then there was the distinguished-looking gentleman who'd asked Cassie Frost out at the Lisbon restaurant.

Ramsey couldn't help wondering if *distinguished looking* was another phrase for gray-haired.

She heard the crunch of wheels on gravel and went to the window. Felt a ribbon of pleasure unfurl when she saw Dev behind the wheel of the car. And although her customary guard was present, it didn't raise as swiftly as usual. Inner alarms didn't shrill when she threw open the door and stepped outside. She watched him stop in his tracks when he saw her, his smile slow and wide and devastating. And the female heart inside her cop's skin gave a stutter.

"So are you just going to stand there with that sappy grin on your face, or should we go next door?" Her voice sounded just a little too breathless for comfort.

"I'm partial to goin' next door." He didn't walk so much as stalk toward her as she pulled the office door shut and unlocked the door to her cabin. And she could feel an answering smile on her face even as she swung the door shut behind him. Felt it grow wider as he caught her around the waist and twirled her into his arms.

His eyes, when they looked down into hers, were wicked. "You look good enough to eat."

"You must be partial to navy drab."

"I'm partial to you."

There was no response to be made to that because his

mouth, that clever intoxicating mouth, was on hers. Inviting a response. Demanding one. And for once in her life, Ramsey gave it freely, without thought of guard or defenses.

His taste ricocheted through her system, pinballs of pleasure racketing off nerve endings along the way. There was urgency here, urgency she shared despite having had him less than forty-eight hours earlier. But it was layered beneath the soft lazy seduction of stroking tongues, clinging lips. He framed her face in both of his hands, kissing her with a single-minded intensity that was all the more powerful for being focused solely on her. And when the nerve-snapping chemistry sparked to life as easily as a match to a gasoline-soaked fuse, that, too, was familiar. She was beginning to accept this was the way it would be between them. At least during the time they could be together.

"I missed you," he murmured against her lips.

She cupped his hands with her palms for a moment. Savored the warmth of flesh against flesh. "You just saw me."

"You're a dangerous woman, Ramsey Clark." His lips were curved, but his eyes were alight with intensity. "You've got a way of working under a man's skin."

"Sounds painful," she managed lightly.

"I had a feeling you might describe this that way, but I certainly wouldn't."

She didn't trust that expression on his face. Smug and supremely male. "And how would you describe *this*?"

"In spite of your better judgment, you and I are having us a romance." Her expression must have looked as stupefied as she felt, because his blasted grin was back. He dropped a kiss on her forehead. "Like it or not, you'll have a hard time denyin' it. But I look forward to you trying to, just the same."

Chapter 19

Because Ramsey's jaw was hanging open, Dev slipped a finger beneath her chin to help her close it.

Not surprisingly, she batted his hands out of the way. "Sex," she croaked.

He gave a meaningful glance toward the bed. "Okay."

"No, I mean we have sex. Had," she corrected herself. "Once."

"Actually, it was three . . ."

"No, one night." She slipped out of his arms. He immediately missed the feel of her. Which meant he had it worse than he thought, but he was still convinced he could handle this.

He was becoming less and less convinced he could handle *her*.

"It would be a mistake to confuse that with romance, something all tied up with hearts and flowers. We don't need that. Neither of us."

He was past the time he could claim that himself, though he was unsurprised she did. And it calmed something inside him to see her reacting just this way. Because he was coming to know her, to predict her reactions, he saw just how close panic was running beneath her normally impassive exterior. "At some point, you and I are gonna have a talk 'bout what it is we do need. But for now . . ." For now, he needed to soothe the nerves that were all but jittering off her. "It's enough you tell me you missed me, too."

The lift of her shoulder was jerky. But she didn't bolt

when he slid an arm around her waist again and pulled her closer. "I gave you a thought a time or two."

"Poetry." He pretended to dab at his eyes with his free hand. Needed quick reflexes to avoid the jab she would have sent to his ribs. "Big-city women like you come down here, turn a simple man's head with your fast talk and smooth lines."

"I have a feeling your head is turned so easily you're lucky it doesn't fly off."

A thread of pure delight ran through him. "Why is it we sensitive sorts always fall for the hard cases?"

"Maybe you can't resist a challenge."

He recognized the underlying seriousness of her words, wondered at it. "Maybe . . ." Dev ducked his head, nipped at the cord on the side of her throat. Was satisfied to feel her body relax a bit more against his. ". . . it's because I recognize the softness beneath is all the more satisfying for bein' disguised." He nipped again, less gently this time. Immediately soothed the area with the tip of his tongue.

"Dev . . ."

A wise man realized when not to push. A smarter one yet knew enough to change the subject when it was apt to turn to something he didn't want to hear.

He gave her bottom an affectionate squeeze and deliberately set her away from him. "Enough. If I let you have your way with me, we'll spend the afternoon rollin' on that lumpy motel bed and not get any work done."

Her look was withering. "You flatter yourself."

"When no one else will." To keep from reaching for her again, he tucked his fingers into his jeans' pockets. "Can't think straight when you're enticin' me that way, and I've got somethin' to tell you. I think it just might prove to be a real lead in our case."

The look that settled over her expression then was pure cop. "*Our* case? You don't have a case, Stryker. You have . . ." She made a gesture with her hand. "Ghosts and readings and dancing lights that may or may not be real lights. This investigation—the police end of it—doesn't concern you."

There was no reason that should have wounded. But it did. A quick vicious burn. "Okay then. Get your purse. We'll go out to lunch instead."

Ramsey didn't move. She was watching him closely, seemingly fighting an inner battle. "I'm not belittling what you do. I can't say I understand it—I don't at all—but I got a little taste of it the other night and can certainly agree that some things aren't easily explained."

He turned toward the door. "The Half Moon doesn't open until four, but The Henhouse serves until two. Unless you want to head over to Kwik Serv for another pizza."

"I'm not hungry."

Maybe not for food, but if he didn't miss his guess, curiosity was already working at her. "You can watch me eat." He headed to the door

"You could still tell me what information you've come across," she said to his back.

"Nope, you're probably right." It took effort to toss a friendly grin over his shoulder. "You don't need me messin' around in your investigation."

"I didn't say . . . shit." She hissed out a breath, jammed her fingers through her hair. "I'm sorry, okay? That was snotty and mean. And automatic." There was a bleakness in her eyes, there and gone so quickly he might have thought he imagined it if he hadn't seen it there before. "The thing is, I'm all those things, Stryker. You've said it yourself. I'm mean-tempered and surly, and other people's feelings are rarely my first consideration."

His ire faded in the face of her misery. He gave a slow nod. "You can be all those things, Ramsey. Can't deny it. But you're more, too. And damned if it isn't the more that trips me up, every time."

"Since you're outside the investigation, discussing the case with you is enough of a stretch. I can't divulge any aspect of the case not already public—"

"When have I asked you to?"

"—but I'm interested in the information you have. I'm just saying it might be a one way street."

The words struck him as ominous only because they so closely paralleled what he feared might end up being the summation of their relationship. He decided then and there he'd be having a beer with his meal. He'd never met a woman who took more energy just to be around than this one.

"In that case, you can buy me lunch. Even up the score."

They ended up settling on pizza, and Dev insisted on eating it in the middle of the town square. Ramsey expressed some uneasiness about him drinking a Bud Lite in the center of town, directly across from the courthouse, but he waved away her concern. They were in far more danger from Mary Sue Talbot if she found out they'd swiped the quilt from the motel bed to spread out beneath the huge boughs of the ancient oak than from an enterprising town cop set to write him a ticket for an open container.

Eventually Ramsey even seemed to get into the mood, although he'd be willing to bet she couldn't name the last time she'd been on a picnic. She'd slipped out of her suit jacket, seeming unconcerned that her shoulder holster showed. He'd managed to talk her into unbuttoning the top two buttons of her short sleeve blouse, but only because there was no one close enough to notice.

And he found he liked this side of her, a little too much, when she relaxed enough to set aside the uptight cop and just enjoy *being*.

Dev set his beer on the pizza box and took a healthy bite of the slice he held in his hand. He reflected that it was just as well Ramsey had had the foresight to buy paper plates, since he'd talked her into a pizza loaded with all the fixings.

As if in response to the thought, a glob of tomato sauce plopped off his pizza to the plate beneath it.

"Okay, give."

He made a show of looking first at the quilt, then at her. "Here?" Then dodged the wadded up napkin she threw at him.

"The information you said you ran across."

"Oh, that." He chewed reflectively, considering the sight she made in the buttoned-down white shirt and navy slacks. "Y'know, if it weren't for the gun, you'd look like a Catholic school girl in uniform. Sorta Mary Katherine Gallagher, packin' heat."

She looked blank. "Who?"

Of course she wouldn't understand a reference to old *Saturday Night Live* reruns. He doubted popular culture headed the list of her personal favorites. And she was far better looking than the comedienne who'd made the *SNL* character famous, with her short streaked brown hair, hazel eyes, and long lithe curves. "Never mind."

He caught a teetering mountain of sauerkraut before it slid from his pizza and resettled it more securely. "We've discussed it before when we went to talk to local healers. How the plant I shouldn't know anythin' 'bout could have somethin' to do with healin', or witchcraft, or religion." He saw the slight wince she gave at his verbal jab and immediately felt petty and mean for slipping it in.

"So I got to thinkin' . . ." He finished off his slice of pizza and reached for another. Ramsey was still working on her first, but only because she was such a finicky eater and she was picking all the toppings she didn't like off and leaving them in a growing mound on her plate. "Coupla people have mentioned this Rufus Ashton fella, the town founder, and how he also started the first church in this area."

She took a careful bite, as if afraid to encounter anything not already preapproved. He imagined she approached life much the same way she did a kitchen-sink pizza. She wasn't one to enjoy meeting the unexpected.

"And I happen to know someone in that line of research. He checked some stuff out for me, and I found out this Rufus Ashton left Pennsylvania back in the early 1870s. Belonged to the Church of Elders. Seems he and several other young men were ordained and given money to buy land in different states to spread the religion. But once in Tennessee, Ashton had a fallin' out with the church bigwigs. Had his own set of beliefs and was eventually kicked out of the church for them. But until that time, there are records of his doin's in the church's name."

He let her digest, both the pizza and his words, and waited for the inevitable questions.

"So Ashton settles Buffalo Springs, starts the town, begins the church. Builds that house where Rose Thornton lives now."

"Actually begins the first bank and the quarry 'mong other things, but seems he didn't cotton to just anyone bein' in his church. Had quite strict standards, did Rufus Ashton, and some of those standards led to the Church of Elders cuttin' him loose years later."

"Must've been bad to have the Church of Elders disagree with him," she observed. He noted that in her distraction, she didn't even seem to notice she'd just bitten into a mushroom that she'd missed in her earlier mining. "Aren't they the ones who believe only thirty-five people a century go to heaven, and the rest of the godly go to like a press box or something?"

He made the mistake of trying to swallow when she'd made that last remark. Almost choked for his efforts. "I believe it's compared more to a waiting room while the holiest in the church prepare the faithful's way into an eternity of paradise."

Ramsey snorted and reached for her Diet Coke. "Sounds like a religious snipe hunt to me."

She had the most fascinating mind. "In a sense. Anyway, I'd always imagined there's some wicked politickin' goin' on tryin' to get to be one of the chosen in that century." He bit off a piece of pizza, chewed reflectively. "I mean, I've seen people get downright nasty just to secure their spot at the annual Buffalo Days Parade. I can't imagine what some would do to wedge their way into eternal paradise." He thought of Reverend Biggers then. Considered it fortunate all around that the man was a Baptist. "Anyway, one of the first instances of Ashton's beliefs departin' from the church's was his enthusiastic way of metin' out punishment for violations of the faith. Another was his view on marriage. Seems he was for it. Over and over and over again."

She paused in the midst of bringing the slice of denuded pizza to her mouth. "He was a bigamist?"

"He was a 'celestial channeler,'" Dev corrected. He wished he'd brought his laptop, where he'd downloaded all the notes Denny had sent, but he thought he remembered that part correctly. "He maintained that he was in direct contact with God. And apparently his being in direct contact with nubile young virgins, in the plural tense, just made the signals stronger."

"What, his penis was a sort of heavenly antenna? A divining rod in the most literal sense?"

That had him bent over in a spate of coughing so violent he vowed to stop trying to eat until this conversation was over. When he recovered his power of speech, he gasped, "You are a dangerous woman to eat 'round. Are you tryin' to kill me?"

She selected another slice of pizza. Her technique was losing some of its earlier finesse: this time, she merely flicked the excess toppings off with her finger. "C'mon, tell me the rest. I fail to see how it remotely connects to this case, but I find myself morbidly fascinated. So this Rufus Ashton guy—a perv of the highest order—starts this harem of women in the name of religion. Then what?"

"Apparently Rufus Ashton, as head of the church, was allowed unlimited wives. The men in his church, the ones he allowed to be a part of it, were allowed wives in direct correlation to their standing with Ashton. Children were raised in a community atmosphere, and the female children were kept separate from the males. Many of the male children were banished from the town between the ages of ten to sixteen for various offenses."

Her voice was caustic. "Here's betting their biggest offense was making the old guys in the church look bad in comparison."

"That's where Denny's research starts moving into supposition, but yeah. That's what he's figurin'. Of course by that time, the main Church of Elders had cut all ties with Ashton, so most of their written records end, at least relatin' to him. But Denny had an undergrad student use this topic as an honor's thesis recently, and there were a few more details uncovered in her research. Ashton did a bit of travelin' and preachin' on the side, in an attempt to gather more church members. In 1888, he was travelin' through what's now southeastern Illinois, and he stayed with a farm couple by the name of Klinkel."

He took a moment to tip his beer to his lips and swallow before he continued. "The Klinkels were quite taken with his preachin'. Seems he'd been 'round that area before. And durin' the course of his stay with them, he took a shine to their daughter, Ruth. Pretty as a speckled pup she was, and Denny's student apparently scared up some photos that proved it."

Ramsey put a hand to her stomach. "Don't tell me. She was his next 'bride.'"

"You guessed it. He convinced her folks it was Ruth's path to salvation, and they agreed to stand up with her as the Reverend Ashton took her hand in marriage. I 'spect it was pretty convenient with him bein' able to say the words over them, while bein' the groom and all."

"How old was she?" Ramsey had given up all pretense of eating. Her gaze was grim.

"Fourteen."

"And he was likely decades older. He prettied it up with religion, but a pedophile is still a pedophile," she muttered.

He was to the part of the story that put him off his own appetite. "Details from here out are sketchy and garnered from genealogy buffs in the modern Klinkel family. Apparently there are letters that still exist between Ruth and her parents. Life in Buffalo Springs was hard. She'd joined thirteen other wives of Rufus Ashton, and the man was a strict taskmaster. Worked them like slaves. The labor of men and women alike was responsible for building the church, startin' the quarry, and other businesses. Ashton expected absolute obedience to him and to the church's guidelines, which of course he dictated. Accordin' to these letters, he retained absolute control over his wives, children—one letter mentioned he had nearly forty—and other members of the church. Dissenters were dealt with harshly."

He heard a slight sound and glanced down. Saw her tight grip on the soda can had crushed in its sides.

"How harshly?"

"Public whippin's and whispers of more private punishment given out by the disciples of the church to the 'sinners.' Some of the people, men and women alike, disappeared and their names were never spoken again."

"I hope that convinced her family to act."

He gave a slow nod. "Thomas Klinkel went down to Tennessee to fetch his daughter home, marriage vows or no marriage vows. But you have to recall what the mail service was like in those days. What travel consisted of. By the time he received that last letter and got to Tennessee, at least a month has passed since his daughter had written it. Probably more. He sent one letter to his wife shortly after he'd gotten to Buffalo Springs. Couldn't get anyone to talk to him about Ruth. The next day he had a meetin' planned with Rufus Ashton, and he promised his wife he'd be bringin' their Ruth back home."

Dev paused a moment, but it was a moment too long. Ramsey interrupted his conclusion by stating, "And neither of them were seen or heard from again."

His eyes narrowed in irritation. "How do you do that?"

"Deduction." She made an impatient gesture. "And it ended there?"

Piqued, he considered not answering. The woman knew how to take the bang out of a good story. "It ended there. With young ones at home and now workin' the farm alone, Matilda Klinkel had no way to find out what happened on her own. She did contact the US Marshal in the region, but the only word she heard was that her husband had never been seen in town and her daughter had died three months earlier of cholera."

"Except she had letters disproving both those statements."

"She did. But she was never able to interest the marshal into followin' up. The secrets surroundin' Thomas Klinkel's and Ruth Ashton's deaths were buried with them."

The fierce frown on her face was contemplative, and he reached for another slice of pizza while she reflected on the tale he'd recounted. Folks sometimes had a way of glorifying the past, as if simpler times made for purer values. But he figured people were people no matter what time period they lived in. And he had to admit the thought of their town father being part of something so grisly made him feel a bit queasy, over a century later.

After several minutes, she shrugged. "There has to be information around we can dig up about this. Every town keeps historical records of details regarding their founding fathers, even if they tend to glorify them a bit."

"Tried that." His bottle empty now, he ran a thumbnail around the edge of the damp label, loosening it. "I spent some rather painful time in the Historical Museum—don't ask—and read the extremely borin' journals talkin' 'bout life in those times and extollin' Ashton's virtues." He'd assumed the authors had been Ashton relatives but suspected now they'd all been dutiful Ashton wives. "I found nothin' that serves as verification for the worst of the story. Even went to the library, where I got only enough information to know what direction to have my buddy start lookin'." Honesty had him adding, "Probably could go back when I have a bit more time and look harder, but I'm doubtin' I'll find anythin' close to describin' Ashton's real actions."

He saw the exact moment she'd reached a decision. Felt a surge of impatience as she said the words he fully expected to hear. "Interesting. Sad even. But this has nothing to do with Cassie Frost's murder. Regardless of what you decide is causing those lights, you're not going to convince me Rufus Ashton rises up again every generation to exact punishment on the unworthy."

"Wouldn't try to."

She reached for her pizza. Chewed ferociously. "Do we

know anything about the church offshoot Ashton started? Sancrosanctity? Does it still exist?"

"Denny says there's no record of it anywhere, although various cult-type religions include a similar belief or two in their own guidelines."

"How many churches are in Buffalo Springs?"

This was an area he definitely wasn't well versed in. "Well, let's see now." He rubbed his chin. "We've got our Southern Baptist, of course. There's the United Methodist over on East Union. They've always been regarded a bit suspiciously by the Baptists, but I figure that's only 'cuz they bring in more tithin' every year despite having half the number of members in the congregation." He searched his memory. Found it embarrassingly empty. "I know there's a Presbyterian. Bet you didn't know Mark Rollins is a deacon there."

When he stopped, he caught her eyes on him, amused, and he shrugged. "Okay. So I'm no expert in the local congregations. I go occasionally with my granddaddy when I'm visitin'. He's a lifelong member of the United Methodist. But if you're really interested in learnin' more 'bout local churches, we can go talk to a pastor. Take 'bout ten minutes."

"Seems like a waste of time. Like I say, it isn't related to my case."

Although there was every reason to agree with her, he couldn't prevent a stab of disappointment. "Not yet."

"Not at all," she said flatly. "The victim's sister said she wasn't a member in any particular church. And certainly nothing else points to a religious bent to the investigation."

"Unless the plant you were interested in turns out to have religious implications." He helped himself to the last slice of pizza, watched her silently wrestle with his words. There wasn't an impulsive bone in Ramsey's body. Every move would be carefully weighed and evaluated before decided on. What made her a good cop could also drive him crazy if he let it.

"You have an idea of a pastor to talk to? I don't have much more than those ten minutes you mentioned. I need to get back to work. And sometime today I have to find a place I can do my laundry."

Satisfied, he hid his smile by ducking his head to gather up the trash. He'd figured on that intelligent curiosity of hers to close the deal. "Might've underestimated the time it will take, but it won't be much longer than that. And I've got a solution to your laundry problem. You can do it at my house. After work," he hastened to add when she threw him a thoughtful look. "I'll fire up the grill. How do you feel about hamburgers?"

"Mildly interested, actually."

"You can bring the wine."

She stood up and slipped back into her suit jacket as he gathered up the trash. "Wine? With hamburgers?" She waited for him to step off the quilt before picking it up, giving it a slight shake, and folding it.

"It's hamburgers. We have to class it up."

"What's the best place around here to buy wine that doesn't come in a box?"

"Hurley's Liquor is on Main across from the police station. They close promptly at five." That brought a slight frown to her face, and he knew she was thinking of having to interrupt her work to shop. He didn't offer to take care of it for her. It was time, he decided, for the woman to start putting herself out a bit for their relationship.

She skated a glance at him. "I wonder if they carry Boone's Farm."

He was pretty sure she was kidding. "Just remember you're drinkin' whatever you buy. But if you need recommendations, all you have to do is ask." They moved in the direction of the car, pausing only so he could dump the trash in the litter can.

"I'm not completely without social graces, Stryker."

He couldn't deny a quick flicker of relief. "In that case, bring two bottles."

Chapter 20

Teddy Molitor, head pastor of United Methodist Church, had one of those faces that would look young well into old age. Apple-cheeked and smooth-faced, he had short brown hair and dark-rimmed glasses covering kind gray eyes. He was exactly as tall as Dev, which meant those eyes gazed directly into his, brimming—at least to Dev's imagination—with quiet reproach.

"Devlin." Because he stuck out his hand, there was nothing for Dev to do but to shake it. "I'd heard you were home. Thought I might see you accompany your granddaddy one of these Sundays."

He swallowed hard around a ball of guilt that was decades in the making. "I 'spect you will. One of these Sundays."

Seemingly satisfied, the man turned his gaze to Ramsey, leaving Dev with a notable feeling of relief. "This is Ramsey Clark. She's workin' with Mark Rollins on the murder of that woman coupla weeks ago."

Teddy's expression went sorrowful. He gripped Ramsey's hand in both of his. "Thank you for that, ma'am. It can't be easy on you, that line of work. Bless you for havin' the strength to do it."

Ramsey looked even more ill at ease than he felt. "I appreciate it. I hope we're not taking you away from anything."

Brows skimming upward, Dev sent her a look of approval. Either holy men put Ramsey on her best behavior, or she was learning the ways of the rural south. That was as close to small talk as he'd ever heard out of her.

Of course she was a product of the south, he reminded himself. Mississippi, she'd said. Although she'd rid herself of the telltale drawl, he recalled that she could summon it whenever it suited her. She'd revealed just enough for him to figure the accent had probably been the easiest part of her past to shed.

"We have a couple questions, but I promise we won't keep you long," she was saying. "Dev wasn't able to tell me how many churches there are in town."

He stifled a wince as Teddy's thoughtful gaze flicked to him. "Always been most familiar with this one," he hastened to put in. The other man didn't look convinced, but he was too polite to dispute him.

Teddy's attention returned to Ramsey. "Are you lookin' for a place to worship, Miz Clark?"

If he wasn't so relieved to have Teddy's focus off him, Dev might have felt sorry for Ramsey. The shock in her expression was quickly followed by horror. "Uh . . . no. Do I need to be a member of the congregation for you to answer questions?"

Teddy laughed easily. "No, ma'am. I was just . . . well the truth of it is, I'm cursed with a curiosity befittin' a cat. Surely your interest doesn't have anythin' to do with the case you're workin'."

"No. Reverend." That last was tacked on, as if unsure exactly how to address a man of the cloth.

"I'm a bit of a crime-show buff," he admitted in a shamefaced aside. "Oh, I know TV is nothin' like real life. But I find myself sittin' in front of the set several times a week anyway, tryin' to solve the crimes before the detectives in the show." He looked at her expectantly. "In your expert opinion, which of the crime shows on TV these days are most realistic?"

"I'm sorry. I don't watch much TV."

"Of course." He waved a hand. "And if you did, why would you choose to watch the same thing you deal with in your work? Let's see." He paused a moment. "You asked about churches in town. At last count we had eleven."

Ramsey gaped at him. Dev was mildly surprised himself. Certainly he was aware of the churches dotting the town even if he couldn't name them all. But he would have been hard pressed to come up with the number.

"There's not even three thousand people in Buffalo Springs." She did some quick math. "That's about two hundred fifty people per church."

"Far less than that, I'm afraid. Even countin' the people who live in the outlyin' areas." Teddy's face had gone businesslike. And Dev supposed this *was* his business. "We're church-goin' folk down here, but of course not everyone attends." Although he never once looked in Dev's direction, Dev couldn't help but take the tinge of disapproval in the man's voice personally. He no longer lived in Buffalo Springs, but he also wasn't a regular churchgoer at home. It suited him to blame that on Reverend Biggers and the long-ago trauma he'd inflicted on a ten-year-old boy, and not sheer laziness on his part.

Teddy went on. "And it would be a mistake to assume all churches have the same size congregations. Take ours. We're half the size of the Southern Baptist at two-hundred ninety, but I'm not bein' prideful tellin' you that we make a pretty good showin' for ourselves at the fall festivals and Fourth of July booths." He gave a boyish smile. "Our ladies' guilds bake all the pies for the pie eatin' contest every Buffalo Days, and they start takin' orders after the county fair that keep them busy clear up to fall festival."

"Which church in town is the one Rufus Ashton built?"

Teddy sent Dev a reproving glance. "I'm surprised you didn't know that, Devlin. It's ours, of course." He turned to follow the direction of their gaze at the structure behind him. "The limestone was quarried locally, I'm told, and all the windows 'cept one are original." He made a face. "I know that 'cause we're constantly lookin' for ways to cut the draft through them. The ladies' guild saved up for nearly a decade in the sixties for that big stained glass window facing Main Street. At least what's now Main Street. Way I hear it, back in Ashton's day Main ran north and south. It wasn't until the early twenties that the town leaders renamed it to coincide with the direction the town was growin'."

"I recall hearin' somethin' 'bout that. Used to have flash

floods on the old Main Street, so people were leery 'bout buildin' there."

But Ramsey had clearly remained footed in their earlier conversation. "Is this part the original structure?"

"Why don't you come closer so I can show you?" They fell into step behind Molitor as he led them across a patch of grass toward the church. "It takes a discernin' eye to tell where the original structure ends. Each time an addition was planned, great pains were taken to match the limestone. But basically everywhere there's a difference in the roof pitch, that indicates a newer addition."

He pointed to each in turn. "I'm told the new front steps and gatherin' area were added in the twenties. Then the sacristy burned in 1941, and here's where the new one was built, about three times the original size." Gesturing to another area, he went on. "A cryin' room and social hall were added in the 1980s. Just paid off the note on that two years ago."

With all the various additions, Dev would have expected more of a hodgepodge effect, but the resulting structure was anything but. The effects of modernization coexisted peacefully with the original sections.

Ramsey moseyed to the front, eyeing the magnificent octagon stained glass window above the double oak doors. A wide expanse of steps led to the doors from the sidewalk. Looking back over her shoulder, she asked, "So when did this structure change from Ashton's church of Sancrosanctity to United Methodist?"

Molitor looked puzzled. "This structure has housed a few different denominations in its time, most recently the Pentecostals before United Methodist moved in durin' the 1940s. But I've never heard Ashton's church called that before. What'd you call it? Sancrosanctity?" He shook his head. "Although truth be told, I don't recollect ever hearin' the name of Ashton's church, if it had one. Back then, there were many more nondenominational churches than organized ones."

"So you wouldn't have complete records on the history of this building?" Ramsey asked. She turned and walked back to rejoin them.

"You mean regardin' the original structure? I suspect there'd be some in the museum. But the only church records I have relate to the United Methodist congregation, as is fittin'."

"So where do records like that go?" she wondered. "I imagine there were notations of births and deaths, marriages. They wouldn't just be destroyed."

"Well . . ." Teddy scratched his chin. "If the congregation merely moved from one buildin' to 'nother, of course, the records would move with them. If it dissolved altogether, and it was an organized religion, chances are it would go to the leadin' church in its district. At least Methodists are divided into districts," he added.

"But Ashton's church was an offshoot of the Church of Elders," Dev put in. "My researcher says there was a rift between Ashton and the parent church, so it's doubtful the records would have gone there."

"You're sure Ashton's church doesn't still exist in one of the other eleven churches here in town?"

Teddy was looking increasingly confused. But he answered Ramsey's question. "I can say with complete certainty there is no congregation affiliated with the Church of Elders in Buffalo Springs. I'd be surprised if one existed anywhere in the state. The other ten here are the Baptist, Flat Rock Christian, Christian Reformed, Presbyterian, Episcopals, First Christian, Christian Alliance, First Alliance, Sunrise Salvation, and Spring County Family Worship."

"I'm not familiar with some of those denominations. Isn't it possible that one of them evolved from Sancrosanctity?"

The reverend shook his head in response to Ramsey's question. "I think you two are followin' up on some faulty information. Granted, I've only been in town nine years, but I'm never heard that church name before." His expression grew thoughtful. "I'm certain you'd find the name of Ashton's church referenced somewhere in local history stored at the museum or library, though."

"You'd think so," Dev agreed. "But I couldn't find it when I checked. I had Denny Pruett, a buddy of mine, look up these details and others for me. He's supposed to be top-notch in his field. I trust his research."

If he'd suggested he donned a cape and flew to the moon in his free time, Teddy couldn't have looked more astounded. "Dennis Pruett? Of the NYU Theology Department?"

"That's right." And it tickled Dev no end to see the utter astonishment on Teddy's face at the attested relationship. "He's now dean of theology there."

The reverend withdrew a handkerchief and wiped at his face, an act that could only be habitual since the temperatures were relatively balmy. "You're friends with Dennis Pruett." He repeated the words as if he were having trouble comprehending them. "He's a leading scholar of theology in this country. How did you two ever . . ." He stopped himself just in time, Dev reckoned, to avoid saying something offensive.

"I did him a favor once." And since he didn't want Teddy to keel over in shock right on the church sidewalk, he'd spare him the details.

The pastor's expression was still dazed. "Well." He folded up the handkerchief meticulously and replaced it in his pocket. "I'm 'fraid my thoughts are goin' ever' which way. But if you say you got this information from Dennis Pruett, I can't disbelieve it. I'd be interested in lookin' it over some-time, if you have a mind to share it."

"Sure." Dev was careful not to promise a timeline. In light of their recent conversation, it was doubtful the man could shed any new light on the material Denny had sent him.

Teddy's gaze went past him then, and he gave a slight wince. "I'm sorry. Musta lost all track of time. Here comes my chess partner to continue our weekly game. I don't want to chase you folks off, though. Maybe you'd like to stay and repeat this information to Reverend Biggers. He's been in town far longer than I have."

Dev glanced behind him, met Biggers's baleful gaze as he approached. "Not likely."

"We'd really appreciate it if you'd keep this conversation to yourself," Ramsey put in. "We'd like to talk to the other . . . ah . . . pastors in town and get their opinions."

"Of course." But Teddy looked disappointed. "Feel free to come back anytime."

Biggers stomped by them, muttering audibly, "Godless sinner."

"Bellicose old hellhound," Dev offered pleasantly.

As Teddy's eyes widened, his gaze swinging between the two of them, Biggers scowled fiercely in Dev's direction before continuing up the walk leading to the home next to the church, which housed Teddy's family.

Molitor coughed, lifting his fist to his lips, but Dev saw the smile he was trying to hide. "I'd best get on inside. It doesn't pay to leave Jay alone with the chessboard too long." Conspiratorially, he leaned forward, lowered his voice. "He cheats."

Dev offered a bland smile. "I'm not surprised."

In the car a few moments later, Ramsey worked her shoulders. "Men of the cloth always give me an itchy feeling between the shoulder blades."

"I'd blame it on a guilty conscience if they didn't make me feel exactly the same way. And, of course, my conscience is pure." She smiled, as he'd meant her to. "Do you believe in an afterlife?"

Her expression went pensive. "I can't say I've ever given much thought to heaven. But I hope there is a hell, if only because I've met so many people who belong there."

Her words sobered him. Times like these, when he gave real thought to what she saw every day on the job, he wondered how she could bear it. And understood, just a little better, what drove her.

His granddaddy, as wise about human nature as anyone Dev had ever met, was fond of saying "we all look out our own window." Dev was pretty certain the view out Ramsey's window could be pretty grim.

He cleared his throat and switched the subject. "I have a hard time believin' records from a church are destroyed once the church ceases to exist. Towns this size put a lot of store by their foundin' fathers and the town history. But I sure never found any direct reference to Ashton's church in the record books I went through at the museum or the library." He put the key in the ignition, checked the nonexistent traffic, and pulled away from the curb.

Ramsey looked at him. "And you're sure you saw every record book?"

He thought of Shirley Pierson and the lack of welcome she'd afforded him at the museum. "I can't be positive of that, no."

"Might be worth making another pass at them," she mused. "But I'm not as convinced as Molitor that Ashton's church ceased to exist. I'd like to spend a little time going around to talk to the other ministers in town." She waited a beat. "It'd probably go smoother if you made the introductions. That is, if you have time."

He felt a flicker of satisfaction. Ramsey's intentions stated better than words that whatever she'd earlier said about the information he'd shared about Ashton having no bearing on the case, she was hooked now.

In the next moment, satisfaction was elbowed aside by discomfit. "I've got the time. I just don't know how much use I'm gonna be to you."

Immediate comprehension filled her expression. "The man who knows everybody doesn't know the ministers? Why am I not surprised?"

He shifted uncomfortably. "I probably know 'em. I'm just sayin' if you gave me a map of all the churches in town, I'm not so sure I can label each with its name and the pastor that goes with the church, if you catch my drift." Her look of amusement had him feeling defensive. "Could you do the same if we were talkin' 'bout your hometown?"

"Point taken." Her voice was dry. "Okay. Let's go back and get Molitor to make us a list. That would be quickest."

Dev turned at the next corner and began to backtrack. "It might be best if you go to the door. I'd be lyin' if I said there was love lost 'tween me and Reverend Biggers."

"Really?" False wonder dripped from the word. "And here I thought his greeting was meant as a term of endearment. Sounded like there's ancient history between you two."

"Mostly. Some of it's recent. He took exception to me bein' in the graveyard the other night, regardless of the fact that I had permission to be there." He gave a lift of his shoulder. "We have differin' views on the sins of the fathers, you could say."

The amusement abruptly faded from her expression. "I could rough him up while I'm in there if you want."

For an offer surely made in jest, there was a note of promise in her words. And it warmed him that she'd take his part, even without the details of the bad blood between him and the reverend.

"Old goat would probably enjoy it," he said lightly. He lifted a hand as they passed Margaret Ann Nierling watering her peonies. "I always sorta figured that the ones who are supposed to be beyond reproach are often the biggest sinners out there."

"Yeah." Her voice went bleak. "I've discovered the same thing."

Slowing at the corner of Nantucket, the street running along the west side of the church, he signaled, preparing to turn. Ramsey was facing the window, but her profile was rigid. Sometime, he vowed, she was going to explain to him exactly what had happened in her past that had formed the shield she'd erected around herself. But because it would be meaningless if she didn't volunteer the information willingly, he resigned himself to waiting.

"Back up."

Sending a quizzical look in her direction, he found her still staring out the window.

"Why?"

She reached out to grip his arm, still not looking at him. "Back up!"

Her urgent tone had him looking in his rearview mirror and slowing even more. There was a car following along behind him, making stopping impossible.

"Dev, I'm serious. I want to . . ."

"Hang on. We've got traffic laws even in a town this size."

He came to a complete halt, powered down his window and waved the vehicle behind him to go around.

When the road was clear, he backed up, coming to a halt before the side of the church. He'd barely slowed the car before Ramsey was tumbling out the door. "Where are you . . ." He threw the vehicle into park and got out to follow her, wondering when he'd ever seen this degree of excitement from her before.

"What do you suppose that is?"

He squinted in the direction she was pointing. Felt a pitch in his gut when he saw the images in the simple stained glass windows on either side of the door. On the right was an image of pinecones, a soft brown against the cloudy yellow glass. On the left . . . he cocked his head. "Is that a flower?"

"It's some sort of plant." Adrenaline fairly shimmered off her. "And this was originally the front of the church. That's what you guys were saying earlier. Before they decided Main Street should run the other way. Molitor said these windows were original, right? Each but the front one."

"That's what he said." Regardless of what he was and wasn't supposed to know about the case, Ramsey was working, they'd spent nearly a full day visiting local healers, and she'd offered a small fortune for samples from Raelynn Urdall. It was clear that a plant of some sort figured largely in Ramsey's investigation.

"See what Molitor can tell you about the windows. I'll take some pictures of them." He had all his equipment still in the trunk from the unproductive time he'd spent at the old Kuemper place earlier in the day.

But he was speaking to Ramsey's back. She was already heading for the minister's home.

———

"I would have figured people in a small town would take more interest in the local history." Frustrated, Ramsey ducked into Dev's car and slammed the door after her.

He started the engine. "No luck?"

"Well, Molitor knew the one window had pinecones, of course. But he seemed to think the plant was a generic symbol of new life. Rebirth." Which, when she thought about it, could take on new meaning to a twisted mind raping and killing women and dumping them in whatever body of water was handy.

She applied a mental brake to her thinking. There was no solid connection yet between the Frost killing and the one near DC. But if Detective Hopwood's evidence was still intact, she might get a link through the hair he'd found entwined in the rope.

A sudden thought occurred to her. "Water."

"You're thirsty?"

She shook her head. "In a church, I mean. Water has symbolism, too, right? Baptism. Cleansing sin, or whatnot."

"Most churches have some sort of baptism." He sounded reflective. "I guess cleansin' is as good a term as any. Was Molitor able to put together that list for you?"

"He was, although he seemed a bit distracted by the hellhound playing chess with him."

"Actually has a proper name. Reverend Jay Biggers of the Southern Baptist Church here in town."

"Didn't seem particularly ministerly." What he'd seemed, from her observations, was the cheat Molitor had called him. While the younger man was rummaging in his desk drawer for a pen and paper to write Ramsey's list, Biggers had been surreptitiously moving his queen. She'd aimed the same look at him that she regularly used on recalcitrant suspects until he'd returned the queen to its earlier position.

"Anyway, if you took pictures of the windows, I'd rather go back to the motel. I'd like to print them out and get them over to my guy in the lab."

"I got some pictures. Camera's in the backseat." He took the next left and headed toward the motel. "You want to use it, though, it's gonna cost you."

"I'm already buying you wine. What more do you want?" She twisted in her seat and tried to get the camera. When she couldn't reach it, she unsnapped her seat belt and shifted position, half diving in the backseat to make another attempt at it.

"Well, that's a start, I s'pose."

When she felt his palm on her butt, she slapped it away. Snagging the camera, she returned to her seat, shooting him a narrowed look. "That's a good way to lose a hand."

"Honey, it just might be worth it."

The lazy good humor in his words had her smiling in spite of herself. The smile abruptly faded when memory intruded. "I can't believe I forgot to tell you." Guilt stabbed through her. "I went to see ex–chief of police Kenner this morning."

If she hadn't been watching so closely she might not have noticed the slight tensing of his body, as if readying for a blow. "What'd he have to say?"

"He didn't want to say much. He seems discreet enough. But he indicated the mystery of your father's drinking prior to the murder might be solved by a conversation with your mother. Sounded like he kept details from the report that he didn't feel were pertinent to the night in question in an effort to avoid some sort of embarrassment."

The muscle in his jaw clenched once. "Well, we're a polite folk down here."

Remorse sprouted fangs, sank deep. "I'm really sorry I didn't tell you earlier."

He turned into the parking lot of the motel and pulled up to the cabin housing the temporary TBI office. "Don't be. It's goin' to take some time to decide how badly I want to know those details." His smile was humorless. "You're not the only one with reason to avoid contact with family."

Because it was locked, Ramsey banged on the door to the lab. Jonesy answered and blocked her entrance. "Uh-uh, you don't come in unless you're sterile."

She looked down at herself. "I haven't exactly been rolling in the dirt today." Although if it hadn't been for the quilt

Dev had snatched from the bed, she would have been close during their picnic. "And don't I always gown up when I come inside?"

But he was adamant. "I'm running tests; there's no reason for you to come in. I don't have anything for you yet. I'm about three quarters done with the comparisons on those plants and no matches yet."

She handed him the batch of photos she'd downloaded from Dev's cameras. "Do any of them look like this?"

He flipped through the pages. Today he was back in jeans and a T-shirt beneath the scrubs. She absolutely didn't want to consider whether he seemed more relaxed or not.

"I never realized how much plant parts can look alike," he muttered. "But yeah, there are a couple that seem similar. You want me to try them next?"

"I'll wait while you do."

When he looked up from the photos to glower at her, she gave him a grim smile. "The only way you're keeping me out of the lab is if you think you can throw me out. Feeling lucky today?"

Apparently he wasn't. Although that didn't stop him from throwing her filthy looks after she donned sterile clothing and made herself comfortable on a chair in the corner.

An hour later she was convinced he was being purposefully slow. Meticulous was one thing, but surely it shouldn't take that long to cut off the roots from the plants, wash them, and slice a part from each to jam under the microscope.

Involuntarily, her thoughts turned to Dev's response to her conversation with Kenner. He was a grown man. It was ridiculous to worry about him. But there had been something in his eyes that told her he expected the upcoming conversation with his mother to be more unpleasant than illuminating. And she could sympathize with his reluctance to tackle it.

What was shocking was the strength of her desire to spare him that. She, who would never thank anyone for attempting to protect her from unpleasantness. Ramsey was reminded then of what Leanne had had to say about Dev's parents a couple days ago.

From all accounts, Lucas Rollins was a lot like Dev. Easy to get along with and not much for gettin' liquored up and carousin'. Which seems sorta ironic. Woman like that would drive most men to drink.

It made her wonder just what sort of woman Celia Ann was.

"Geez, you asleep over there or what? I expected some sort of reaction, at least."

Her attention snapped to Jonesy, who was looking a bit crestfallen. "What?"

He gave an exaggerated sigh of patience. "Like I told you a minute ago. We've got a match."

Chapter 21

"It's called turmeric." Ramsey spelled the name for Powell as she looked down at the printouts before her. She'd spent hours doing research on the Internet before calling the agent with what she had. The excitement buzzing through her had grown with each new discovery and was now impossible to contain. "It has numerous healing properties. Ulcers, for one thing." She thought the man would appreciate that detail. "It's said to detoxify the liver, balance cholesterol levels, stimulate digestion . . . there's a whole list. The root is ground up and used as a spice. It's native to India."

"But none of the local healers you talked to recall sellin' any recently."

"I haven't been able to get in contact with Rose Thornton yet," she admitted. There'd been no sign of the woman anywhere on her property when Ramsey had driven out there. And after knocking, she'd tried the woman's door only to find it locked. "But I made personal contacts with the other women I'd spoken to. All say they have only an occasional call for it, and none think they've sold any in the last year."

There was a silence on the line, and she wondered what the agent was thinking. Eventually he said, "Well, we can be certain Frost didn't take it for medicinal purposes since it was ingested shortly before death. So that means the UNSUB brought it with him. You said it wouldn't be found outdoors?"

"In Tennessee it would have to be grown inside," she affirmed. "But I don't think the offender's reasons for using it have anything to do with its alleged healing powers. I did some research on plant symbolization. Apparently, turmeric symbolizes purification. The other window on the church I told you about? It had pinecones on it. In religion, pinecones symbolize immortality."

"Have you found any verification that the plant on the church window really is an image of turmeric?" Powell asked.

Somewhat deflated, Ramsey leaned back in the desk chair. "Not yet. I'll continue looking into that end."

"I'm no nature expert, but one plant can look a lot like 'nother. An image on a window, especially, can be imprecise."

"There must be a county horticulturist around here somewhere." She looked at her watch. Noted that it was nearing five, when most county employees would be heading home.

And when the town's only liquor store would be closing.

Banishing the errant thought, she continued. "I'll start delving into the church history. Try to get verification that the plant image on the church window really does depict turmeric. But this fits, Powell. It all fits. That ViCAP hit I was telling you about? The homicide four years ago in DC? She had some sort of undigested plant root in her system, too. She was also dumped in water, which might be symbolic if we stay with the religious connection."

Powell grunted. "Well, if we can get our hands on that hair in the detective's evidence log, and it matches the one found in Frost's apartment, we'll know the two cases are linked. Too soon to get excited over the possibility yet. But good job, Clark. Work up a profile usin' the religious link for the perp. I'll head back in a day or two to go over it with you."

"Already got started on it." All of Raiker's consultants were cross-trained in various aspects of investigation and profiling. Since joining his team, Ramsey couldn't imagine carrying out an investigation without developing a profile. "How's it going with Sanders?"

She could hear the shrug in Powell's voice. "He's shut down, probably on his attorney's orders. But the forensic accountin' done so far shows he's in deeper than he wants to admit. The money from the life insurance policy wouldn't make all his credit problems go away, but it would buy him some needed time. The place he opened has been a money pit and is bleedin' red ink. I'd say he knows we've got motive and he's sweatin' it."

"I'll touch base with Rollins. See if anything's come from that search he was going to do to find a connection between Sanders and someone in the area."

"He's next on my list to call, so I'll ask him. Seems like I'm spendin' all my time on the phone these days. But Jeffries is pleased with our progress so far."

The moment the call was over Ramsey headed for the door, already dialing directory assistance. She went through several queries as she drove to the liquor store and made her selection a few minutes before it was due to close. Was back in the car again when she'd finally connected with the local county extension office.

"I'm sorry, ma'am, it's 'bout one minute to closin' time. Perhaps you can call back tomorrow." The woman's drawl was thick enough to cut with a knife.

"I don't think you understand." Ramsey let civility slip a notch and steel took its place. "I'm working with the TBI investigation." She gave no details, but knew she didn't have to. Everyone in the area had heard about the murder victim discovered on county property recently. "I'm certain your office will want to extend us every courtesy."

"But . . ."

"In a timely manner," she added firmly.

Which was how she happened to be standing fifteen minutes later on the sidewalk, once again staring up at the stained glass windows. This time with a prematurely balding young man at her side by the name of Lonny Beaumont.

"Huh," he said reflectively.

Ramsey shifted from one foot to the other with barely concealed impatience. "Do you recognize the plant or not?"

"Huh," he repeated. "Y'know, it's funny how a fella can pass by a place ever' day, and never really 'see' it, y'know what I mean?" He scratched his balding pate, fell to contemplating again. "Those are pinecones over t'other side, of course."

"Yeah. That I was able to figure out on my own."

He obviously wasn't a student of sarcasm. Hers seemed to sail right over his head, which was, with its scarcity of hair, visibly too small for his gangly large-framed body. Lonny rocked back on his heels and pulled at his lower lip, squinting up at the window with the plant on it.

"Can you make an educated guess what that plant is?"

"We-e-ll," he drawled out the word long enough to have Ramsey ready to reach in his mouth and pull out the rest of the sentence. "I could. Problem is, a guess is all it would be. Tucker's actually more of what you'd call a horticulturist. That'd be Tucker Green, and he's at a meetin' all day today." He fell silent, cocking his head to study the window from another angle. "Might be I could bring him by tomorrow, get his take on it."

"Wait." She strode to the car and grabbed the sheets of photos Dev had already taken of the window. Burning off a tinge of her frustration by slamming the door, she approached him and held them out. "Here are some pictures. Maybe you can show them to him and he can do a little research." She reached into her pocket and withdrew a card and extended that, too. "Have Tucker call me tomorrow once he's had a chance to look at these."

Lonny took the card, studied it. "Work does tend to pile up when we're gone." He glanced up again. "I can't promise that he'll . . ." A look at her unflinching expression had him swallowing. "I'll tell Tuck it's urgent."

"You tell Tuck it's urgent," she agreed. "Tell him it'd be better that he call me before I come looking for him." She was almost sorry for that last statement when Lonny's gaze widened, fixing on the bulge beneath her jacket.

He swallowed hard again. "I'll do that ma'am. Or . . ." he glanced at the card again. "Miz Clark?"

Was it her imagination or was everybody younger than she was these days? Younger and too damn easily intimidated. Giving an inner sigh, she relented, sent him a genuine, if small, smile. "I'd appreciate it. And thanks for meeting me here after work hours."

Lonny seemed to relax a bit. Turned to look at the church again as if the answers to Ramsey's questions were emblazoned on it. "T'weren't no problem. United Methodist is right on my way home. I was born and raised in a house over on Grant, three blocks south of here. Maybe you've gone by it. Gray house with pink shutters? Funny story 'bout them shutters. See they was s'posed to be maroon, but the man at the paint store, he . . ."

Ramsey headed for the Ford. He didn't seem to realize he was alone. She could still hear him talking as she got in and turned on the ignition. There was no telling how far he'd get into the story before realizing his audience had left.

She pulled away from the curb, feeling a tiny flicker of guilt. Then her glance fell to the purchase she'd made earlier. The wine was getting warm. She still needed to drive back to the motel for her laundry, which was going to make her late for those hamburgers with Dev.

Just that easily, the guilt vanished and a feeling of warm anticipation took its place. Because she didn't want to examine that emotion too closely, she resolved for once just to let it be.

———

"You get the dryer runnin' okay?" Dev walked through the back door with a platter piled with enough hamburgers to feed a small village for a week.

"I'm not completely without domestic skills." She put down the book she'd been examining and moved the wineglasses out of the way so he could place the platter on the table.

"So I see."

She'd been left with the job of setting the table and readying vegetables she'd never eat to top the burgers. Oh, and opening a bag of chips to pour into a bowl. Which, if truth be known, was pretty much the extent of her prowess in the kitchen. It wasn't a matter of not knowing how to cook as much as rarely bothering. It was far easier to rely on takeout, especially with the hours she kept.

Still, this was nice. Cozy. Her side of labor for the meal hadn't entailed much, so she'd gone wandering around the house. Spied the book near the computer with Dev's name emblazoned across the front and picked it up.

She was still reeling with impressions. "Somehow you failed to mention your doctorate."

He was rummaging in the refrigerator, before he straightened with bottles of ketchup and mustard in his hands. Approaching her, he set them on the table. "Doesn't come up much. Unless . . ." He sent her a look filled with mock hope. "Does the thought of advanced degrees by any chance make your clothes fall off?"

Ramsey smirked. "You'll have to expend a little energy to that end yourself."

"There you go. I knew it wouldn't impress you, so there was no need to mention it." He stabbed a burger and set it on her plate before rounding the table to his own seat.

She flipped open the back jacket again, studied his photo. It showed him unsmiling, wearing glasses she'd never seen him in. He looked serious and scholarly. Befitting of the accolades in the bio beneath. "Best-selling and award-winning author, huh?"

He lifted a shoulder easily and piled two hamburgers with all the fixings, with the smooth dexterity of a man used to fending for himself in the kitchen. "My agent puts that together. It's always a mistake to believe your own press, I always say."

Studying him shrewdly, she was certain he was underestimating his success. That in itself wasn't surprising. But she was coming to suspect that his lazy good humor and self-deprecating manner were as much a defense as the admittedly prickly shield she'd erected around herself. And it was amazingly effective. She'd met him several times herself before she'd thought to look deeper for more.

The admission was accompanied by a tinge of shame. "I'd like to read the book."

"Tomatoes?" When she shook her head, he put that plate down and picked up another to offer. "Lettuce?"

"Just ketchup. Can I borrow this one?"

He watched her closely, something unidentifiable in his eyes. "It's probably not goin' to be your thing." When she didn't answer, he merely shrugged, reached over to take the book and look at it. "Sure, if you want to. This one took place in Louisiana. Lots of atmosphere in Louisiana. An old plantation house was s'posed to be haunted. I went down there to decide." Without getting up out of his chair, he reached behind him and pulled open a drawer. Rummaging inside it, he withdrew out a pen.

"Was it?"

His grin was wicked. "Guess you'll find out when you read it." He flipped open the front cover, and with a flourish, wrote a message and signed it. Then he handed it to her. "There. It's yours."

Curiously touched, she took the book from him. "Thank you." Most of her reading, even in her off hours, consisted of case studies, procedural texts, and true crime, which was really little more than an extension of her job. Dev's book was going to be a welcome change from that. She suspected it would give her a clearer picture of the man.

"You just goin' to eat ketchup on that burger?" Wincing, he reached for a few chips to add to the growing mound of food on his plate.

"Why cover up the taste?" she countered. "Especially with a bunch of stuff I don't eat under any circumstances."

His eyes danced as he looked at her over the rim of his wineglass. When he set it down he said, "Your eatin' habits rival a five-year-old's. We're goin' to have to do somethin' to . . ."

A hammering at the back door interrupted him. Glancing at the clock, he said, "I had a surprise arranged for you, but she's earlier than I expected."

She? Ramsey's curiosity was piqued as Dev got up to pull open the door. Curiosity transformed to surprise at the sight of Leanne Layton on the back porch, her manner circumspect.

"I put them in bags to smuggle them out more discreetlike, but you can carry them in the house because I'm here to tell you, they are heavy. Hi, Ramsey." The woman sent her a gay wave. "Guess that first date the other night went all right, huh?"

"Yeah, it was fine." She got up to join the woman at the door, and watched, mystified, as Dev went out to reach into the open trunk of Leanne's car. He hauled out a shopping bag in each hand. Ramsey stepped aside so he could get through the door. He headed into the dining room to set the bags on the table with a thud. Then he made a return trip.

"What's in the bags? Dev mentioned a surprise, but he didn't say you were bringing it."

"Well, that's just like him. He always did enjoy springin' things on people." To Dev she said, "Those last two bags are it, honey. Just go on and shut the trunk lid."

Turning her attention back to Ramsey, she said, "They're the record books, of course. From the museum. Dev said y'all were in a hurry to look through them and that pinched-up Shirley Pierson was no help a'tall when he went in to do research." She smiled prettily when Dev dropped her keys in her outstretched hand as he went by her with the last of the bags.

Still at a loss, Ramsey said, "They let you check those things out of the museum?"

Leanne's laugh tinkled out of her. "No, silly. Well, you could say I 'checked them out' on your behalf. And I'm so excited at bein' able to help you on your case this way that I'm just practically ready to burst!" As if to prevent just that, she hugged her arms around her sides and gave a little hop. "The museum isn't even open today. I just used the key I had made back in high school and let myself in the back."

"I figured you'd wait until dark," Dev observed, rejoining them in the kitchen. "Less chance of anyone noticin'."

"It just so happens that I'm headed out of town this evenin', so I couldn't. But I was real careful, and no one saw me. I do want to put them back inside early mornin' tomorrow, though, so Dev, you'll need to meet me in back of the museum around four-thirty."

Although his expression looked pained, he agreed. "I'll be there."

"Does Donnelle know about this?" But Ramsey was certain she already knew the answer to that question.

"No, and she better never learn 'bout it, either. I'd hate to have to explain after all these years how I came to have that key."

"Leanne used the museum for a make-out place for years in high school," Dev inserted wickedly. "Gotta say, for some of those fellas she took in there, it was probably the education of their lives. In more ways than one."

The woman didn't seem embarrassed in the least by the revelation. "Least I didn't roll in the grass with whoever'd have me down near Hitchy Creek. Or in a haymow. 'Course once you could drive, backseats were more your style."

At Ramsey's raised brows, he shrugged. "In my defense, I have to point out that although the majority of my dates lacked an interest in history, they did end up with an education of sorts."

Leanne gave a hoot at that, and even Ramsey had to smile. "I don't doubt it." She looked at the other woman. "I really appreciate this, Leanne. We'll make sure the record books are back where they belong tomorrow morning."

"After the night I'm plannin', I'll be draggin' at that hour, but we all make our sacrifices. And I'll expect a full accountin' with all the juicy details just as soon as you can talk 'bout this case."

Ramsey was half surprised to hear herself say, "You've got it." She followed the woman out the back door to the porch. "Did that dress do the job the other night?" Remembering the woman's words, she asked, "Did your ex bleed when he saw you in it?"

"Sliced and diced." Leanne's smile was feline. "I'd be lyin' if I said that didn't make my night."

When Dev closed the door behind the woman, Ramsey walked over to him and slid her arms around his waist. Tipping her head back, she murmured, "You have a devious mind, Stryker." She gave him a quick kiss. Settled in for a more lingering one. "I'm finding it's one of my favorite things about you."

He wasn't a man to waste an opportunity. His lips warmed on hers and hazed her mind pleasantly. "Nice to know that my penchant for crime meets your approval."

When his hands grew more inquisitive, she wedged her palms between them and gave his chest a light push. "You ever pull anything like that, and it jams up one of my investigations, I'll slap the cuffs on you myself."

His smile was wicked. "I think I just might enjoy that."

Ramsey blew out a sigh. "Yeah, you probably would."

———

It was a good thing, she concluded three hours later, that Dev had insisted they finish their meal before tackling the records. Ramsey rubbed the heels of her palms against her burning eyes. They were only halfway through the pile, and they hadn't come up with anything really valuable yet.

They'd run across several references to turmeric, buried amidst a mind-numbing host of other herbs, plants, and crops in the endless cycle of planting and harvesting detailed in the records. There were the minutiae of preparing everything for use, whether it was cutting off and cleaning roots, pulverizing them to powder, or grinding grain and corn for food. None of it was remotely helpful, and she lowered her hands to gaze at the heavy leather-bound records balefully.

"So these almost have to have all been written by his wives, huh?" She glanced at the running list she was keeping of author names and dates. "Given the timeline we have placing Ashton in this area, it's doubtful they're relatives. Or children."

"I'm guessin' so. Look at this one." Dev shoved a record over to her from his seat beside her. "It details more of what their property looked like. That clearin' of Rose Thornton's didn't hold just the main cabin, but several structures."

"With fourteen wives, the man would need several structures," she muttered, scanning the page he indicated. "A curing barn. For the meat, I guess. Oh, a planting shed." She read silently for a moment, the close, cramped writing hurting her eyes. "Clever, even back then. They were growing plants out of season, out of climate even, in a crude temperature-controlled building." And turmeric, she noted, was on the list of plants grown there. "A celestial chapel for their devotions. Spent a ton of time in it, from the looks in those records." Every meticulously recorded day mentioned devotions before dawn and again after nightfall. "Doesn't look like all the time Ashton spent in church did him any good."

"God can be a dangerous weapon in the hands of the wrong person." At her surprised look, Dev shrugged. "The things some people have done in the name of religion over the history of mankind are pretty horrifying."

She couldn't disagree. Not when it was appearing more and more possible that someone had raped and killed Cassie Frost with some sort of god complex in his mind. Ramsey wondered where someone like Quinn Sanders would have met up with a man like that.

Handing the book back to him, she resumed studying the list she'd made. "We're missing a record."

"No, this is it," he said, without lifting his head from the record he was studying. He was wearing those glasses he'd had on in the book photo, she noted, which he'd sheepishly admitted to need for reading. She'd snuck more than one look at him in them throughout the night. She thought she just might strip him naked when they were done, all but those rimless glasses. On him, they looked sexy.

Jerking her attention back to the list she made, she cleared her throat. "Yeah, but each record book was written by a different woman, recording the daily activities of the Ashton clan for a calendar year. And one year's missing."

Finally, he lifted his head. "I asked Leanne specially. She says these are all of them. And she's had the run of that museum since she was in grade school, what with Donnelle's devotion to the place. She'd know."

Once she'd discovered how they were arranged, she'd flipped the front of each open and noted the name and year covered. Silently, she began jotting the years down in chronological order.

Once done, Ramsey looked up, satisfied. "Like I said. We're missing one. 1892. The records run from 1882 to 1898, so it didn't start right away when Ashton went down there. That's seventeen years. We've got sixteen books. And if our assumption is true and these are written by Ashton's wives, he must have acquired a few wives after his marriage to Ruth."

"Goes to figure, given his history," Dev agreed. "Probably had even more than that. Could be he just gave his favorites the honor of writin' the annual records."

"So where's the missing book?"

They looked at each other for a moment. "Could have been lost through the years, I s'pose. Or ruined." He gave a quick grin. "Maybe someone spilled a beer on it or somethin'."

"Or maybe it was destroyed." Her mind was working rapidly. "Maybe someone wrote something in it that Ashton didn't like."

Dev looked dubious. "What would that be, that they didn't write borin' enough? Because I gotta tell ya, readin' this stuff the first time had my eyeballs bleedin'. It's not any better tonight. I can't for the life of me figure how people got the strength to face 'nother day if this"—he thumped the book in front of him for emphasis—"is all they had to look forward to."

"When did Ruth Ashton disappear?"

He paused. Then, without a word he got up from the table and went to his computer desk in the next room, began rummaging through the notes stacked there. When he went still, she knew she had her answer.

"Eighteen ninety-two."

Her mind was a jumble with pieces of the puzzle, and she gave them time to click into place before speaking. "So what if she displeased Ashton somehow? Maybe he found out about the letters she'd written home." And how, she wondered for the first time, had Ruth managed to smuggle them out for mailing in the tight-knit community in the first place?

"That may have given him reason to kill her, but not to destroy the record she created."

"Unless he got his hands on a letter, discovered she was selling him out to her parents, and then took a closer look at the records she was writing." Driven to move, she shoved her chair back and paced the length of the room. "There had to be constant supervision in their life. These people lived in each other's pockets. Ruth would have had to be smart to conceal something in the records that was escaping everyone else's attention." But the fact she'd somehow managed to write and mail those letters home proved she'd been plenty smart.

"Eighteen ninety-two." Dev looked pensive, staring into space.

When he didn't go on, she said, "What?"

"Thinkin' back to what Donnelle told us 'bout the legend. The red mist is sighted every generation or so. The first time was in 1922." He paused a beat. "The way I count it, that's exactly thirty years later. Maybe the legend of the red mist originated from acts a generation earlier than we've been thinkin'."

Everything inside her reared away from his conjecture. Facts. He'd gotten her facts about the existence of the religion. Facts suggesting that Rufus Ashton had been one very sick fuck. But she was nowhere close to embracing the local superstition or using the information they'd uncovered to support it.

She was here to solve a murder. One in *this* century. Her only interest in Sancrosanctity, Ashton's church, was that it gave her background for the profile she'd be developing.

A man acting on the beliefs taught by a cult—damned if she'd call it a religion—originating in the 1870s. A man who used its beliefs to condone his own twisted pleasures.

Ramsey was on shaky ground, and she was glad she didn't have Raiker here, challenging her at every turn, forcing her to defend her conclusions. His tactics kept his consultants sharp, made them exacting in their deductions. But there was nothing exact about what she was considering now. They were light on evidence, heavy on speculation. And as a professional, that made her more than a little uneasy.

"Okay." She shot him a look that was half apologetic, half defiant. "I'm not ready to go there. But the rest of it . . . yeah, it could fit. Where's that last record book? Have we looked in it?"

Dev reached for it, and she rounded the table to peer over his shoulder as he flipped through it. The careful writing halted midway through the book. Both of them read silently.

"So Ashton died in March, 1898."

"Again, here's hoping there's a hell," she muttered. "Sounds like they built a special crypt for him."

"I know that mausoleum," he said pensively. "The cemetery butts up against Rose's land. It's in the oldest corner of the area. Used to play around there when I was a kid."

The entries grew more random after that. Instead of daily, one day might be recorded, and then the next entry would be weeks later. Until August of that year, where a full month's worth of entries were entered.

"They left the area under the direction of the new leader," she murmured, peering harder at the writing. "Pages and pages indicating the area was getting increasingly intolerant—said the pot to the kettle—and they were going west to find a more moral place to settle."

"And then nothin' after that." Dev closed the book slowly. "Apparently the new leader wasn't interested in keepin' records."

"Or if he was, those new records stayed with them. Rufus Ashton's history remained here in the town he started."

She insisted on finishing the other books since they hadn't looked at them chronologically, but very little new information came to light. Ramsey was on the last of them when a word seemed to jump off the page at her. Turmeric.

Slowing, she began to read more carefully. Finally she

said, "The author of this record seems like one of those un-
bearably smug people, you know? The kind that thinks she
works harder than anyone else. Does more than her share."

"A martyr," Dev offered. He had his glasses off and was
rubbing his eyes.

Checking the clock, Ramsey saw it was near midnight.
"Yeah, I guess. But she also goes into even greater detail
about her days, to prove just how busy she kept. Listen."
Ramsey began to read from the journal. "'My service today
was to prepare the basket for the casting out ceremony. I
carefully cut away the root of the turmeric and laid it among
the most perfect pinecones I could gather.'" She looked up at
Dev. "Casting out ceremony. She's mentioned it several times
in here but doesn't define it."

"Maybe when they threw the undesirable males out of
their place," suggested Dev. "Cast them out because they were
too much competition for female attention, or they didn't
make the religious cut in some way."

Funny how her impression was always several shades
darker than his. Or, perhaps, not so odd, given her occupation. "What else do you cast out in religion? Demons, sin."

"Evil."

"And if you're casting out evil, what do you hope to re-
place it with? Purity, right?"

There was a slight smile on his face as he watched her
work through it, but his nod was immediate. "Goes to figure."

"Turmeric to symbolize purification. Pinecones to symbolize immortality." And the only people in need of immortality, she thought, were the dead or the dying. "This is it,"
Ramsey said surely. "Or at least as close as we're going to
get to verification about the plant on the church window."

"Is it enough?"

"It's enough for me."

"Good." He shoved the books in front of him away to
stretch. "'Cuz I have to have these records back in a little
over four hours, and there's the little matter of some sleep
'tween now and then."

She considered him. He didn't look all that tired to her. Her lips curved slowly. "I can see you're exhausted. So I'll just stick around long enough to get you tucked in bed before I go back to the motel."

There was a gleam in his eye that no woman in her right mind would trust. "Would you?" His chair scraped the floor as he pushed back from the table and rose. "I am feelin' a bit weak in the legs. Probably goin' to need some help just gettin' back to my bedroom."

"You are in sorry shape." She rose, slid an arm around his waist, and was rewarded with a quick squeeze as he hugged her to his side. "I wouldn't feel right if I didn't offer every bit of assistance I could."

"You're a givin' sort of woman, Ramsey." The words were rife with amusement. Slowly, arms wrapped around each other, they moved down the hallway. "I've always recognized it."

It would serve him right, she thought with a flash of humor, to do exactly as she'd stated. Get him all primed and ready in bed and then kiss him on the forehead and go for the door. Just to hear what he'd come up with next.

He nudged her to the left, and they entered a shadowy bedroom. He bent to turn on a lamp on the bedside table. Its soft glow pushed gently at the darkness, relegating it to the corners of the bed where they hovered like inky curtains.

There'd been no lamp on the last time they'd ended up in Dev's bed, she recalled. She had a fleeting impression of a high school boy's room, with posters on the wall of muscle cars and pinup girls. Trophies lining the shelves. Knew the room had been kept as it had been when Dev had occupied it full time.

There was a temptation to explore that further. To take a look at the boy he'd been in order to get a better handle on the man he'd become.

But the strength of that temptation couldn't begin to compete with the urge she felt when she looked in Dev's eyes. When he lowered his head and brushed his lips down the curve of her jaw. Whisper soft. Too light a gesture to be responsible for her pulse revving to instant life.

Her immediate response was troubling on one level. Because no man had been allowed that power over her. Sex was a mutual give and take, but she was always careful about what she gave. She didn't look back. Not ever. But she knew he wouldn't be so easily forgotten. He was dangerous for that fact alone.

His mouth cruised along her chin, down her throat to linger at the hollow at the base of her neck. And she knew, even as her head lolled back to provide him greater access, that if she didn't take control of this interlude, his tenderness would be her undoing.

She placed her hands on his chest and exerted enough pressure to have them both tumbling on the bed. The springs of the mattress creaked as they landed on the bed, then rolled, limbs entwined.

"Pushy." Dev's lips curved. "I kinda like it."

"You've incredibly high standards." With swift movements, she divested him of his shirt and went to work on his belt. "I'll try to live up to them."

Her sudden urgency fed his, and he tugged at her clothing until their hands were engaged in a battle as they fought to divest each other of their garments. And that first sweet feel of flesh against flesh had Ramsey sighing in satisfaction.

Her hands streaked over him, testing, exploring. Rediscovering the surprisingly solid muscle roped along his arms. Layered beneath his chest and stomach. And recalled again the pleasure to be had from his body.

They rolled until she was above him and he used the position to nuzzle her breast, taking the nipple into his mouth and sucking, scraping it lightly with his teeth.

Colors kaleidoscoped behind her closed eyelids. This was what she wanted. Sensation rearing up, rollicking through her system, making it easy only to feel. Battening back all thought, all logic, until it was only the act itself that mattered.

He switched his attention to her other breast, and she went on her knees above him, pressing closer. His hand wandered over the curve of her hip and slipped between her legs, rubbing softly at the dampness there, his touch eliciting even more heat.

Last time he'd reduced her to a shuddering mass. This time she was determined to return the favor. But first she had to evade those clever stroking hands. That knowing, seeking mouth.

When she pulled away from him, he made a move to stop her. But his movements halted when she embarked on a sensual journey of discovery.

There were intriguing hollows on his chest, where sinew met bone, and she used her lips to trace each one. Moving lower, she swirled her tongue in the slight indentation of his navel. Used her finger to follow the trail of hair, a couple shades darker than that on his head, to where it arrowed toward his sex.

The muscles in his belly clenched and jumped beneath her touch, the evidence of his reaction firing little pinwheels of desire through her system. His penis was engorged, quivering. And when she took him in her mouth, his hips jerked helplessly.

She wrapped her fingers around his shaft to stroke as she used her tongue to lash at the sensitive tip. And let the dark flavor of him work through her, until it joined the fever in her blood.

It was less about control now. The thought formed, fragmented. It was more about wanting to return the pleasure in kind. To bring him to the brink of trembling need. To hone his desire to the same painfully keen edge as her own.

He withstood the sensual torment for long moments. But when her intent changed, when the soft suction grew stronger, his fingers tightened on her shoulders. Urged her higher.

"Not without you, sugar," he murmured against her lips.

It pleased her that his voice was thick. Ragged. "That can be easily arranged."

He guessed her intention when she straddled him, and he sat up, one arm around her waist to keep her steady while he sent a hand in search of the other bedside table. She heard a drawer open. The crinkle of a foil wrapper.

She took it from him and opened it. Made the act of rolling the latex over his thick sex an act of excruciating promise.

The desire steadied. Was no less fierce for being tamped down, but it was no longer in danger of slipping its leash. That was important, wasn't it? That she retain something of herself even as she drove them both crazy. So she wouldn't be searching for splinters of herself to re-form once the act was over.

But when she paused in position over him, took him in, she made the mistake of looking into Dev's eyes. Found them narrowed and glittering. And realized with a start that he knew exactly what she was about.

To distract them both, she started moving, her eyelids sliding shut in pleasure at the delicious friction. She slid from slow and easy to a mad frenetic pace that had them both gasping. Flesh slapping against flesh in a frantic speed that promised to hurtle them both to completion in record time.

Until he slowed beneath her. His movements halted completely, even as his body quivered against hers like a tiger ready to spring. "Ramsey." The word was drenched in emotion. "Look at me."

His plea punched through the fog of desire and she dragged open her eyes, her body still attuned to the feel of him pulsing and throbbing inside her. It took a moment to focus. Another to comprehend the very different sort of need in his gaze.

"Look at us. *See* us." His palms left her hips. Found her hands. Threaded his fingers with hers against the mattress.

She shook her head, a ribbon of panic unfurling down her spine. He was asking for more than she could give. More than she *wanted* to give.

But then his hips began to thrust, establishing a languid rhythm that had the need streaking through her again, so sharp, so ripe, that it burned. She met him glide for glide, the pace slower but no less intense.

His deep blue eyes were blurred with passion. She wanted to deny the request she saw there. Wanted to pretend she'd never noticed it at all.

But she was caught. Helplessly mesmerized by the promise and plea she'd identified. Terrified her expression would give away just how very much she wanted to give him the answer he sought.

Their pace quickened. Breathing thickened. And still her eyes remained fixed on his. When he'd swim out of focus, she fought to clear her vision, wanting to watch him as the pleasure took him. Watch him watching her.

The world shifted, narrowing crazily, until it pinpointed this moment. Only the two of them engaged in a race to be first to drive the other over the edge. And if there was more here, more that threatened to ensnare and entangle, Ramsey was certain she could avoid it. Shake free of it.

Dev smiled then, and her heart stuttered. But before her reaction could summon panic, he lunged beneath her, driving home with hard rapid thrusts.

She shattered, riding the release in a long endless rainbow of unspeakable pleasure. His climax followed seconds later as their bodies shuddered together.

And through it all, her gaze never left his.

Chapter 22

Collapsed on top of Dev, Ramsey felt no particular compulsion to move. Given the lazy stroke of his hands over her still-trembling flesh, he was in no hurry for her to do so.

The jangle of her cell brought a snarl to her lips. An epithet tumbling off her tongue.

"Is that yours?"

"Of course." Reluctantly, she disengaged from him. Sitting up in bed without him entwined around her was strangely disorienting.

The cell went silent as the call switched to voice mail. Then it immediately began to ring again. It took a moment for her to fumble though the pile of their clothes. Another to retrieve it from the pocket of her suit jacket. By the time she squinted at the screen, it had gone silent again. Two missed calls.

It took only a second to ascertain that they both came from Cripolo.

"Gonna deal with that tonight?"

She turned her head to find Dev close enough to read the cell screen. There was no judgment in his expression. No sign of his opinion of a woman who'd rather chase down a murder suspect than deal with her own family.

But he had a little experience in that area, too, she recalled. He'd be the last to offer empty platitudes.

The cell began to ring again as if in answer. And she recognized that she'd put this moment off as long as she could. Flipping the phone open, she said shortly, "What do you want?"

There was a moment of silence on the line, before the familiar voice sounded. "Well, well. Miss High and Mighty finally decided to answer my call. Guess I should be grateful."

"I don't have time for this, Luverne. Say your piece and get it over with." As if the messages he'd left hadn't been enough already. After the first couple, she hadn't bothered to listen to the rest. She knew exactly what her brother was. She always had.

"Did I interrupt somethin'? Hope you're takin' it rough up the ass, you stinkin' cunt."

"As usual, your brotherly sentiment is overwhelming. You've got ten seconds. What do you want?"

There was a pause. She could hear him haul in a breath, as if to rein in temper. "You cost me a sweet li'l deal with that Realtor. You're gonna have to pay for that."

"Seems to me I was going to pay anyway," she said drily. Sitting on the edge of the bed in the near darkness, spine straight, heart hardened, the sense of déjà vu was dizzying. It washed over her with an accompanying blanket of hopelessness.

She shook it off. "That's my house. I bought it for Hilda. If she doesn't want to live there, wants to milk it for the rent money, well I guess I'll let that go." She had a feeling that surprised him, as if they hadn't suspected she knew what they used the property for. "But my name is still on the deed. How the hell did you think you'd ever get away with selling it?"

"Almost did. Would have if that dipshit Realtor hadn't gotten it in his head to call after I convinced him right and proper."

"Yeah, you're real clever. That sort of theft would constitute a felony. A brainy move for someone only out of prison, what? Twenty-one months?"

"Wouldn't a had to try it if'n you gave me money when I asked. You're a tight-fisted bitch. You want your own family crawlin' 'round on our knees, beggin'."

"I've given you money," she pointed out futilely. Luverne—

for that matter her mother and sister as well—remembered only what suited them. "Got tired of throwing dollars down the same rat hole. I told you last time you wouldn't be getting anymore so, true to form, you decided to steal it instead. There goes my faith in the rehabilitative nature of prison."

"Oh, I think you'll give me more."

There was a tone in his voice, sneaky and satisfied. The sense of déjà vu returned. Stronger this time.

"I ain't takin' this layin' down. You'll give me money every damn month. Exactly as much as I say. Or I'm gonna have me a little confab with Reggie Masterson."

The name was like a punch to the gut. It shouldn't have been. Masterson and his buddies were in the past. A past she'd buried long ago.

A past that had a nasty way of rearing up at random moments to prove it still retained some power.

"He's law down here, y'know. Sheriff, just like his daddy was. How's that for a kick in the ass?"

She had to wait until her throat eased enough to force the words out. "Your ten seconds are up."

"Wait!" A new note of threat entered Luverne's voice. "You want to know what I'm gonna tell 'em? I'm gonna waltz right into his office and slap a paper on his desk with your address and phone number."

There was no way to prevent the quick shuddering breath at the words. And no way for Luverne to have missed it.

"That's right. I hear he's still harboring a grudge over the way you shot that paint gun at his family jewels. And then tryin' to get him in trouble with his daddy by cryin' to the cops . . . well, folks 'round here still talk 'bout it sometimes. How you lured them boys into the woods, offerin' to spread your legs for 'em, and then got all pissy when they wouldn't pay for it."

An unnatural calm settled over her. "Is that what they say?"

"Most do. 'Course there's 'nother side to it that got spread 'round agin when Everett Grout was runnin' 'gainst him in the sheriff's race. Reggie won anyways, but he was mighty pissed it got told. I hear he has a powerful bitterness 'gainst you. The story is, you cost him one of his balls."

The fierce stab of satisfaction at the words hadn't lessened after all these years. "If you owned a pair yourself, maybe you could loan him one."

Luverne's voice went ugly as the leash on his temper snapped. "You listen to me, you smart-mouthed whore. You think you're somebody now? You're the same li'l tramp you was down here, shakin' your ass for anyone who'd pay you for it. You ain't *nuthin'*."

"Oh, I'm something," she protested mildly. She was numb now, walled off from feeling. Maybe she wouldn't feel anything at all anymore. It would be so much simpler. "I'm the one with the money, remember? And you're still not getting a dime."

The names he called her then slid harmlessly off her. She'd heard worse. Some from him. "Y'all think I'm kiddin'?" Rage had his words ragged. "I'll do it. And maybe I'll come on up to your place myself first. Pound some damn respect into you. Then I'll let Reggie do the rest."

"You might want to recall that I have the name of your parole officer. I'm sure the Realtor would be pleased to tell him how you tried to bilk me out of my property. And if you talk to Reggie, be sure to tell him and his friends that I don't use branches and paint guns to defend myself anymore. I use bullets. And I'm a helluva shot. Come to think of it, you might want to remember that yourself."

She disconnected the call, but then the strength seemed to leave her limbs. She sat there, knowing she had to move. Unable to. As if words would summon the energy she needed, Ramsey said, "I should be getting back to the motel."

In response, Dev simply reached for the cell she still held and set it on the bedside table. Then, with one arm around her waist he repositioned her in bed, cradled close to him. "I don't think so."

She wanted to struggle, but the feat was beyond her. So

she lay there. Listening to the steady and solid sound of his heartbeat, and waiting for her knees to stabilize enough to hold her upright again.

"I don't want to talk about it."

"You don't have to."

Did he mean he wouldn't press or that he'd heard enough of the conversation to piece it together? It didn't matter, she thought wearily. It had all ceased to matter once she'd left Cripolo, Mississippi, behind. Maybe time had taught her she couldn't carve away the past with the precision of an emotional surgeon, but it was over. She was often grateful for that.

Minutes melded into an hour. They laid there awake, motionless, save for the hand Dev brushed soothingly over her back. Sleep would have been as impossible to summon as the strength needed to head back to the motel.

"Maybe you ought to give your brother's parole officer a call anyway. Save yourself some headaches," he suggested in a murmur.

She gave a little shake of her head, her hair brushing his chest. "He'll land back in prison soon enough. I'll keep that as an ace in the hole." Black humor filled her. "With Luverne, it always pays to have something to fight back with."

"He should've protected you." For the first time, she identified the tone in his voice, and she felt a jolt of surprise. Suppressed fury. "He's your brother, and he should have been watchin' out for you back then."

"Familial loyalty isn't a cultivated Hawkins family trait." The note of humor she tried for came out flat. "We were trash, Dev. The sort you have here in town, too, I imagine, who everyone pities or looks down on. My mama was never too proud to take charity. We were so low that the people I envied were the ones who lived in the double-wide trailers on the other side of the park. The ones with the decks and porches built on. Compared to us, they lived like kings."

"You're a long way from the trailer park now."

She didn't dispute him. Not even as she recognized the trailer park was a big part of who she'd been. What had formed her. Was part of the darkness that lived inside that had once threatened to swallow her whole.

"I knew what everybody in Cripolo thought of my family," she whispered, eyes burning. "Had a hard time looking anyone in the eye because of it. It took Masterson two weeks to even get me to return his hellos. But he was persistent."

And she was stupid. Her eyelids slid shut in pity for the naïve fifteen-year-old she'd been. Kids these days seemed wiser, didn't they? Older than their years. But she'd grown up in a hurry once Reggie Masterson had taken an interest in her.

"A month later he convinced me to let him show me the prettiest place in the area to look at the stars." And she'd been young enough, dumb enough, to daydream that their first kiss might ensue. "Turns out he had something else in mind. A little naked hunting in the woods, followed by a gang rape. First one to hit me with the paint gun was first on, I guess." She shrugged. "They ended up with a bit more than they could handle." But not before they'd terrified her with a scene that, if she were honest, still lived in her nightmares.

"And his dad was the town cop."

"He was the sheriff. And since it was county land, that's who we were sent to." Hilda Hawkins had marched her into Sheriff Masterson's office, still bruised and weeping. But Ramsey had been thrilled, in some tiny part of herself, that her mother was acting like a parent. Taking her side.

"My mother accepted eight hundred dollars from the sheriff to forget all about it. I got labeled as the town slut. She bought two new chairs for her beauty parlor and a fancy dryer. And it all went away."

"Holy Christ, Ramsey." His arm tightened around her, making it difficult to breathe. The weight of it warmed something inside her.

He went up on one elbow, still holding her close, his face near hers. "You're the strongest woman I know. Too strong, I thought sometimes. I can admire that about you while hatin' like hell how that strength was formed."

His kiss was soft as gossamer. It shouldn't have had the

power to heal, just a little, the tangle of raw-edged emotion she carried inside.

"I don't want you to matter." Her voice was a whisper, but when he stilled, she knew he'd heard it. "It'd be so much easier if you didn't."

"It'd be easier if you didn't feel," he countered. "But you do, Ramsey. You can pretend differently, but you do. And none of us can will ourselves to not feel a certain way." His hand moved from her waist to stroke her hair, the gesture tender. "All I'm askin' is that you not run away from your feelin's. Least not 'til you give yourself the time to figure out what they are."

She pressed her face closer to his chest. Her eyes were dry, but they still stung.

All I'm askin' is that you not run away from your feelin's.

He had no idea what he was requesting. If she could find a way to get through life without feeling at all, she'd take it in a heartbeat.

But the risk here wasn't in the suggestion he made. She knew that even as she tried to reject it.

The real danger lay in how powerfully tempted she was to forget a lifetime of defenses and do exactly what he asked.

———

He stepped through the woods, his footing sure despite the almost absolute darkness. Kathleen Sebern's personal belongings were shoved in the backpack he wore. It was time to get rid of them before someone found them. Leaving loose ends was just sloppy.

The sound at his side had him bringing his rifle up in one smooth motion. "Who's there?"

Only the sounds of night creatures surrounded him. But he wasn't fooled. With one hand, he reached up and fitted the night vision goggles over the eye slit in the face mask. The interior of the woods took on a ghostly green glow. He saw a coon do a fast waddle to a nearby bush, and he breathed a little easier. But still he stayed motionless for a few more minutes. Watching.

He didn't tolerate carelessness. Not from others. Not from himself.

When he didn't see anything suspicious, he continued walking again. Hadn't gotten more than a couple steps before the words were hissed behind him.

"Yer bad. You made her scream, and I'm gonna tell."

He whirled around, the gun raised again as he scanned the area. He saw no one. Just brush and trees and yellow eyes blinking at him. "Who's out there?" Squinting at the trees above him, he wondered if someone was lodged in one nearby.

"Yessiree. Yer bad. Bad men get dead."

He looked again, more carefully. Was that an elbow showing around that pine's trunk? He moved to take cover himself.

"You'll hafta go to the bad place. You made her dead. Dead is dead."

He let out a breath. It was that freak Ezra T. He peered around the tree. Yeah, he was hiding around that pine all right. Skinny as a rail, he was almost undetectable behind it. "I'm not sure what you mean, Ezra T. Why don't you come out here and we'll talk 'bout it?"

There was a long silence. Then, "You got gum?"

What an idiot. Why was he allowed to run around loose? "Yeah, I got gum. Juicy Fruit. You like Juicy Fruit?"

"Dubble Bubble. I like me some Dubble Bubble."

"Well, let's see." He pretended to check his pockets while he kept an eye on the pine. Ezra T. shifted, showing the edge of his shoulder. Not enough for a shot. "Well, lookee here, I do have some Dubble Bubble. Why don't you come on over and you can have it."

The loon actually moved closer. Quicker, though, than he expected, and heading for another tree. But it was enough time to bring the shotgun up to fire.

An ear-splitting screech told him he'd hit the freak straight on, too. Stepping away from the tree, he scanned the terrain to see where he'd fallen.

His goggles hazed. He rubbed them with one gloved

hand, but when his vision didn't improve, he pulled them off to check them.

And found himself surrounded by fog. It seeped up from the ground in a cloud of red vapor, thick and deep and suffocating.

Shock morphed to panic. He tried to wave it away. Took a few steps, attempting to find his way out of it. But it enveloped him. Blinded him to everything in his path. And with every passing second, it grew denser. The color of blood.

The red mist. His bowels turned to ice. He clawed at it when it seemed to wrap around his throat. Cut off his breath. His lungs strangled and his hands went up to claw ineffectually at his throat.

Almighty God, save your servant!

He forgot about Ezra T. Forgot about disposing of Kathleen Seburn's belongings. All he could think about was escape. He couldn't see. Couldn't breathe. The blood was pounding in his ears. There was a fist in his chest squeezing the oxygen from his lungs.

Turning, he stumbled through low-hanging branches and trees. The fog seemed to wind around his feet, nearly causing him to fall to the ground. Dear God, it was up his nose, in his throat, seeming to expand so he couldn't haul in air.

Carefulness forgotten, he ran, clumsy and blind, from the woods, his hands futilely trying to loosen the grip the red mist seemed to have on his throat.

"Where you off to this afternoon, Dev?"

Clem Leesom had ambled out of the Gas 'n' Go to run a damp squeegee over Dev's windshield in a desultory fashion. His place didn't run to full service, but he provided it just the same if he was in the mood for a gossip, which he often was.

Dev regarded him out of the open driver's window. "Just up to Knoxville for a few hours to see my mama."

"Pretty day for a drive. You gonna spend the night?"

"Naw." He was getting a later start today than he'd planned, but there was no way he'd consider more than a few hours in Celia Ann's company. No way she'd welcome more.

"Ain't been up to Knoxville in a coon's age." Finished with the windshield, Clem rounded the vehicle to draw closer to the window. "By the time you get up there and back, won't leave much time for visitin'."

"It'll be time enough." When the digits on the pump finally halted, Dev reached into his wallet and pulled out three twenties. "Damned oil companies. Robbin' us all blind."

"And squeezin' folks like me right along with ya. I'll go get your change."

While Clem ambled into the shop, Dev shoved aside impatience. It wasn't like he was anxious for the upcoming scene with his mama. She hadn't been exactly open to the idea of him stopping in for a bit today, but he was unwilling to have this conversation over the phone.

When he'd gotten up to return the records to Leanne, Ramsey had insisted on rising, too, and gathering up her laundry before heading back to the motel. While he would have preferred to return home and slip back into bed with her, he knew he should be thankful she'd spent the night. At least the few hours that had constituted night. She wasn't a woman it paid to push, and she'd been through a wringer with that phone call from her brother.

His chest went tight. He had as much empathy as the next person, but he didn't ever recall this overwhelming surge of rage that squeezed his heart in a vise when he thought about someone hurting her. She'd been let down by the very people in her life who should have protected her. It was no wonder she'd built defenses. After what she'd been through, most people would have constructed a damn fortress.

Clem strolled back at a pace only a notch above snail-like. Ponderously, he counted back Dev's change. "There you go. You have yerself a nice day."

He peeled off a five and handed it to the man. "Thanks, Clem. You do the same."

A genuine smile settled on the man's seamed face. "That's

right mannerly of you, Dev. I 'preciate it. You tell your granddaddy hey for me, will ya?"

"I'll do that." He paused to return the rest of the cash to his wallet, unsurprised that the news about Benjamin had already reached Clem. A scare with his granddaddy was actually the reason he was late today. The assisted living facility had called to inform him they were taking Benjamin in for heart pains.

Dev had been experiencing heart pains himself by the time he got to Doc Theisen's clinic. They hadn't eased until Doc had finally put the equipment aside and agreed with his granddaddy's assessment that he'd just had a bad case of heartburn. Brought on, Benjamin had insisted darkly, more by the unexpected company of Bunny Franzen and her damn dog than the fresh peach cobbler she'd brought him.

He'd accompanied his granddaddy back to the Manor Apartments and seen him inside. Made him comfortable. Not for the world would he have admitted his part in Bunny's visit.

With a wave to Clem, who was still watching from the window, he pulled away from the station and took the county road that would lead out of town. And tried to dissolve the ball of dread tightening in his gut.

It was a couple hours drive to Knoxville, least the way he drove. Somehow in that time he'd figure out exactly what he was going to say to his mama.

———

As Dev pulled away from his station, Clem picked up the phone and squinted at the number scribbled on the piece of paper. He really needed glasses. Hettie was always nagging on him about that. He just hated to admit that the woman was right.

The call rang twice before a man answered. "That you, Banty? This here is Clem at the Gas 'n' Go. You said I was to call ya anytime I noted Devlin Stryker headin' outta town. Well, he just left and said he's goin' on up to Knoxville today. Plannin' on comin' back tonight, too."

"You sure 'bout that, Clem? That he's comin' back tonight?"

"Sure as sure. He said it hisself. Now that I called you, we're square, hear? You said you'd wipe out that twenty dollars I owe you from pinochle."

"We're square, Clem. You done good."

Clem hung up pleased with the way the day had turned out. He'd made himself an extra twenty-five dollars, more or less, and there weren't many days a body could claim that.

Whistling, he went to get the hose to spray off the drive in front of the station. While he worked, he wondered what practical joke Banty was going to pull on Dev. That Banty Whipple was a caution.

Clem couldn't wait to hear about the prank he came up with this time.

———

Mark read the copy of the latest e-mail from the DC detective that Ramsey handed him. "I'll send my chief deputy up there to get the evidence from Hopwood. I think you met him before. Stratton? First desk outside my door?"

Ramsey nodded. He was the same deputy who'd come to fetch someone to the morgue when Jim Grayson had contacted Mark, certain he would be identifying his daughter's body.

"I trust him the most." The sheriff grimaced, cracked his knuckles. "Which means I can spare him the least. But I'll gladly take on extra hours while he's gone if it gets us a step closer to solvin' this thing."

"Let's hope." She sipped from her coffee. Having tasted the brew Letty made here, she'd picked up two coffees from The Henhouse on her way over.

"Sure 'preciate this." Mark indicated his cup. "Letty's brew is strong enough to separate paint. Even though drinkin' that swill is probably what's goin' to have her out-livin' both of us."

"Did Powell call you?"

He gave a slow nod. "Sure did. Sounds like they've got

Sanders dead to rights. But can't say I'm any closer to findin' a relation of his here in town. I've actually been usin' Kendra May's online genealogy programs to find a match. They're slick as snot. But nothin's turned up yet."

He hadn't yet broached the topic she most wanted to discuss. "Did Powell tell about the possible link to Ashton's church? Sacrosanctity?"

Rollins nodded again. "He said you were lookin' for proof that the plant in the stained glass window at United Methodist was this turmeric you were talkin' 'bout." He rubbed the back of his neck with his free hand. "Did you find it?"

"Well, the guy I met with this morning from County Extension couldn't be sure, although it was one of the plants on the list of possibilities he gave me. But . . ." She caught herself just before telling him that she and Dev had looked at the records last night. ". . . I went through the Ashton record books from the museum, and there are enough references to it to make me pretty certain."

He looked mildly interested. "I'm not sure I knew there were record books from Ashton's time in the museum. Huh." Mark contemplated his coffee a moment. "I'm not goin' to lie, it's tough to wrap my mind 'round it." He held up his free hand to stem any protest she would have made. "Not takin' anythin' away from your work, mind you. But landsakes, Ramsey. It was hard 'nough considerin' that we have a murderer in our midst. Then came the possibility that the perp might be an honest-to-God serial killer."

"We're a ways from establishing that."

He went on as if she hadn't spoken. "Now you want me to consider that our town's foundin' father was some sort of whack job, killin' folk in the name of Jesus, and someone with ties to the area has that same bent of mind?"

"It's a lot to take in," she allowed. And wondered what he'd have to say if she repeated Dev's speculation linking Ruth Ashton to the red mist. "Lots of loose threads and not enough tying them together." She leaned forward in her chair, both hands clasped around her cup. "But you know as well as

I do that things start coming together all at once. And I have a feeling that we're getting close, Mark. We're getting real close."

"I hope to God you're right. We finally saw the last of the reporters a coupla days ago, and I'm hopin' they're gone for good. Folks have a right to feel peaceful in their homes. We need to bring this thing to an end, let people get back to their lives."

"Let's hope it's soon."

Mark took another sip from his coffee, his eyes sliding shut for a moment in appreciation. "Powell also said he was headin' back here tomorrow. That you had a profile the two of you were goin' over."

"I *will* have a profile." With that reminder, she rose. "I'm not done with it yet, but when I am, you'll get a copy."

He nodded. "And I 'preciate that, too."

She left his office, stopping only to exchange a few words with the taciturn Deputy Stratton. Then she headed for her car. She wanted to look over her work before showing it to Powell, and the mention of the man's name had ignited a feeling of urgency.

It occurred to her as she drove back to the motel that under ordinary circumstances she would have stayed up all night to get the details polished in the profile.

But last night had been anything but ordinary circumstances. And she couldn't find it in herself to regret that.

Chapter 23

Celia Ann Stryker hurried out of the house as Dev pulled up at the curb. Anyone else might think their mama was anxious to see them. But he knew better than to expect a warm welcome.

He got out of the car and strolled up the pretty brick drive. His mama had done real well for herself. This new house she shared with his stepdaddy wasn't in a gated community, but it was the next thing to it, with those stone pillars and somber dark metal signs at the entrance informing newcomers that they were entering Wedgewood Estates. He'd never been invited to this house before, although he thought his mama and stepdaddy had moved here nearly a year ago.

And that, too, wasn't unexpected.

"Mama." He bent to brush a kiss on the cool cheek she offered. "You're lookin' pretty as a picture, as always."

That much was true enough. She was trim and attractive, in a black and white sundress and heels. Her blond hair was carefully kept the same shade as his own. And if age had the indecency to show up in her face, she had whatever discreet procedure necessary to banish it.

"Devlin." Her smile was forced. "I expected you hours ago."

"Granddaddy had a spell. I had to meet him at the doctor's."

Her eyes slid to the house. "That's too bad. But the fact is, I set aside time this afternoon for a nice visit and now, well, now it's later. Howard's home. And, well, you know seein' you always upsets him."

He felt something inside him go cold. "Granddaddy's fine, mama. He'll appreciate you askin'."

Her brown gaze returned to his with a start and she had the grace to flush. "Well, how you do go on, Devlin. As if I don't care 'bout my own daddy's health. I'll call him before Howard and I go out tonight."

"I won't keep you long." He shoved his hands in the pockets of his jeans and wondered why the hell it was so difficult to talk to his own mother. To feel anything at all for her, outside a dutiful sort of love that had nothing to do with earned devotion. "It's 'bout that night. The night they arrested daddy."

Her face went as white as her dress. And her voice sounded a bit shrill. "Honestly, Devlin, we went over that once, just recently. I told you everythin' I know, and I don't 'preciate you dredgin' it all up again!"

He rocked back on his heels and surveyed her. "Well, actually you didn't. You refused to discuss it, remember?"

Celia Ann had a convenient memory when it was called for. "I recall no such thing. We had a long discussion and . . ."

"Ex–Chief of Police Kenner seems to think you can solve one mystery 'bout that night." Manners had him taking her arm when she swayed, but she shook off his touch as if it burned. "Said he'd left somethin' out of the police report to save embarrassin' you. Somethin' that has to do with why daddy was drinkin' so much that night."

"I have no idea what he's talkin' 'bout." The color had returned to her face now. Twin flags of red flushed her cheeks. "And I refuse to have this conversation with you."

Dev gave a slow nod. "That's your right, I 'spect." And certainly her usual method to avoid anything unpleasant. "Just means I'll go directly to John Kenner myself. I don't think he'd object to tellin' me."

She moistened her lips. Glanced in the direction of the house and back again. Following the path of her gaze, Dev noted a blind at the front window twitch. "It was such a long time ago."

"I don't reckon it's somethin' you're likely to have forgotten."

"You have to understand, I was young. Younger than you are now, actually. With a baby that needed constant attention. And Lucas workin' all the time tryin' to make more money. I would have been happy doin' with less," she hastened to add.

"Of course you would have," he murmured cynically. Celia Ann was high maintenance. Apparently she'd had that quality even back then.

Her immaculate nails gleaming against the fabric as one hand smoothed over her dress. "I made a mistake back then, Devlin. One I'm not proud of, but there were all those factors drivin' me to it."

His entire system slowed. Blood. Heart. Lungs. A terrible sort of trepidation filled him. "What'd you do, Mama?"

"I hated that town with a passion even when I was growin' up there," she said, a flash of heat in her eyes. "People do more talkin' than workin', seems like. And there'd been talk . . . Lucas claimed it wasn't true, but that didn't stop some folks from repeatin' it just the same. His name had been mentioned as the one who'd been steppin' out with Sally Ann Porter before she disappeared. Even her mama, Jessalyn, asked him 'bout it." Her hand lifted to cover her heart. "You just don't know what that did to me, hearin' such a thing. Wonderin' if it were true that Lucas had been unfaithful."

The picture forming in his mind was an ugly one. "So you decided to get even. Just in case it was true."

Celia Ann hesitated. "There was a man who was sweet on me. Not important who it was, and it wasn't many times that we met." Her eyes filled with tears that he wished he could believe were genuine. "Your daddy came home early that night and caught us."

Even half expecting the revelation, the news caught him like a swift right jab in the solar plexus. No child should have to know this much about his parents' private lives.

"Okay." He swallowed hard. Reached wildly for the objectivity that served him so well in his research. "I imagine things got . . . unpleasant."

"There was a terrible row. Lucas and . . . the other man busted up the place before your daddy ran him off. Then we had ourselves a terrible screamin' match. He started drinkin'. We didn't keep much liquor in the house, but we'd had a barbecue 'bout a month earlier. There were a few bottles people had left, and he started in on them. He got . . ." She gave a quick shudder. "He wasn't himself. I was scared and called his family. Scooped you out of bed and ran over to my daddy's house. I never knew the rest 'til the police came knockin' at our door the next day."

He stared at her, emotions careening and colliding inside him. "Pretty quick to give up Lucas, too, weren't you, once the news broke."

Guiltily, she flushed. "You didn't see him that night. It wasn't the man I knew. He was violent. And so angry. I really can't say what he might have been capable of."

And that really was the crux of it, Dev thought numbly. Maybe no one was what they seemed. Scratch the surface, and all sorts of nastiness oozed forth. "I guess the same can be said for all of us, Mama. But you're hardly blameless in all this."

The moisture in her eyes had miraculously cleared. They were flinty now. "You've got more than a bit of your daddy in you, Devlin. Always expectin' more of people than they can give. Makes you hard to be 'round, knowin' I can never live up to your expectations."

If she'd thrust a knife in his chest, she couldn't have wounded him more deeply. He took a deep breath. Blew it out. When he was able to speak, he said, "Maybe that's true. Or maybe you just don't have more to give. Whichever the case, I don't think either of us needs to pretend anymore." He nodded toward the house and said with heavy irony, "Tell Howard hey for me."

She didn't try to call him back as he headed for the car. Would it have helped if she did? He didn't know, but he doubted it. Whatever fragile pretense of a relationship they'd managed to tiptoe around for the last couple decades had been irrevocably altered.

But he sat in his car for several minutes after Celia Ann had disappeared into the house. His fingers clenched and unclenched on the steering wheel. Seemed like the more he discovered, the more questions he had. Problem was, he was losing his stomach for hearing the answers.

He started the vehicle and pulled away from the curb. He couldn't help wondering about something his mama had said. About him wanting more than people could give.

And whether Ramsey just might agree with her.

The UNSUB is a power-assertive offender, using a value system from a century-old religious sect to condone his act. The trappings of the religion, i.e., the plant the victim was forced to ingest, are part of his signature. His approach probably includes the con or surprise, and he is likely to use force to ensure compliance. Evidence suggests he didn't act alone.

The victim's death was a predetermined outcome of the attack itself, but the UNSUB would likely use sexual torture to "punish" the victim for some perceived unworthiness during the duration of the assault.

The offender is likely to be of above-average intelligence, Caucasian, between the ages of thirty-five to fifty. Given the strength of the value system he uses to justify his act, it is doubtful this is his first offense. He is extremely high risk for offending again.

Ramsey reread part of her completed profile and wondered yet again if she was taking a step off a steep cliff with this one. But she couldn't get beyond the part turmeric had played in Ashton's religion. And that frightened her.

It was her job to look at all possibilities. To weigh them carefully and to retain objectivity. The greatest flaw an investigator could have was to be blinded by a mind already made up.

And there were a lot of questions still unanswered.

Sanders obviously believed Frost was "unworthy" since he'd chosen her sister over his former fiancée. Not to mention the motivation that life insurance policy gave him. But what possible connection did he have with the sick perp who had carried out the crime? The one with a link to Spring County? Matthews hadn't found one. Rollins hadn't either. And Sanders was liable to walk away from this thing if they didn't discover it.

She looked at the clock as her cell rang, startled to discover it was nearing eight thirty. Food hadn't been uppermost on her mind while she'd completed the profile, but she was starving now. Hopefully the call was from Dev with ideas for dinner.

But the voice on the other end of the line wasn't Dev's. It was Rollins.

"I've found it, Ramsey. Damn, I still can't believe it." His tone was a mingle of urgency and incredulity. "Started workin' on that genealogy software of Kendra May's again after dinner, and there it was, big as you please."

Anticipation torched her system. "You've found Sanders's connection to someone here in town?"

"It's loose." He sounded as though he were trying to tamp down his own excitement. "Mighty loose. Third or fourth cousin—I never can make hide nor hair of that. But the relationship is there, all right."

"Who is it?"

"You'll never believe it. Wouldn't myself if I wasn't sitting here starin' at the screen with my own eyes." Just when she was getting ready to scream the question at him again, Mark took a breath. "Quinn Sanders is some sorta kinfolk to Reverend Jay Biggers."

Stunned, it took her a moment to digest the news. The crotchety pastor who held such a dim view of Dev? Then her gaze dropped to her profile again. Because this shot the first hole in her conclusions. She wouldn't hazard a guess to Biggers's age, but he was older than fifty-five.

"Shit. I started talking to all the ministers in town today, but was leaving him for last because I'd sort of met him once already."

"Don't feel bad." Mark sounded disgusted. "I've known the man practically all my life, and this 'bout has me pole-axed. I'm headin' out to his place to have a word with him. Figured you'd want to come along."

Ramsey was already out of her chair. "Damn straight."

Full dark had fallen as they drove down a familiar road on the outskirts of town. "I think we need to go at him easy-like at first." Rollins slanted her a glance. "He's not the friendliest man at the best of times, and I'd like to see if I can get him to admit to the relationship with Sanders himself."

"I'll follow your lead." At least at first. But if Biggers was unforthcoming, she was more than ready to turn up the heat.

"I called Powell on the way over here. He was pretty excited about the find. He's on his way back first thing tomorrow mornin'."

"Let's hope we have something for him by then." She looked out the window. "Where's he live out here?"

"Just over that next knoll. He moved out of town after his wife left him. Sorta curious, for a pastor, come to think of it," Mark said reflectively. "Most live near their church so as to be more accessible to their congregation." He sent her a quick glance. "I'm sorta hopin' to find him at home. I'd hate like fire to have to drag him out of some church function with witnesses all 'round to start all kinds of talk. Say what you want, but it's my job to keep that sort of thing to a minimum."

His voice cut off then as the car slowed. A rare obscenity escaped him.

Ramsey looked over. "What?"

"Switched vehicles with Stratton for his trip to DC because he'd been havin' trouble with his."

"What sort of trouble?"

Rollins stomped on the accelerator a couple times to no avail. "That kind of trouble. Shit." He pulled over and rammed the vehicle into park, his movements jerky with frustration. "Let me see what he carries in the way of tools."

Damn. Ramsey looked at the illuminated clock on the dash. It wasn't like there was real urgency to get to Biggers. The man obviously wasn't going anywhere; had every right, in fact, to believe he'd gotten away with killing Cassie Frost.

The urgency came from within. A burn to bring the offender to justice. To make him pay for this crime. And maybe to discover others he'd committed.

Mark slammed the trunk lid. When he pulled open the door and got in the Jeep again, she asked, "Are you going to be able to fix the problem?" She looked at him, and a sheet of pure ice kissed her skin.

The hand aiming the Smith & Wesson at her was steady. "Technically, Ramsey, *you're* the problem. But I reckon I can fix you easy 'nough."

———

The ride back from Knoxville was a blur. Because he preferred not to think, Dev had found a classic rock station and adjusted the radio to an ear-splitting level. The distraction hadn't totally worked, but it had been a start.

It was with a feeling of relief that he turned onto the county road leading into Buffalo Springs. The place his mama couldn't wait to escape. The place where his daddy had lost his head and done the unspeakable.

He couldn't say it was easier knowin' the truth. That Jessalyn Porter had given Lucas a reason to dislike her. That an even-tempered man could be driven out of his head by events that had nothing to do with the older woman. But that had eventually led to her death anyway.

His mama was all wrapped up in the fault of that, though she'd never see it. And rather than feeling satisfied by knowing the truth, the only thing he felt was an overwhelming sadness.

He'd been ignoring the headlights that had been behind him for the last little while as he brooded. But there was no ignoring the lights in front of him. They flashed across the road, disorienting him for a minute. Had there been an accident?

Comprehension hit just a moment too late. There were two vehicles crossways in the road, blocking his path. His first thought was that neither of them were police cars.

His second thought was that one of them was a black souped-up dually.

Stomping on the brakes, he skidded around, meaning to head back the way he came, at whatever speed necessary. The day he couldn't outrun Banty Whipple was the day he needed to hang up his car keys.

But there were two vehicles blocking his path to the east, as well. And the sides of the road were so heavily wooded, there would be no alternate route there.

As Dev fought to control the car as it skidded into another one-eighty, he thought with black humor that this night would be a fitting ending for his horseshit day.

And if the earlier pain had been emotional, at least this was something he could fight back against.

Even if it was more than likely to leave very different sorts of bruises.

———

The only thing that could have compelled Ramsey to enter the dark woods was the shotgun at her back. Rollins nudged her violently with it, sent her stumbling to her knees.

"Get up."

With effort, she obeyed. He had her legs bound loosely with a zip cord. Her wrists were trussed behind her with another, making her hope of wresting control of one of his weapons a futile one.

"You're not stupid, Rollins." Delusional. One very sick fuck. But not stupid. "If I end up missing, how long do you think you'll avoid scrutiny? All kinds of people saw me riding with you out of town."

"And I can get a coupla people to swear they saw me drop you later at your motel. So you're right 'bout one thing, Ramsey. I'm not stupid. When questioned, I'll recollect you talkin' 'bout the meth labs you saw out in the woods. Everyone's goin' to think you went out on your own to make an arrest."

The barrel pressed against her back again, stronger this time. "That'll be believable 'cuz the big-name forensic Mindhunt-er," he drawled the word sarcastically, "thinks she's better than all the rest of us lowly law enforcement." He grabbed her hair, bent her head back painfully. "Only you and I will know who the best cop was, won't we Ramsey? Because it sure won't be pieces of me that the wildlife are goin' to be dinin' on tonight."

"It's only a matter of time before Powell and Matthews put this thing together for themselves. I've told Powell everything about what we've discovered."

"I know exactly what you've told Powell. I gave him a call before I picked you up, remember? 'Fraid I let somethin' slip 'bout you spendin' too much energy worryin' 'bout the meth activity we got goin' on 'round here. Sorta primed the pump, you might say. And when Stratton gets back with the evidence from the DC cop, evidence he's goin' to switch, well . . . the hair won't match the one found in Frost's apartment. And your ideas will be discredited all 'round."

A stick cracked beneath her foot. The woods surrounding them seemed unnaturally quiet. "You are smarter than I gave you credit for, Rollins." It was an effort to imbue her words with sarcasm when panic was doing a fast sprint up her spine. "Of course, that's not saying much. But giving credit where it's due, I'm guessing you got away with murder at least twice now. Once in DC, and once with Cassie Frost. That takes a bit of intelligence."

One minute she was upright, and the next he'd tripped her and her face was pressed in the dirt. His booted foot was on her back. "Damn right it does. And I'd like to tell you all 'bout just how smart I am. But more than that, I'd like to show you." The rifle barrel caressed a cool path over her cheek. "Because if there was ever a woman who needed spiritual cleansing, it's you."

Inhaling the damply sweet scent of decay, Ramsey fought

to push back terror. "And to think I never realized just how special you were. Rufus Ashton's disciple. Purifying the world one woman at a time."

"But you know it now." He reached for her and dragged her upright by her hair until she was in a standing position again. Then he gave her a push forward. "Rufus Ashton was a prophet. His mistake was believin' there was a place in this country that was sinless 'nough to embrace his teachin's. His congregation might've scattered at his death, his secrets buried with him, but his true believers have flourished in secret. Your disappearance would be hard to explain, so your death has to be different. No one will ever connect you to Frost." He made a sound of amusement. "Or the last one."

The last one? Ramsey seized on the words. There'd been another victim, and they hadn't even realized it?

He yanked her to a stop. Strode a few paces away to kick at some leaves at the base of a rock pile. "Here we go. Meth heads can always be counted on to leave their shit behind when they move on."

A dull sort of horror bloomed. She knew exactly how dangerous abandoned labs could be.

"Where is it? Put it here myself the other night."

"What are we looking for? Your conscience?"

He was quicker than she'd expected. The rifle barrel caught her across the side of her head, sending her to her knees again. Had her blinking dazedly at the yellow eyes staring out from beneath the shadowy bush.

"You won't bait me," he said silkily, hauling her up to a standing position. She swayed as he continued, "It's the Lord's will to be done here. My human inclinations cannot supersede his plan for you."

He shoved her over to face a massive tree trunk. She heard him rummaging in the backpack he wore. "Someone made off with the anhydrous I stashed here, so you'll have to wait a while. But when I get back with more, I'm gonna fix it so it blows you to hell."

"Good to know," she said between gritted teeth. If she didn't clench them tightly, they'd be chattering, and she was damned if she'd give him the satisfaction of hearing the sound of her fear. "I like to be able to plan my evening."

He gave a short laugh. "Always the smart-ass." She felt him work at the bonds on her wrists. "Maybe the red mist will take care of you so I don't have to. Choke the life right out of you." He slipped another zip cord through the one binding her hands, and then continued stringing more together until it circled the tree. Then he secured it tightly.

She felt him searching her jacket pocket. Draw out her cell phone. There was a crunch followed by a rustle, and she could only assume he'd destroyed it before tossing the pieces.

"I won't be long. Spend the time repentin' your sins, Ramsey. 'For this is the time of the Lord's vengeance.'"

"I'm going to spend the time thinking of a way to cut your balls off and feed them to you."

She felt his hand in her hair, yanking her head back before slamming it forward against the tree trunk. Pain rocketed through her skull.

And then everything went black.

"Welcome to the party." Banty Whipple grinned at Dev as he got down out of the cab of his shiny dually. He held a short club in his hands, tapping one end lightly against his palm. "Holdin' it in your honor. It'd be a shame for you to miss it, right boys?"

The three goons joining Banty in the circle of headlights all wore ear-splitting grins. One of them cackled in agreement.

"He don't look like he's in the mood for a party." This from the guy Dev assumed was Zach Harris, since he'd gotten out of a piece-of-shit red truck, the twin for the one he'd seen after the brick had been heaved at his house.

He studied them all in the dim light. "Hey, Zach. Guess you got tired of throwin' bricks through windows, huh?" The grin abruptly faded from the man's face. One man was a stranger to Dev. He figured it was someone Banty worked with at the mill. The third was Arvin Tester, from north of town. As ornery a bastard as ever drew a breath.

"Doesn't seem hardly fair," Dev said mildly, taking mental inventory of the contents of his car. The most lethal thing in it was a plastic soft drink bottle. "None of my friends got invited."

Banty spit a wad of chew on the asphalt. "Shee-it. Tried to tell you once, you ain't got no friends 'round these parts. But I know I've been wantin' to tie your asshole in a knot for some time."

"Sounds like you've been thinkin' of me." Dev veered in the direction of the road's shoulder, looking for a stray tree limb. "Can't say you've crossed my mind."

"Your kind don't belong in Buffalo Springs." This from Tester. And there was nothing on his face but pure mean. "Dipshit cops can't seem to figure out that when your family's 'round, women die. But we got your number, Stryker."

The four were approaching steadily. "Good to know. Save me a fortune in analyst fees." Why the hell did the county have to pick now to clear the shoulders free of debris? There wasn't more than a good-sized pebble to be seen.

Dev stopped scanning the area for a weapon and surveyed Whipple's friends. "You boys here to do what Banty can't himself or just to watch the fun?" The men sent quick looks at each other as Dev went on. "'Cuz Banty here, well, he's always been a li'l fella. Probably not a fair fight 'tween the two of us, even him with that club."

"Keep my damn name outta your mouth, Stryker!" There was fire in Whipple's eyes, evident even in the dim light afforded by their headlights. "I don't need no one else's help to whip tar outta you. I'm a gonna jerk you through a knot all by myself."

The other three faded back then, as if to watch the start. But Dev had no doubt about their plans to leave without getting involved themselves.

Banty came closer, whipping the club back and forth in front of him in short slicing motions. "I'm gonna stave in your ribs, Stryker."

"You're goin' to have to get closer than that to do it." The rest of the scene faded as his focus narrowed to Banty. On getting the sawed-off little shit close enough to inflict some damage on him.

Whipple took the bait and jumped forward, the club singing through the air. Dev dodged, waited until the weapon had finished its arc, and grabbed it. Yanked forward. When he'd pulled Banty off balance, he planted a fist in the man's face before dancing away.

"Yowsa!" One of the onlookers shouted. "You gonna let him get 'way with that shit, Banty?"

Banty's nose was gushing. "You're dead, Stryker." He rushed him, catching Dev in the chest with the short end of the club and driving the breath from his lungs. He grasped the club again, but he lacked the strength to hang on to it when Banty moved away.

"I reckon that might've stung a little." Whipple's voice was smug.

Dev still couldn't get a deep breath. "That li'l tap? That all you got?" He straightened, fists curled. He needed to get that club away from Banty. And he had to stay on his feet. The idiot would beat him to death with it before realizing he was dead.

"Talked to your wife the other day," he said in a conversational tone. "She told me all 'bout your trouble satisfyin' her in bed." He sent a silent apology to Emma Jean Whipple, who had always seemed a decent enough sort, short of her lamentable taste in men. "Seems it's not just your legs that are short."

There were hoots from the other men at this, but the gibe had the necessary effect. Banty came in swinging, then paused to aim a vicious kick at Dev's privates. Dev jumped aside and delivered a roundhouse to the side of Banty's head, knocking the man to the pavement. Then he wasted no time dropping on top of him.

They rolled, each grasping for purchase. Banty landed the first punch, a clip to the jaw that had Dev's head snapping back. He returned a fist to the man's face and followed it with another. There was a ringing in his ears as he pummeled the man. A gray haze over his vision. But when it occurred to him Banty had all but stopped fighting back, he hauled in a deep breath and staggered to his feet.

He shook his head to clear it, discovered the problem was blood running in his eyes. Dev swiped at his face with his shirt, searching for the club Whipple had dropped.

Then saw it a moment later in Tester's hand. The man was standing a couple feet away, a sneer on his face.

"Figure you must be warmed up by now, Stryker." And he took a step toward him.

"What sort of foolishness are y'all up to?" The unexpected voice split the scene like a surgeon's scalpel.

Everyone, Dev included, turned to face the newcomer.

Rose Thornton was standing on the opposite shoulder of the road, wearing the same coat and hat he'd seen her in the last time he'd spoken to her. Carrying the shotgun that never seemed to be very far away.

"Rose." Dev felt like laughing crazily. Would have if not for the likelihood he had a broken rib.

"You mind your manners, Devlin Stryker, and address me proper." She moved closer but never left the shoulder of the road. "I should've known you were behind all this."

"Get on outta here, old lady. This don't concern you."

She peered fiercely at the speaker. "That you, Arvin Tester? You no 'count poachin' thief. Think I don't know who it is goes huntin' on my property once it gets dark?"

The man looked taken aback but stood his ground. For the first time, a sliver of concern for the old lady filtered through Dev. "Maybe you better head home, Miz Thornton."

"Well, that's 'xactly what I plan to do once all these cars get out of my way. How's a body s'posed to get home from town with you id'jits blockin' the road?"

The words gave Dev pause. This wasn't the road leading to Rose's place. But her next move caught his attention. And everyone else's, including Banty's, who had just staggered to his feet.

Hefting her shotgun threateningly, she said, "I have half a mind to call the law on all of ya. Get on out of here, or y'all be pickin' lead out of your butts 'til the next blue Tuesday." She waited a moment, and when no one moved, she sited the shotgun. "Go on now, git!"

As if in slow motion, one man after another drifted toward his vehicle. Started it up. Pulled away.

"Not so fast, Stryker."

Without the gleam from headlights of multiple cars, Rose's shape was shadowy. "I want to know what that woman of yours was doin' in my woods tonight."

"Ramsey?" He gave a moment to contemplate just how much she'd hate that description. "You must be mistaken."

"I've got eyes, don't I? Saw her myself. Her and that no-good sheriff who keeps gettin' himself reelected."

"That's impossible. I can't explain why, but there's absolutely no way Ramsey would willingly go into the woods at night." He recalled all too easily what had happened the last time he'd taken her there.

Rose's voice went testy. "Didn't say she was willin', did I? He was doin' the forcin', looks like to me. I warned her she was baitin' trouble. Looks like she found it where she least expected it."

She walked away. Dev's head was spinning, trying to make sense of what she'd said.

Ramsey . . . and Mark? Why would they be in trouble? It didn't make sense. "Wait." He started after the elderly woman, who was already vanishing into the darkness.

"Time's runnin' out, Stryker." The words drifted behind her.

Turning on his heel, he sprinted for his car. He could make sense of it as he drove. He cast one last look behind him. Could no longer make out the shape of Rose in the darkness. He wondered how far down the road she'd parked.

And then he forgot the woman completely as a feeling of urgency filled him. He started up the car and headed east again, away from Rose, away from the scene of the ambush.

He'd go around the other way. He couldn't afford to be slowed if Banty and his idiot friends were waiting for him closer to town.

Without thought to speed limits, he took a left on the first gravel road and raced toward the blacktop that would lead to the woods near Rose's house. His heart was pounding like a sprinter after a hundred-meter dash.

Ramsey. There was a boulder-sized knot in his throat threatening to choke him. She was in some kind of trouble, her and Mark. He should alert the sheriff's office. Have some of his cousin's deputies . . .

But wait. He flipped on his brights and pressed down on the accelerator. Mark was with her. According to Rose, Mark had forced her into those woods.

He shoved away the inference. Dev had forced her into the woods, too, not so long ago. Before he understood just what he was asking of her. Rose had misinterpreted what she'd seen, that's all.

The mental argument ping-ponged inside him all the way to the Thornton property. He tried calling Ramsey on the way there. None of his calls went through. He scanned the roadside as he neared Rose's place. No sign of any vehicles. Bringing his car to a stop along the side of the blacktop, he got out. Stood there indecisively.

This was impossible. How was he supposed to find Ramsey? Even in the daylight, it'd be a helluva feat.

Dev's hand went to the cell phone in his pocket. Best thing would be to call Mark, explain Rose's crazy talk . . . His hand hovered over the phone.

I warned her she was baitin' trouble. Looks like she found it where she least expected it.

Slowly, he dropped the cell back in his pocket.

It was then he saw the lights.

Brilliant dancing balls of illumination, halfway between him and the edge of the woods. Dev took a step closer, his gaze never moving off them.

Orbs. He hadn't disproved that they were anything else. Hadn't proved these were paranormal entities, either, but damned if they didn't seem to be beckoning him. Flickering closer for several yards, and then dancing away.

As if leading him somewhere.

Without taking his focus off them, he fumbled for the switch on his key ring to unlock his trunk. Searched one-handed inside it for the Mag-Lite before closing the lid again.

And without further thought, he plunged through the clearing. Followed the lights as they led the way to the fringe of the woods.

Chapter 24

Ramsey stilled again, straining her ears. In the darkness every sound seemed magnified. Nightmares, past and present, crashed together in her mind. Every time she heard a noise, she was convinced it was Rollins coming back for her. How long had he been gone? Twenty minutes? Thirty?

She redoubled her efforts. She'd been working at the binds since she'd regained consciousness. Her position made it impossible for her to scrape the zip cord against the tree bark, hoping to fray it. Her only hope was to work her wrists out of the cord securing them.

A twig cracked. A sob of fury escaped her. She'd be damned if she'd make this easy for Rollins. He'd have to take the binds off before setting off his little meth bomb. He couldn't take the chance that a piece of her was found with a zip cord still dangling from it.

When he released her, she'd be ready. If she was going to die in these woods tonight, she was going do her damnedest to take him with her.

"Ramsey! Sugar, where are you?"

She stilled. What trick was this? Did Rollins have Dev now? Was he going to kill them both?

And then there was someone behind her, tearing the duct tape from her mouth. Fumbling for the binds at her wrists. "Who did this to you? Rose said she saw you come in here with Mark, but that makes no sense at all. Hold still, baby. Hold still and let me figure out how these things work."

Ramsey rested her forehead against the tree as her knees

went to water. "Dev?" His name shuddered out of her. "What are you doing here? Did you see Rollins? It's him. He's Ashton's disciple." Too late she recalled the two men were cousins. What if he didn't believe her?

She felt the binds fall away, and turned around to find herself in his arms.

"Oh, sugar, your poor face."

A smile hurt too much to attempt. "Yours doesn't look much better." There was a cut over his eye that was oozing sullenly. His bottom lip was swollen and split.

"Yeah, that's a story. Can you walk?" His hands were running over her, as if checking for broken bones. His touch felt real. For the first time, she let herself believe they just might get out of these woods alive.

"I'm fine." Her wrists were numb. But she could move. And she was in a hurry to get out of here. "I don't get it. How did you ever . . ."

"Long story, and not one you're goin' to believe right off," he muttered. He ducked down, worked at the cord around her legs until she was freed. "For now let's get you the hell out of here."

"Wait." She tried to grab his shirt. Found her arms didn't work. They were alive with pins and needles as circulation made a sluggish return, but heavy. Useless. "Where's your car?"

"In front of Rose's place."

She nodded, started moving forward with him. "That's good. Rollins will return any minute, but we came in the back way. Let's hope he uses that same approach."

Dev stopped, threw a look over his shoulder. "You came in from that direction?"

She used her shoulder to nudge him forward again. She wasn't anxious to still be here when Rollins came back. Not before she was better shape to defend herself. "Yeah."

His voice was grim as he grabbed her arm and pulled her into a run. "Well, none of this makes a damn bit of sense. Not the least the bit 'bout Mark. But what really baffles me is how the hell Rose Thornton could have seen the two of you go into the woods if you didn't go by her place?"

———

"Absolutely not." Ramsey shoved shells into the ancient shotgun Dev had taken from his granddaddy's closet shelf. "You're in danger because of me. Think I don't realize that? You have to find a place to hole up until this thing is over. Somewhere you'll be safe."

"Ramsey." There was a note in his voice she didn't recognize. When she looked up, she saw it mirrored in his face. Determination. "Do you really think I'm goin' to let you ride on out of here like the Lone Ranger while I hide under the bed in the meantime?"

She knew better than to tell him that was exactly what she hoped for. "He said there were others," she repeated her argument, hoping he'd find it more convincing this time around. "There's no way to be sure who they are. Where they are. I know at least one of his deputies is in on this. With no way of being sure whether I can trust his officers or even the local police, we're seriously fucked until Powell gets TBI reinforcements to town."

He was watching her steadily. "So get to the part that makes me likely to let you walk out of here to hunt down Mark on your own."

"You're not armed. You're not trained." She dropped her gaze because it was easier to revert to the professional she was when she wasn't looking at him. "He can use you against me, Dev." It took more courage than it should have to admit that. "He's got to know we've spent time together. If he can get to you, he gets to me. I can't take that chance."

Because she wasn't looking at him, she was shocked by the brush of his swollen lips against her forehead. "I know what that cost you. But you have no idea what it would cost me to let you walk out that door alone. So the answer is still no."

Furious, her gaze snapped to his. And when she saw the steely light in his eyes, she knew further argument was futile.

"Mark loves me like a brother." There was a catch in his

voice, but his expression remained determined. "He'll hesitate before hurting me. If push comes to shove, that hesitation might give you the second we need."

His argument sucked. He'd still be in danger. But short of binding and gagging him and hauling him to the basement—an idea that had merit—she couldn't figure out a way to get out of here without him.

"There's no way you're leavin' without me." His words mirrored her thoughts. "I'd just follow you anyway. Besides . . ." His grin was lopsided. "Two of us stand a better chance than one, right?"

She heaved out a breath and accepted the inevitable. Hoped like hell she wasn't making a mistake she'd regret the rest of her life. Dropping extra shotgun shells in her jacket pocket, she headed for the door.

"For Godsakes," she threw over her shoulder grimly, "try to keep your head down."

———

"Explain to me again what we're doin' here."

Ramsey dropped lightly down to the ground from the gate she'd scaled at the Buffalo Springs cemetery. She accepted the shotgun Dev handed her through the bars and waited for him to join her.

Her ears sharpened at the sound of pain he made when he landed. "Are you sure you're all right?" She'd cleaned up his face as best she could, relieved to discover nothing in need of stitching. Then he'd done the same for her. But it was the bruises on his chest that had her worried. She wasn't convinced nothing had been broken.

"I'm dandy." The words sounded as though they were gritted through his teeth. But by the time she'd moved to his side, he'd picked up the bag of tools he'd brought and was striding away, leaving her no choice but to follow.

"Rollins mentioned that Ashton's secrets were buried with him. I got to thinking he might be talking about Ruth's missing record. While we're waiting for backup, we may as well check it out."

The inky darkness of the cemetery, with its looming tomb-stones and eerie shadows, had little effect on her. It wasn't the woods. And she wasn't helpless, waiting for a madman's return.

"The Ashton mausoleum is in the back corner in the old-est section. This way."

Silently they crossed the quiet space. Dark clouds scudded across the sky, blotting out all but occasional glimpses of the moon. When there was a glimmer of illumination, it turned the branches of the old oaks into skeletal fingers.

There was more than one mausoleum in the area, she noted, but Dev seemed to know which one to go to. When occasional headlights would spear the darkness on the road beyond, they took cover, waiting for the vehicle to go by. It always did.

Where was Rollins? The question burned across her mind. How long after they'd left the woods had he returned to find her gone? He'd have known she'd had help escaping. Even she could admit now, away from the hope inspired by panic, that there had been little chance of her freeing herself on her own. He might think a poacher came across her. Or maybe even Ezra T.

But he probably realized her rescuer was Dev.

A fist clenched in her belly. If she encountered Rollins to-night and Dev got in the middle of it, she'd never forgive herself. If she'd struck out on her own, and the sheriff grabbed up Dev to flush her out . . . She sighed. She'd never forgive that, either. They'd been sitting ducks at his grandfather's house. And anywhere else they'd have tried to hide would have drawn more people into danger.

She'd had few choices. And with over two hours, mini-mum, before Knoxville agents could get here, she couldn't be sure what Rollins might be driven to do.

Because she wasn't paying attention, she nearly plowed into Dev's back when he halted. He was holding out his cell, which was still vibrating in his palm. "For you."

She snatched it up to answer. There'd been little choice but to give Powell his number with her phone destroyed.

The agent didn't waste time with preliminaries. "I've got state police hittin' town as we speak. They'll spread out, lookin' for Rollins. They've been informed to trust no one on the local level in the search. Where are you?"

"Chasing down a lead."

"For Godsakes, Ramsey, don't be a damned hero." The man's voice was stern. "You're Rollins's likeliest target. Get somewhere safe and stay out of sight until we get reinforcements there."

"I'll do that," she said drily. Flipping the phone shut, she slipped it in her pocket rather than giving it back to Dev.

"That TBI?" They started moving again.

"Yeah." The state police might be here, but they wouldn't find the sheriff. She was certain of that. If she had to guess, he'd be taking shelter in the same place where Cassie Frost had been killed. And the other victim he'd alluded to earlier. They'd need a door-to-door search, which would take extra manpower and a whole lot of time to accomplish. She could only hope he didn't slip out of town in the meantime.

"Here we are." Dev stopped before a small dark building. When he played the light over its front, the first thing she noticed was *Ashton* in faint, aged letters. The second thing she observed was the padlock on the door.

She blew out a breath. "Nothing's ever easy, is it? I need to get in that bag."

He set it down and aimed the light so she could see what she was searching for. Benjamin Gorder hadn't had much in the way of lock-picking equipment in his toolbox, but he'd had paper clips. If she needed more than that, she was losing her touch. But just in case she'd overestimated her skills, she'd brought the older man's hacksaw.

It took longer than it should have, but a few minutes later she had the padlock open and out of the hasp. She took one more look around before pulling the door open. The hinges opened without a sound.

"Someone keeps these well-oiled," she murmured. It took more effort than it should have to step into the small building. Dev's light didn't do much more than punch a hole in the darkness within. The open door behind them helped marginally.

She took a couple steps farther inside. The center was taken up by a huge stone vault, in which, she assumed, was Ashton's casket. She had the caustic thought that his wives were probably buried somewhere in pine boxes. But nothing so simple for the big man himself.

Ramsey stepped out of the beam so she could look at Dev. "Only one hiding place in here." And she was slightly queasy at the thought of moving aside that lid. Sticking her hand inside.

"Unless there's a loose stone somewhere. An opening at the base of the vault itself." Dev got on his hands and knees to look. He almost managed to hide the hiss of pain the action cost him.

"For Godsakes, get up." Concern had her rounding the vault to go to him. Until a shadow moved across the door. "Stay down!"

"Just like a woman. Can't make up her mind."

Ramsey brought the shotgun up in one smooth movement but was blinded by the light Rollins shone in her face. When she stepped out of the beam, she saw the sheriff holding a light that could have been the twin of Dev's in one hand. The S&W he'd aimed at her earlier was in the other.

"Ramsey, Ramsey, Ramsey." He tutted. "So predictable. After our little conversation, I imagined exactly where you'd go next."

"You have a better imagination than I do. Can't say I'd pictured what you looked like in a gray wig." Coupled with whatever he'd rubbed on his eyebrows, the shapeless flannel shirt, and suspenders, the getup added at least fifteen years to his appearance.

Rollins set the light on the floor at his feet, the gun never once wavering from her. Stay down, Dev, she pled silently as she inched along the wall, keeping the sheriff in her sites. Just one more minute. Just until I can . . .

The next moment Dev dove at Rollins's feet, but the man was waiting for him. He heaved a kick at his side, and Ramsey heard a sickening crack.

"Now that didn't have to happen, son." Mark's voice was reproving. "Sounds like you mighta had something loosened up in there already. But I don't like that you're takin' this li'l bitch's side over your family. That just isn't right."

"This is between the two of us, Rollins." She hoped her desperation didn't leak into her voice. "Dev has nothing . . ."

"He shouldn't have had anythin' to do with it. This *is* on you, Ramsey. All I did was invite him home as an ace in the hole. If things got too warm, well who better to point the finger at than Lucas Rollins's son."

Dev raised his head slowly up to face his cousin's. "My mama said she called his family that night. The night they had a fight and he started drinkin'."

"That's right. She called my daddy."

Disbelief filled her. "He set up his own brother that night? Framed him for Jessalyn's death?"

"Daddy saw a chance to get rid of that old bitch and shut her slanderous mouth for good. Her slut of a daughter got exactly what was comin' to her, but she wouldn't let go with her vicious talk. It could've cost him the election. Lucas was a sacrifice." The fervency in his voice sent a chill spiraling down Ramsey's spine. "In the Bible, Abraham was willing to give up his own son. Daddy gave up his brother. God's will had to continue. And that kind of reputation is hard to beat, a man willin' to see justice done, even when it implicates his own family. Got him reelected, too."

Mark gave Dev's foot a nudge with his boot. "Get on up here, son. You know I was hopin' involvin' you wasn't goin' to be necessary. Always loved you like a brother."

"Given your family's idea of loyalty, that's hardly comforting. Stay down, Dev." She knew exactly what Rollins was planning. And once he had Dev as a human shield, their chances diminished greatly.

She wished like hell Rollins hadn't taken her gun. Even Dev couldn't be sure when the shotgun had last been fired. What if it malfunctioned? What if the shells were too old?

Her thoughts fragmented at Rollins's next words. "I swear if you don't get up here, I'll shoot the bitch where she stands.

It's not the way she needs to die. In a state of impurity. But if that's what I have to do, that's on you."

"No!"

But Dev was already rising, slowly, painfully, to his feet. He had time to send her one glance, take one step, before Rollins pulled him in front of him, one arm around his neck.

And then he pressed the gun against Dev's temple. "Put down the gun, Ramsey. You're not that good."

Never surrender your weapon. How many times had Raiker drilled that into them? *Never leave yourself completely defenseless.*

"You don't know how good I am, Mark. It's been a long time since we worked together."

"But you haven't changed. You're a godless whore. I only wish I'd taken the opportunity to purify you when I had the chance. Too bad the red mist didn't choke the life out of you back in the woods. The way it almost did to me."

The way the man was rambling, she wondered if he'd suffered a complete break from reality. But Dev was trying to get her attention. His gaze fixed on hers then on the floor at his feet. She frowned, uncomprehending.

"Took some liberties with Sancrosanctity's casting out ceremonies, didn't you?" Was Dev signaling he was going to distract Rollins some way? "Wonder what the rest of your cult would think about you raping and killing women on your own. Like that woman in DC. I'll bet you were at a conference there and just couldn't resist going hunting."

"God is channeling in me. Through me." She winced when she saw him pressing the gun harder against Dev's head. "I'm the elder of the church now. Like my daddy and granddaddy were before me. I don't have to wait for the group's decision. They don't need to be part of every castin' out ceremony."

No, he couldn't wait. Because the taste of it had gotten in his blood. And the church-sanctioned ceremonies of rape and murder had left him craving more.

Ramsey didn't have a clear shot. She cocked her head,

trying to find a better angle. Dev's eyes widened for a moment.

A split second later, he let his head loll to the side and went limp in Rollins's arms, his weight pulling the man off balance. She had a split second before the sheriff recovered. Turned the gun. Brought it up . . .

Ramsey fired. The sound reverberated in the small enclosure, deafening her. She was aware of Dev falling to one side. Rollins to another. She dove and squeezed off another shot.

It was a moment before she recognized that the sheriff had fallen backward to land outside the door of the mausoleum. "Dev, are you hit?" She couldn't take her eyes off Rollins as she advanced on the open doorway. But she was inwardly reeling in horror at what might have just happened. "Answer me, dammit!" Panic surged, threatening to drown her. "Are you hit! Damn you, you better not be dead."

She stood over Rollins, weapon ready. But he was no longer a threat. He'd never be a threat again. The old shotgun had blasted most of his face away.

"Well, I guess I'm not dead if I can still hear you yellin' at me."

Her knees went boneless. Turning, she walked into his arms. Felt them tighten around her. "I was afraid I'd hit you. Or that he had. . . ."

"He was aimin' at you for a while there. Gotta say that gave me a few bad moments." She couldn't tell which of them was trembling more.

Gently, he took the gun out of her hand. "Let's put this down, sugar. It's all over now."

She nodded against his chest, let her eyes slide shut in one brief moment of giddy relief. "Yeah. It's over."

Chapter 25

Ramsey stood next to Dev at the edge of Ashton's Pond, watched the divers and dredgers at work. "Some people need to get new priorities." She was referring to the small cluster standing well back of the police tape holding signs protesting the work being done. "Who the hell cares about saving some spotted toad when we've got bodies to bring up?"

She heard the humor in his voice when he answered. "Well . . . nature lovers, I guess."

"Nature's overrated."

"I couldn't agree more." She turned as she heard Adam Raiker's voice.

The uneven terrain had to be hell on his leg. But as usual, there was no flicker of expression on the man's face. She noticed more than one sidelong glance in his direction from the law enforcement officers scattered around the area. But Ramsey figured their interest was motivated as much by his reputation as his appearance.

His last case with the Bureau had cost him dearly. A jagged scar bisected his throat. A black patch covered the eye he'd lost. And she'd never seen him walk without the cane he carried now. But no one who'd ever met him would pity him for the injuries he'd suffered. The man was too formidable.

He came to a halt beside them. Ramsey made the introductions. "Devlin Stryker, my boss, Adam Raiker."

She was a bit surprised when Raiker accepted Dev's outstretched hand. Was downright shocked when her boss's good eye narrowed in thought. "Stryker. The parapsychologist. I've read a couple of your books. Intriguing."

Her expression must have given away her thoughts because Raiker raised his brows. "What? You didn't think I could read?"

She exchanged a quick look with Dev, noted the small smile he wore. "No," she said in belated response to Raiker's question. "I mean yes. I'm just glad you recognize quality writing when you see it."

"Thanks, sugar." Dev brushed a kiss against her hair before he began to move away. "I'll let you two catch up. I see a friend over there. Nice to meet you, Mr. Raiker."

When her attention returned to her boss, he was watching her with an expression that had wariness flickering.

"You better not be thinking of leaving the agency, Clark."

Real amazement flared at the words. "Why would I do that?"

Her response seemed to satisfy him, and they watched in silence for a time as the divers broke the surface, carefully towing something between them. "How many does that make?"

"Eleven." The governor wasn't going to get his wish. Buffalo Springs was in the national news again. And this time, the notoriety wasn't likely to fade anytime soon.

"I keep thinking of this man who came to the morgue. He thought the victim might be his missing daughter." The thought of Jim Grayson's anguish made her chest go tight. "And all the time, she was lying at the bottom of the pond."

The missing record book had been in Ashton's vault, just as Ramsey had suspected. And when they'd discovered the simple code Ruth had written it in, she was filled with new admiration for the woman who had attempted to stop Ashton well over a century ago. At the very least, she'd tried to record for the ages what the man was. But her attempt had lasted only a few months before it had been discovered. Before she'd become the man's next victim.

"They won't find all the remains intact," Raiker observed. "Going to be a process bringing them up. I've got Fleming on her way. Hard to guess how long it'll take her to sort all the bones out and identify which belong to which victims."

She nodded. Caitlin Fleming was a colleague, a forensic

anthropologist as well as an investigator. She made a mental note to ask her if nearly a century in the pond would have destroyed the remains of Ashton's original victims. Ruth had recorded the sect members' names. Dates. And the "sins" that had condemned them to death.

The original record had been updated over the generations with lists of those sacrificed. But Ramsey doubted all the victims' names would be found there.

"There's bound to be some surprises brought out of the pond, too," she added. "All the group members participated with Frost, it sounds like. But Rollins indicated he killed someone after that, and her death wasn't noted. He can't be the first member to chafe at waiting for the sect members to decide on the next selection. They got a taste of it. They liked the rape. Didn't mind the murder. And when it gets in the blood . . ."

"It's a heady power," Raiker agreed. "Rollins likely wouldn't have been the first elder to strike out on his own when the urge came over him."

She saw Dev standing at the fringe of trees beyond the pond, looking as though he were talking to himself. In the next moment, she saw a flash of a flannel shirt, and realized he'd gone to check on Ezra T., who was watching from afar.

The man's words came back to her from the first time they'd met. She'd asked what he'd observed near the pond, and he said he'd seen the cops. She'd assumed he meant the police working the crime scene. But after hearing how he'd been shot in the woods by Rollins and left to die, she had to wonder if he'd encountered the sheriff or Stratton the night of the murder. Possibly recognized them.

At any rate, she owed the man her life. According to what he'd told Dev a few days ago, it was he who'd removed the anhydrous Rollins had hidden in the woods. The man's motives were of less interest to her than was the fact it had bought her needed time to escape.

"You've finished with the evidence from the tunnel, I hear."

With a start, she returned her attention to Raiker. "Jonesy's identified blood from eighteen different victims. The records indicate nearly three dozen since Ruth's time. Hopefully Caitlin will be able to match the blood to the remains from the pond."

And the tunnel itself had been one of the grisliest sites she'd encountered yet. It ended on Thornton's property, directly beneath the spot where records indicated Ashton's celestial chapel had sat. One entrance was cleverly secreted on the forest floor, only a few yards into the woods beyond her property. Another narrow passage led to Ashton's crypt in the graveyard. When they'd moved the vault lid, they'd found no remains from the town's founding father. The vault floor was missing save for steps that led to the passage.

"Your work's done here, Clark. Fleming will be using the mobile lab, but I've dispatched Jonesy back to headquarters."

"Good riddance," she muttered.

There was a ghost of a smile playing across his lips. "He shared a similar sentiment. Always good to know my people play nice together when they're away from the office."

Agents Powell and Matthews were conversing with some state police nearby. Both men broke away at that moment to veer over in their direction to introduce themselves to Adam.

"Well, Powell." Ramsey didn't trust that tone of her boss's voice. "You almost had Sanders wrapped up for this. Good thing Ramsey didn't let go of that turmeric lead."

Powell flushed, but Ramsey put in, "If we hadn't been leaning on Sanders, we might not have discovered Frost being stalked in Lisbon by a gray-haired man. I would never have thought much of the stray gray hair found in her apartment. Never made the connection to the one found with the ViCAP victim in DC."

"Still, Sanders is a scumbag," Matthews put in. He gazed at the scene of the pond moodily. "Hate to see him profit off Frost's death, even if he didn't have anything to do with it."

She went silent as the men continued to talk, her mind still on the night she'd killed Rollins. The church members' names were listed in the record book, too. A father passed the duty down to his eldest son. It had taken them three days to make all the arrests. She'd been shocked by the listing for Beau Simpson, the man who'd supposedly committed suicide. But it had been Doc Thiesen's arrest that had shaken her the most.

She imagined his stint as county coroner had come in handy when mistakes were made and victims were discovered.

One name they hadn't found in the records, much to Dev's disappointment, was that of Reverend Biggers. The man wasn't exactly a role model as a church leader, but he hadn't been involved in the secret sect. Which just went to show, she considered, that evil lingered far deeper below the surface than did mere unpleasantness.

"Ramsey."

She turned at Dev's voice, immediately concerned by his expression.

"What is it?"

He drew her away from the group. "I heard one of the deputies say he'd just come from Rose Thornton's place. She's been found dead."

It took a moment to make sense of the words. "Not murdered."

He shook his head, his expression a little dazed. "No. But Ramsey . . . they say she's been dead at least three months."

"It's impossible." Dusk was falling as they made their way toward Rose's property, avoiding the emergency vehicles in the rutted overgrown drive. "You just didn't remember what she looked like and we were talking to someone else, that's all. You said yourself you hadn't seen her for years."

"It was her," he said flatly. "Her that we talked to at her place. It was Rose that I spoke to on the road the night she warned me you were in danger. I'm tellin' you, they're carrying the wrong body out of that cabin. It's not Rose's."

The medics were carrying out a stretcher holding a long black-zippered bag. Dev stopped the car behind a state police vehicle and Ramsey got out. Jogged over to the stretcher.

Flashing her temporary badge, she said, "I'd like to ID the victim."

"That's already been done, ma'am."

"I need to see for myself."

The two medics looked at each other. Shrugged. "Ain't gonna be pretty," one said as he reached down to partially unzip the top of the bag. "There were so many flies in that cabin we had to go out and get masks."

It wasn't the sight of the partially eaten away remains of the face that had Ramsey taking a step back. It was the fact that she recognized it.

Dev slipped an arm around her waist as the medics continued toward the ambulance. "It's impossible," she said again, but weakly this time. "How can that be? We saw her. We talked to her."

"We thought we did."

The emergency vehicles were starting to pull out. Dev pulled her toward the side of the house. Ramsey was still shaking her head as they made their way to the back of the cabin. "Maybe she hasn't been dead as long as they think. Insects inflict a lot of damage. Closer examination might have the ME revising time of death."

"But I'm tellin' you, she was there on the road that . . ."

When his words halted, she turned to look at him. Followed the direction of his gaze to the area beyond the cabin's back porch.

Rose was standing there. Floating, really. The woman she'd just seen in the body bag. In the same clothes she'd worn the one time Ramsey had met her.

It looked like Rose Thornton. But the image of her wavered at the edges, like a reflection in a clear pond. And in the next moment her image melded into that of a young woman in a high-necked buttoned-up gown. Her eyes were filled with sorrow.

"Ruth," Dev breathed.

As if his voice banished it, her image trembled. Faded. And then there was nothing but the lights. Dancing balls of illumination that flickered and skipped across the yard.

Burning bright and brighter. Over the garage. Above the brush. Into the woods before they vanished.

"Shit." She was holding on to Dev's arm so tight she had to be hurting him, but Ramsey couldn't bring herself to let go. "What the hell was that? What *was* that?"

"That," he released a shaky breath, his voice filled with a wonder she was far from mirroring, "was one of those things that can't be explained by science. I have a feeling the residents of Buffalo Springs have seen the last of the red mist."

Her mind was still grappling with implications she couldn't let herself fathom. He turned her to face him. "See, that's what I've been sayin'." The curve of his lips was belied by the serious light in his eyes. "You can't analyze everythin' in this world. Some things you just have to accept for what they are. For what they could be."

Her voice was shaky. "I think someone told me that once."

Dev nodded. "Sounds like a wise man. Here's some facts for you to think 'bout. We both do some travelin', but when I'm writin', I can do that 'bout anywhere. I'm not fussy 'bout where I live." His smile hadn't faded. Neither had the intensity in his gaze. "I *am* fussy 'bout who I live with. Guess I'm hopin' you're not quite as fussy, 'cuz I'd like to be livin' with you."

She sensed he was feeling his way with her. Offering only as much as it took to keep her from running like hell. Away from what he offered. Away from what he wanted.

Her palms dampened. There was a hammering in her heart. A thundering in her ears. "I'm not a good bet."

"Honey, I chase ghosts for a livin'. You're the one takin' a risk here."

A laugh escaped at that, although she knew it wasn't true. Of the two of them, she was the one terrified to disappoint. Terrified that whatever she gave could never be enough.

But when she looked at him, she knew what her answer would be. Because whatever else she felt, the biggest fear that loomed was elicited by the thought of never seeing him again.

"I've taken the easy way most of my life. Easier not to feel anything at all. What I feel now, for you . . ." She drew in a breath. "It scares me to death. But the thought of losing it, losing you, scares me even more."

The bruises on his face still lingered, but it was the pure joy in his expression that had her heart stuttering. "We'll take it slow," he promised, his head lowering to hers. "How do you feel 'bout namin' our firstborn after my daddy?"

She started, the panic at peak alert, until she saw the wicked light in his eyes. "We'll take it slow," Ramsey repeated firmly.

But as her lips met his, she knew that she was going to find a way to accept every last thing Dev was offering.

And offer him the same.

Turn the page for a preview of
the third book in Kylie Brant's
exciting Mindhunters series

WAKING THE DEAD

Available November 2009
from Berkley Sensation!

Seven stainless steel gurneys were lined up in the morgue, each occupied by a partially assembled skeleton and a large garbage bag. The bones gleamed under the fluorescent lights. At the base of the last gurney was a heap of stray bones that had been found lying separately. Caitlin Fleming's first thought was that they looked forlorn. Deprived of their dignity, until they could be rejoined to form the remnant of the person they'd once belonged to.

Her second thought was that without the skulls, the chances of identifying those persons decreased dramatically.

"What do you think?" Sheriff Marin Andrews demanded. Her booted feet sounded heavily as she walked from one gurney to the next. "The bones were pretty much loose in the bags, but the medical examiner made an attempt to reassemble them. We brought out the bones scattered on the bottom of the cave floor in a separate body bag. Recovery operation was a bitch, I'm telling you. The cave branches off from the original vein, gets wider and higher. Then it drops off to a steep chamber about seven feet down. These were probably dumped from above into that chamber." She must have caught Cait's wince, because she added, "We had an anthropologist from the university supervise the removal process."

Cait nodded. She was rarely brought onto a case in time to help process the crime scene. But that didn't stop her from questioning what might have been destroyed or overlooked in the recovery. "I'll want to see the cave."

Andrews's expression first revealed shock, then amusement. "Fortunately for you, that won't be necessary. It's on the face of Castle Rock and not easily accessible. Either you climb down from the top, or you scale upwards nearly eight hundred feet. There are trails, of course, but they could be tricky for an inexperienced climber. We don't need an injury on our hands before we even get started."

"I'm not inexperienced." Cait knew exactly what the sheriff saw when she looked at her. It was, after all, the appearance she'd cultivated for well over a decade. But her days on the runways of New York, Milan, and Paris were long behind her. She was as comfortable these days in a room exactly like this one as hiking in the Blue Ridge Mountains.

The other woman shrugged. She was probably about fifteen years Cait's senior. Her looks were nondescript. A sturdy build filling out a beige uniform. Close-cropped light brown hair and hazel eyes. But Cait knew better than anyone that appearances could be deceiving. Marin Andrews had a reputation for being an excellent, if ambitious cop. And that ambition, along with her father's millions, were rumored to be priming her for a chase to the governor's mansion.

Cait's help in solving this case would provide a steppingstone to that end.

"Figured you'd want to see the area, anyway. That forest fire in the eastern Cascades has depleted the personnel at the forestry stations, but we've hired Zach Sharper to stay available during the course of the investigation. He's the outdoors guide who found the bodies. Said he was preparing for a client who wanted to spelunk some out-of-the-way caves, so Zach explored a few off the beaten path. Thought he'd discovered a new one when he stumbled on this." Andrews waved a hand at the skeletons. "He runs a outfitting company. Rafting, kayaking, mountain climbing, hiking, that sort of thing." The assessing look in her eye said better than words that she didn't believe Cait's assertion of her outdoor experience. "He's also on the search and rescue team when campers and hikers go missing. He's got some rough edges, but he's supposed to be the best in the state."

"I can handle rough edges." Cait walked around the gurneys to peer more closely at the nearly identical junctures where the skulls had been separated from each skeleton. She looked around then, spotted a magnifying loupe on a set of metal shelves in the corner, and retrieved it before continuing her examination.

"The guy from the university said it looked like a knife or saw was used to decapitate them."

Cait moved to another gurney to peer at the vertebra. "I'd say a saw. With luck I may be able to narrow the type down for you." Straightening, she scanned the remains lined up on the stainless steel tables. "You've got four men and three women, but I suspect the medical examiner told you that."

"He did. He also tried, and failed, to find a cause of death for any of them. But this thing is way out of his league and he knows it. He's a pathologist, not a forensic anthropologist. When I saw what we had here, I immediately thought of Raiker Forensics. Adam Raiker assures me you're the best in this field."

Cait used the loupe to take a close look at the femur of the second skeleton. The guy had suffered a fracture to it at some point in his life. It had knit cleanly, suggesting certain medical attention. "I am," she responded absently. She looked up then to arrow a look at Andrews. "My assistant will be arriving at dawn tomorrow with our equipment. Will this facility remain available to us?"

"It will. The building is less than a year old and state of the art." The look of satisfaction stamping the sheriff's face told Cait better than words that the other woman had been a driving force behind the new morgue. "Anything you need, talk to the Lane County medical examiner. His name is Steve Michaels. You'll have to meet him tomorrow." Cait followed the direction of the woman's gaze to the clock on the wall. Eight P.M. And she'd left home at six in the morning in order to catch her flight from Dulles. Weariness was edging in, warring with hunger.

"I've arranged two rooms for you and your assistant at the Landview Suites here in Eugene. You've rented a vehicle?"

"Picked it up at the airport." The compact SUV looked perfect for the ground she'd be covering in the course of this investigation. "I'd like all the maps you can provide for the area. Roads, forests, surrounding towns . . ." A thought struck her then and she looked at the other woman. "And thanks for arranging for the weapon permit so quickly." Raiker refused to let any of his consultants work without one.

Andrews lifted a shoulder. "Your boss made it clear that condition wasn't up for discussion. I doubt you'll need it. These bones may have been in that cave for decades. Even if foul play is determined, the unknown subject is probably long gone by now. The threat should be minimal."

"Maybe. Maybe not. It certainly doesn't take decades for a corpse to be reduced to a skeleton. In some climates it'd be a week if the body were left out in the elements. In Oregon it'd take several weeks or months, depending on where the body's dumped, the season, the temperature, insect and animal access. Maybe you're right and these bones have been there for that long. But not necessarily."

When she saw the satisfied gleam in the sheriff's eye, Cait knew she'd read the woman correctly. Whatever the outcome of this case, Andrews was going use it to vault her political career. And solving a current crime spree would make for a lot better press than some old murders that had happened long ago.

But the woman only said, "I've got a copy of the case file for you in the car. You'll be reporting directly to me, but in the field you may be working with my lead detective, Mitch Barnes. You can meet him tomorrow, too."

Cait's attention had already returned to the skeletons. There was a lot of preparatory work to be done on them, but it would have to wait until tomorrow when Kristy arrived. Although she'd be supervising the lab work, these days Cait was an investigator first, a forensic anthropologist second. And she was anxious to get a look at the secondary scene.

"I'll want to get my assistant started first thing tomorrow morning. Have Barnes meet me here at nine and tell Sharper to stand by. We'll head up to . . ."

"Castle Rock," the other woman supplied.

". . . and he can show me how he happened to discover the

remains of seven people." She shot a glance at the sheriff as they headed to the door. "How did Sharper react to the discovery? Is he pretty shaken up?"

Andrews gave a bark of laughter, real amusement showing in her expression. "Nothing shakes up Sharper, unless it's people wasting his time. He'll be steady enough, don't worry. But he won't win any congeniality contests."

Cait shrugged. "I don't need congenial. I'll be satisfied with competent."

Andrews led the way out of the morgue, the echo of her booted footsteps ringing hollowly. "I may need to remind you of those words after you meet him."

———

Her first stop had been an office supply store. The next was a fast food drive-through for a grilled chicken salad with definite wilting around the edges. Cait had eaten in between setting up her work area. The crime scene photos were tacked to the white display boards sitting on top of the desk. A collection of labels, index cards, markers, and Post-it notes sat neatly at the base.

Now she sat on the bed leaning against the headboard, the contents of the fat accordion file folder scattered across her lap and on the mattress. The photographs taken in the cave chamber had been taken with a low-light lens, but they were still darker than she'd like. While she was able to easily make out the bags' proximity to one another, it was more difficult to read the plastic numbered evidence markers that had been set in front of each to tell which one was which.

There was a preliminary report from the ME, Steve Michaels, and it appeared to be solid work. Measurements of each set of bones were included, as was a thorough examination for evidence of trauma. None of the skeletons showed recent signs of injury. Perhaps the missing skulls would. Or maybe the deaths were the result of poison. Cait narrowed her eyes, considering. She found herself hoping for the victims' sakes that the decapitation had been enacted posthumously.

Had the skulls been removed to impede identification of the victims? To prevent investigators from detecting the method of death? Or were they kept by the perp as trophies?

Taking a look at her watch, Cait began gathering up the materials and replacing them in the file. But it occurred to her that if she could answer those questions, she'd be a long way toward profiling the UNSUB they were searching for.

———

Kristy Jensen was a full foot shorter than Cait at four-eleven, a wispy ethereal creature with an otherworldly air. Slap a pair of wings on her, and with her elfin features and blonde wavy hair, she'd looked like a fairy in a kid's story-book.

Once she opened her mouth, however, that notion would be dispelled forever.

"There is no fucking good way to get to this fuck dump of a town, you know that, don't you?" Kristy sipped at her Star-bucks coffee and aimed a gimlet stare over the rim from cornflower blue eyes. "Charter plane, my ass. Eight fucking hours it took me from Dulles. I could have walked faster. I could have parachuted half way here, hitched a ride on a mother-fucking migrating duck and still gotten here before that damn plane."

"So the plane ride was good?" Cait laughed as her diminu-tive friend gave her the finger as they entered the morgue. "And you owe me four bucks. I'm giving you a pass on the 'damn,' and the one-finger salute because at least that's si-lent."

"We haven't even started work yet," Kristy complained. But she was already digging in her purse to pull out the money. "I think we should change the rules so it only counts during work time."

"Tough love." Cait snatched the five from the woman's hand and dug in her purse until she found a one for change. "You wanted help cleaning up your language. Can't change the rules midcourse."

"Why not? Nothing else has changed, except for my disposable income. I'm still swearing like a one-legged sailor."

They showed their temporary ID to the clerk at the front desk and headed down the long hallway to the room where Andrews had brought Cait the evening before.

"Discipline," she chided. But there was no heat to the word. She could care less whether or not Kristy swore like a seasoned dock worker, as long as she did her job to Cait's exact specifications. And since Kristy was the best tech she'd ever been assigned, Cait was satisfied. "Anyway you'll cheer up quick enough once you see what we have to work with." She paused in front of the door at the end of the hall before opening it with a dramatic flourish.

"Sweeeeet," Kristy breathed, when she got a glimpse of the remains on the gurneys. "Very sweet. What do we have, mass burial? Mass murder," she corrected as she got closer and noted the lack of human skulls attached.

"I suppose we have to allow for the possibility that someone stumbled upon that cave long before the guide did," mused Cait. The thought had occurred belatedly, once she'd gone to bed, her mind still filled with the contents of the files. "Someone with a sense of the macabre who took the skulls as souvenirs."

Kristy was practically salivating as she walked between each gurney. "So I'll double-check them, right? Make sure the right parts are with the proper skeleton?"

"I want you to start a photograph log first," Cait corrected. "I need a notebook kept of images of each skeleton throughout each step of the process." It would be easier to correct mistakes that way, especially in the tricky process of reassembling the full remains of each, which was often a matter of trial and error. "The ME should be around somewhere. Get him to give you a copy of the measurements he's done." She'd left her copy in her case file back at the motel.

"But you'll want me to do my own."

Cait sent her a look of approval. "I doubt he had a caliper to do the measurements with. Then you can ensure each bone is with the right remains." And when Kristy was done, Cait would go over them carefully again, just to be certain. "We've got assorted bones on the last gurney that will have to be matched, as well. Then we'll see exactly what we've got here."

"What should I do in my spare time?" But her sarcasm was checked. Kristy was hooked by the enormity of their task, just as Cait was. Anticipation was all but radiating off her.

"I heard voices." At the sound of the newcomer the women turned toward the door. The man approaching them was average height, with hair as dark as Cait's. He wore blue scrubs, shoe covers, and a slight smile that faded as he got closer. Then his face took on that slightly stunned expression that was all too familiar. He stared from Cait to Kristy and back again, with the look of a starving man surrounded by a steaming banquet. "Ah . . . Michaels." He held out his hand to each of them in turn, visibly wrestling to get the words out in proper order. "Steve. I am, that is."

He looked chagrined, but Cait spared him no slack. "Well, Michaels Steve, I'm Cait Fleming." She jerked a thumb at the other woman. "My assistant, Kristy Jensen. I've got your preliminary report. Appreciate it. Kristy will be working down here most of the time. I've been assured that whatever she needs, she can come to you."

While she spoke the man seemed to have regained his powers of speech. But twin flags of color rode high on his cheeks and his dark eyes still looked dazed. "Certainly." He dragged his gaze away from Cait and fixed it on Kristy. "Certainly," he repeated.

"Then I'll leave you to get started." She didn't know if Barnes would be here yet, but she wasn't anxious to spend any more time with the ME who looked like he'd just cast them in a low-budget porn fantasy involving a threesome and a stainless steel coroner's station. She started out of the room, throwing a look at Kristy over her shoulder. "Keep me posted."

As she headed through the door she heard her assistant

say sweetly, "So Michaels Steve, why don't we go out to the truck and you can help unload the mother-fucking equipment."

A smirk on her lips, Cait decided to let it slide. Nothing was more guaranteed to shatter a guy's X-rated fantasy than a pint-sized angelic blonde with a mouth like a sewage plant. She almost felt sorry for him. Would have if she weren't still annoyed at his all too common reaction. As it was, she figured he was going to get exactly what he deserved working with Kristy.

When she stepped out of the morgue doors she saw the Lane County sheriff patrol car pulling up to the curb a full fifteen minutes early. Her good humor restored, Cait rounded it to approach the driver's door. A stocky deputy got out, extended his hand. "Mitch Barnes, Ms. Fleming."

Belatedly, Cait realized she was still wearing the morgue temporary ID. She snatched it off with one hand and she offered him the other. "Looking forward to working with you, Mitch."

The man came to her chin, had receding blond hair and brown eyes that were pure cop. And it'd been her ID that drew his attention rather than her face or figure. She liked him immediately for that fact alone.

"Sheriff says you want to head up toward McKenzie Bridge. Over to Castle Rock."

She nodded as she dropped her ID into her purse. "I'd like to get a look at the dump site. Get a feel for it."

"You got the pictures?"

Understanding what he was getting at, she nodded. "Still want to see it."

Shrugging, he leaned into his front seat only to withdraw a moment later with an armful of maps. "Andrews said you asked for these."

"I did, thanks." She took the stack from him. "If you want to lead the way up to the McKenzie Bridge area, I'll follow this time. That way you don't have to wait around while I go through the cave if you don't want to."

"Sounds good. It's about a forty-five minute drive. I'll call

Sharper on the way and let him know we're coming by." A smirk flashed across the man's otherwise professional demeanor. "He'll be thrilled to take you to the cave."

Coupled with the sheriff's comments the night before, Cait had the distinct impression that the guide they kept mentioning was light on social graces. The thought didn't bother her nearly as much as it would if he were another ogler like the ME.

Men like that rarely brought out the best in her.

———————

How the hell had he gotten into this mess?

Fuming, Zach Sharper threw another look at the rearview mirror and the empty ribbon of road behind him. The answer was swift in coming. Ever since he'd reported his findings from that cave, Andrews had had him wrapped up like a damn trick monkey. First he'd had to lead law enforcement to the place. Hang around while they did their thing. Then there'd been the endless questioning.

And now he found himself forced to be at the beck and call of some consultant hired by the sheriff's office. Playing glorified nursemaid to a cop—or close enough to it—promised to be worse than the biggest pain-in-the-ass client he ran across from time to time. At least he had a choice when taking on the clients.

Yeah, not being given a choice here rankled the most.

He saw the county car headed toward him. Zach put on his sunglasses and got out of his Trailblazer. Damned if he'd been about to travel down to Eugene and then back again once he'd heard what the consultant wanted. And he sure as hell wasn't going to arrange for the cops to meet him at his place. Whispering Pines was his getaway. His refuge. Guests were rarely invited.

A navy SUV pulled off the road in back of the sheriff's car. He was unsurprised to see Mitch Barnes get out of the lead car. The way Zach heard it, Barnes did most of the grunt work for Andrews while she got all the glory. He'd been the first of the cops to follow Zach into that cave. The sheriff sure hadn't gone in, though she'd been present, running things on top Castle Rock while her people had hauled the bones out. If Barnes wanted another pass at the cave he sure as hell didn't need Zach. He knew where it was located.

Made a guy wonder if this was just one more way for Andrews to yank his chain, show him who was calling the shots.

He walked toward the deputy, who was approaching on the shoulder. The driver of the SUV got out, too, but it was Barnes Zach concentrated on. He wasn't a bad sort, for a cop. Maybe he could talk him into a change of plans. Zach was resigned to the fact that he wasn't going to get out of this forced alliance with the sheriff's office. But Andrews wouldn't necessarily have to know whether he was the one playing nursemaid or if one of Zach's employees fulfilled the duty.

Although he wasn't sure he had an employee he disliked enough to saddle with this job.

"Barnes," he said by way of greeting. The other man gave him a nod. Wasting no time, he continued, "Maybe you and I can reach an . . ."

"Sharper, I want you to meet Caitlin Fleming, a consultant for the sheriff's department. She's with Raiker Forensics."

The inflection in the man's voice imbued his last words with meaning. But it was his earlier words that had Zach halting in disbelief. Tipping his Julbo sunglasses down he looked—really looked—at the woman approaching.

The mile-long legs could be right. And she was tall enough; only a few inches shorter than his six-three height. The kiss-my-ass cheekbones were familiar. But it was the thick black hair that clinched it, though shorter now than it'd been all those years ago. He didn't need her to remove her tinted glasses to know the eyes behind them were moss green and guaranteed to turn any breathing male into an instant walking hard-on.

His voice terse, he turned his attention to the deputy and said, "Is this some kind of a joke?"

Barnes blinked. "What?"

"I mean are there going to be TV trucks and cameras following our every move?" Christ, what a clusterfuck. He could already imagine it. TV channels were filled with so-called entertainment featuring desperate cultural celebrities and he could anticipate what was going on here. "I'm not about to get involved in a reality TV show or whatever the hell she's part of. You can tell the sheriff the deal is off." Andrews had threatened to jam him up with the constant renewal of permits needed to take his clients camping or kayaking. But maybe he could bribe someone at the permit department to circumvent her meddling. He was willing to take his chances.

"What the hell are you talking about?"

"He's talking about me." The voice was smoke, pure sex. He'd never heard her speak before, but he'd imagined it often enough years ago in his adolescent fantasies. "Probably recognizes me from some of my modeling work, isn't that right, Sharper? A long time ago. If you want me to believe you've changed from a sweaty hormone-ridden teenage boy who undoubtedly used one of my posters to fuel your juvenile wet dreams, then you'll have to credit that I too grew up and moved on. I want a first-hand look at that cave. You're going to take me there."

Somehow when he'd imagined her talking decades ago it had been without that tone of withering disdain. His disbelief dissipated, the skepticism remained. He slanted a glance at the deputy. "Seriously, Barnes. *This* is the department's consultant?"

The man's manner was stiff. "Like I said, she's from Raiker Forensics. *The Mindhunters.* That might not mean anything to you, but in law enforcement circles it carries a helluva lot of weight."

Caitlin Fleming as a cop. The implausibility of it still rang in his mind. But then he gave a mental shrug. Most people in these parts used to be something else. Many were reluctant to talk about their pasts. Including him.

Especially him.

He looked her over again, noting the jeans, tennis shoes, and long-sleeve navy T-shirt. "Either we hike down Castle Rock or climb up it. Either way, it's not a walk in the park.

Mitch here can tell you that. You might want to rethink visiting it in person."

Instead of responding, she looked at the deputy. "You coming along?"

He shook his head. "Once was enough for me. I've been stopping in at the forest service stations in the area to look at the citations they've issued in the last few years. There might be a pattern. Maybe some common names."

She nodded. "I'll be anxious to hear what you find. See you back in Eugene, then. This will probably take most of the day." She walked back to her SUV and pulled a pack out of the back end. Then she locked it and headed back to where they stood waiting for her.

"We'll use your vehicle, Sharper. I'll want to explore both approaches to the cave." She headed toward where he'd left his Trailblazer parked on the shoulder of the road. Her voice drifted behind her as she walked away. "I'd already been warned you were an asshole, so your attitude isn't much of a surprise. But it'll be up to you to convince me that you're as good at your job as I've heard. Right now, I've got to say, I have my doubts."

About the Author

Kylie Brant is the bestselling author of nearly thirty contemporary romantic suspense novels, including *Waking Nightmare*, *Waking Evil*, and *Waking the Dead*. She's a two-time Rita nominee and a Romantic Times Career Achievement award winner. One of her books is listed by *Romantic Times* magazine as an all-time favorite.

Kylie lives in the Midwest with her husband and a very spoiled Polish Lowland sheepdog. Visit her website at www.kyliebrant.com or contact her at kylie@kyliebrant.com.

COMING NOVEMBER 2009

WAKING THE DEAD

BY **KYLIE BRANT**

A Killer in the Wilderness

When seven headless sets of skeletal remains are found in the Oregon wilderness, forensic anthropologist Caitlin Fleming is the first one called. Now she must piece together the clues and repress her growing attraction for outdoor guide Zach Sharper. But will she unmask the killer before he terminates the investigation?

"Kylie Brant is destined to become a star!"
—*New York Times* bestselling author Cindy Gerard

penguin.com

M468T0509